UNDER THE GU~

D1149997

THE BOLDEST STORIES FROM T~~ ~~~~
TALENTS—IN AN OUTSTANDING COLLECTION OF
MYSTERY AND SUSPENSE

STUART KAMINSKY, "The Buck Stops Here"—This Edgar
Award-winning author is best known for his 1930s Hollywood private
eye Toby Peters, but the famous hero of this riveting tale is exactly
whom you suspect.

DEAN KOONTZ, "Twilight of the Dawn"—Crossing over from
fantasy/horror to psychological suspense, bestselling writer Koontz
once again creates totally believable characters experiencing very out-
of-the-ordinary things.

SUE GRAFTON, "Non Sung Smoke"—Winner of a Shamus Award
and three Anthony Awards, Grafton and her hard-boiled female P.I.
Kinsey Millhone show us the state-of-the-art in this perfect gem of
the genre.

BILL PRONZINI, "Incident in a Neighborhood Tavern"—From the
master of the P.I. story and his famous "Nameless" detective comes
a gritty tale of quick violence and fast justice in a San Francisco bar.

ANTONIA FRASER, "Jemima Shore at the Sunny Grave"—One
of the several increasingly popular females in detection, Britisher
Jemima Shore lands in the Caribbean for a murder in the heat of the
night.

PETER LOVESEY, "The Wasp"—Best known for his Victorian-
era mysteries, Silver Dagger-winner Lovesey pens a poignant but
macabre modern tale of a perfect murder.

These are but six of the twenty-one twisting tales awaiting lovers of
edge-of-the-seat mystery and suspense—in a riveting collection of the
year's very best.

EDWARD GORMAN is a Shamus Award-winning mystery writer
and creator of the murder series featuring ex-cop Jack Dwyer, as well
as being one of the Editor/Publishers of *Mystery Scene* magazine.

ROBERT J. RANDISI, author of the Miles Jacoby mystery series
and the mystery/western "Gunsmith" series, is the other Editor/Pub-
lisher of *Mystery Scene* magazine.

UNDER THE GUN

Mystery Scene
**Presents
the Best Suspense
and Mystery**
First Annual Collection

Edited by
Ed Gorman,
Bob Randisi
and
Martin H. Greenberg

A PLUME BOOK
NEW AMERICAN LIBRARY
A DIVISION OF PENGUIN BOOKS USA INC., NEW YORK
PUBLISHED IN CANADA BY
PENGUIN BOOKS CANADA LIMITED, MARKHAM, ONTARIO

NAL BOOKS ARE AVAILABLE AT QUALITY DISCOUNTS WHEN USED TO PROMOTE PRODUCTS OR SERVICES. FOR INFORMATION PLEASE WRITE TO PREMIUM MARKETING DIVISION, NEW AMERICAN LIBRARY, 1633 BROADWAY, NEW YORK, NEW YORK 10019.

This book is also available in an NAL BOOKS hardcover edition, published by New American Library and simultaneously in Canada by Penguin Books Canada Limited.

Acknowledgments

"Jemima Shore at the Sunny Grave," by Antonia Fraser. Copyright © 1988 by Antonia Fraser. First published in *Ellery Queen's Mystery Magazine*, June issue. Reprinted by permission of the author and the author's agents, Curtis Crown, Ltd. (London).

"The Owl in the Oak," by Joseph Hansen. Copyright © 1988 by Davis Publications, Inc. First published in *Alfred Hitchcock's Mystery Magazine*, March issue. Reprinted by permission of the author.

"How Dangerous Is Your Brother?" by William Bankier. Copyright © 1988 by William Bankier. First published in *Ellery Queen's Mystery Magazine*, September issue. Reprinted by permission of the author.

"Incident in a Neighborhood Tavern," by Bill Pronzini. Copyright © 1988 by Bill Pronzini. First published in *An Eye for Justice*, edited by Robert J. Randisi, Mysterious Press. Reprinted by permission of the author.

"The Case of the Pietro Andromache," by Sara Paretsky. Copyright © 1988 by Davis Publications, Inc. First published in *Alfred Hitchcock's Mystery Magazine*, December issue. Reprinted by permission of the author.

"Flicks," by Bill Crenshaw. Copyright © 1988 by Davis Publications, Inc. First published in *Alfred Hitchcock's Mystery Magazine*, August issue. Reprinted by permission of the author.

"The Buck Stops Here," by Stuart M. Kaminsky. Copyright © 1988 by Stuart M. Kaminsky. First published in *Mr. President, Private Eye*, edited by Francis M. Nevins, Jr., and Martin H. Greenberg, Ballantine Books. Reprinted by permission of the author.

"The Wasp," by Peter Lovesey. Copyright © 1988 by Peter Lovesey. First published in *Ellery Queen's Mystery Magazine*, November issue. Reprinted by permission of the author.

"State of Grace," by Loren D. Estleman. Copyright © 1988 by Loren D. Estleman. First published in *An Eye for Justice*, edited by Robert J. Randisi, Mysterious Press. Reprinted by permission of the author.

"Death of a Romance Writer," by Joan Hess. Copyright © 1988 by Davis Publications, Inc. First published in *Alfred Hitchcock's Mystery Magazine*, March issue. Reprinted by permission of the author.

"Marble Mildred," by Max Allan Collins. Copyright © 1988 by Max Allan Collins. First published in *An Eye for Justice*, edited by Robert J. Randisi, Mysterious Press. Reprinted by permission of the author.

"Faces," by F. Paul Wilson. Copyright © 1988 by F. Paul Wilson. First published in *Night Visions IV*, Dark Harvest. Reprinted by permission of the author and the author's agent, Writers House, Inc. .

SIGNET, SIGNET CLASSIC, MENTOR, ONYX, PLUME, MERIDIAN and NAL BOOKS are published *in the United States* by New American Library, a division of Penguin Books USA Inc., 1633 Broadway, New York, New York 10019, and *in Canada* by Penguin Books Canada Limited, 2801 John Street, Markham, Ontario L3R 1B4

LIBRARY OF CONGRESS CATALOGING-IN-PUBLICATION DATA

Under the gun : Mystery scene presents the best suspense and mystery :
    first annual collection / edited by Ed Gorman, Bob Randisi and
    Martin H. Greenberg.
        p.   cm.
    ISBN 0-453-00713-9
    1. Detective and mystery stories, American.   2. Detective and
mystery stories, English.   I. Gorman, Edward.   II. Randisi, Robert
J.   III. Greenberg, Martin Harry.
PS648.D4U54   1990
813'.087208—dc20
                                                                89-13226
                                                                CIP

Designed by Sherry Brown

First Plume Printing, February, 1990

1 2 3 4 5 6 7 8 9

PRINTED IN THE UNITED STATES OF AMERICA

Contents

CONTENTS

INTRODUCTION

The Year in Mystery: 1988

1988 was the year of the woman.

It was a hot ticket to be a woman mystery writer in 1988. Along with the normal success of Mary Higgins Clark, Barbara Michaels, Ruth Rendell, P. D. James, and others, some new women writers moved to the forefront of the mystery world. Sara Paretsky, Sue Grafton, Marcia Muller, Charlotte MacLeod, and Nancy Pickard became the "hot" writers, and there are other women on the way up as the trend continues into 1989.

In 1982 the Private Eye Writers of America (PWA) was born, and along with it the Shamus Award for the best in private eye fiction. It was *probably* a coincidence that 1982 was the year that the P.I. novel became the hot item. Robert B. Parker was just the tip of the iceberg, and the other names are too numerous to mention here, as the P.I. novel's success in the early eighties is simply an analogy. As successful as the P.I. novel was in the early to mid-eighties, that is how successful the mystery written by a *female* writer is in the late eighties. Is it also a coincidence that this coincides with the birth of Sisters in Crime, an organization formed for the benefit of women mystery writers? (I believe they disdain the initials for the full name. After all, who wants to be known as SIC?)

Perhaps we'll never know for sure.

Although the mystery novel flourished, there were some publishers who fell by the wayside—as has started to happen every year. The Pageant line, which was published by Crown in partnership with Waldenbooks, passed on, as did Paperjacks, a publisher who was just beginning to publish a line of mysteries, called "Bogie's Mysteries," in conjunction with Bogie's Restaurant in New York. Bart also fell by the wayside.

Continuing to flourish were the fine mystery lines of The Mysterious Press, St. Martin's Press, Scribners, Ballantine, Fawcett, Bantam, and Pocket Books, which started their line in 1987. There are, of course, many publishers doing mysteries, but the above-mentioned publishers provide the bulk of the material.

As far as particular books, naturally, the works of Elmore Leonard, Robert B. Parker, and Mary Higgins Clark continued to appear on the best-seller list; Thomas Harris (*The Silence of the Lambs*) and William Diehl (*Thai Horse*) reappeared; and Tony Hillerman (*A Thief of Time*) made the *New York Times* list for the first time. But it is the category mysteries, the books that never make the various best-seller lists, that support the genre and keep it going. The books of Loren D. Estleman (*Downriver*), Sara Paretsky (*Bloodshot*), Sue Grafton (*E is for Evidence*), Charlotte MacLeod (*The Silver Ghost*), Nancy Pickard (*Dead Crazy*), James Ellroy (*The Black Dahlia* and *The Big Nowhere*), and Stuart M. Kaminsky (*A Cold Red Sunrise*) all fared well in the marketplace, and these writers are all considered in various quarters to be on the brink of stardom. (In point of fact, the first mystery bestseller list was created in 1988 by *Mystery Scene* magazine—culled from more than a dozen mystery bookstores, as well as the big chains—and all of these authors appeared on it at one time or another.)

1988 was a year for mystery conferences and conventions. The 1988 Bouchercon—the nineteenth such convention—held in San Diego, was among the most successful of the series. There was also the 4th International Crime Writers Congress in New York City—which received mixed reviews: The Americans, specifically the New York mystery writers, loved it, but the foreign attendees felt somewhat slighted. Still, it was the first such meeting since Sweden in 1981, and continues to be a noble idea. The more recently formed International Association of Crime Writers had its first meeting, *Semana Negra*, in Gijon, Spain, and was, by all accounts, a success. The group intends to repeat it in 1989.

On the short story scene, *A Matter of Crime* finally fell by the wayside after two incarnations, but not before producing some fine stories from established writers in the field. *Ellery Queen* and *Alfred Hitchcock's Mystery Magazine* continued to prosper, both increasing in circulation; the small semi-pro publication, *Hardboiled*, limped along, combatting financial problems to continue to provide a forum for newer writers, while also publishing stories by established pros. Publisher Wayne Dundee assures the field that *Hardboiled* will continue into 1989 and, hopefully, further. *Hardboiled* was joined by *Detective Story* magazine (three issues in 1988) and *Two Fisted De-*

tective Stories (two issues.) All indications are that they will continue into the next year.

On the anthology scene there was almost an explosion of anthologies. The Fourth PWA Anthology (all have been anthologies of *original* stories), *An Eye for Justice*, appeared, along with original anthologies such as *Raymond Chandler's Philip Marlowe*, a handsome volume of Raymond Chandler stories written by top mystery authors; *Mr. President, Private Eye*, edited by Martin H. Greenberg; and *Crime at Christmas*, edited by Jack Adrian.

Reprint anthologies were *Masterpieces of Mystery and Suspense*, edited by Martin H. Greenberg, and *The Mammoth Book of Private Eye Stories*, edited by Greenberg and Bill Pronzini; *English Country House Murders*, edited by Thomas Godfrey; and *The Second Black Lizard Anthology of Crime Fiction*, edited by Edward Gorman.

To further illustrate what a fine year it was for short mystery fiction, there were four single-author collections of note: Loren D. Estleman's *General Murders*, a collection of Amos Walker stories; *Small Felonies*, a collection of fifty short-shorts by Bill Pronzini; *Better Mousetraps*, a collection of short stories by John Lutz; and *Timothy's Game*, three novellas with a common protagonist by Laurence Sanders.

Call 1988 a banner year for short fiction.

Television saw the return of Peter Falk and Burt Reynolds to series duty. Falk returned with *Columbo* while Reynolds portrayed Florida P.I. *B. L. Stryker*. They alternated with Lou Gossett, who appeared as *Gideon Oliver*. Of course *L.A. Law* and *Murder She Wrote* continued to rate highly, along with *Hunter*.

In the theater the mystery flourished, as *Mississippi Burning* heads the list of films with a mystery or crime elements that includes: *Frantic, Off Limits, D.O.A., Colors, White Mischief, Stormy Monday, Who Framed Roger Rabbit, The Dead Pool, Midnight Run, Married to the Mob, Betrayed, Eight Men Out, Patty Hearst, The Accused, Without a Clue, A Cry in the Dark, Tequila Sunrise*, and *Dirty Rotten Scoundrels*.

The saddest duty of an examination of a year in any genre is listing those authors who passed away. We could do it quickly, but that would not do them justice.

They are: *Ed Mathis*, the author of the Dan Roman series, who may have left us, but left behind a legacy of unpublished manuscripts to delight us for a few years to come; *Charles Willeford* was taken just when his star was on the rise, but he left us with four wonderful novels featuring Hoke Mosely; *Elizabeth Linington*, author of countless mysteries under her own name, and others written as Dell Shannon; *Louis L'Amour*, whose mystery contributions were limited to short stories; *William R. Cox*, a legend of the old pulps; and *John Ball*, author of *In the Heat of the Night*, which, ironically, came to the TV screen in 1988.

They will all be sorely missed.

Big deals are, of course, a matter of standpoint. They are bigger to the author who is getting them than to anyone else, and only the author knows *how* big they are, but here are some people who signed some big deals in 1988: Robert B. Parker, who switched from Delacorte to Putnam for a cool million, and who also signed to finish Raymond Chandler's unfinished Philip Marlowe novel, *The Poodle Springs Murder*, also for a cool mil; Nancy Pickard signed a two-book hard/soft deal with Pocket Books for her Jenny Cain series; Bill Pronzini signed a three-book hard/soft deal with Delacorte for three Nameless novels.

Was Parker's deal hard/soft? Who cares!

Six awards were given out in 1988, possibly the most of any year. Two were professional awards—MWA's Edgar and PWA's Shamus—and four were nonprofessional—*Mystery Scene*'s American Mystery Award, Bouchercon's Anthony Award, the Mystery Readers Macavity Award, and Malice Domestic's new Agathas.

The Edgar Awards went to: Best Novel, *Old Bones* by Aaron Elkins; Best First Mystery Novel, *Death among Strangers* by Deidre S. Laiken; Best Paperback Novel, *Bimbos of the Death Sun* by Sharyn McCrumb; Best Short Story, "Soft Monkey" by Harlan Ellison.

The Shamus Awards went to: Best Novel, *A Tax in Blood* by Benjamin M. Schutz; Best First Novel, *Death on the Rocks* by Michael Allegretto; Best Paperback Original Novel, *Wild Night* by L. J. Washburn; Best Short Story, "Turn Away" by Edward Gorman.

The American Mystery Awards went to: Best Traditional Mystery Novel, *The Corpse in Oozak's Pond* by Charlotte MacLeod; Best Private Eye Novel, *A Trouble of Fools* by Linda Barnes; Best Romantic Suspense Novel, *Trojan Gold* by Elizabeth Peters; Best Crime Novel, *Bandits* by Elmore Leonard; Best Paperback Original Novel, *Wild Night* by L. J. Washburn; Best Police Procedural Novel, *Tricks* by Ed McBain; Best Short Story, "Soft Monkey" by Harlan Ellison.

The Anthony Awards went to: Best Novel, *Skinwalker* by Tony Hillerman; Best First Novel, *Caught Dead in Philadelphia* by Gillian

Roberts; Best Paperback Mystery Novel, *The Monkey's Raincoat* by Robert Crais; Best Short Story, "Breakfast Television" by Robert Barnard.

The Macavity Awards went to: Best Novel, *Marriage Is Murder* by Nancy Pickard; Best First Novel, *The Monkey's Raincoat* by Robert Crais; Best Nonfiction Critical Article, "Son of Gun in Cheek" by Bill Pronzini; Best Short Story, "The Woman in the Wardrobe" by Robert Barnard.

The Agatha Awards went to: Best "Domestic" Mystery Novel, *Something Wicked* by Carolyn Hart; Best First Novel, *A Great Deliverance* by Elizabeth George; Best Short Story, "More Final Than Divorce" by Robert Barnard.

—Robert J. Randisi

Story introductions by Jim Frenkel

ANTONIA FRASER

Lady Antonia Fraser is a multitalented writer who has excelled in every one of the endeavors in which we've been able to detect her participation. Her biography of Mary Stuart, *Mary, Queen of Scots* (1969), won the Black Memorial Prize for biography and brought her work to a vast audience. Her history of dolls is acknowledged as an authoritative work in the field; and her mysteries hold sway over a large and growing audience.

Jemima Shore has been the protagonist of many mysteries by Fraser. The following tale amply illustrates the keen eye for the dynamics of relationships and the effortlessly pleasing narrative style that have made Fraser's work so popular. At the same time, the story sheds light on two basic motives for murder: greed and revenge.

Jemima Shore at
the Sunny Grave

"This is your graveyard in the sun—" The tall young man standing in her path was singing the words lightly but clearly. It took Jemima Shore a moment to realize exactly what message he was intoning to the tune of the famous calypso. Then she stepped back. It was a sinister and not particularly welcoming little parody.

> "This is my island in the sun
> Where my people have toiled since time begun—"

Ever since she had arrived in the Caribbean, she seemed to have had the tune echoing in her ears. How old was it? How many years was it since the inimitable Harry Belafonte had first implanted it in everybody's consciousness? No matter. Whatever its age, the calypso was still being sung today with charm, vigor, and a certain relentlessness on Bow Island, and on the other West Indian islands she had visited in the course of her journey.

It was not the only tune to be heard, of course. The loud noise of music, she had discovered, was an inseparable part of Caribbean life, starting with the airport. The heavy, irresistible beat of the steel band, the honeyed wail of the singers, all this was happening somewhere if not everywhere all over the islands late into the night: the joyous sound of freedom, of dancing, of drinking (rum punch), and, for the tourists at any rate, the sound of holiday.

It wasn't the sound of holiday for Jemima Shore, Investigator. Or not officially so. That was all to the good, Jemima being one of those people temperamentally whose best holidays combined some work with a good deal of pleasure. She could hardly believe it when Megalith Television, her employers, had agreed to a program which took her away from freezing Britain to the sunny Caribbean in late January. This was a reversal of normal practice, by which Cy Fred-

2

ericks, Jemima's boss—and the effective boss of Megalith—was generally to be found relaxing in the Caribbean in February while Jemima herself, if she got there at all, was liable to be despatched there in the inconvenient humidity of August. And it was a fascinating project to boot. This was definitely her lucky year.

"This is my island in the sun—" But what the young man facing her had actually sung was "your *graveyard* in the sun." Hers? Or whose? Since the man was standing between Jemima and the historic grave she had come to visit, it was possible that he was being proprietorial as well as aggressive. On second thought, surely not. It was a joke, a cheerful joke on a cheerful, very sunny day. But the young man's expression was, it seemed to her, more threatening than that.

Jemima gazed back with that special sweet smile so familiar to viewers of British television. (These same viewers were also aware from past experience that Jemima, sweet as her smile might be, stood no nonsense from anyone, at least not on her program.) On closer inspection, the man was not really as young as all that. She saw someone of perhaps roughly her own age—early thirties. He was white, although so deeply tanned that she guessed he wasn't a tourist but one of the small loyal European population of Bow Island, a place fiercely proud of its recent independence from a much larger neighbor.

The stranger's height, unlike his youth, was not an illusion. He towered over Jemima and she herself was not short. He was also handsome, or would have been except for an oddly formed, rather large nose with a high bridge to it and a pronounced aquiline curve. But if the nose marred the regularity of his features, the impression left was not unattractive. He was wearing whitish cotton shorts, like more or less every male on Bow Island, black or white. His orange T-shirt bore the familiar island logo or crest: the outline of a bow in black and a black hand drawing it back. Beneath the logo was printed one of the enormous variety of local slogans—cheerful again—designed to make a play upon the island's name. This one read: THIS IS THE END OF THE SUN-BOW!

No, in that friendly T-shirt, he was surely not intending to be aggressive.

In that case, the odd thing about the whole encounter was that the stranger still stood absolutely still in Jemima's path. She could glimpse the large stone Archer Tomb just behind him, which she recognized from the postcards. For a smallish place, Bow Island was remarkably rich in historic relics. Nelson in his time had visited it with his fleet, for like its neighbors Bow Island had found itself engulfed in the Napoleonic Wars. Two hundred or so years before that, first British, then French, then British again had invaded and settled the island which had once belonged to Caribs, and before that Arawaks. Finally, into this melting pot, Africans had been brought forcibly to work the sugar plantations on which its wealth depended. All these elements in various degrees had gone to make up the people now known casually among themselves as the Bo'landers.

The Archer Tomb, the existence of which had in a sense brought Jemima across the Atlantic, belonged to the period of the second—and final—British settlement. Here was buried the most celebrated Governor in Bow Island's history, Sir Valentine Archer. Even its name commemorated his long reign. Bow Island had originally been called by the name of a saint, and while it was true the island was vaguely formed in the shape of a bow it was Governor Archer who had made the change: to signify ritually that this particular archer was in command of this particular bow.

Jemima knew that the monument, splendidly carved, would show Sir Valentine Archer with Isabella, his wife, beside him. This double stone bier was capped with a white wood structure reminiscent of a small church, done either to give the whole monument additional importance—although it must always have dominated the small churchyard by its sheer size—or to protect it from the weather. Jemima had read that there were no Archer children inscribed on the tomb, contrary to the usual seventeenth century practice. This was because, as a local historian delicately put it, Governor Archer had been as a parent to the entire island. Or in the words of another purely local calypso:

"Across the sea came old Sir Valentine—
He came to be your daddy, and he came to be mine."

In short, no one monument could comprise the progeny of a man popularly supposed to have sired over a hundred children, legitimate and illegitimate. The legitimate line was, however, now on the point of dying out. It was to see Miss Isabella Archer, officially at least the last of her race, that Jemima had come to the Caribbean. She hoped to make a program about the old lady and her home, Archer Plantation House, alleged to be untouched in its decoration these fifty years. She wanted also to interview her generally about the changes Miss Archer had seen in her lifetime in this part of the world.

"Greg Harrison," said the man standing in Jemima's path suddenly. "And this is my sister, Coralie." A girl who had been standing unnoticed by Jemima in the shade of the arched church porch stepped rather shyly forward. She, too, was extremely brown and her blonde hair, whitened almost to flax by the sun, was pulled back into a ponytail. His sister. Was there a resemblance? Coralie Harrison was wearing a similar orange T-shirt, but otherwise she was not much like her brother. She was quite short, for one thing, and her features were appealing rather than beautiful—and, perhaps fortunately, she lacked her brother's commanding nose.

"Welcome to Bow Island, Miss Shore," she began. But her brother interrupted her. He put out a hand, large, muscular, and burnt to nut color by the sun.

"I know why you're here and I don't like it," said Greg Harrison. "Stirring up forgotten things. Why don't you leave Miss Izzy to die in peace?" The contrast between his apparently friendly handshake and the hostile, if calmly spoken words was disconcerting.

"I'm Jemima Shore," she said, though he obviously knew that. "Am I going to be allowed to inspect the Archer Tomb? Or is it to be across your dead body?" Jemima smiled again with sweetness.

"*My* dead body!" Greg Harrison smiled back in his turn. The effect, however, was not particularly warming. "Have you come armed to the teeth, then?" Before she could answer, he began to hum the famous calypso again. Jemima imagined the words: "This is your graveyard in the sun." Then he added: "Might not be such a bad idea, that, when you start to dig up things that should be buried."

Jemima decided it was time for action. Neatly sidestepping Greg Harrison, she marched firmly toward the Archer Tomb. There lay the carved couple. She read: "Sacred to the memory of Sir Valentine Archer, first Governor of this island, and his only wife, Isabella, daughter of Randal Oxford, gentleman." She was reminded briefly of her favorite Philip Larkin poem about the Arundel Monument, beginning, "The Earl and Countess lie in stone—" and ending, "All that remains of us is love."

But that couple lay a thousand miles away in the cloistered cool of Chichester Cathedral. Here the hot tropical sun burnt down on her naked head. She found she had taken off her large straw hat as a token of respect and quickly clapped it back on again. Here, too, in contrast to the very English-looking stone church with pointed Gothic windows beyond, there were palm trees among the graves instead of yews, their slender trunks bending like giraffes' necks in the breeze. She had once romantically laid white roses on the Arundel Monument. It was as the memory of the gesture returned to her that she spied the heap of bright pink and orange hibiscus blossoms lying on the stone before her. A shadow fell across it.

"Tina puts them there." Greg Harrison had followed her. "Every day she can manage it. Most days. Then she tells Miss Izzy what she's done. Touching, isn't it?" But he did not make it sound as if he found it especially touching. In fact, there was so much bitterness, even malevolence, in his voice that for a moment, standing as she was in the sunny graveyard, Jemima felt quite chilled. "Or is it revolting?" he added, the malevolence now quite naked.

"Greg," murmured Coralie Harrison faintly, as if in protest.

"Tina?" Jemima said. "That's Miss Archer's—Miss Izzy's—companion. We've corresponded. For the moment I can't remember her other name."

"She's known as Tina Archer these days, I think you'll find. When she wrote to you, she probably signed the letter Tina Harrison." Harrison looked at Jemima sardonically but she had genuinely forgotten the surname of the companion—it was, after all, not a particularly uncommon one.

They were interrupted by a loud hail from the road. Jemima saw a young black man at the wheel of one of the convenient roofless minis everyone seemed to drive around Bow Island. He stood up and started to shout something.

"Greg! Cora! You coming on to—" She missed the rest of it—something about a boat and a fish. Coralie Harrison looked suddenly radiant, and for a moment even Greg Harrison actually looked properly pleased.

He waved back. "Hey, Joseph. Come and say hello to Miss Jemima Shore of BBC Television!"

"Megalith Television," Jemima interrupted, but in vain. Harrison continued:

"You heard, Joseph. She's making a program about Miss Izzy."

The man leapt gracefully out of the car and approached up the palm-lined path. Jemima saw that he, too, was extremely tall. And like the vast majority of the Bo'landers she had so far met, he had the air of being a natural athlete. Whatever the genetic mix in the past of Carib and African and other people that had produced them, the Bo'landers were certainly wonderful-looking. He kissed Coralie on both cheeks and patted her brother on the back.

"Miss Shore, meet Joseph—" but even before Greg Harrison had pronounced the surname, his mischievous expression had warned Jemima what it was likely to be "—Joseph Archer. Undoubtedly one of the ten thousand descendants of the philoprogenitive old gentleman at whose tomb you are so raptly gazing." All that remains of us is love indeed, thought Jemima irreverently as she shook Joseph Archer's hand—with all due respect to Philip Larkin, it seemed that a good deal more remained of Sir Valentine than that.

"Oh, you'll find we're all called Archer round here," murmured

Joseph pleasantly. Unlike Greg Harrison, he appeared to be genuinely welcoming. "As for Sir Val-en-tine—" he pronounced it syllable by syllable like the calypso "—don't pay too much attention to the stories. Otherwise, how come we're not all living in that fine old Archer Plantation House?"

"Instead of merely my ex-wife. No, Coralie, don't protest. I could kill her for what she's doing." Again Jemima felt a chill at the extent of the violence in Greg Harrison's voice. "Come, Joseph, we'll see about that fish of yours. Come on, Coralie." He strode off, unsmiling, accompanied by Joseph, who did smile. Coralie, however, stopped to ask Jemima if there was anything she could do for her. Her manner was still shy but in her brother's absence a great deal more friendly. Jemima also had the strong impression that Coralie Harrison wanted to communicate something to her, something she did not necessarily want her brother to hear.

"I could perhaps interpret, explain—" Coralie stopped. Jemima said nothing. "Certain things," went on Coralie. "There are so many layers in a place like this. Just because it's small, an outsider doesn't always understand—"

"And I'm the outsider? Of course I am." Jemima had started to sketch the tomb for future reference, something for which she had a minor but useful talent. She forbore to observe truthfully, if platitudinously, that an outsider could also sometimes see local matters rather more clearly than those involved—she wanted to know what else Coralie had to say. Would she explain, for example, Greg's quite blatant dislike of his former wife?

But an impatient cry from her brother now in the car beside Joseph meant that Coralie for the time being had nothing more to add. She fled down the path and Jemima was left to ponder with renewed interest on her forthcoming visit to Isabella Archer of Archer Plantation House. It was a visit which would include, she took it, a meeting with Miss Archer's companion, who, like her employer, was currently dwelling in comfort there.

Comfort! Even from a distance, later that day, the square, low-built mansion had a comfortable air. More than that, it conveyed an impression of gracious and old-fashioned tranquility. As Jemima drove her own rented mini up the long avenue of palm trees—much taller than those in the churchyard—she could fancy she was driving back in time to the days of Governor Archer, his copious banquets, parties, and balls, all served by black slaves.

At that moment, a young woman with coffee-colored skin and short black curly hair appeared on the steps. Unlike the maids in Jemima's hotel who wore a pastiche of bygone servants' costume at dinner—brightly colored dresses to the ankle, white-muslin aprons, and turbans—this girl was wearing an up-to-the-minute scarlet halter-top and cutaway shorts revealing most of her smooth brown legs. Tina Archer: for so she introduced herself.

It did not surprise Jemima Shore one bit to discover that Tina Archer—formerly Harrison—was easy to get on with. Anyone who left the hostile and graceless Greg Harrison was already ahead in Jemima's book. But with Tina Archer chatting away at her side, so chic and even trendy in her appearance, the revelation of the interior of the house was far more of a shock to her than it would otherwise have been. There was nothing, nothing at all, of the slightestly modernity about it. Dust and cobwebs were not literally there perhaps, but they were suggested in its gloom, its heavy wooden furniture—where were the light cane chairs so suitable to the climate?—and above all in its desolation. Archer Plantation House reminded her of poor Miss Havisham's time-warp home in *Great Expectations*. And still worse, there was an atmosphere of sadness hanging over the whole interior. Or perhaps it was mere loneliness, a kind of somber, sterile grandeur you felt must stretch back centuries.

All this was in violent contrast to the sunshine still brilliant in the late afternoon, the rioting bushes of brightly colored tropical flowers outside. None of it had Jemima expected. Information garnered in London had led her to form quite a different picture of Archer Plantation House, something far more like her original impression, as she drove down the avenue of palm trees, of antique mellow grace.

Just as Jemima was adapting to this surprise, she discovered the figure of Miss Archer herself to be equally astonishing. That is to say, having adjusted rapidly from free and easy Tina to the moldering, somber house, she now had to adjust with equal rapidity all over again. For the very first inspection of the old lady, known by Jemima to be at least eighty, quickly banished all thoughts of Miss Havisham. Here was no aged, abandoned bride, forlorn in the decaying wedding-dress of fifty years before. Miss Izzy Archer was wearing a coolie straw hat, apparently tied under her chin with a duster, a loose white man's shirt, and faded bluejeans cut off at the knee. On her feet were a pair of what looked like child's brown sandals. From the look of her, she had either just taken a shower wearing all this or been swimming. She was dripping wet, making large pools on the rich carpet and dark, polished boards of the formal drawing room, all dark-red brocade and swagged, fringed curtains, where she had received Jemima. It was possible to see this even in the filtered light seeping through the heavy brown shutters which shut out the view of the sea.

"Oh, don't fuss so, Tina dear," exclaimed Miss Izzy impatiently—although Tina had, in fact, said nothing. "What do a few drops of water matter? Stains? What stains?" (Tina still had not spoken.) "Let the government put it right when the time comes."

Although Tina Archer continued to be silent, gazing amiably, even cheerfully, at her employer, nevertheless in some way she stiffened, froze in her polite listening attitude. Instinctively Jemima knew that she was in some way upset.

"Now don't be silly, Tina, don't take on, dear." The old lady was now shaking herself free of water like a small but stout dog. "You know what I mean. If you don't, who does—since half the time I don't know what I mean, let alone what I say. You can put it all right one day, is that better? After all, you'll have plenty of money to do it. You can afford a few new covers and carpets." So saying, Miss Izzy, taking Jemima by the hand and attended by the still-silent Tina, led the way to the farthest dark-red sofa. Looking remarkably wet from top to toe, she sat down firmly in the middle of it.

It was in this way that Jemima first realized that Archer Plantation House would not necessarily pass to the newly independent government of Bow Island on its owner's death. Miss Izzy, if she had her way, was intending to leave it all, house and fortune, to Tina. Among other things, this meant that Jemima was no longer making a program about a house destined shortly to be a national museum—which was very much part of the arrangement that had brought her to the island and had, incidentally, secured the friendly cooperation of that same new government. Was all this new? How new? Did the new government know? If the will had been signed, they must know.

"I've signed the will this morning, dear," Miss Archer pronounced triumphantly, with an uncanny ability to answer unspoken questions. "I went swimming to celebrate. I always celebrate things with a good swim—so much more healthy than rum or champagne. Although there's still plenty of *that* in the cellar."

She paused. "So there you are, aren't you, dear? Or there you will be. Here you will be. Thompson says there'll be trouble, of course. What can you expect these days? Everything is trouble since independence. Not that I'm against independence, far from it. But everything new brings new trouble here in addition to all the old troubles, so that the troubles get more and more. On Bow Island, no troubles ever go away. Why is that?"

But Miss Izzy did not stop for an answer. "No, I'm all for independence and I shall tell you all about that, my dear"—she turned to Jemima and put one damp hand on her sleeve—"on your program. I'm being a Bo'lander born and bred, you know." It was true that Miss Izzy, unlike Tina for example, spoke with the peculiar, slightly sing-song intonation of the islanders—not unattractive to Jemima's ears.

"I was born in this very house eighty-two years ago in April," went on Miss Izzy. "You shall come to my birthday party. I was born during a hurricane. A good start! But my mother died in childbirth, they should never have got in that new-fangled doctor, just because he came from England. A total fool he was, I remember him well. They should have had a good Bo'lander midwife, then my mother wouldn't have died and my father would have had sons—"

Miss Izzy was drifting away into a host of reminiscences—and while these were supposed to be what Jemima had come to hear, her thoughts were actually racing off in quite a different direction. Trouble? What trouble? Where did Greg Harrison, for example, stand in all this—Greg Harrison who wanted Miss Izzy to be left to "die in peace?" Greg Harrison who had been married to Tina and was no longer? Tina Archer, now heiress to a fortune.

Above all, why was this forthright old lady intending to leave everything to her companion? For one thing, Jemima did not know how seriously to treat the matter of Tina's surname. Joseph Archer had laughed off the whole subject of Sir Valentine's innumerable descendants. But perhaps the beautiful Tina was in some special way connected to Miss Izzy. She might be the product of some rather more recent union between a rakish Archer and a Bo'lander maiden. More recent than the Seventeenth Century, that is.

Her attention was wrenched back to Miss Izzy's reminiscing monologue by the mention of the Archer Tomb.

"You've seen the grave? Tina has discovered it's all a fraud. A great big lie, lying under the sun—yes, Tina dear, you once said that. Sir Valentine Archer, my great great great—" An infinite number of greats followed before Miss Izzy finally pronounced the word "grandfather," but Jemima had to admit that she did seem to be counting. "He had a great big lie perpetuated on his tombstone."

"What Miss Izzy means—" This was the first time Tina had spoken since they entered the darkened drawing room. She was still standing, while Jemima and Miss Izzy sat.

"Don't tell me what I mean, child," rapped out the old lady; her tone was imperious rather than indulgent. Tina might for a moment have been a plantation worker two hundred years earlier rather than an independent-minded girl in the late twentieth century. "It's the inscription which is a lie. She wasn't his only wife. The very inscription should have warned us. Tina wants to see justice done to poor little Lucie Anne and so do I. Independence indeed! I've been independent all my life and I'm certainly not stopping now. Tell me, Miss Shore, you're a clever young woman from television. Why do you bother to contradict something unless it's true all along? That's the way you work all the time in television, don't you?"

Jemima was wondering just how to answer this question diplomatically and without traducing her profession when Tina firmly, and this time successfully, took over from her employer.

"I read history at university in the U.K., Jemima. Genealogical research is my specialty. I was helping Miss Izzy put her papers in order for the museum—or what was to be the museum. Then the request came for your program and I began to dig a little deeper. That's how I found the marriage certificate. Old Sir Valentine *did* marry his young Carib mistress, known as Lucie Anne. Late in life— long after his first wife died. That's Lucie Anne who was the mother of his youngest two children. He was getting old, and for some reason he decided to marry her. The church, maybe. In its way, this has always been a God-fearing island. Perhaps Lucie Anne, who was very young and very beautiful, put pressure on the old man, using the church. At any rate, these last two children of all the hundreds he sired would have been legitimate!"

"And so?" questioned Jemima in her most encouraging manner.

"I'm descended from Lucie Anne—and Sir Valentine, of course." Tina returned sweet smile for sweet smile. "I've traced that, too, from the church records—not too difficult, given the strength of the church here. Not too difficult for an expert, at all events. Oh, I've got all sorts of blood, like most of us round here, including a Spanish grandmother and maybe some French blood, too. But the Archer descent is perfectly straightforward and clear."

Tina seemed aware that Jemima was gazing at her with respect. Did she, however, understand the actual tenor of Jemima's thoughts? This is a formidable person, Jemima was reflecting. Charming, yes, but formidable. And ruthless, maybe, on occasion. Jemima was also, to be frank, wondering just how she was going to present this sudden change of angle in her program on Megalith Television. On the one hand, it might now be seen as a romantic rags-to-riches story, the discovery of the lost heiress. On the other hand, just supposing Tina Archer was not so much an heiress as an adventuress? In that case, what would Megalith—what did Jemima Shore—make of a bright young woman putting across a load of false history on an innocent old lady? In those circumstances, Jemima could understand how the man by the sunny grave might display his contempt for Tina Archer.

"I met Greg Harrison by the Archer Tomb this morning," Jemima commented deliberately. "Your ex-husband, I take it."

"Of course he's her ex-husband." It was Miss Izzy who chose to answer. "That no-good. Gregory Harrison has been a no-good since the day he was born. And that sister of his. Drifters. Not a job between them. Sailing. Fishing. As if the world owes them a living."

"Half sister. Coralie is his half sister. And she works in a hotel boutique." Tina spoke perfectly equably, but once again Jemima guessed that she was in some way put out. "Greg is the no-good in that family." For all her calm, there was a hint of suppressed anger in her reference to her former husband. With what bitterness that marriage must have ended!

"No-good, the pair of them. You're well out of that marriage, Tina dear," exclaimed Miss Izzy. "And do sit down, child—you're standing there like some kind of housekeeper. And where is Hazel, anyway? It's nearly half past five. It'll begin to get dark soon. We might go down to the terrace to watch the sun sink. Where is Henry? He ought to be bringing us some punch. The Archer Plantation punch, Miss Shore—wait till you taste it. One secret ingredient, my father always said—"

Miss Izzy was happily returning to the past.

"I'll get the punch," said Tina, still on her feet. "Didn't you say Hazel could have the day off? Her sister is getting married over at Tamarind Creek. Henry has taken her."

"Then where's the boy? Where's what's-his-name? Little Joseph." The old lady was beginning to sound petulant.

"There isn't a boy any longer," explained Tina patiently. "Just Hazel and Henry. As for Joseph—well, little Joseph Archer is quite grown up now, isn't he?"

"Of course he is! I didn't mean that Joseph—he came to see me the other day. Wasn't there another boy called Joseph? Perhaps that was before the war. My father had a stable boy—"

"I'll get the rum punch." Tina vanished swiftly and gracefully.

"Pretty creature," murmured Miss Izzy after her. "Archer blood. It always shows. They do say the best-looking Bo'landers are still called Archer."

But when Tina returned, the old lady's mood had changed again.

"I'm cold and damp," she declared. "I might get a chill sitting here. And soon I'm going to be all alone in the house. I hate being left alone. Ever since I was a little girl I've hated being alone. Everyone knows that. Tina, you have to stay to dinner. Miss Shore, you must stay, too. It's so lonely here by the sea. What happens if someone breaks in?—Don't frown, there are plenty of bad people about. That's one thing that hasn't gotten better since independence."

"Of course I'm staying," replied Tina easily. "I've arranged it with Hazel." Jemima was wondering guiltily if she, too, ought to stay. But it was the night of her hotel's weekly party on the beach—barbecue followed by dancing to a steel band. Jemima, who loved to dance in the Northern Hemisphere, was longing to try it here. Dancing under the stars by the sea sounded idyllic. Did Miss Izzy really need extra company? Her eyes met those of Tina Archer across the old lady's strawhatted head. Tina shook her head slightly.

After a sip of the famous rum punch—whatever the secret ingredient, it was the strongest she had yet tasted on the island—Jemima was able to make her escape. In any case, the punch was having a manifestly relaxing effect on Miss Izzy herself. She became rapidly quite tipsy and Jemima wondered how long she would actually stay awake. The next time they met must be in the freshness of a morning.

Jemima drove away just as the enormous red sun was rushing down below the horizon. The beat of the waves from the shore pursued her. Archer Plantation House was set in a lonely position on its own spit of land at the end of its own long avenue. She could hardly blame Miss Izzy for not wanting to be abandoned there. Jemima listened to the sound of the waves until the very different noise of the steel band in the next village along the shore took over. That transferred her thoughts temporarily from recent events at Archer Plantation House to the prospect of her evening ahead. One way or another, for a brief space of time, she would stop thinking altogether about Miss Isabella Archer.

That was because the beach party was at first exactly what Jemima had expected—relaxed, good-natured, and noisy. She found her cares gradually floating away as she danced and danced again with a series of partners, English, American, and Bo'lander, to the beat of the steel band. That rum punch of Miss Izzy's, with its secret ingredient, must have been lethal because its effects seemed to stay with her for hours. She decided she didn't even need the generous profferings of the hotel mixture—a good deal weaker than Miss Izzy's beneath its lavish surface scattering of nutmeg. Others, however, decided that the hotel punch was exactly what they did need. All in all, it was already a very good party long before the sliver of the new moon became visible over the now-black waters of the Caribbean. Jemima, temporarily alone, tilted back her head as she stood by the lapping waves at the edge of the beach and fixed the moon in her sights.

"You going to wish on that new little moon?" She turned. A tall man—at least a head taller than she was—was standing beside her on the sand. She had not heard him, the gentle noise of the waves masking his approach. For a moment she didn't recognize Joseph Archer in his loose flowered shirt and long white trousers, so different did he look from the fisherman encountered that noon at the graveside.

In this way it came about that the second part of the beach party was quite unexpected, at least from Jemima's point of view.

"I ought to wish. I ought to wish to make a good program, I suppose. That would be a good, professional thing to do."

"Miss Izzy Archer and all that?"

"Miss Izzy, Archer Plantation House, Bow Island—to say nothing of the Archer Tomb, old Sir Valentine, and all that." She decided not to mention Tina Archer and all that for the time being.

"All that!" He sighed. "Listen, Jemima—it's good, this band. We're saying it's about the best on the island these days. Let's be dancing, shall we? Then you and me can talk about all that in the morning. In my office, you know."

It was the distinct authority with which Joseph Archer spoke quite as much as the mention of his office which intrigued Jemima. Before she lost herself still further in the rhythm of the dance—which she had a feeling that with Joseph Archer to help her she was about to do—she must find out just what he meant. And, for that matter, just who he was.

The second question was easily answered. It also provided the answer to the first. Joseph Archer might or might not go fishing from time to time when he was off-duty, but he was also a member of the newly formed Bo'lander government. Quite an important one, in fact. Important in the eyes of the world in general, and particularly important in the eyes of Jemima Shore, Investigator. For Joseph Archer was the minister dealing with tourism, his brief extending to such matters as conservation, the Bo'lander historic heritage, and—as he described it to her—"the future National Archer Plantation House Museum."

Once again it didn't seem the appropriate moment to mention Tina Archer and her possible future ownership of the plantation house. As Joseph himself had said, the morning would do for all that. In his office in Bowtown.

They danced on for a while, and it was as Jemima had suspected it would be: something to lose herself in, perhaps dangerously so. The tune to "This is my island in the sun" was played and Jemima never once heard the graveyard words in her imagination. Then Joseph Archer, most politely and apparently regretfully, said he had to leave. He had an extremely early appointment—and not with a fish, either, he added with a smile. Jemima felt a pang which she hoped didn't show. But there was plenty of time, wasn't there? There would be other nights and other parties, other nights on the beach as the moon waxed to full in the two weeks she had before she must return to England.

Jemima's personal party stopped, but the rest of the celebration went on late into the night, spilling onto the sands, even into the sea, long after the sliver of the moon had vanished. Jemima, sleeping fitfully and visited by dreams in which Joseph Archer, Tina, and Miss Izzy executed some kind of elaborate dance, not at all like the kind of island jump-up she had recently been enjoying, heard the noise in the distance.

Far away on Archer Plantation's lonely peninsula, the peace was broken not by a steel band but by the rough sound of the waves bashing against the rocks at its farthest point. A stranger might have been surprised to see that the lights were still on in the great drawing room, the shutters having been drawn back once the sun was gone, but nobody born on Bow Island—a fisherman out to sea, for example—would have found it at all odd. Everyone knew that Miss Izzy Archer was frightened of the dark and liked to go to bed with all her lights blazing. Especially when Hazel had gone to her sister's wedding and Henry had taken her there—another fact of island life which most Bo'landers would have known.

In her room overlooking the sea, tossing in the big four-poster bed in which she had been born over eighty years ago, Miss Izzy, like Jemima Shore, slept fitfully. After a while, she got out of bed and went to one of the long windows. Jemima would have found her nightclothes, like her swimming costume, bizarre, for Miss Izzy wasn't wearing the kind of formal Victorian nightdress which might have gone with the house. Rather, she was "using up," as she quaintly put it, her father's ancient burgundy-silk pajamas, purchased many eons ago in Jermyn Street. And as the last Sir John Archer, Baronet, had been several feet taller than his plump little daughter, the long trouser legs trailed on the floor behind her.

Miss Izzy continued to stare out of the window. Her gaze followed the direction of the terrace, which led in a series of parterres, once grandly planted, now overgrown, down to the rocks and the sea. Although the waters themselves were mostly blackness, the Caribbean night was not entirely dark. Besides, the light from the drawing-room windows streamed out onto the nearest terrace. Miss Izzy rubbed her eyes, then she turned back into the bedroom, where the celebrated oil painting of Sir Valentine hung over the mantel-piece dominated the room. Rather confusedly—she must have drunk far too much of that punch—she decided that her ancestor was trying to encourage her to be valiant in the face of danger for the first time in her life. She, little Isabella Archer, spoilt and petted Izzy, his last legitimate descendant—no, not his last legitimate descendant, but the habits of a lifetime were difficult to break—was being spurred on to something courageous by the hawklike gaze of the fierce old autocrat.

But I'm so old, thought Miss Izzy. Then: But not *too* old. Once you let people know you're not, after all, a coward—

She looked out of the window once more. The effects of the punch were wearing off. Now she was quite certain of what she was seeing. Something dark, darkly clad, dark-skinned—What did it matter, someone dark had come out of the sea and was now proceeding silently in the direction of the house.

I must be brave, thought Miss Izzy. She said aloud: "Then he'll be proud of me. His brave girl." Whose brave girl? No, not Sir Valentine's—Daddy's brave girl. Her thoughts began to float away again into the past. I wonder if Daddy will take me on a swim with him to celebrate?

Miss Izzy started to go downstairs. She had just reached the door of the drawing room and was standing looking into the decaying red-velvet interior, still brightly illuminated, at the moment when the black-clad intruder stepped into the room through the open window.

Even before the intruder began to move softly toward her, dark-gloved hands outstretched, Miss Izzy Archer knew without doubt in her rapidly beating old heart that Archer Plantation, the house in which she had been born, was also the house in which she was about to die.

"Miss Izzy Archer is dead. Some person went and killed her last night. A robber, maybe." It was Joseph Archer who broke the news to Jemima the next morning.

He spoke across the broad desk of his formal office in Bowtown. His voice was hollow and distant, only the Bo'lander sing-song to connect him with Jemima's handsome dancing partner of the night before. In his short-sleeved but official-looking white shirt and dark trousers, he looked once again completely different from the cheer-ful ragged fisherman Jemima had first encountered. This was indeed the rising young Bo'lander politician she was seeing: a member of the newly formed government of Bow Island. Even the tragic fact of the death—the murder, as it seemed—of an old lady seemed to strike no chord of emotion in him.

Then Jemima looked again and saw what looked suspiciously like tears in Joseph Archer's eyes.

"I just heard myself, you know. The Chief of Police, Sandy Marlow, is my cousin." He didn't attempt to brush away the tears. If that was what they were. But the words were presumably meant as an explanation. Of what? Of shock? Grief? Shock he must surely have experienced, but grief? Jemima decided at this point that she could at least inquire delicately about his precise relationship to Miss Izzy.

It came back to her that he had visited the old lady the week previously, if Miss Izzy's rather vague words concerning "Little Joseph" were to be trusted. She was thinking not so much of a possible blood relationship as some other kind of connection. After all, Joseph Archer himself had dismissed the former idea in the graveyard. His words about Sir Valentine and his numerous progeny came back to her: "Don't pay too much attention to the stories. Otherwise, how come we're not all living in that fine old Archer Plantation House?" At which Greg Harrison had commented with such fury: "Instead of merely my ex-wife." The exchange made more sense to her now, of course, that she knew of the position of Tina Harrison, now Tina Archer, in Miss Izzy's will.

The will! Tina would now inherit! And she would inherit in the light of a will signed the very morning of the day of Miss Izzy's death. Clearly, Joseph had been correct when he dismissed the claim of the many Bo'landers called Archer to be descended in any meaningful fashion from Sir Valentine. There was already a considerable difference between Tina, the allegedly sole legitimate descendant other than Miss Izzy, and the rest of the Bo'lander Archers. In the future, with Tina come into her inheritance, the gap would widen even more.

It was extremely hot in Joseph's office. It was not so much that Bow Island was an unsophisticated place as that the persistent breeze made air-conditioning generally unnecessary. The North American tourists who were beginning to request air-conditioning in the hotels, reflected Jemima, would only succeed in ruining the most perfect kind of natural ventilation. But a government office in Bowtown was rather different. A huge fan in the ceiling made the papers on Joseph's desk stir uneasily. Jemima felt a ribbon of sweat trickle down beneath her long loose white T-shirt, which she had belted as a dress to provide some kind of formal attire to call on a Bo'lander minister in working hours.

By this time, Jemima's disbelieving numbness on the subject of Miss Izzy's murder was wearing off. She was struck by the frightful poignancy of that last encounter in the decaying grandeur of Archer Plantation House. Worse still, the old lady's pathetic fear of loneliness was beginning to haunt her. Miss Izzy had been so passionate in her determination not to be abandoned. "Ever since I was a little girl I've hated being alone. Everyone knows that. It's so lonely here by the sea. What happens if someone breaks in?"

Well, someone had broken in. Or so it was presumed. Joseph Archer's words: "A robber, maybe." And this robber—maybe—had killed the old lady in the process.

Jemima began hesitantly: "I'm so sorry, Joseph. What a ghastly tragedy! You knew her? Well, I suppose everyone round here must have known her—"

"All the days of my life, since I was a little boy. My mama was one of her maids. Just a little thing herself, and then she died. She's in that churchyard, you know, in a corner. Miss Izzy was very good to me when my mama died, oh, yes. She was kind. Now you'd think that independence, *our* independence, would be hard for an old lady like her, but Miss Izzy she just liked it very much. 'England's no good to me any more, Joseph,' she said, 'I'm a Bo'lander just like the rest of you.' "

"You saw her last week, I believe. Miss Izzy told me that herself."

Joseph gazed at Jemima steadily—the emotion had vanished. "I went to talk with her, yes. She had some foolish idea of changing her mind about things. Just a fancy, you know. But that's over. May she rest in peace, little old Miss Izzy. We'll have our National Museum now, that's for sure, and we'll remember her with it. It'll make a good museum for our history. Didn't they tell you in London, Jemima?" There was pride in his voice as he concluded: "Miss Izzy left everything in her will to the people of Bow Island."

Jemima swallowed hard. Was it true? Or rather, was it still true? Had Miss Izzy really signed a new will yesterday? She had been quite circumstantial on the subject, mentioning someone called Thompson—her lawyer, no doubt—who thought there would be "trouble" as a result. "Joseph," she said, "Tina Archer was up at Archer Plantation House yesterday afternoon, too."

"Oh, that girl, the trouble she made, tried to make. Tina and her stories and her fine education and her history. And she's so pretty!" Joseph's tone was momentarily violent but he finished more calmly. "The police are waiting at the hospital. She's not speaking yet, she's not even conscious." Then even more calmly: "She's not so pretty now, I hear. That robber beat her, you see."

It was hotter than ever in the Bowtown office and even the papers on the desk were hardly stirring in the waft of the fan. Jemima saw Joseph's face swimming before her. She absolutely must not faint— she never fainted. She concentrated desperately on what Joseph Archer was telling her, the picture he was recreating of the night of the murder. The shock of learning that Tina Archer had also been present in the house when Miss Izzy was killed was irrational, she realized that. Hadn't Tina promised the old lady she would stay with her?

Joseph was telling her that Miss Izzy's body had been found in the drawing room by the cook, Hazel, returning from her sister's wedding at first light. It was a grisly touch that because Miss Izzy was wearing red-silk pajamas—her daddy's—and all the furnishings of the drawing room were dark-red as well, poor Hazel had not at first realized the extent of her mistress's injuries. Not only was there blood everywhere, there was water, too—pools of it. Whatever— whoever—had killed Miss Izzy had come out of the sea. Wearing rubber shoes—or flippers—and probably gloves as well.

A moment later, Hazel was in no doubt about what had hit Miss Izzy. The club, still stained with blood, had been left lying on the floor of the front hall. (She herself, deposited by Henry, had originally entered by the kitchen door.) The club, although not of Bo'lander manufacture, belonged to the house. It was a relic, African probably, of Sir John Archer's travels in other parts of the former British Empire, and hung heavy and short-handled on the drawing-room wall. Possibly Sir John had in mind to wield it against unlawful intruders but to Miss Izzy it had been simply one more family memento. She never touched it. Now it had killed her.

"No prints anywhere," Joseph said. "So far."

"And Tina?" asked Jemima with dry lips. The idea of the pools of water stagnant on the floor of the drawing room mingled with Miss Izzy's blood reminded her only too vividly of the old lady when last seen—soaking wet in her bizarre swimming costume, defiantly sitting down on her own sofa.

"The robber ransacked the house. Even the cellar. The champagne cases Miss Izzy boasted about must have been too heavy, though. He drank some rum. The police don't know yet what he took—silver snuff-boxes maybe, there were plenty of those about." Joseph sighed. "Then he went upstairs."

"And found Tina?"

"In one of the bedrooms. He didn't hit her with the same weapon—lucky for her, as he'd have killed her just like he killed Miss Izzy. He left that downstairs and picked up something a good deal lighter. Probably didn't reckon on seeing her or anyone there at all. 'Cept for Miss Izzy, that is. Tina must have surprised him.

Maybe she woke up. Robbers—well, all I can say is that robbers here don't generally go and kill people unless they're frightened."

Without warning, Joseph slumped down in front of her and put his head in his hands. He murmured something like: "When we find who did it to Miss Izzy—"

It wasn't until the next day that Tina Archer was able to speak even haltingly to the police. Like most of the rest of the Bow Island population, Jemima Shore was informed of the fact almost immediately. Claudette, manageress of her hotel, a sympathetic if loquacious character, just happened to have a niece who was a nurse. But that was the way information always spread about the island—no need for newspapers or radio, this private telegraph was far more efficient.

Jemima had spent the intervening twenty-four hours swimming rather aimlessly, sunbathing, and making little tours of the island in her mini. She was wondering at what point she should inform Megalith Television of the brutal way in which her projected program had been terminated and make arrangements to return to London. After a bit, the investigative instinct, that inveterate curiosity which would not be stilled, came to the fore. She found she was speculating all the time about Miss Izzy's death. A robber? A robber who had also tried to kill Tina Archer? Or a robber who had merely been surprised by her presence in the house? What connection, if any, had all this with Miss Izzy's will?

The will again. But that was one thing Jemima didn't have to speculate about for very long. For Claudette, the manageress, also just happened to be married to the brother of Hazel, Miss Izzy's cook. In this way, Jemima was apprised—along with the rest of Bow Island, no doubt—that Miss Izzy had indeed signed a new will down in Bowtown on the morning of her death, that Eddie Thompson, the solicitor, had begged her not to do it, that Miss Izzy *had* done it, that Miss Izzy had still looked after Hazel all right, as she had promised (and Henry who had worked for her even longer), and that some jewelry would go to a cousin in England, "seeing as Miss Izzy's mother's jewels were in an English bank anyway since long back." But for the rest, well, there would be no National Bo'lander Museum now, that was for sure. Everything else—that fine old Archer Plantation House, Miss Izzy's fortune, reputedly enormous but who knew for sure?—would go to Tina Archer.

If she recovered, of course. But the latest cautious bulletin from Claudette via the niece-who-was-a-nurse, confirmed by a few other loquacious people on the island, was that Tina Archer *was* recovering. The police had already been able to interview her. In a few

days she would be able to leave the hospital. And she was determined to attend Miss Izzy's funeral, which would be held, naturally
enough, in that little English-looking church with its incongruous
tropical vegetation overlooking the sunny grave. For Miss Izzy had
long ago made clear her own determination to be buried in the
Archer Tomb, along with Governor Sir Valentine and "his only
wife, Isabella."

"As the last of the Archers. But she still had to get permission
since it's a national monument. And of course the government
couldn't do enough for her. So they gave it. Then. Ironic, isn't it?"
The speaker making absolutely no attempt to conceal her disgust
was Coralie Harrison. "And now we learn that she wasn't the last
of the Archers, not officially, and we shall have the so-called Miss
Tina Archer as chief mourner. And while the Bo'lander government
desperately looks for ways to get round the will and grab the house
for their precious museum, nobody quite has the bad taste to go
ahead and say no—no burial in the Archer Tomb for naughty old
Miss Izzy. Since she hasn't, after all, left the people of Bow Island
a penny."

"It should be an interesting occasion," Jemima murmured. She
was sitting with Coralie Harrison under the conical thatched roof
of the hotel's beach bar. This was where she first danced, then sat
out with Joseph Archer on the night of the new moon—the night
Miss Izzy had been killed. Now the sea sparkled under the sun as
though there were crystals scattered on its surface. Today there were
no waves at all and the happy water-skiers crossed and recrossed
the wide bay with its palm-fringed shore. Enormous brown pelicans
perched on some stakes which indicated where rocks lay. Every now
and then, one would take off like an unwieldy aeroplane and fly
slowly and inquisitively over the heads of the swimmers. It was a
tranquil, even an idyllic scene, but somewhere in the distant peninsula lay Archer Plantation House, not only shuttered but now,
she imagined, also sealed by the police.

Coralie had sauntered up to the bar from the beach. She traversed
the few yards with seeming casualness—all Bo'landers frequently
exercised their right to promenade along the sands unchecked (as
in most Caribbean islands, no one owned any portion of the beach
in Bow Island, even outside the most stately mansion like Archer
Plantation House, except the people). Jemima, however, was in no
doubt that this was a planned visit. She had not forgotten that first
meeting, and Coralie's tentative approach to her, interrupted by
Greg's peremptory cry.

It was the day after the inquest on Miss Izzy's death. Her body
had been released by the police and the funeral would soon follow.

Jemima admitted to herself that she was interested enough in the whole Archer family, and its various branches, to want to attend it, quite apart from the tenderness she felt for the old lady herself, based on that brief meeting. To Megalith Television, in a telex from Bowtown, she had spoken merely of tying up a few loose ends resulting from the cancellation of her program.

There had been an open verdict at the inquest. Tina Archer's evidence in a sworn statement had not really contributed much that wasn't known or suspected already. She had been asleep upstairs in one of the many fairly derelict bedrooms kept ostensibly ready for guests. The bedroom chosen for her by Miss Izzy had not faced onto the sea. The chintz curtains in this back room, bearing some dated rosy pattern from a remote era, weren't quite so bleached and tattered since they had been protected from the sun and salt.

Miss Izzy had gone to bed in good spirits, reassured by the fact that Tina Archer was going to spend the night. She had drunk several more rum punches and had offered to have Henry fetch some of her father's celebrated champagne from the cellar. As a matter of fact, Miss Izzy often made this offer after a few draughts of punch, but Tina reminded her that Henry was away and the subject was dropped.

In her statement, Tina said she had no clue as to what might have awakened the old lady and induced her to descend the stairs—it was right out of character in her own opinion. Isabella Archer was a lady of independent mind but notoriously frightened of the dark, hence Tina's presence at the house in the first place. As to her own recollection of the attack, Tina had so far managed to dredge very few of the details from her memory—the blow to the back of the head had temporarily or permanently expunged all the immediate circumstances from her consciousness. She had a vague idea that there had been a bright light, but even that was rather confused and might be part of the blow she had suffered. Basically, she could remember nothing between going to bed in the tattered, rose-patterned four-poster and waking up in hospital.

Coralie's lip trembled. She bowed her head and sipped at her long drink through a straw—she and Jemima were drinking some exotic mixture of fruit juice, alcohol free, invented by Matthew, the barman. There was a wonderful soft breeze coming in from the sea and Coralie was dressed in a loose flowered cotton dress, but she looked hot and angry. "Tina schemed for everything all her life and now she's got it. That's what I wanted to warn you about that morning in the churchyard—don't trust Tina Archer, I wanted to say. Now it's too late, she's got it all. When she was married to

Greg, I tried to like her, Jemima, honestly I did. Little Tina, so cute and so clever, but always trouble—"

"Joseph Archer feels rather the same way about her, I gather," Jemima said. Was it her imagination or did Coralie's face soften slightly at the sound of Joseph's name?

"Does he? I'm glad. He fancied her, too, once upon a time. She is quite pretty." Their eyes met. "Well, not all that pretty, but if you like the type—" Jemima and Coralie both laughed. The fact was that Coralie Harrison was quite appealing, if you liked *her* type, but Tina Archer was ravishing by any standards.

"Greg absolutely loathes her now, of course," Coralie continued firmly, "especially since he heard the news about the will. When we met you that morning up at the church he'd just been told. Hence, well, I'm sorry, but he was very rude, wasn't he?"

"More hostile than rude." But Jemima had begun to work out the timing. "You mean your brother knew about the will *before* Miss Izzy was killed?" she exclaimed.

"Oh, yes. Someone from Eddie Thompson's office told Greg— Daisy Marlow, maybe, he takes her out. Of course, we all knew it was on the cards, except we hoped Joseph had argued Miss Izzy out of it. And he *would* have argued her out of it given time. That museum is everything to Joseph."

"Your brother and Miss Izzy—that wasn't an easy relationship, I gather."

Jemima thought she was using her gentlest and most persuasive interviewer's voice, but Coralie countered with something like defiance: "You sound like the police!"

"Why, have they—?"

"Well, of course they have!" Coralie answered the question before Jemima had completed it. "Everyone knows that Greg absolutely hated Miss Izzy—blamed her for breaking up his marriage, for taking little Tina and giving her ideas!"

"Wasn't it rather the other way around—Tina delving into the family records for the museum and then my program? You *said* she was a schemer."

"Oh, I *know* she was a schemer! But did Greg? He did not. Not then. He was besotted with her at the time, so he had to blame the old lady. They had a frightful row—very publicly. He went round to the house one night, went in by the sea, shouted at her. Hazel and Henry heard, so then everyone knew. That was when Tina told him she was going to get a divorce and throw in her lot with Miss Izzy for the future. I'm afraid my brother is rather an extreme person—his temper is certainly extreme. He made threats—"

"But the police don't think—" Jemima stopped. It was clear what she meant.

Coralie swung her legs off the bar stool. Jemima handed her the huge straw bag with the archer logo on it and she slung it over her shoulder in proper Bo'lander fashion.

"How pretty," Jemima commented politely.

"I sell them at the hotel on the North Point. For a living." The remark sounded pointed. "No," Coralie went on rapidly before Jemima could say anything more on that subject, "of course the police don't *think*, as you put it. Greg might have assaulted Tina— but Greg kill Miss Izzy when he knew perfectly well that by so doing he was handing his ex-wife a fortune? No way. Not even the Bo'lander police would believe that."

That night Jemima Shore found Joseph Archer again on the beach under the stars. But the moon had waxed since their first encounter. Now it was beginning to cast a silver pathway on the waters of the night. Nor was this meeting unplanned as that first one had been. Joseph had sent her a message that he would be free and they had agreed to meet down by the bar.

"What do you say I'll take you on a night drive round our island, Jemima?"

"No. Let's be proper Bo'landers and walk along the sands." Jemima wanted to be alone with him, not driving past the rows of lighted tourist hotels, listening to the eternal beat of the steel bands. She felt reckless enough not to care how Joseph himself would interpret this change of plan.

They walked for some time along the edge of the sea, in silence except for the gentle lap of the waves. After a while, Jemima took off her sandals and splashed through the warm receding waters, and a little while after that Joseph took her hand and led her back onto the sand. The waves grew conspicuously rougher as they rounded the point of the first wide bay. They stood for a moment together, Joseph and Jemima, he with his arm companionably round her waist.

"Jemima, even without that new moon, I'm going to wish—" Then Joseph stiffened. He dropped the encircling arm, grabbed her shoulder, and swung her around. "Jesus, oh sweet Jesus, do you see that?"

The force of his gesture made Jemima wince. For a moment she was distracted by the flickering moonlit swathe on the dark surface of the water. There were multitudinous white—silver—horses out beyond the land where high waves were breaking over an outcrop of rocks. She thought Joseph was pointing out to sea. Then she saw the lights.

"The Archer house!" she cried. "I thought it was shut up!" It seemed that all the lights of the house were streaming out across the promontory on which it lay. Such was the illumination that you might have supposed some great ball was in progress, a thousand candles lit as in the days of Governor Archer. More somberly, Jemima realized that was how the plantation house must have looked on the night of Miss Izzy's death. Tina Archer and others had borne witness to the old lady's insistence on never leaving her house in darkness. The night her murderer had come in from the sea, this is how the house must have looked to him.

"Come on!" said Joseph. The moment of lightness—or loving, perhaps?—had utterly vanished. He sounded both grim and determined.

"To the police?"

"No, to the house. I need to know what's happening there."

As they half ran along the sands, Joseph said, "This house should have been *ours*."

Ours: the people of Bow Island.

His restlessness on the subject of the museum struck Jemima anew since her conversation with Coralie Harrison. What would a man— or a woman, for that matter—do for an inheritance? And there was more than one kind of inheritance. Wasn't a national heritage as important to some people as a personal inheritance to others? Joseph Archer was above all a patriotic Bo'lander. And he had not known of the change of will on the morning after Miss Izzy's death. She herself had evidence of that. Might a man like Joseph Archer, a man who had already risen in his own world by sheer determination, decide to take the law into his own hands in order to secure the museum for his people while there was still time?

But to kill the old lady who had befriended him as a boy? Batter her to death? As he strode along, so tall in the moonlight, Joseph was suddenly a complete and thus menacing enigma to Jemima.

They had reached the promontory, had scrambled up the rocks, and had got as far as the first terrace when all the lights in the house went out. It was as though a switch had been thrown. Only the cold eerie glow of the moon over the sea behind them remained to il-luminate the bushes, now wildly overgrown, and the sagging bal-ustrades.

But Joseph strode on, helping Jemima up the flights of stone steps, some of them deeply cracked and uneven. In the darkness, Jemima could just see that the windows of the drawing room were still open. There had to be someone in there behind the ragged red-brocade curtains which had been stained by Miss Izzy's blood.

Joseph, holding Jemima's hand, pulled her through the center window.

There was a short cry like a suppressed scream and then a low sound, as if someone was laughing at them there in the dark. An instant later, all the lights were snapped on at once.

Tina was standing at the door, her hand at the switch. She wore a white bandage on her head like a turban—and she wasn't laughing, she was sobbing.

"Oh, it's you, Jo-seph and Je-mi-ma Shore." For the first time, Jemima was aware of the sing-song Bo'lander note in Tina's voice. "I was so fright-ened."

"Are you all right, Tina?" asked Jemima hastily, to cover the fact that she had been quite severely frightened herself. The atmosphere of angry tension between the two other people in the room, so different in looks yet both of them, as it happened, called Archer, was almost palpable. She felt she was in honor bound to try to relieve it. "Are you all alone?"

"The police said I could come." Tina ignored the question. "They have finished with everything here. And besides—" her terrified sobs had vanished, there was something deliberately provocative about her as she moved toward them "—why ever not?" To neither of them did she need to elaborate. The words "since it's all mine" hung in the air.

Joseph spoke for the first time since they had entered the room. "I want to look at the house," he said harshly.

"Jo-seph Archer, you get out of here. Back where you came from, back to your off-ice and that's not a great fine house." Then she addressed Jemima placatingly, in something more like her usual sweet manner. "I'm sorry, but, you see, we've not been friends since way back. And, besides, you gave me such a shock."

Joseph swung on his heel. "I'll see you at the funeral, Miss Archer." He managed to make the words sound extraordinarily threatening.

That night it seemed to Jemima Shore that she hardly slept, although the threads of broken, half remembered dreams disturbed her and indicated that she must actually have fallen into some kind of doze in the hour before dawn. The light was still grey when she looked out of her shutters. The tops of the tall palms were bending— there was quite a wind.

Back on her bed, Jemima tried to recall just what she had been dreaming. There had been some pattern to it: she knew there had. She wished rather angrily that light would suddenly break through into her sleepy mind as the sun was shortly due to break through the eastern fringe of palms on the hotel estate. No gentle, slow-developing, rosy-fingered dawn for the Caribbean: one brilliant low ray was a herald of what was to come, and then, almost immediately, hot relentless sunshine for the rest of the day. She needed that kind of instant clarity herself.

Hostility. That was part of it all—the nature of hostility. The hostility, for example, between Joseph and Tina Archer the night before, so virulent and public—with herself as the public—that it might almost have been managed for effect.

Then the management of things: Tina Archer, always managing, always a schemer (as Coralie Harrison had said—and Joseph Archer, too). That brought her to the other couple in this odd, four-pointed drama: the Harrisons, brother and sister, or rather *half* brother and sister (a point made by Tina to correct Miss Izzy).

More hostility: Greg, who had once loved Tina and now loathed her. Joseph, who had once also perhaps loved Tina. Coralie, who had once perhaps—very much perhaps, this one—loved Joseph and certainly loathed Tina. Cute and clever little Tina, the Archer Tomb, the carved figures of Sir Valentine and his wife, the inscription. Jemima was beginning to float back into sleep, as the four figures, all Bo'landers, all sharing some kind of common past, began to dance to a calypso whose wording, too, was confused:

"This is your graveyard in the sun
Where my people have toiled since time begun—"

An extraordinarily loud noise on the corrugated metal roof above her head recalled her, trembling, to her senses. The racket had been quite immense, almost as if there had been an explosion or at least a missile fired at the chalet. The thought of a missile made her realize that it had in fact been a missile: it must have been a coconut which had fallen in such a startling fashion on the corrugated roof. Guests were officially warned by the hotel against sitting too close under the palm trees, whose innocuous-looking fronds could suddenly dispense their heavily lethal nuts. COCONUTS CAN CAUSE INJURY ran the printed notice.

That kind of blow on my head would certainly have caused injury, thought Jemima, if not death.

Injury, if not death. And the Archer Tomb: my only wife.

At that moment, straight on cue, the sun struck low through the bending fronds to the east and onto her shutters. And Jemima realized not only why it had been done but how it had been done.

Who of them all had been responsible for consigning Miss Izzy Archer to the graveyard in the sun.

The scene by the Archer Tomb a few hours later had that same strange mixture of English tradition and Bo'lander exoticism which had intrigued Jemima on her first visit. Only this time she had a deeper, sadder purpose than sheer tourism. Traditional English hymns were sung at the service, but outside a steel band was playing at Miss Izzy's request. As one who had been born on the island, she had asked for a proper Bo'lander funeral.

The Bo'landers, attending in large numbers, were by and large dressed with that extreme formality—dark suits, white shirts, ties, dark dresses, dark straw hats, even white gloves—which Jemima had observed in churchgoers of a Sunday and in the Bo'lander children, all of them neatly uniformed on their way to school. No Bow Island T-shirts were to be seen, although many of the highly colored intricate and lavish wreaths were in the bow shape of the island's logo. The size of the crowd was undoubtedly a genuine mark of respect. Whatever the disappointments of the will to their government, to the Bo'landers Miss Izzy Archer had been part of their heritage.

Tina Archer wore a black scarf wound round her head which almost totally concealed her bandage. Joseph Archer, standing far apart from her and not looking in her direction, looked both elegant and formal in his office clothes, a respectable member of the government. The Harrisons stood together, Coralie with her head bowed. Greg's defiant aspect, head lifted proudly, was clearly intended to give the lie to any suggestions that he had not been on the best of terms with the woman whose body was now being lowered into the family tomb.

As the coffin—so small and thus so touching—vanished from view, there was a sigh from the mourners. They began to sing again: a hymn, but with the steel band gently echoing the tune in the background.

Jemima moved discreetly in the crowd and stood by the side of the tall man.

"You'll never be able to trust her," she said in a low voice. "She's managed you before, she'll manage you again. It'll be someone else who will be doing the dirty work next time. On you. You'll never be able to trust her, will you? Once a murderess, always a murderess. You may wish one day you'd finished her off."

The tall man looked down at her. Then he looked across at Tina Archer with one quick savagely doubting look. Tina Archer Harrison, his only wife.

"Why, you—" For a moment, Jemima thought Greg Harrison would actually strike her down there at the graveside, as he had struck down old Miss Izzy and—if only on pretense—struck down Tina herself.

"Greg darling." It was Coralie Harrison's pathetic, protesting murmur. "What are you saying to him?" she demanded of Jemima in a voice as low as Jemima's own. But the explanations—for Coralie and the rest of Bow Island—of the conspiracy of Tina Archer and Greg Harrison were only just beginning.

The rest was up to the police, who with their patient work of investigation would first amplify, then press, finally concluding the case. And in the course of the investigations, the conspirators would fall apart, this time for real. To the police fell the unpleasant duty of disentangling the new lies of Tina Archer, who now swore that her memory had just returned, that it had been Greg who had half killed her that night, that she had had absolutely nothing to do with it. And Greg Harrison denounced Tina in return, this time with genuine ferocity. "It was her plan, her plan all along. She managed everything. I should never have listened to her!"

Before she left Bow Island, Jemima went to say goodbye to Joseph Archer in his Bowtown office. There were many casualties of the Archer tragedy beyond Miss Izzy herself. Poor Coralie was one: she had been convinced that her brother, for all his notorious temper, would never batter down Miss Izzy to benefit his ex-wife. Like the rest of Bow Island, she was unaware of the deep plot by which Greg and Tina would publicly display their hostility, advertise their divorce, and all along plan to kill Miss Izzy once the new will was signed. Greg, ostentatiously hating his ex-wife, would not be suspected, and Tina, suffering such obvious injuries, could only arouse sympathy.

Another small casualty, much less important, was the romance which just might have developed between Joseph Archer and Jemima Shore. Now, in his steamingly hot office with its perpetually moving fan, they talked of quite other things than the new moon and new wishes.

"You must be happy you'll get your museum," said Jemima.

"But that's not at all the way I wanted it to happen," he replied. Then Joseph added: "But you know, Jemima, there has been justice done. And in her heart of hearts Miss Izzy did really want us to have this National Museum. I'd have talked her round to good sense again if she had lived."

"That's why they acted when they did. They didn't dare wait, given Miss Izzy's respect for you," suggested Jemima. She stopped, but her curiosity got the better of her. There was one thing she had to know before she left. "The Archer Tomb and all that. Tina being descended from Sir Valentine's lawful second marriage. Is that true?"

"Yes, it's true. Maybe. But it's not important to most of us here. You know something, Jemima? I, too, am descended from that well known second marriage. Maybe. And a few others maybe. Lucie Anne had two children, don't forget, and Bo'landers have large families. It was important to Tina Archer, not to me. That's not what I want. That's all past. Miss Izzy was the last of the Archers, so far as I'm concerned. Let her lie in her tomb."

"What *do* you want for yourself? Or for Bow Island, if you prefer."

Joseph smiled and there was a glimmer there of the handsome fisherman who had welcomed her to Bow Island, the cheerful dancing partner. "Come back to Bow Island one day, Jemima. Make another program about us, our history and all that, and I'll tell you then."

"I might just do that," said Jemima Shore.

JOSEPH HANSEN

For over twenty years Joseph Hansen has been writing fine mystery stories. Since the first Dave Brandstetter novel, *Fadeout*, Hansen has shown a consistent ability to entertain while also writing thoughtful, intriguingly different tales.

"The Owl in the Oak" features Hack Bohannon, Hansen's favorite short-form protagonist. Bohannon has survived a lot over the years, but in this story he goes beyond being merely beleaguered before catching up with the cause of a marvelously varied series of criminal consequences. Sometimes things may actually be simpler than they seem, though not necessarily in the direction indicated by the most obvious evidence. As you will discover shortly.

The Owl
in the Oak

Alice Donovan was a small woman, past forty but brisk, with an open way about her, a smile and a perky word for just about everybody. She called her shop Ye Olde Oak Tree for the very good reason that an old oak sheltered it. Like a good many shops in Madrone, a tiny foothill town on California's central coast, hers had been converted from a spindly frame dwelling with jigsaw-work porches and bay windows. Most of these places sported fresh paint nowadays. Ye Olde Oak Tree was green with yellow trim.

The last time Hack Bohannon had noticed, Alice sold cheap china and pewter knickknacks, T-shirts and souvenir scarves, picture postcards, sunglasses, snapshot film, chewing gum, cigarettes—and cookies, when she felt like baking. She kept antiques that needed work. Bohannon recollected a treadle sewing machine in the front yard, an old wooden Maytag with hand-cranked wringers. A wagon wheel had leaned against the trunk of the oak. Bad oil paintings slumped on the porch, seascapes mostly—the ocean was over yonder, on the far side of the highway.

All this was gone now. Neat beds of pansies and petunias lay to either side of the footpath. Bohannon's boot heels knocked across an empty porch. And when he opened the door and stepped inside, he didn't recognize the place. New paint, wallpaper, carpet on the floor. The antique rockers, highboys, commodes were sleekly refinished. Not a postcard rack remained, no T-shirts, visor hats, suntan lotion. Good Mexican terra cotta pots stood on shelves. Fine baskets occupied corners. Soft serapes in natural wool colors hung against the walls. On velvet in glass cases lay bracelets, necklaces, rings in hand-wrought silver set with turquoise and jade.

The shop took up the two front rooms of the little house, parlor, sitting room. He stepped behind a counter and opened an inner door. Built-in diamond-paned sideboards said this had been a dining room. Magazines, books, cassettes, a camera and boxes of film crowded them now. The room had only space enough for two wing chairs, a coffee table, a television set—and these were all it held. He pushed a swinging door and was in the kitchen. A deputy had used a black magic marker on the pale vinyl tile of the floor to outline where and how Alice Donovan's small body had lain when her hulking son Howard had found it last night. Next to a glass of white wine on a counter, slices of apple and a wedge of yellow cheese lay on a saucer, a paring knife in the sink.

The back door stood open, and he frowned at that. Gerard ought to have posted an officer here. Bohannon squinted at the door and the frame. A deadbolt had been broken. Someone had wanted badly to get in. Early this morning, as soon as news of the murder got on the radio. A size twelve shoe had forced the door, a shoe muddy from the dew in the brush out back. He scowled around him. Had big-foot found what Bohannon was here to look for? That would be a hell of a note.

Morning sunlight came cheerfully through a window over the sink and slanted onto the place where Alice Donovan had died. The patch of dried blood there was the size of a dinner plate. Someone had smashed her skull in, unhooked a cast-iron skillet from its place in a row of pans over the stove and hit her from behind. Lieutenant Gerard of the Madrone sheriff's office figured big, shambling Howard had done it. Howard was sitting in a cell. He claimed he had been on the beach, alone all evening, thinking. He had killed eight cans of beer. The empties were there, bobbing in the surf among the rocks to prove it, if anyone cared to check.

"And many more besides," Gerard grunted, "I have no doubt. Christ, people love to make the world ugly, don't they?" He wadded the last bite of a cruller into his mouth and washed it down with coffee from a chipped mug. "No, Howard and Alice had been on a collision course since he was born. She babied him through years one to thirteen, then made him the man in her life, right? Except he could never do what he wanted, only what she wanted."

"You could say—" Bohannon tilted back in a straight oak chair "—he went direct from the nursing bottle to the whisky bottle."

Howard had spent times away from Madrone in hospitals that promise to cure addictive personalities and sometimes succeed—though not with Howard. He wasn't much more than twenty, but no peace officer who'd ever had to deal with him, Bohannon not excepted, figured him for less than a dangerous drunk for life—or at least for as long as he lasted. He was quite a driver when he drank. He had totaled two cars of his mother's, and others that had belonged to former friends.

"His buddies don't want him around," Bohannon said.

"Except Beau Larkin," Gerard said. "Worse than Howard. Beau'd be in Folsom if his dad wasn't a San Luis cop."

"Howard never got violent with Alice. Not once."

"There's always a first time." Gerard crumpled the white paper sack the cruller had come in and dropped it into a wastebasket. "Nothing was stolen, Hack. Whoever did it didn't have to force entry. No, Howard came home drunk, and they had another argument—their last one."

"Fred May doesn't think so," Bohannon said.

"Right. And that's why you're here." Gerard pawed the files, photographs, reports on his desk and found cigarettes. He lit one and looked at Bohannon through the smoke. "Fred wants you to find evidence that somebody else killed Alice Donovan." He gave a thin smile. "You do as much police work as you used to when you were on the payroll here, Hack. Why don't you just come back, and stop being so stubborn?"

Bohannon had been a deputy for fourteen years; then it had gone sour for him, he'd quit, and opened boarding stables up Rodd canyon. He liked the company of horses better than that of men, but people in trouble kept coming to him for help, so he'd taken out a private investigator's license. He didn't know how to turn folks away. But he would never come back to work here. He hated the very sounds and smells of the place, the desks, files, jangling phones, even the lighting. He and Gerard had been partners, friends. They weren't enemies now, but they'd never be the same again.

"Give me the keys," Bohannon said. "I'll go see if Fred's got a case or not."

When Bohannon passed it, May came waddling out of his office and walked beside him down the hallway. May, on the staff of the county attorney, was a public defender when the need arose. He was no papershuffler but a bright lawyer with a belief in justice nothing could shake—certainly not offers of money. He would have been better paid almost anyplace else. Luckily, his wife and kids were decent as he was. If a battered VW bug was wheels enough for him, if he could get through the days in sweatshirts, cheap jeans, and worn-out tennis shoes, so could they, and cheerfully. Bohannon pushed open the side door of the substation, and the fat man followed him out to the parking lot where patrol cars stood collecting leaves and pods from the towering eucalyptus that hedged the tarmac. May said:

"You know what bothers me? Not that nothing was stolen. What bothers me is that Alice Donovan had anything worth stealing. Where did she get the money to upgrade the place so suddenly?"

"Why not from the bank?" Bohannon had lately wrecked his faithful old GM pickup, and the one parked out here now was new, shiny, apple green. He pulled open the door and climbed up into it. It didn't smell of alfalfa and dried manure yet. It still smelled new. He kept thinking it didn't belong to him. "She owned the property, didn't she? Why didn't she take out a loan on it?"

"I don't know—" May's moon face winced up at him "—but she didn't. Not in this area. We checked it out. See what you can find, Hack. There's an answer someplace."

"She didn't tell Howard?" Bohannon slammed the door of the pickup and slid the key into the ignition. "Or is he too hung over to talk?"

"He's not hung over, but she said it was a secret. She teased him, like he was five years old: 'I've got a secret, I won't tell—' "

"Don't sing, Fred," Bohannon said.

"Sorry about that. But he did say something interesting. Said he saw her hide something. If it was money, Howard wanted it. For booze, right? When he thought it was safe, he dug it out, but she caught him before he could open it."

"So he doesn't know if it was money or what." Bohannon started the truck. Over the smooth hum of the engine May said:

"A cardboard box with rubber bands around it. He looked for it again, every chance he got, but he never found it."

"Maybe I'll have better luck." Bohannon released the parking brake. "I won't have to worry about Alice walking in on me, will I?" He lifted a hand, and drove off.

Now, in the silent kitchen, he got down on hands and knees to probe low cupboards that smelled of soap powder. He climbed a flimsy aluminum step stool to grope on high shelves among cobwebby cut glass, cracked plates, forgotten gift boxes of fancy teas. In a shadowy hallway he unloaded sheets, pillowcases, towels from a linen closet. Nothing. He got the step stool and poked his head through a ceiling trapdoor. Nothing but rafters, dust, and heat.

Alice Donovan's bedroom was neat and smelled faintly of sandalwood perfume. He found nothing that didn't belong there. She wouldn't hide whatever it was in Howard's room, but he searched that anyway. Empty pint vodka bottles rattled among the cleated shoes on the closet floor. The closet smelled of the sweaty jeans, shirts, jackets that hung there. On the shelf lay shoulder pads, helmets, a catcher's mitt, and a stack of dog-eared magazines with photos of naked young women. The bed was unmade. In the dustballs under it lay empty beer cans and crumpled potato chip bags.

The bedside stand held a lamp and a digital clock whose red numerals read 3:00. Plainly Howard hadn't bothered setting it again after the last power outage. Maybe time, along with everything else but his thirst, had ceased to have meaning for Howard. Bohannon opened a drawer in the table. Candy bar wrappers, scratched California lottery tickets, rubber bands, a broken pencil. And photographs. Half a dozen. Of a red-haired young woman who looked tall. Taken someplace among boats—Morro Bay? She wore tight jeans, a striped tank top, sunglasses that didn't hide her exceptional good looks. He tucked the photos into a shirt pocket and went to check out the bathroom.

It was shiny clean, and Alice Donovan had not hidden anything there. Back in the kitchen, he opened the refrigerator. He'd never seen so many cans of beer outside a market. He took one, figuring Howard wouldn't mind, since Bohannon was trying to save his sizeable hide. A noise came from the shop. He must have left the door unlocked. He set down the beer can and jogged for the front rooms. A large, expensively dressed woman was peering into one of the glass cases. She turned and stared at him in surprise. He understood. In his Levi's, cowboy boots, sweaty stained Stetson, he plainly was no dealer in jewelry and antiques.

"Who—who are you?" A thick envelope was in her hand. She poked it hastily into a large handbag. "What are you doing here?"

"Investigator for the county attorney," he said. "Bohannon is my name. What's yours?"

"Where's Mrs. Donovan?" She came toward him, peering past his shoulder through the open door into the living quarters. She called out, "Alice? It's Margaret Weems." She looked at Bohannon. "We had an appointment." She read a tiny jewelled watch on a wrist strong enough to control an eight horse hitch. "For twelve noon." She blinked. "Investigator?"

"Mrs. Donovan met with an accident," Bohannon said.

Margaret Weems went very still. Fashion wasn't doing her kind any favors. The exaggerated shoulders of the moment made her look like a linebacker in drag. Her tongue touched her lips. He couldn't read the look in her eyes. "Is she—all right? An automobile accident, you mean?"

Bohannon shook his head. "Assault. She's dead."

"My God." The woman's knees gave. Bohannon stepped out from behind the counter to catch her arm, but she didn't want that. She sat down, breathing hard, clutching the purse tight against her. She managed a pale, apologetic smile. "Excuse me. I'll just sit here a moment, if I may. It's such a shock."

"Get you anything?" he asked. "Water? Brandy?"

Eyes closed, she shook her head. "Assault. How dreadful." She opened her eyes. "She was so tiny."

"Were you a friend?" Bohannon said.

"Friend?" Her brief laugh had no humor in it. "No. Just a—customer." Her gaze caressed the jewelry, pottery, weaving. "She had such lovely things, didn't she?"

"You used her first name," Bohannon said. "If you were a friend, I thought maybe you could help me here."

Her look was guarded. "Help you how? With what?"

He shrugged. "If you talked together, maybe she said something—was she frightened of anything, anyone?"

Margaret Weems snorted. "Have you met her son?"

Bohannon grinned. "He once lifted me up over his head and threw me into the ocean. He and his high school friends got a little rowdy that night. Howard's a big, strong boy."

"I don't know how she could bear having him here."

"He's been locked up for the murder," Bohannon said. "I'm supposed to find evidence he didn't do it."

Margaret Weems gave a wry laugh. "I wish you luck," she said, and got off the chair, and walked out. Bohannon wanted to ask her what was in that envelope she'd stuffed so hurriedly into her handbag. But it would be smarter to wait. He watched her settle into a Mercedes that looked as if it got washed and waxed every day. He watched it roll off down the dusty trail, then went back to the kitchen to finish off his beer and nail shut the back door.

He found the box twenty minutes later, in a spring-operated compartment hidden behind a beautifully mitered drawer in a General Grant lowboy with a marble top. He sat on the fresh crimson velvet of a carved walnut chair, twanged the rubber bands from around the box, and lifted the lid. A sour smell came out. Inside lay a stack of small envelopes, note size, fastened by another rubber band. When he lifted them out, he saw a little packet of olive drab velvet, the same fabric that lined Alice Donovan's glass display cases.

He unfolded the velvet from around a piece of Navajo jewelry, a buckle. Not new like the stuff the Donovan woman was selling. Old. The stone was brown, not blue or green, and the heft of the piece, its time-worn smoothness, told him it was special. He rewrapped it and tucked it into his shirt pocket with the snapshots of the redhaired girl. Then he snapped the rubber band off the envelopes and shuffled through them. They were stained and gritty to the touch.

All were addressed in ballpoint pen to an Estella Hernandez at a post office box in Guadalupe. There was no return address. He pulled a letter out of its envelope. It was signed only G. He read it and blinked. G seemed pretty worked up. He folded that letter and put it back in its envelope and read the others, one by one. G evidently thought he was in love. Starlight and birdsongs and the moon shining on a midnight ocean got into the letters, but so did steamy sexual stuff. One of the letters, the first one, was signed Galen. The postmarks were all Madrone. He rubber-banded the envelopes, stuffed them into a pocket of his Levi jacket, put the empty box back into the lowboy, closed the drawer, and left Alice Donovan's silent shop, locking the door behind him.

Halfway down the path, he paused to squint up at the oak. Crows were making a racket there, flapping around, diving at something hidden in the leafage. It was an owl, a big Western horned owl. He hunched on a branch, and looked like he meant to stay there, like it was his tree, and the crows could do their damnedest but he wasn't leaving. He glared up at them with round yellow eyes and clacked his beak at them from time to time, and now and then spread his wings and bounced up and down as if on springs. Then he'd crouch again, screwing his head around to face them, this way, that way, no matter from what angle they came at him. Bohannon wished him luck and climbed into his new pickup.

Deputy T. Hodges was seated at a little square table on the screened porch of a luncheonette in Madrone. The table top was Formica in a red gingham pattern. A red paper napkin lay crumpled beside T. Hodges' plate. The remains of a hamburger and a scattering of french fries lay on the plate. She was nursing what Bohannon guessed was cold coffee. When he banged in at the screen door, her shiny dark eyes lit up for a second in a smile. She didn't often smile with her mouth. She had the notion that her front teeth stuck out, which they did a little, and this embarrassed her. By the time he pulled the empty chair out at her table, she was frowning. She read her watch.

"I've only got ten minutes left," she said.

"Sorry." He sat down. "I was looking for something and I wasn't too quick about finding it. You haven't had dessert. Shall we eat peach pie together?"

A fat girl in a sweatshirt stenciled RAIDERS came to the table and took a pencil from behind her ear. "Mr. Bohannon. Hi. How's my pal, Geranium?"

Geranium was a broad-backed, placid old buckskin mare who never put a big hoof wrong, and Cassie felt safe on her when she came up to the stables with one of her assorted boyfriends to ride the canyon trails on Mondays, when the cafe was closed.

"She missed you the other day," Bohannon said.

"I went swimming." She made a face. "Tony said we were going sailing in his boat, but he kept tipping it over. What will you have?"

"Peach pie for both of us," Bohannon said. "And Deputy Hodges needs a refill, and I'll have coffee, too, please."

"You got it," Cassie said, took T. Hodges' plate, and padded away.

"Looking for what?" T. Hodges said.

He told her. Then he laid the snapshots in front of her. "Ever see that girl before?"

"Howard had these?" Marveling, she shuffled them. "Yes, it's Andrea Norse." She gave an exaggerated sigh of envy and laid the photos down. "Stunning."

"College girl?" he said.

"She's past thirty, Hack, believe it or not. No, she's a psychological counselor for the county, family relations, that kind of thing. I suppose—" she touched the photos, lining them up "—that was how Howard met her, right?"

"Sounds logical." Bohannon scooped up the pictures and put them away. "Only what was she doing on a date with him? Letting him take her picture?"

"Maybe he didn't," she said. "Why not ask her?"

"I will." Bohannon laid the little packet of velvet on the table and unfolded it. "What does this suggest to you?" T. Hodges' eyes opened wide. She picked up the Navajo piece and studied it. "Stolen," she said.

"You're sure?"

She nodded. "From a private collection of old Indian jewelry in San Luis. The Kanter collection. By housebreakers six months ago. Every piece had been photographed, of course, for insurance company records. The San Luis police sent out fliers illustrated with the photos. I can dig ours out for you if you want."

"Valuable then," Bohannon said. Cassie came with the coffee pot and two slices of pie. She filled their mugs and admired the Navajo piece. "That's pretty." She looked enviously at T. Hodges. "He giving you that? What is it—your birthday or something?"

"It's stolen," T. Hodges said. "He's under arrest."

"I'll phone the TV news," Cassie said, and went away.

"In the neighborhood of a hundred thousand dollars." T. Hodges wrapped the piece up again. "For the whole collection, I mean." She held the little packet out, and Bohannon put it back into his shirt pocket. She cut into her pie. "What was Alice Donovan doing with something so valuable?"

"Why wasn't she the thief?" Bohannon said.

"Because the thief is in jail and the collection is back with the Kanters, all but this piece, which the thief insists he didn't sell. He didn't have time."

Bohannon ate pie, drank coffee, and thought. "Some kind of insurance scam on the part of the owners?"

"I think Mr. Kanter owns most of San Luis."

"Do you know exactly when Alice upgraded that shop?"

"About a year ago," T. Hodges said. "Mmm. This pie is heavenly."

"About a year ago a local man named Galen had an affair with a Guadalupe woman called Estella Hernandez."

"Ah—those letters you mentioned?"

"You know any man named Galen in Madrone?" Bohannon lit a cigarette and drank coffee. "It's not a common name."

"No Galens," she said. "You'll have to ask Estella Hernandez, won't you?"

"If I can find her. From the letters, I take it she lived in a trailer, mobile home. She could be long gone by now." He gave his head a shake. "What do you think? Was Alice Donovan into extortion? Freddy May says she didn't borrow the money to fix up the business. She couldn't have saved anything from the operation the way it was, nickels and dimes. And Howard must have cost a lot, smashing cars and having to be dried out in hospitals."

"So she blackmailed this Galen?" T. Hodges polished off her pie. "And Galen finally got fed up and stepped into the kitchen last night and bashed her head in with a skillet? Then why didn't he take the letters away with him?"

"I told you—they were hidden. No time to look for them. Howard got home very soon after she was killed. The killer would have had to hightail it not to be caught." Bohannon finished his coffee, took a long last drag from the cigarette, put it out. "Maybe it was Galen who came back early this morning and kicked in the back door, hoping to find the letters."

"And never found them," T. Hodges said.

"We better go." Bohannon got to his feet, slid bills from a worn wallet, laid them on the table for Cassie. He held open the screen door for T. Hodges. At the foot of the steps, on the crooked little trail, she read her watch again and looked woebegone.

"I'm really late," she said.

"I'll drive you back," he said.

He wanted to report to Fred May, but May was in court. So Bohannon drove down through the dunes, headed for Guadalupe. He didn't get there. He found a trailer park in a swale on the land side of the beach highway. The office had a temporary look to it, plywood and studs, but it had been there a while—the wood had darkened from rain, sun, wind, and salt spray. It had warped, too. When someone called, "Come in," from behind the door, he had to shoulder the door to get it open. It scraped the floor. The plywood counter had little bonsai trees on it, and a tiny Japanese woman in a wash-faded housedress was snipping at the branches of the trees, craftily, keeping them stunted, and perfect. Her face was like a withered apple. She smiled at him with crooked brown teeth and gave a little bow.

Bohannon touched his hat brim. "One of your tenants an Estella Hernandez?"

Her answer made him think of an owner's manual he'd got with a stereo he and Linda had bought some years back. It was in English, all right, but neither of them had been able to understand it. But the little lady was used to this, it looked like. She laughed at herself, came from behind the counter, took his elbow, led him back outside, and pointed out the Hernandez trailer to him.

It was like the rest of them there, half-hearted efforts at looking like tract houses. Like the rest, it had been some time since it had rolled down any highway on wheels. A tin awning held up by spindly pipes sheltered the side of the place. A skinny brown boy of maybe ten sat on the doorstep with a scuba diver's mask in his hand. When he heard the crunch of gravel under Bohannon's boots, he looked at him, got off the steps, and walked away, glum resignation in the slump of his shoulders, the way he scuffed the ground. Bohannon pulled open a flimsy screen and knocked on the door.

From inside, a woman's voice called to him in Spanish.

"It's Galen," he said. "Open up, Estella."

She opened the door, a dark, slim young woman, heavy breasts in a flower print halter, a very tight pair of jeans, bare feet with crimson toenails. She blinked long furry black lashes at him, and gave a short, mocking laugh. "One thing I do know is voices," she said. "Galen has a high voice." She tilted her head and smiled while her glance ran up and down him. "If you sang, you would sing bass." She frowned, puzzled. "Did Galen send you?" She glanced up at the sun. "It is early in the day."

"Galen didn't send me," he said, and took out his wallet. "And I'm not a client." He showed her his license. "I'm with the county attorney. I need to find Galen."

"What for?" She waved a mocking hand at the wallet. "You don't mean to tell me Galen has committed a crime." She laughed. "He would not have the courage."

"What's his last name, Estella? Where does he live?"

"How do you know about him and me?"

Bohannon showed her the letters.

"I threw those in the garbage," she said.

"That's what they smell like," Bohannon said.

She made a bitter face. "That is what they are."

"You know Galen wouldn't have sent me or any other man here. He was in love with you."

"He is a crazy fool. He nearly got both of us killed with his stupid jealousy."

"He didn't like your line of work?" Bohannon said.

She snorted. "A romantic teenager of fifty years of age. A married man. With a grandchild."

"His last name, please, Estella?"

She narrowed her eyes. "What is it worth to the county attorney's office?"

"Worth not getting busted for prostitution," Bohannon told her, "and for keeping a child on unfit premises."

She sighed grimly. "Why did I think you would be different? It don't matter how goodlooking, a cop is a cop. His name is Worthy. Isn't that a joke?"

"And what's his line of work?" Bohannon said.

"He is a dentist." Her laugh was dry. "Galen, the first Galen in history, you know, was a famous Roman physician. He told me this. So his parents wanted him to be a doctor, but he failed medical school. You've got to have brains to be a doctor."

G. B. Worthy's offices were on the second floor of a brick business building in Madrone that didn't show its brick to the street any more. The front had been dressed in pecky cedar boards. The notion was to make the town look like the Wild West of 1880. Bohannon didn't much like that. The waiting room had bland framed prints on the walls, a pair of couches, a coffee table, a rack of magazines, a green tank of lazily swimming tropical fish. With a knuckle he touched the opaque glass of a service window. The woman who slid the glass back he pegged as Mrs. Worthy. She was stout, middle-aged, and fixed her hair around her head in bulky braids, yellow hair tinged with gray. She smiled with stunning teeth. "Have you an appointment?"

"I need some help from the doctor," Bohannon said, and showed her his license. "It's a law enforcement matter. It shouldn't take long."

She nodded knowingly, as if law enforcement matters were daily occurrences around there, as if the doctor were consulted by peace officers routinely, said, "One moment, please," closed the sliding glass. Voices murmured, then an inner door opened and a good-looking man, trim, slim, mustached, smiled and held out a hand. He said, "Whose dental charts do you want to see, Mr. Bohannon?"

Bohannon took the hand, gave Galen Worthy a conspiratorial look, and drew him out into the waiting room. He said softly, "Tell her we're going for coffee."

Worthy frowned and pulled his hand away. "What for? I don't understand. A police matter, my wife said."

Bohannon murmured, "The death of Alice Donovan. You want to discuss that here?"

"I—I don't know what you're talking about." Worthy's Adam's apple pumped. He turned a bad color. "Alice who?"

Bohannon pulled the smelly letters from his pocket and held them out so the dentist could get a good look. "Donovan. These were in her possession. You wrote them. Or so Estella Hernandez says."

The glass panel slid open. Mrs. Worthy said, "Galen, is everything all right?" She eyed Bohannon dubiously.

Her husband gave her a nervous smile. "It's all right, dear. But I have to go out for a few minutes."

"I won't keep him long," Bohannon told her.

He drove the dentist in his new pickup truck out of town, which didn't mean far in a little place like Madrone. They parked on a dusty foothill road. Worthy had been silent. Now he burst out:

"There are supposed to be two kinds of luck. Why do I always have the bad kind?"

"They say we make our own." Bohannon lit a cigarette.

"You'll kill yourself with those," Worthy snapped at him. "Worse than that, you'll kill those around you."

"I won't, but those letters could," Bohannon said. "How did the Donovan woman get hold of them, anyway?"

Worthy made a sour noise meant for a laugh. "Found them. You know how people dump their trash up in the canyons? Just drive along to a lonely spot and heave it out off the edge of the road. Disgusting."

"Go on," Bohannon said.

Worthy rolled down the window and waved a hand in front of his face to fend off the smoke. "Well, Alice had sent Howard on some errand, and he was hours late getting back. It was going to be dark soon. Knowing him, she figured he'd gotten drunk and passed out somewhere. So she borrowed a neighbor's car and went to find him. He'd driven off the road down a steep embankment. The car had come to rest in a huge pile of plastic trash bags."

"From Estella's trailer camp, right?" Bohannon said.

Worthy's mouth twitched. "And bags had split open and spilled, hadn't they? And here were my letters strewn around for all the world to read. And the rest you know, don't you? How my money smartened up that shop for her?"

"To save your marriage?" Bohannon patted the letters in his side pocket. "I thought you loved Estella."

"Doris—Mrs. Worthy—put me through dental school after my own family gave up on me. I owe her everything."

"And it doesn't matter if you're a good dentist or not," Bohannon said, "she keeps you in style, right?"

"I didn't kill Alice Donovan," Worthy said.

"What size shoe do you wear, doctor?" Bohannon said.

Worthy blinked. "What kind of question is that?"

"Somebody heard on the early morning news that Alice was dead and hustled over to her shop and kicked in the back door with a size twelve shoe. Why wasn't it you, trying to get hold of these letters ahead of the sheriff?"

"It wasn't me." Worthy shook his head hard. "I drove straight to the office. You found the letters, not me."

"I didn't say you found them, only looked for them."

"I wasn't anywhere near there. I didn't know she was dead until you told me. We don't put the TV on in the mornings. Ask Doris."

Bohannon looked at him with his eyebrows raised.

"No. I don't mean that. She mustn't know."

"You and she go to work in the same car?" Bohannon said.

"She goes first to get things ready. I follow later."

"So you can't prove you didn't detour past Alice's."

Worthy said stubbornly, "And you can't prove I did." He read his watch. "I have to get back. I have appointments."

"What about last night?" Bohannon crushed out his cigarette in the dashboard ashtray and pushed the little metal drawer shut. "Around midnight. You weren't at Alice's then, either?"

"I was in bed, asleep."

Bohannon twisted the key in the ignition and the new engine hummed to life. He couldn't get used to its quiet after the clatter of his old truck. It took him by surprise every time. Sometimes he didn't know the damned thing had started at all. He glanced at the dentist.

"You know, if you were there, either last night or this morning, chances are somebody saw you. Alice's place isn't the only one on that road. There are neighbors. It's not a dead end. It's on the way. People drive it. So if you'd like to change your story before it begins to fall apart, now is the time to do it."

Worthy stared straight ahead through the clean windshield. "It isn't a story," he said, "it's the truth."

"Then you've got nothing to be tense about." Bohannon reached over and touched the tight fist on the dentist's knee. Worthy jerked the hand away as if from an electric shock. "Relax," Bohannon said. "If anybody tells your wife, it won't be me."

"Give me back those letters," Worthy pleaded.

"Later," Bohannon said.

"What you have to know," he told Fred May, "is that somebody big got there before me this morning and broke the lock on the back door."

"And it wasn't Howard," the fat man smiled. "Good work, Hack. Who was it?" He touched the stained envelopes on his desk. "The dentist?"

"His feet are too small." Bohannon stared out the window, smoking, a can of beer in his hand. "And he claims he wasn't there. If he was, he didn't find the letters."

"It couldn't have been the Weems woman?" Fred May rocked back in his oak swivel chair and the spring twanged. "You say she's big."

"She still doesn't wear size twelve shoes." Bohannon took a swallow of beer, watched smoke from his cigarette drift out the window into the warm, late afternoon air. "And I don't think she knew Alice Donovan was dead."

"You really think she came to make a payment to her?" He poked with a fat finger at the Navajo buckle that lay on its ragged little square of velvet among the typed, blue-papered briefs and law books on the desk. "To keep Alice from revealing she was in possession of stolen property?"

Bohannon frowned and shook his head. "It doesn't make sense, Fred." He flicked the spent cigarette out the window into a flowerbed and dropped onto an oak chair. "Why pay a blackmailer when you could easily explain to the San Luis police that you'd bought it innocently? It would be cheaper to take the loss on what she'd paid for it than to keep shelling out to Alice for the rest of her life."

"Then there's something Alice had around the place you didn't find." May drank diet soda from a can. "Or did the early riser who kicked in the door find it?"

"There wasn't any sign anybody had done any searching for anything." Bohannon finished his beer and tossed the empty can into the brown metal wastebasket beside May's desk, and made a face. "If bigfoot even came inside, he found what he wanted right there in the kitchen, or what he thought was there wasn't."

"What would it be?" May's forehead wrinkled.

"When I find him, I'll ask him." With a sigh, Bohannon got to his feet. It had been a long day. He was tired. "Meantime, I need the key to Alice's cash register."

May said, "Right here," opened a drawer, and took out a little flat key. Bohannon held his hand out, and May put the key into it. "What do you expect to find?"

Bohannon grinned and tossed the key in his hand. "Photographs of a very large, middle-aged lady," he said, "doing something she shouldn't."

The house was an expensive one on the beach, stone and beams and gloomy smoked glass on the road side. From the road where he left the pickup, he looked down on the flat roof of the house that was covered in rocks white as chalk. He went down sandy stone steps into a cavelike entryway and put his thumb on a bell push. He stood listening to the silky rush and retreat of waves on the beach, and then the door opened. It wasn't the Weems woman. It was a young man, dressed in next to nothing. He was smooth and tan. His lean musculature looked carved. His hair was curly and black and he wore it long. Bohannon wondered on what beach Margaret Weems had found him.

Bohannon wasn't a type he'd encountered before. He looked puzzled, but he didn't say anything.

"Mrs. Weems here?" Bohannon gave his name. "We met this morning. Tell her. She'll remember me."

The young man blinked. Something was happening under all that theatrical hair. Maybe he was thinking. At last, with a small shrug, he turned and went down a long room whose far end had a wall of glass that showed the beach and the sea. The sun was lowering and the light on the water was turning flame-colored. The young man stepped outside, Bohannon stepped inside, shut the door behind him, went down the long room. The young man was back in the open panel of the glass wall in no time.

"What do you want?" he said in a French accent.

"I have something for Mrs. Weems from Alice Donovan's shop." He raised his voice, in case Margaret Weems was within earshot. "She'll want to see it."

The young man stepped toward him. "You must telephone and make the appointment." He reached for Bohannon's arm. Bohannon didn't want to knock him down, but he wasn't about to leave. He shook the hand off. The youth tried again, and a voice reached them both. Margaret Weems stood in the open glass panel. Her white terry cloth robe made her look like a polar bear.

"Oh, Mr. Bohannon." Her smile was nervous, and she lied. "I misunderstood. Jean-Marie's accent puzzles me sometimes." She

tried for a laugh and missed. She came to them, gently but firmly
pried the youth away from Bohannon, and aimed him at an inner
doorway. "Dear Jean, be a darling and find us all some bubbly,
will you?"

"Beer," Bohannon said, "thanks."

Jean-Marie scowled like a six-year-old, but after a second's pause,
he grumbled away, glancing back menacingly at the pair of them.
A jealous lover in the authentic Gallic mode, out of a silent movie.
Funny.

Margaret Weems put a finger to her lips and led Bohannon out
onto the deck, across the deck, down to the sand. She took his arm
and hustled him along the sand. "You've got the pictures. That's
what you found at Alice's shop, isn't it? Those dreadful pictures.
Give them to me."

"You were paying Alice to keep quiet about them."

"I'll pay you. The money's in the house. Only give them to me.
And the negatives? She said I could have the negatives this time."

"I don't think so," Bohannon said.

Her face fell. She let him go. "What?"

"I don't think she'd give you those." He gestured at the house.
"You're well fixed, it appears to me. No, I think she'd bleed you
with those pictures forever."

She sighed. "Of course. You're right. Awful woman."

"Where were you at midnight last night?" he said.

"We had a party," she said. "It was very lively. Young people.
Music. Jean-Marie is a singer, you know. And a song writer. Guitar.
Piano. He has a wonderful future. Everyone says so."

"Good," Bohannon said. "How late did this party run?"

"Until almost sunrise," she said.

"And you stayed until the last guest left?"

She gave him a rueful laugh. "Those were the days, weren't they?
No, I was in bed by one thirty, two. You can ask any of them—
and you will, won't you?"

"When you give me the guest list," he said.

"Right away," she said.

Jean-Marie came along the sand, carrying a tray on which glasses
glittered. All by his lonesome he turned this stretch of beach into
the Côte d'Azure. There should have been a bevy of bikini-clad
nymphets in his wake. Bohannon looked at Margaret Weems. She
was watching the French lad as if she'd never seen anything so
delicious in her life—and maybe she hadn't.

"Is it him Alice Donovan was threatening to show those photos
to?" The photos had been taken in supermarkets and department
stores. Alice must have followed her around for weeks with that

camera hidden in a shopping bag. Margaret Weems was a shoplifter. Not the first person-who-had-everything Bohannon had run into who couldn't keep from stealing. It was some kind of emotional short circuit. A bid for attention? Maybe once Jean-Marie came along, she'd given it up. "Would he leave you?"

She flushed. "Of course not. No, she'd have shown them to my husband. He'd divorce me. I'd lose everything."

"He doesn't object to Jean-Marie?"

"I'm only helping Jean-Marie with his career."

"Where is Mr. Weems these days?" Bohannon said.

"In Hong Kong. He owns electronics parts firms there. Also in Taiwan and South Korea. He's away much of the time."

"Too bad," Bohannon said.

Jean-Marie arrived with his tray. She beamed at him. "Dear boy," she said, and took a tulip champagne glass from the tray. While the French lad filled it, the Weems woman turned her smile on Bohannon. "I miss Henry, of course, but I manage to struggle along without him—somehow."

Bohannon took a glass and a bottle of Beck's from the tray. "I see that you do," he said, and poured his beer.

They sat down on the sand. Mrs. Weems rubbed a big terry cloth shoulder against the boy's naked one. She said, "Mr. Bohannon works for the—uh—county attorney, and for reasons I can't hope to understand, he needs a list of our guests last night. Will you find it, please?"

The boy didn't turn to her. He watched leggy little shore birds getting in their last long-beaked probings of the glassy sand before nightfall. Maybe he was making up a song. He certainly wasn't worried. "Oui," he said.

Bohannon got in and out of his truck often in the next three hours. Each time he was behind the steering wheel again, he unfolded the list Jean-Marie had given him, and at the end the paper was coming apart. He sighed and tucked it away. He was on a twisty road with few street lamps in Settlers Cove, a section of houses hidden among pines on hills beside the sea. Because they were farthest off, he had first checked on the partygoers in Morro Bay and Los Osos. So far as any of them remembered—a skinny girl painter, a fortyish male dancer who wore mascara, a squat bald screenwriter in flowered knee-length surfer shorts—Margaret Weems had not only been highly visible in the house and on the beach at her place until the wee hours, but had been the life of the party. They all liked good old Margaret. Oysters chilled on the half shell, duck pate, lobster, and all the champagne you could drink.

Really, Margaret was something else. And the story had been the same among the sighing night pines of Settlers Cove. He'd heard it here from a reed player with spiky blue hair, from a music video producer with one leg in a cast, from Mitch Russell, the big, bushy-bearded man who ran the little theater in Madrone. No point bothering anyone else. Bohannon started the truck and headed for home, food, a shower, and bed.

When Bohannon stopped the truck at the far end of the long, white, green-trimmed stable building, pulled the parking brake, and killed the engine, George Stubbs came out of his sleeping quarters next to the tackroom. He was an ex-rodeo rider, a fat old man now, who hobbled, his bones and joints remembering long-ago breaks and sprains. Bohannon climbed wearily down out of the truck and slammed the door in the night silence. Horses stirred in their dark box stalls behind closed doors and nickered softly. Mountains loomed above the place, dark and shaggy. The air was cool.

Stubbs limped up, looking a little peeved. His thick fingers, with their arthritis-swollen joints, were smudged with charcoal. Likely he'd been drawing in his room. He loved to draw—most commonly horses—and did it well and took pride in it. "Where you been all day and half the night? Couldn't you find a phone?"

"A crisis, was there?" Bohannon started for the house. "Anybody dead?"

Stubbs followed him. "Pretty dead supper in the oven, but I reckon that's my own fault, bothering about you."

"I'm sorry I didn't phone, George. I won't let it happen again." A long covered plank walk fronted the ranch house. Bohannon went along it to the kitchen, pulled the screen door, walked over to the big stove rearing up in a corner. He pulled open the door to the warming oven and squinted inside. Stubbs put a quilted mitten in his hand. Bohannon peeled foil off a beef, green pepper, noodle casserole, set it on a counter, shoveled it onto a plate. "This will be fine." He threw the skeptical-looking Stubbs a smile and carried the plate with a fork to the table. He sat down, began to eat—he was hungry—and a sheet of paper lying just outside the circle of light from the lamp in the center of the table caught his eye. "What's this?"

"T. Hodges was here tonight." Stubbs brought a mug of coffee to the table, sat down with a suppressed groan. "She stayed almost an hour, hoping you'd show up." He pried a bent cigarette from a crumpled pack, lit it with a kitchen match. "Finally says she had to go, and wrote you that."

The handwriting was just what he'd have expected of the deputy—

firm and without flourishes, straight up and down, easy to read. It said a woman's dog had been struck and its leg broken on Pleasant Trail this morning early. Pleasant Trail was where Alice Donovan's shop was. And the woman lived across and just down the road from there. She said the car that hit the dog was a new red Suzuki Samurai but she didn't get the license number. It came out of the driveway at Ye Olde Oak Tree hell-for-leather, and caromed down the dusty little road. The driver was a tall, young-looking man with a deep tan and a trim little beard. The woman, Gladys Tyndall, didn't know him, never saw him before. But she would like to get her hands on him. Her dog was going to be okay, but he could as easily be dead for all that driver cared.

Bohannon scraped the fork around on the plate for the last taste of his supper. "That was good," he said. "Hardly dried out at all. Thank you, George."

Stubbs grunted. "You want some coffee now?"

"Any of that blueberry cobbler of yours left?"

Stubbs brought the cold cobbler and a mug of hot coffee. Bohannon got up and trudged to the sideboard for a whisky bottle, came back with it, added a jolt of whisky to his coffee, and sat down. He picked up T. Hodges' note and rattled it at Stubbs. "You know any young man with a trimmed beard, a suntan, who drives one of those new little Japanese jeeps?"

"I thought you'd never ask," Stubbs said. He twisted out his smoked-down cigarette in the big glass ashtray that lived on the table. "Him and that red-haired tall girl been up here a couple times to ride the trails."

"Her name—" Bohannon had a mouthful of cobbler; he swallowed, gulped some coffee "—is Andrea Norse. What's his?"

"Beats me," Stubbs said. "It was her that signed in."

"So her address is in our records," Bohannon said.

"If it ain't," Stubbs said, "I'm slipping, and I better start thinking about the old folks' home."

Bohannon got to his feet and went into the shadows for the scuffed gray cardboard box of file cards.

The Samurai stood high on its wheels under drooping blue wisteria beside a rickety white frame cottage among a lot of others like it. This was one of the earliest spots built up in Settlers Cove. Bohannon got down from his truck, ducked under the wisteria that showered him with dew. He pulled open an aluminum screen door and rapped at a brightly varnished wooden door. It was just past seven in the morning. So quiet he could hear the surf breaking, many streets away. Nobody stirred inside the house. He lit a cigarette and knuckled the door again, harder this time. After a ten second pause, he heard the thump of footfalls, and the tall, redheaded girl opened the door, tugging down a big, loose sweater, shaking back her hair. She had on tight jeans and was barefoot. She winced in the morning light.

"What is it?"

"You know the owner of this vehicle?" Bohannon had his wallet out and open to show his license. He closed the wallet and pushed it away. "It struck a dog yesterday morning about this time, over on Pleasant Trail."

She looked wary. "Who are you, exactly?"

He told her. "Working for the public defender. On the Alice Donovan case? Did you know her, Miss Norse?"

She paled. "I—yes, I counseled her son, Howard." Her smile was thin and didn't last. "He had problems."

"You didn't counsel his mother?" Bohannon said. "Wasn't she behind those problems?"

Her tone hardened. "She didn't see it that way."

"That's how I see it." Bohannon gave her his best smile. "Don't you agree with me?"

"It's very early in the morning, Mr. Bohannon. I have to get ready for work. If you'll excuse me—"

"The Samurai is not your car, is it?" he said.

A bearded young man, naked to the waist, buttoning brown walking shorts, came to the door. His dark hair was tousled from sleep. He blinked and yawned. He was tall enough to reach over Andrea Norse's head and take hold of the door she was holding open. "What's this all about?" he said.

Bohannon told him about the dog. "What's your name?"

"Wolfe. I'm sorry about the dog. I didn't know I'd hit anything. I'll pay the woman."

"You didn't know you hit anything because you came tearing out of Alice Donovan's driveway in a sweat. Why? What were you doing there? Why did you kick in her back door? What was it you were after?"

Wolfe squinted. "Who's Alice Donovan?"

Looking mournful, Andrea Norse touched his chest. "It's no use, Zach. He knows we know her." She turned to face Bohannon. "We heard on the early morning radio news that Alice had been murdered. I was over there the night before, to plead with her to change her tactics with Howard. I'd tried before. Howard used to come to me in tears."

"Drunken tears?" Bohannon said.

"Not always, but always heartbroken. That sunny little woman.

She was a monster, you know. Sex-starved, smothering, seductive—as mixed up and dangerous as they come.''

"Should I quote you on that?" Bohannon twitched her a half smile. "It doesn't sound exactly clinical."

"No." She looked ashamed of herself. "But I couldn't stand by and not try to change the situation. She was destroying her own son. He was very disturbed when he came to this door night before last."

"So disturbed he killed her," Wolfe said, and swung away. "I need coffee."

"I don't think so," Bohannon said. And to the Norse woman, "So you went over to try to talk to her? When?"

"Howard stayed here spilling out his woes to me for hours. When I'd got him calmed down and he left, I drove over to Madrone. What time? Ten? A little past."

"And she was all right?" Bohannon said.

"Self-righteous, smug, superior. Did I think you learned about human nature from books? What was I—thirty years old? Had I raised children of my own? She tried to keep him straight. But he wasn't bright, and boys like that awful Beau Larkin kept getting him into trouble."

"You knew Howard. Could he have killed her?"

"She was his god. We don't kill our gods."

"She wasn't your god. You didn't use that skillet?"

"No, of course not. I'd taken Howard's case folder with me—his history. I wanted to go through it point by point, episode by episode, to show her just how she—"

"And she wouldn't listen, and you walked out," Bohannon said, "and in your anger you left the file behind, and the next morning you remembered, and sent Zach to get it before the sheriff could connect you to the killing."

"He got it," she said wryly, "but it seems it didn't help. What am I, now? Under arrest for murder?"

Bohannon shook his head. "I don't arrest people. I just ask questions. Can you prove you weren't there at midnight? What time did you get home? Was anyone here?"

"Zach and a friend, Sonny Snyder. When? Eleven? Zach put *Diva* on the VCR. He knows it always calms me down."

Bohannon turned away. "Tell him to stop in at the sheriff's about the dog before he goes to work." He ducked under the wisteria. In the road he dropped his cigarette and stepped on it. And a bullet slammed into his shoulder. He heard the report of the rifle as he fell. It echoed off the hills. A second shot kicked grit into his face but that was all. Then Zach Wolfe was kneeling beside him.

"It's all right," he said, "I'm a doctor."

* * *

Gerard said, "We'll handle it from now on. Okay?" He sat on a chrome and wicker chair in a hospital room. Clear noon sunlight fell on him from a window. It gleamed off his scalp. Gerard was developing a bald spot. Bohannon hadn't noticed that before. He sat up in the high bed, left arm in a sling, lunch on a tray in front of him. He laid the fork down. The food was tepid and tasteless.

"Did you let Howard go? Obviously, he didn't shoot me."

Gerard shrugged. "Alice was blackmailing people. You were tracking those people down. It made somebody nervous. It doesn't change Howard's status."

"More than nervous," Bohannon said. "Deadly."

"We found the shell casings up the hillside in a tangle of brush and ferns and trees. They could have come from a thousand rifles around here. Thirty-thirty. No dwellings up there. We can't find anybody who saw him."

Bohannon stuck with his thought. "If he was willing to kill me, he was willing to kill Alice Donovan."

"It wasn't Dr. Worthy." Gerard pushed back the crisp cuff of his tan uniform shirt to read his watch. "It wasn't Mrs. Weems." He stood up. "That was sharp of you, having Andrea Norse check on them right then by phone."

"Oh, I'm a hee-ro, I am. Lying there bleeding in the dust and gasping out orders with my dying breath."

"Don't let it go to your head." Gerard opened the door. From the hallway came the squeak of nurses' shoe soles, the jingle of medication trays, the clash of lunch dishes being collected. "Fred May wants us to give you a medal."

"He was here earlier," Bohannon said. "He feels worse than I do about it. He takes things hard."

"We'll find who did it," Gerard said.

"Unless I find him first," Bohannon said.

Gerard turned back. "You stay where you are, damn it. It's the only way we can protect you." He spoke to the young deputy, posted on a chair outside Bohannon's door. "Don't let him trick you, Vern. He's sneaky."

Vern poked his yellow-haired head around the doorframe and grinned at Bohannon. "I'll watch him, sir," he said.

Looking half amused, half grim, Gerard went away.

The phone by the bed was almost as good as freedom. He rang T. Hodges to confirm a suspicion about the Kanter case. He rang Andrea Norse to bring the new truck down to the hospital. And Manuel Rivera, at the stables, to bring him clothes without blood-

stains and a packet of little firecrackers that had lain in a drawer of
the kitchen sideboard for years.

Rivera appeared in his soutane. He was preparing for priesthood
and had supported himself while he studied at the seminary up on
the ridge by working part time for Bohannon. Bohannon was going
to be sorry to lose him. He was a good worker and an even better
friend.

"Close the door," Bohannon told him. "Help me get dressed."
It was tricky. There was the arm in the sling to work around, and
he was slow from the painkillers they'd given him. But they managed
it. "Okay," he said. "Now, you open the door, say goodbye to me,
go on down the hall and around the corner, then light the firecrackers, drop them, and walk out as if you had nothing to do with it."

Rivera regarded him with doubtful brown eyes.

"It will work," Bohannon said. "Who's going to suspect a priest?"

"No one will be harmed?" Rivera asked.

"It will just make a racket."

"I don't feel good about it," Rivera said.

"Do it anyway," Bohannon said. "A postulant should learn what
it's like to sin. Manuel, go on. It's important."

The slim lad sighed, shook his head, but he went.

Bohannon's only worry was that the firecrackers were so old they
wouldn't go off. But they did. A few of them, and made sufficient
noise to send Vern racing down the hall and out of sight. Bohannon
went the other direction. He found the truck with the keys in it in
the parking lot. By the time he was rolling down the street, his
shoulder had begun to throb. But he was under way. He laughed
to himself.

He could hear the music a block off when he halted the truck at
a stop sign. The neighborhood was one of ranch style houses on
comfortable lots with well-grown trees. How were they taking that
clamor—the thud of drums, the snarl of electric guitars? And the
crowd noises that went with it, shouts, raucous laughter, four-letter
words? The street was parked up, too. How did the neighbors like
that? He turned a corner, found an alley, parked there, and entered
the uproar through a back gate. The rock music hit him like an
eighteen wheeler.

The crowd he could see was all male, teenage, college age, town
boys, ranch boys, jeans, surfer trunks, workshoes, jogging shoes,
baseball caps, straw hats, and crazily shaved heads with no hats at
all. They stamped their feet to the roaring music, howled and
whooped, pushed and tripped each other. At a brick outdoor bar-

becue a fat boy scorched hamburger patties. Beside the grill a plastic
tub held beer cans on ice. Empty cans kicked around underfoot.
Everybody had a can in his hand except three boys who lay passed
out on the grass. The smell of mesquite smoke was strong in the
windless air of the hot afternoon. But so was the smell of marijuana.

Nobody noticed Bohannon. He looked around for the kid hosting
this shindig. He would stand out. He was almost as big as Howard
Donovan. Then Bohannon saw him. He came out the back door of
the house, surrounded by squealing girls, carrying hamburger buns,
ketchup, mustard, barbecue sauce. Drunken cheers went up as they
pushed through the crowd toward the red-faced fat boy in the smoke.
Bohannon followed, and waited until the girls scattered. He poked
the big boy's ribs. Beau Larkin swung around and stared at him.
The color drained from his face. He licked his lips. He stammered.

"Hey, where did you come from?"

"Come on." Bohannon caught his arm and hauled him out the
back gate into the alley.

"You can't touch me, my father's a police officer."

"And he was on the Kanter robbery case, that collection of Navajo
Indian jewelry. And one piece disappeared from the collection. I
know your father. He's an honest cop. He didn't take it. I think
you took it. And tried to sell it to Alice Donovan, only she recognized it for what it was, and she's been blackmailing you with it
ever since. Making you pay her not to tell your father."

Larkin reeked of beer. He peered glassily down at Bohannon.
He swayed. His speech was slurred. "Howard said she'd buy it off
me. I didn't know where else to go."

"Why did you kill her, Beau?"

"Because I was behind on my payments. My old man got sore
and cut off my cash flow. I couldn't pay her. But she didn't care.
She was going to tell him. I had to kill her. I thought I was out of
trouble. But then you got the thing from where she had it hid. Cassie
at the cafe told Tony about this stolen Indian buckle you had, and
he told me. And I heard how smart you are, and I knew you'd be
after me soon. So I had to kill you, too. And now I have to do it
again." He lunged. His big hands grabbed Bohannon's throat.

Bohannon struggled. His shoulder screamed pain. He put an open
hand against the boy's face and pushed. He kicked. He kneed.
Nothing helped. The boy's thumbs were cutting off his air. The light
was going out. His ears rang. Then a shout sliced through the back
yard noise. A gun went off. Larkin let him go, and Bohannon staggered a few steps, gasping, choking, until his legs wouldn't hold
him. He slumped against a fence, and blurrily saw Larkin lying face

down in weeds and cinders, and Vern bending over, snapping hand-cuffs on the boy's thick wrists.

"Hack, were you crazy?" T. Hodges made the rocker in Bohan-non's pine plank bedroom creak angrily. "Going after a giant like that—with only one good arm, just out of surgery? How did you expect to even get there?"

He lay in his own bed. That was the good part. The bad part was how sore his throat was. He couldn't swallow food. It even hurt to talk. The sound that came out was hoarse, no more than a whisper. "It's over now. Calm down."

"You were lucky Vern got there when he did."

Vern gave his toothy kid grin. "Lieutenant Gerard warned me he was tricky." He stood gangly at the foot of the poster bed. "Soon as I saw those firecrackers, I knew it was Mr. Bohannon back of it. He didn't get much of a start on me. Broke a lot of speed laws, though. With that old patrol car I had, I almost lost him a couple of times."

"I was drugged," Bohannon whispered, "didn't know what I was doing." He heard voices in the hallway and looked at the door. Fred May came in, wearing a pup-tent-size pink sweatshirt that had once been red. He did his best to smile, but worry for how Bohannon felt spoiled the attempt. As if Bohannon were hovering near death, he looked for advice to the two young deputies.

"Is it okay?" he said. "I brought somebody."

"Fred, I'm all right." Bohannon hoped he was more successful with his try at smiling than May had been. "Who is it?"

Who it was filled the doorway. Howard Donovan. He held there, shy as a five-year-old, trying to find the words to thank Bohannon for getting him out of jail. "They all thought I killed my mother." Tears brimmed his eyes, and he used big fists to knuckle the tears away. "You knew I didn't do that. You knew I wouldn't."

"I was betting on it."

Howard grinned unexpectedly. "Even if I did pick you up that night and throw you in the water."

"It's not the same," Bohannon said.

"That was only funning, wasn't it?" Howard said. He looked grave again. "She made me very mad sometimes, but I wouldn't hurt her. I never did hurt her. Even when she hit me. Not once." He frowned to himself. "It wouldn't be right. She was too little." He paused, and abruptly the small boy that lived in his head changed the subject. Excited. Eyes shining. "There's a big old owl up in our tree. Did you know that? And the crows been pestering him."

"Yes," Bohannon said, "I knew that."

"Well, guess what? When I came home from jail, there's black feathers all over the yard. Crow feathers. Guess that old owl showed them who's boss, didn't he?"

"It's his tree," Bohannon said. "We both knew that."

"And it's my house," Howard said. "Isn't it?"

WILLIAM BANKIER

William Bankier, one of Canada's best-known suspense writers, has written short stories for *Ellery Queen's Mystery Magazine* for over twenty years. His work has featured a variety of protagonists, including his musician/detective, Harry Lawson.

Here he turns his hand to a small, quirky story that features a disc jockey as its protagonist. Murder plays no favorites, but frequently repeats itself. Sometimes, murder is a matter beyond personal control. When the line between murder and madness is crossed, the police usually find out. But when the murder is still only a potentiality, police have little recourse but to assume the logical chain of events. One sometimes can't tell when sure signs of murder are true or false, until it's too late. In the case of the brother, you're on your own as judge and jury.

How Dangerous Is Your Brother?

Mary Lawrence heard a kitten crying as she locked the back door of the radio station after midnight. She found it under a shrub between two parked cars. "Come out of there!" She managed to grasp and lift the fragile creature, exposing china-blue eyes, pink mouth, needle teeth. Its pounding heart overflowed her hand.

"Are you lost? I can't leave you here and I can't go knocking on doors."

Mary headed home on foot, carrying the animal. The apartment she rented was an easy walk from the studios of CBAY. Arriving in Baytown three weeks ago, she had lucked out with her accommodation. There might be a problem if Jessie Hay downstairs objected to a cat in her house. But it wouldn't be a major difficulty since Mary didn't intend to keep it.

Watching it lap milk from a saucer, Mary wondered if it could become the station cat. Clement Foy, the chief announcer, would have to give his permission. She had done Clem a favor by working tonight, allowing him to play a gig at The Cedars with his danceband. They could set up a litterbox in the newsroom. Plates of food and milk could be left in a corner. The cat would probably enjoy being fussed over by the staff.

"Were you abandoned?" Mary asked as the kitten finished feeding and began to explore the apartment, looking for a hiding place. Observing its brave helplessness, Mary experienced a protective urge. Be careful, she warned herself. You just finished with a lame duck up north. A clear image of Tim Melton's handsome, drunken face surfaced in her mind. He was one reason she had left the radio station in Pitfall and moved down here to CBAY. But not the only reason. Her aim was eventually to land a job at one of the big stations in Montreal. Baytown was a step closer.

* * *

Mary woke early. The kitten was on the bed. Playing with it and then feeding it was more than satisfying. Her emotional deadline for getting rid of it, she figured, was probably sundown of that day.

Shopping at the market on Front Street, she found herself picking up tins of special food for kittens. And a litter tray and a sack of litter. Interesting implements hung on hooks—flea combs, brushes, flea collars, catnip toys. A trip to the vet for a round of shots would soon be on. Followed, eventually, by the neutering operation. Money going out, diversion of energy and concentration—Tim Melton all over again. Tim oozed charm so that most women wanted to grab him and hold him. But he did exactly as he wished—he was a lot like a cat.

Lining up at a checkout counter, Mary found herself looking at a familiar back. It was Jessie Hay, her landlady, who had a job at the local high school. She was with a young man Mary had never seen before. Jessie turned and saw Mary. Her sharp eyes did an inventory of Mary's shopping cart before she said, "This is my brother. Harry, meet Mary Lawrence, the girl upstairs."

Harry Hay had the family freckles, but fewer of them than his sister. With her ginger hair locked in an excruciating perm, Jessie peered out from behind a screen of the tiny spots. Harry wore his like a spattering of mud on the face of a child. He was a head taller than his sister, with darker hair and eyes. His mood was solemn, mouth held slack.

Mary decided to air the situation. "I found a stray kitten last night. I don't intend to keep it. Do you know anybody wants to give a kitten a home?"

Harry clasped his hands and turned to Jessie. "May I have it, Jess? Please?"

"A kitten needs looking after."

"I'll take care of it, you won't have to do a thing. Please, Jess?" Sounding like a schoolboy, Harry seemed to grow in size. He loomed over his sister, who peered up at him with peevish amusement.

"You may as well, if she wants to give it to you."

The Hays drove while Mary walked home, thanking Jessie for her offer of a lift. With all their starting and parking, she was at the house ahead of them. They were loading their groceries in through the kitchen door when Mary came down the back stairs carrying the kitten in her arms.

Harry received it with moans of solicitude, shouldering it against his cheek, murmuring as he bore the animal away, "Little Annabella—little Annabella."

Mary said the obvious. "It's the first I've seen your brother."

"He's been away." Jessie grabbed the last plastic bag from the car and slammed the door.

"In school?"

"Sort of."

That afternoon, Mary ran into Clement Foy in the record library. She was getting together the music for her program, *Town Topics*. Clem was searching out a few disks for his jazz program. "Thanks for covering for me last night," the chief announcer said. Broad-shouldered, in an expensive but ancient suit, and slick-haired, Foy had a kind of silent-screen charm. Not at all bad, was Mary's reaction on first meeting her boss. But he treated her as a valued colleague instead of as dating material. And wasn't that worth a lot more than dinner and dancing?

"You almost got a kitten out of it." She told him about her discovery.

"If you find a stray announcer out there," Foy said, "send him to me. I don't intend to go on handling the night shift."

Mary did her show, fielding some interesting telephone calls, extending the feature on single-parenting, putting together yet another edition of the best magazine program CBAY had ever produced. After work, she wandered home, picking up some tonic water to dilute the remains of her long-standing bottle of gin.

She was watching the news on one of the U.S. channels from across Lake Ontario when she heard footsteps on the stairs. She got up and opened the door. It was Harry Hay with Annabella clinging to his Viyella shirt. "Look how she's grown," he crowed.

Mary couldn't detect any change in size, although the animal was obviously thriving. "Come in. I was going to make myself a drink. Have one with me."

Harry sipped his gin and hardly took his eyes off the kitten. He was the most soft-spoken, courteous young man Mary had ever run across. It was as if the gods had warned him he would die if he raised his voice. Yes, he told her, he had been away. In Southern California, spending a lot of Jessie's hard-earned money. Los Angeles was a fine place, but to succeed there you needed more energy and talent than he could muster.

Mary asked him why he wanted to work in the United States, anyway—there was all that hassle with Immigration and work permits.

"Because they owe me. Because I volunteered for their Army."

"You were in the American Army?"

"In Vietnam. I lost a lot of friends there." He lowered a finger.

Annabella savaged it with four sets of claws. "I still dream about the blood."

Mary was doing some mental arithmetic. The Vietnam conflict had been over for years. "How old are you, Harry?" When he said he was twenty-four, she knew something was wrong. No way he could have been in that war. "You have dreams?"

"Recurring nightmares." He produced his sheepish smile. "Don't worry, I won't describe them. I save all that stuff for my shrink."

To change the subject, Mary asked if Jessie enjoyed her work at the high school.

"She hates it," Harry said calmly. "When you're a student, you can goof off. And you get summer vacations. The principal's secretary is a permanent slave."

Mary contracted cabin-fever around nine o'clock. It was a short walk down Front Street to the Coronet Hotel. The blind pianist was playing jazz in the back lounge, which prompted Mary to look around for Clem Foy. He wasn't there, but Jessie Hay was by herself at the end of the bar, pouring a beer.

Mary slid onto the next stool and bought a round. They listened to an airy rendition of "Fools Rush In" that brought them to the brink of tears. Then the piano-man was gone behind the dog with the handle on its back, and they were left with nothing to talk about but life.

Mary led off with ten minutes on her adventures at the radio station. Jessie ate it up and responded with a point-by-point assessment of the high-school principal's incompetence. By this time, Mary was finishing her second G&T, and the bartender seemed to be pouring doubles. During a lull in the conversation, the question just came rolling out.

"How dangerous is your brother?"

Jessie turned her head. She looked at the woman on the next stool for three full beats. "What's that supposed to mean?"

"He came up to show me how fast the kitten's growing. We were talking and he told me about his military service in Vietnam. He isn't old enough, surely?"

"Harry fantasizes. But he's under the care of a good doctor and it's going to be all right."

"I'm glad to hear it." That sounded glib. Why, Mary asked herself, was she trying so hard to alienate the owner of the apartment she lived in?

"As for dangerous," Jessie said, gathering up her cigarettes and her lighter and her change, "I'm the one you have to worry about. I'm ten times more dangerous than Harry."

* * *

As the Baytown summer sauntered on, Mary worked her shifts and wished she was back home in Montreal. Maybe someday. That year's course in broadcasting at Tennyson Institute in Toronto had promised much, but the reality—working for low wages at the radio station in Pitfall—soon became tedious. Baytown seemed better, but that might be the season.

Harry Hay brought the kitten upstairs every day for a visit. Mary provided drinks after dark, or coffee and biscuits if the sun had not yet reached the yardarm. The young man didn't seem to have a job. One evening when she asked him about work, he said he was starting on a new project, then ran downstairs and returned with three watercolor paintings—explosions of red and orange.

Harry was hanging around another evening when Tim Melton showed up unexpectedly. The Pitfall broadcaster arrived with rucksack and bedroll, saying not to worry, he would crash on the living-room carpet. Mary was both annoyed by his brassy intrusion and pleased to see him. Now there would be hours of gossip about the station up north. As for Harry, he responded not only to Melton but to the visitor's effect on Mary. It was as if the disturbed young man's parents had been separated and now they were back together. Their embrace when Tim appeared at the top of the stairs left Harry beaming, his eyes moist.

"Who's your lapdog?" Melton asked when Harry excused himself and took Annabella away.

"I won't have you insulting him. He's my landlady's brother. Tell me about Pitfall."

"I did the entire morning show drunk." Melton's square face carried a few days' worth of dark beard. Unwashed, untrimmed, he had the presence of the scruffy twin who is cleaned up and becomes king. "I adlibbed all the commercials. Duffy's Used Cars was on the telephone, screaming. I read 'Casey at the Bat' with Beethoven's Ninth Symphony as background music. I called the station manager at half past five—woke him up and put him on the air without telling him."

"It sounds self-destructive to me, Timothy."

"Absolutely. I obviously need somebody to take care of me."

"I wish you luck."

"I was hoping you might get me in at CBAY."

"They don't need anybody." If she told Tim there was an opening, he would clean himself up and get the job. She might find herself slipping back into the relationship she had been so wise to abandon. "You can crash here for three nights. This is the law." She fended off his kiss—feeling none of the old electricity, thank goodness. "Then you have to move on."

"Who's your house guest?" Jessie asked.

Mary was collecting her mail from the box by the front gate. "A former colleague of mine from another station."

"I never allow tenants to bring men into my house." Jessie had been edgy since Mary's unthinking question at the Coronet.

"You didn't say that when I rented the apartment," Mary said. "Come on, Jessie. This isn't Victorian England."

"When is he leaving?"

"None of your business, really. But I've told him he can stay three nights."

As she headed upstairs, Mary saw Harry watching from the kitchen window. Ten minutes later, he was knocking on her door. "I heard what Jessie said. I want you to know I'm on your side."

"It's a tempest in a teacup, Harry. But thanks."

"My sister can be a monster. She's capable of terrible things. I could tell you stories you wouldn't believe."

"I'm sure you could."

"But I won't let her do anything to you, Mary. I'll stop her if she tries."

Tim Melton did one of his pub crawls through the fleshpots of Baytown and came home after midnight, singing as he fumbled with the gate, falling on the front lawn, and lying there blinking at the moon. By the time Mary got some clothes on and ran down to bring him inside, Jessie was on the scene.

"This is how your colleague comes home?" She was down on one knee, staring down into his jubilant face.

"I've died and gone to heaven," Melton crooned. "It's the face of an angel."

"Get up, Tim," Mary snapped. "It isn't funny."

The drunken announcer used Jessie as a crutch, dragging his weight up and leaning on her as he staggered to the house. "Make my bed soon," his throaty baritone rumbled in her ear, "for I'm weary wi' hunting—"

Jessie relinquished him to Mary at the foot of the stairs. "Three nights, you told me."

"Or less," Mary said grimly.

Tim packed his gear and moved out the next afternoon. "Very cold here in the deep freeze," he said. "You could hang turkeys in this place." He left on foot, heading for the highway and a lift to anywhere.

Jessie knew he was gone before Mary could tell her. She had a way of pronouncing the word "colleague." "Your *colleague* left me a note. He said he's going back to where he came from. Where did you say that is?"

"Pitfall. Up near Thunder Bay."

"I can't see that man apologizing and getting his old job back, can you?"

"I'm not concerned."

It was going to be difficult to repair the relationship between herself and Jessie. Mary was half inclined to let it end. There were other apartments for rent in Baytown. But this one was comfortable, damn it. And she could walk to work in less than ten minutes.

"When in doubt, do nothing" was one of Mary's axioms and she obeyed it when it suited her. For the next week, she came and went, avoiding Jessie. Harry paid his daily visit with Annabella, who had become a small cat. Then, on a Friday evening, Jessie launched her rocket.

"You'll have to go," she said. "I'm going to need this apartment. Harry will be living up here."

"You can't do that."

"There's no lease. You pay by the week." Jessie avoided Mary's eyes. "I'll give you till next weekend and then I want you gone."

Mary ran downstairs after Jessie to pursue the argument and got the kitchen door slammed in her face. Harry's head was in the window, his eyes disturbed.

At the station on Monday, Mary asked Clement Foy if the landlady could get away with putting her out. He thought she could. "Anyway, since things are unpleasant, why not move?"

"I hate to give in to her, she isn't being fair—but I suppose I'll have to."

But it was Jessie Hay who disappeared from the house on Station Street. And Harry began keeping to himself. For three days, there was none of the normal sound from downstairs. Finally, late on Thursday morning, Mary went to the kitchen door and knocked. It took Harry a while to answer.

"Oh, hi," he said. His eyes were shifting.

"Is everything all right?"

"You bet."

"I haven't seen Jessie in a while."

"That's right." It was as if he was concentrating on saying what Mary wanted to hear.

"She told me to leave. But I don't want to."

"Don't worry about it," Harry said.

"What do you mean?"

"You won't have to leave. I've taken care of it."

"Did Jessie change her mind?"

"Forget about Jessie. I had some trouble with her." Harry seemed to be sorting himself out. "I've put her in her place."

As Mary concluded her program that afternoon, Clem Foy watched her through the studio window. When she signed off, he came in and said, "What's on your mind?"

"Does it show?" She described Jessie's disappearance and her brother's cryptic comments. "He's so spooky. He's gentle with the kitten, but he has a mind full of violence. He sees a psychiatrist and he's been institutionalized."

"You think he's *killed* her?"

"There's a big garden behind the house. He loves the kitten I gave him. He wants to help me. Yes, I think he's killed her."

"Are you going to tell the police?"

"What's your advice?"

"Tell the police."

Chief Greb's wife listened to *Town Topics* and had raved to her husband about the new broadcaster. Greb took it upon himself to hear Mary's story. He was impressed. "Harry Hay gave us some trouble when he came back from California. He was off his medication. His sister called us in and we ended up driving him down to the Ontario Hospital in Kingston."

"Do you think he may have done something with her?"

The chief came out from behind his desk. "Let's go and find out."

Harry must have seen the police car pull up and park outside. He was in the front doorway as Greb approached with Mary at his heels. "Where's your sister, Harry?"

Harry's eyes darted back and forth between the visitors. "She isn't here."

Mary said, "Are you trying to help me?"

"She shouldn't have ordered you to move out."

Greb said, "I want the truth from you, Harry."

Annabella, rangy now and fast, darted between Harry's legs and out onto the lawn. Harry ran after her. Then, when he was within reach of her, he changed direction. Before the policeman could react, Harry was through the gate and behind the wheel of a battered sedan parked in front of the cruiser. He switched on, pulled out, and raced away up Station Street.

"Stay here," Greb ordered. He left Mary watching as he got into the police car and drove off in pursuit.

Mary went looking for Annabella—with no luck. She started up the back stairs, then changed her mind. She was too nervous to go inside. What made Harry run? It looked suspicious for him to take off when the chief began questioning him. There was no way he could escape in such a wreck of a car.

The garden behind the house was not well tended. Halfway up the stairs, Mary noticed a clear patch in the tangle of weeds. Somebody had been working there.

The hair stood erect on the back of her neck as she walked through deep grass and stood looking at obvious signs of digging. Fresh earth lay in a mound beside rose bushes run riot. Her heart pounding, she fled to her apartment.

The telephone rang. It was Chief Greb. "I'm at the General Hospital. He's asking for you."

"What happened?"

"I think the kid is suicidal. He drove that wreck faster than it went when it was new. I chased him down 401, almost as far as Napanee. He lost control and went into a concrete overpass. Or maybe he did it on purpose. Can you get here?"

It was too far to walk. Mary called a taxi and arrived at the hospital on Dundas Street within the half hour. Greb was waiting outside Intensive Care. He spoke to a nurse and obtained permission for Mary to go to Harry's bedside.

Harry's head was bandaged and i.v. tubes were taped to both arms. His eyes were closed.

"Harry?"

He recognized her. He smiled. "A whole platoon got through the perimeter in the night," he whispered. "There was a hell of a firefight. Did you get a body count?"

"Not yet." She squeezed his hand. "You sleep now."

Outside in the corridor, she said, "He believes he's been wounded in Vietnam. He's told me stories before."

"Believe it or not, they say he should pull through." Greb said he'd drive Mary home. On the way out of the building, he said, "Having Harry in this condition delays my investigation into his sister's disappearance."

"Lord, I forgot," Mary said. She described the recent digging in the back garden.

The chief said nothing, but on the way to Station Street, he radioed for another car to meet him at the address.

A younger officer with a shovel made short work of the excavation behind Jessie's house. It wasn't a grave at all—but it did contain some of Jessie's dresses, some costume jewelry, articles of makeup, and a framed photograph of Jessie and Harry taken years ago, all of it buried in a shallow hole.

Mary shivered. "This freaks me more than if Jessie was in there."

"Where the hell is she?" Greb wondered.

Several days went by. The disappearance of Jessie Hay was now a topic of conversation around town. Greb told Mary he was convinced Harry had killed his sister. When he became lucid enough to respond to questioning, he would tell what he had done with her. Mary wasn't so sure. "I think her clothing in the ground is symbolic," she said.

Greb blinked at that and soon made his goodbyes.

Clem Foy asked again about possible candidates to fill the vacancy on CBAY's announcer staff. Mary felt guilty about not recommending Tim Melton, but the feeling lasted only a few moments. She had trouble enough in her life without importing more. And she grieved for Annabella, who seemed to have run off for good.

The house at night was quiet as the grave. When she turned off the television before bed, or popped Berlioz or Dvorak out of the cassette player, there was nothing to be heard except the occasional car passing on Station Street. With her head on the pillow, she could listen to her own heartbeat. The old frame building creaked and settled as the temperature changed. Sleep would come eventually, she would be patient.

The door slammed downstairs. People were moving around. Mary sat up in the dark. She could hear muffled voices. Somebody had got in! There was the scrape of something heavy on the floor—what was that, burglars shifting the stereo? And how long before they decided to come up here?

Mary quietly lifted the bedside telephone, dialed the operator, and asked for the police. She told the answering officer what was happening, adding that Chief Greb was investigating a possible murder up here. The policeman on the line knew all about Jessie Hay's disappearance, and where her home was. He said he'd have a car there fast.

Mary hurried into a sweater and jeans and waited at the top of the back stairs with the door open. An occasional sound from below indicated the intruders were still there. When headlights swept the road, Mary crept down the steps and moved around the side of the house to meet the uniformed officer as he got out of the car.

"They've put a light on," she said. "I could still hear them."

"Stay back here." The cop unsnapped the cover on his holster and rested a hand on the butt of his gun as he approached the door and knocked.

"Who's that?" Jessie Hay's voice sounded full of joy. She opened the door. She knew the policeman by sight. "Keith Miller! What's up?"

"Hi, Jessie." The young man was abashed. "We got a report somebody was messing around inside your house."

"And you checked it out. Good for you. And you found it's me." She sounded a little tipsy. "You can be the first to congratulate me, Keith. I'm not Jessie Hay any longer. I'm Mrs. Melton. Meet my husband, Tim."

The door of the police car was open. Mary sank onto the upholstered front seat. Tim was in the doorway, shaking hands with the officer. Miller was giving the bride a kiss, refusing a drink because he was on duty. Mary decided to sneak away upstairs before she could become further involved, but the front door closed and Keith Miller spotted her moving across the lawn as he headed back to the car.

"It wasn't intruders," he said. "Jessie's got married and—"

"I know, I heard," Mary cut him off. "Sorry I brought you out." She went upstairs to bed.

She could have predicted what would happen next. Clem Foy didn't have to come looking for Tim Melton. Since there was only one radio station in town, the newlywed announcer made his way there almost as soon as the confetti was washed out of his hair. With his experience in the business and his abundance of charm, he was hired on the spot.

Encountering Mary in the record library while he was being shown around, he whispered, "You should get more involved in what's happening. You said there were no jobs going here. Clem just told me he's been looking for somebody since April."

On her way up the back stairs later in the week, Mary saw Jessie working in the garden with clippers and mower and rake. Mary got in the first shot.

"Concealing the evidence of Harry's aberration?"

"My brother was stressed to the max when I told him I might be getting married. His imagination took over and he reacted. Big deal. Anyway, a neat garden will help when I sell the cottage. And you don't have to bother moving. With Harry in the hospital, I don't need the apartment." She went on to say, "Tim tells me you consider him to be the worst thing that's happened to Canadian broadcasting since rock-and-roll."

"Tim's okay."

"He's a diamond in the rough. All he ever needed was somebody to take care of him." Jessie radiated triumph as she bent to her clipping.

She did sell up and move before the end of the year and Mary wasn't affected. An old couple moved in downstairs, and they were delighted to have CBAY's lady broadcaster living in their new house.

Mary didn't see Harry again. He went from Baytown Hospital to a convalescent home for six months, and then to Jessie's new residence on the south shore where there was plenty of room for him.

But she heard his voice. Getting ready for bed one night, she tuned in *Melton's Magic*, the new late-night DJ show Foy had added to the schedule. The music was appealing, she gave Tim credit for that. There was often a guest in the studio. Tim had a flair for scouting out characters who had something to say. Mary propped herself against two pillows with a magazine and a cup of hot chocolate while Tim's resonant voice rumbled out of the bedside radio.

"My guest tonight is a local lad who has been there and back. He admits to suffering long bouts of psychiatric illness. Good therapy and medication have left that in the past. Harry, you once believed you had fought in Vietnam, although you were too young for the war."

"That's true, Tim." Harry's voice sounded equally laid back. From his hospital bed, the little faker had risen to become a media person. "I dreamed of firefights, of being wounded, of losing my friends in battle." Harry went on at length, dissecting his own case as if he were reading from a medical journal.

Mary's eyes became heavy. She turned out the light and snuggled down. But, too fascinated to miss a word of the interview, she left the radio on.

It was much later, and perhaps she had dozed off, when something in Harry Hay's voice caused her to sit bolt upright, awake and shaking.

"The sane world isn't much better than the crazy one I used to inhabit," he was saying. "Can you imagine a person sick enough to give somebody a kitten infected with rabies? The giver knowing it and not mentioning it?"

"That's incredible."

"But it's true," Harry said in a tone Mary recognized from before, only it was darker, much darker, than when he'd spoken to her of his sister. "I know a person who did this. Right here in Baytown."

Within minutes, Tim had smoothly ended the interview and eased into some slumber-inducing music. But Mary didn't sleep. Instead, she found herself wondering over and over and over how dangerous Harry Hay really was.

BILL PRONZINI

Bill Pronzini has been a fixture in the mystery field for a number of years, winning Shamus Awards, Edgar Award nominations, editing anthologies, collaborating with Marcia Muller, helping to start the Private Eye Writers of America and serving as its first president, and generally being a terrific writer of hardboiled detective fiction.

Best known for his Nameles Detective series, Pronzini weighs in here with a story set in Nameless territory, in a particular bar, upon the premises of which rests the story's McGuffin. This story, which has been nominated for awards, will only help enhance his reputation as a rising star in the field. It's tough-minded, but human in its view of an ugly situation.

Incident in a
Neighborhood Tavern

When the holdup went down I was sitting at the near end of the Foghorn Tavern's scarred mahogany bar talking to the owner, Matt Candiotti.

It was a little before seven of a midweek evening, lull-time in working-class neighborhood saloons like this one. Blue-collar locals would jam the place from four until about six-thirty, when the last of them headed home for dinner; the hard-core drinkers wouldn't begin filtering back in until about seven-thirty or eight. Right now there were only two customers, and the jukebox and computer hockey games were quiet. The TV over the back bar was on but with the sound turned down to a tolerable level. One of the customers, a porky guy in his fifties, drinking Anchor Steam out of the bottle, was watching the last of the NBC national news. The other customer, an equally porky and middle-aged female barfly, half in the bag on red wine, was trying to convince him to pay attention to her instead of Tom Brokaw.

I had a draft beer in front of me, but that wasn't the reason I was there. I'd come to ask Candiotti, as I had asked two dozen other merchants here in the Outer Mission, if he could offer any leads on the rash of burglaries that were plaguing small businesses in the neighborhood. The police hadn't come up with anything positive after six weeks, so a couple of the victims had gotten up a fund and hired me to see what I could find out. They'd picked me because I had been born and raised in the Outer Mission, I still had friends and shirttail relatives living here, and I understood the neighborhood a good deal better than any other private detective in San Francisco.

But so far I wasn't having any more luck than the SFPD. None of the merchants I'd spoken with today had given me any new ideas, and Candiotti was proving to be no exception. He stood slicing limes

74

into wedges as we talked. They might have been onions the way his long, mournful face was screwed up, like a man trying to hold back tears. His gray-stubbled jowls wobbled every time he shook his head. He reminded me of a tired old hound, friendly and sad, as if life had dealt him a few kicks but not quite enough to rob him of his good nature.

"Wish I could help," he said. "But hell, I don't hear nothing. Must be pros from Hunters Point or the Fillmore, hah?"

Hunters Point and the Fillmore were black sections of the city, which was a pretty good indicator of where his head was at. I said, "Some of the others figure it for local talent."

"Out of this neighborhood, you mean?"

I nodded, drank some of my draft.

"Nah, I doubt it," he said. "Guys that organized, they don't shit where they eat. Too smart, you know?"

"Maybe. Any break-ins or attempted break-ins here?"

"Not so far. I got bars on all the windows, double dead-bolt locks on the storeroom door off the alley. Besides, what's for them to steal besides a few cases of whiskey?"

"You don't keep cash on the premises overnight?"

"Fifty bucks in the till," Candiotti said, "that's all; that's my limit. Everything else goes out of here when I close up, down to the night deposit at the B of A on Mission. My mama didn't raise no airheads." He scraped the lime wedges off his board, into a plastic container, and racked the serrated knife he'd been using. "One thing I did hear," he said. "I heard some of the loot turned up down in San Jose. You know about that?"

"Not much of a lead there. Secondhand dealer named Pitman had a few pieces of stereo equipment stolen from the factory outlet store on Geneva. Said he bought it from a guy at the San Jose flea market, somebody he didn't know, never saw before."

"Yeah, sure," Candiotti said wryly. "What do the cops think?"

"That Pitman bought it off a fence."

"Makes sense. So maybe the boosters are from San Jose, hah?"

"Could be," I said, and that was when the kid walked in.

He brought bad air in with him; I sensed it right away and so did Candiotti. We both glanced at the door when it opened, the way you do, but we didn't look away again once we saw him. He was in his early twenties, dark-skinned, dressed in chinos, a cotton windbreaker, sharp-toed shoes polished to a high gloss. But it was his eyes that put the chill on my neck, the sudden clutch of tension down low in my belly. They were bright, jumpy, on the wild side, and in the dim light of the Foghorn's interior, the pupils were so small they seemed nonexistent. He had one hand in his jacket pocket and I knew it was clamped around a gun even before he took it out and showed it to us.

He came up to the bar a few feet on my left, the gun jabbing the air in front of him. He couldn't hold it steady; it kept jerking up and down, from side to side, as if it had a kind of spasmodic life of its own. Behind me, at the other end of the bar, I heard Anchor Steam suck in his breath, the barfly make a sound like a stifled moan. I eased back a little on the stool, watching the gun and the kid's eyes flick from Candiotti to me to the two customers and back around again. Candiotti didn't move at all, just stood there staring with his hound's face screwed up in that holding-back-tears way.

"All right all right," the kid said. His voice was high pitched, excited, and there was drool at one corner of his mouth. You couldn't get much more stoned than he was and still function. Coke, crack, speed—maybe a combination. The gun that kept flicking this way and that was a goddamn Saturday Night Special. "Listen good, man, everybody listen good. I don't want to kill none of you, man, but I will if I got to, you believe it?"

None of us said anything. None of us moved.

The kid had a folded-up paper sack in one pocket; he dragged it out with his free hand, dropped it, broke quickly at the middle to pick it up without lowering his gaze. When he straightened again there was sweat on his forehead, more drool coming out of his mouth. He threw the sack on the bar.

"Put the money in there Mr. Cyclone Man," he said to Candiotti. "All the money in the register but not the coins; I don't want the fuckin' coins, you hear me?"

Candiotti nodded; reached out slowly, caught up the sack, turned toward the back bar with his shoulders hunched up against his neck. When he punched No Sale on the register, the ringing thump of the cash drawer sliding open seemed overloud in the electric hush. For a few seconds the kid watched him scoop bills into the paper sack; then his eyes and the gun skittered my way again. I had looked into the muzzle of a handgun before and it was the same feeling each time: dull fear, helplessness, a kind of naked vulnerability.

"Your wallet on the bar, man, all your cash." The gun barrel and the wild eyes flicked away again, down the length of the plank, before I could move to comply. "You down there, dude, you and fat mama put your money on the bar. All of it, hurry up."

Each of us did as we were told. While I was getting my wallet out I managed to slide my right foot off the stool, onto the brass rail, and to get my right hand pressed tight against the beveled edge of the bar. If I had to make any sudden moves, I would need the leverage.

Candiotti finished loading the sack, turned from the register. There was a grayish cast to his face now—the wet gray color of fear. The kid said to him, "Pick up their money, put it in the sack with the rest. Come on come on come on!"

Candiotti went to the far end of the plank, scooped up the wallets belonging to Anchor Steam and the woman; then he came back my way, added my wallet to the contents of the paper sack, put the sack down carefully in front of the kid.

"Okay," the kid said, "okay all right." He glanced over his shoulder at the street door, as if he'd heard something there; but it stayed closed. He jerked his head around again. In his sweaty agitation the Saturday Night Special almost slipped free of his fingers; he fumbled a tighter grip on it, and when it didn't go off I let the breath I had been holding come out thin and slow between my teeth. The muscles in my shoulders and back were drawn so tight I was afraid they might cramp.

The kid reached out for the sack, dragged it in against his body. But he made no move to leave with it. Instead he said, "Now we go get the big pile, man."

Candiotti opened his mouth, closed it again. His eyes were almost as big and starey as the kid's.

"Come on Mr. Cyclone Man, the safe, the safe in your office. We goin' back there *now*."

"No money in that safe," Candiotti said in a thin, scratchy voice. "Nothing valuable."

"Oh man I'll kill you man I'll blow your fuckin' head off! I ain't playin' no games I want that money!"

He took two steps forward, jabbing with the gun up close to Candiotti's gray face. Candiotti backed off a step, brought his hands up, took a tremulous breath.

"All right," he said, "but I got to get the key to the office. It's in the register."

"Hurry up hurry up!"

Candiotti turned back to the register, rang it open, rummaged inside with his left hand. But with his right hand, shielded from the kid by his body, he eased up the top on a large wooden cigar box adjacent. The hand disappeared inside; came out again with metal in it, glinting in the back bar lights. I saw it and I wanted to yell at him, but it wouldn't have done any good, would only have warned the kid . . . and he was already turning with it, bringing it up with both hands now—the damn gun of his own he'd had hidden inside the cigar box. There was no time for me to do anything but shove away from the bar and sideways off the stool just as Candiotti opened fire.

The state he was in, the kid didn't realize what was happening until it was too late for him to react; he never even got a shot off. Candiotti's first slug knocked him halfway around, and one of the three others that followed it opened up his face like a piece of ripe fruit smacked by a hammer. He was dead before his body, driven backward, slammed into the cigarette machine near the door, slid down it to the floor.

The half-drunk woman was yelling in broken shrieks, as if she couldn't get enough air for a sustained scream. When I came up out of my crouch I saw that Anchor Steam had hold of her, clinging to her as much for support as in an effort to calm her down. Candiotti stood flat-footed, his arms down at his sides, the gun out of sight below the bar, staring at the bloody remains of the kid as if he couldn't believe what he was seeing, couldn't believe what he'd done.

Some of the tension in me eased as I went to the door, found the lock on its security gate, fastened it before anybody could come in off the street. The Saturday Night Special was still clutched in the kid's hand; I bent, pulled it free with my thumb and forefinger, broke the cylinder. It was loaded, all right—five cartridges. I dropped it into my jacket pocket, thought about checking the kid's clothing for identification, didn't do it. It wasn't any of my business, now, who he'd been. And I did not want to touch him or any part of him. There was a queasiness in my stomach, a fluttery weakness behind my knees—the same delayed reaction I always had to violence and death—and touching him would only make it worse.

To keep from looking at the red ruin of the kid's face, I pivoted back to the bar. Candiotti hadn't moved. Anchor Steam had gotten the woman to stop screeching and had coaxed her over to one of the handful of tables near the jukebox; now she was sobbing, "I've got to go home, I'm gonna be sick if I don't go home." But she didn't make any move to get up and neither did Anchor Steam.

I walked over near Candiotti, pushed hard words at him in an undertone. "That was a damn fool thing to do. You could have got us all killed."

"I know," he said. "I know."

"Why'd you do it?"

"I thought . . . hell, you saw the way he was waving that piece of his . . ."

"Yeah," I said. "Call the police. Nine-eleven."

"Nine-eleven. Okay."

"Put that gun of yours down first. On the bar."

He did that. There was a phone on the back bar; he went away to it in shaky strides. While he was talking to the Emergency operator I picked up his weapon, saw that it was a .32 Charter Arms revolver. I held it in my hand until Candiotti finished with the call, set it down again as he came back to where I stood.

"They'll have somebody here in five minutes," he said.

I said, "You know that kid?"

"Christ, no."

"Ever see him before? Here or anywhere else?"

"No."

"So how did he know about your safe?"

Candiotti blinked at me. "What?"

"The safe in your office. Street kid like that . . . how'd he know about it?"

"How should I know? What difference does it make?"

"He seemed to think you keep big money in that safe."

"Well, I don't. There's nothing in it."

"That's right, you told me you don't keep more than fifty bucks on the premises overnight. In the till."

"Yeah."

"Then why have you got a safe, if it's empty?"

Candiotti's eyes narrowed. "I used to keep my receipts in it, all right? Before all these burglaries started. Then I figured I'd be smarter to take the money to the bank every night."

"Sure, that explains it," I said. "Still, a kid like that, looking for a big score to feed his habit, he wasn't just after what was in the till and our wallets. No, it was as if he'd gotten wind of a heavy stash—a grand or more."

Nothing from Candiotti.

I watched him for a time. Then I said, "Big risk you took, using that .32 of yours. How come you didn't make your play the first time you went to the register? How come you waited until the kid mentioned your office safe?"

"I didn't like the way he was acting, like he might start shooting any second. I figured it was our only chance. Listen, what're you getting at, hah?"

"Another funny thing," I said, "is the way he called you 'Mr. Cyclone Man.' Now why would a hopped-up kid use a term like that to a bar owner he didn't know?"

"How the hell should I know?"

"Cyclone," I said. "What's a cyclone but a big destructive wind? Only one other thing I can think of."

"Yeah? What's that?"

"A fence. A cyclone fence."

Candiotti made a fidgety movement. Some of the wet gray pallor was beginning to spread across his cheeks again, like a fungus.

I said, "And a fence is somebody who receives and distributes stolen goods. A Mr. Fence Man. But then you know that, don't you, Candiotti? We were talking about that kind of fence before the kid came in . . . how Pitman, down in San Jose, bought some hot stereo equipment off of one. That fence could just as easily be operating here in San Francisco, though. Right here in this neighborhood, in fact. Hell, suppose the stuff taken in all those burglaries never left the neighborhood. Suppose it was brought to a place nearby and stored until it could be trucked out to other cities—a tavern storeroom, for instance. Might even be some of it is *still* in that storeroom. And the money he got for the rest he'd keep locked up in his safe, right? Who'd figure it? Except maybe a poor junkie who picked up a whisper on the street somewhere—"

Candiotti made a sudden grab for the .32, caught it up, backed up a step with it leveled at my chest. "You smart son of a bitch," he said. "I ought to kill you too."

"In front of witnesses? With the police due any minute?"

He glanced over at the two customers. The woman was still sobbing, lost in a bleak outpouring of self-pity; but Anchor Steam was staring our way, and from the expression on his face he'd heard every word of my exchange with Candiotti.

"There's still enough time for me to get clear," Candiotti said grimly. He was talking to himself, not to me. Sweat had plastered his lank hair to his forehead; the revolver was not quite steady in his hand. "Lock you up in my office, you and those two back there . . ."

"I don't think so," I said.

"Goddamn you, you think I won't use this gun again?"

"I *know* you won't use it. I emptied out the last two cartridges while you were on the phone."

I took the two shells out of my left-hand jacket pocket and held them up where he could see them. At the same time I got the kid's Saturday Night Special out of the other pocket, held it loosely pointed in his direction. "You want to put your piece down now, Candiotti? You've not going anywhere, not for a long time."

He put it down—dropped it clattering onto the bartop. And as he did his sad hound's face screwed up again, only this time he didn't even try to keep the wetness from leaking out of his eyes. He was leaning against the bar, crying like the woman, submerged in his own outpouring of self-pity, when the cops showed up a little while later.

SARA PARETSKY

Sara Paretsky's latest V. I. Warshawski novel, *Blood Shot*, won the British Crime Writers Association's Silver Dagger for Best Novel. Since the apprearance of *Indemnity Only*, Ms. Paretsky has been rising rapidly in the field, her sharp portrayals of life in the eighties in Chicago striking a chord with growing numbers of readers. Ms. Paretsky has been one of the most successful young writers in this decade and has been a catalyst in the formation of Sisters in Crime.

In the current story she has neatly placed temptation in front of a fascinating array of characters, letting the chips fall where they may. The outcome is, of course, murder.

The Case of the
Pietro Andromache

"You only agreed to hire him because of his art collection. Of that I'm sure." Lotty Herschel bent down to adjust her stockings. "And don't waggle your eyebrows like that—it makes you look like an adolescent Groucho Marx."

Max Loewenthal obediently smoothed his eyebrows, but said, "It's your legs, Lotty; they remind me of my youth. You know, going into the Underground to wait out the air raids, looking at the ladies as they came down the escalators. The updraft always made their skirts billow."

"You're making this up, Max. I was in those Underground stations, too, and as I remember the ladies were always bundled in coats and children."

Max moved from the doorway to put an arm around Lotty. "That's what keeps us together, *Lottchen*: I am a romantic and you are severely logical. And you know we didn't hire Caudwell because of his collection. Although I admit I am eager to see it. The board wants Beth Israel to develop a transplant program. It's the only way we're going to become competitive—"

"Don't deliver your publicity lecture to me," Lotty snapped. Her thick brows contracted to a solid black line across her forehead. "As far as I am concerned he is a cretin with the hands of a Caliban and the personality of Attila."

Lotty's intense commitment to medicine left no room for the mundane consideration of money. But as the hospital's executive director, Max was on the spot with the trustees to see that Beth Israel ran at a profit. Or at least at a smaller loss than they'd achieved in recent years. They'd brought Caudwell in part to attract more paying patients—and to help screen out some of the indigent who made up twelve percent of Beth Israel's patient load. Max wondered how long the hospital could afford to support personalities as di-

vergent as Lotty and Caudwell with their radically differing approaches to medicine.

He dropped his arm and smiled quizzically at her. "Why do you
hate him so much, Lotty?"

"*I* am the person who has to justify the patients I admit to this—
this troglodyte. Do you realize he tried to keep Mrs. Mendes from
the operating room when he learned she had AIDS? He wasn't even
being asked to sully his hands with her blood and he didn't want
me performing surgery on her."

Lotty drew back from Max and pointed an accusing finger at him.
"You may tell the board that if he keeps questioning my judgment
they will find themselves looking for a new perinatologist. I am
serious about this. You listen this afternoon, Max, you hear whether
or not he calls me 'our little baby doctor.' I am fifty-eight years old,
I am a Fellow of the Royal College of Surgeons besides having
enough credentials in this country to support a whole hospital, and
to him I am a 'little baby doctor.' "

Max sat on the daybed and pulled Lotty down next to him. "No,
no, *Lottchen*: don't fight. Listen to me. Why haven't you told me
any of this before?"

"Don't be an idiot, Max: you are the director of the hospital. I
cannot use our special relationship to deal with problems I have
with the staff. I said my piece when Caudwell came for his final
interview. A number of the other physicians were not happy with
his attitude. If you remember, we asked the board to bring him in
as a cardiac surgeon first and promote him to chief of staff after a
year if everyone was satisfied with his performance."

"We talked about doing it that way," Max admitted. "But he
wouldn't take the appointment except as chief of staff. That was the
only way we could offer him the kind of money he could get at one
of the university hospitals or Humana. And, Lotty, even if you don't
like his personality you must agree that he is a first-class surgeon."

"I agree to nothing." Red lights danced in her black eyes. "If he
patronizes me, a fellow physician, how do you imagine he treats his
patients? You cannot practice medicine if—"

"Now it's my turn to ask to be spared a lecture," Max interrupted
gently. "But if you feel so strongly about him, maybe you shouldn't
go to his party this afternoon."

"And admit that he can beat me? Never."

"Very well then." Max got up and placed a heavily-brocaded wool
shawl over Lotty's shoulders. "But you must promise me to behave.
This is a social function we are going to, remember, not a gladiator
contest. Caudwell is trying to repay some hospitality this afternoon,
not to belittle you."

"I don't need lessons in conduct from you: Herschels were attending the emperors of Austria while the Loewenthals were operating vegetable stalls on the Ring," Lotty said haughtily.

Max laughed and kissed her hand. "Then remember these regal Herschels and act like them, *Eure Hoheit.*"

II

Caudwell had bought an apartment sight unseen when he moved to Chicago. A divorced man whose children are in college only has to consult with his own taste in these matters. He asked the Beth Israel board to recommend a realtor, sent his requirements to them— twenties construction, near Lake Michigan, good security, modern plumbing—and dropped seven hundred and fifty thousand for an eight-room condo facing the lake at Scott Street.

Since Beth Israel paid handsomely for the privilege of retaining Dr. Charlotte Herschel as their perinatologist, nothing required her to live in a five room walkup on the fringes of Uptown, so it was a bit unfair of her to mutter "Parvenu" to Max when they walked into the lobby.

Max relinquished Lotty gratefully when they got off the elevator. Being her lover was like trying to be companion to a Bengal tiger: you never knew when she'd take a lethal swipe at you. Still, if Caudwell were insulting her—and her judgment—maybe he needed to talk to the surgeon, explain how important Lotty was for the reputation of Beth Israel.

Caudwell's two children were making the obligatory Christmas visit. They were a boy and a girl, Deborah and Steve, within a year of the same age, both tall, both blond and poised, with a hearty sophistication born of a childhood spent on expensive ski slopes. Max wasn't very big, and as one took his coat and the other performed brisk introductions, he felt himself shrinking, losing in self-assurance. He accepted a glass of special *cuvée* from one of them— was it the boy or the girl, he wondered in confusion—and fled into the melee.

He landed next to one of Beth Israel's trustees, a woman in her sixties wearing a grey textured mini-dress whose black stripes were constructed of feathers. She commented brightly on Caudwell's art collection, but Max sensed an undercurrent of hostility: wealthy trustees don't like the idea that they can't out-buy the staff.

While he was frowning and nodding at appropriate intervals, it dawned on Max that Caudwell did know how much the hospital needed Lotty. Heart surgeons do not have the world's smallest egos: when you ask them to name the world's three leading practitioners, they never can remember the names of the other two. Lotty was at the top of her field, and she, too, was used to having things her way. Since her confrontational style was reminiscent more of the Battle of the Bulge than the Imperial Court of Vienna, he didn't blame Caudwell for trying to force her out of the hospital.

Max moved away from Martha Gildersleeve to admire some of the paintings and figurines she'd been discussing. A collector himself of Chinese porcelains, Max raised his eyebrows and mouthed a soundless whistle at the pieces on display. A small Watteau and a Charles Demuth watercolor were worth as much as Beth Israel paid Caudwell in a year. No wonder Mrs. Gildersleeve had been so annoyed.

"Impressive, isn't it."

Max turned to see Arthur Gioia looming over him. Max was shorter than most of the Beth Israel staff, shorter than everyone but Lotty. But Gioia, a tall muscular immunologist, loomed over everyone. He had gone to the University of Arkansas on a football scholarship and had even spent a season playing tackle for Houston before starting medical school. It had been twenty years since he last lifted weights, but his neck still looked like a redwood stump.

Gioia had led the opposition to Caudwell's appointment. Max had suspected at the time that it was due more to a medicine man's not wanting a surgeon as his nominal boss than from any other cause, but after Lotty's outburst he wasn't so sure. He was debating whether to ask the doctor how he felt about Caudwell now that he'd worked with him for six months when their host surged over to him and shook his hand.

"Sorry I didn't see you when you came in, Loewenthal. You like the Watteau? It's one of my favorite pieces. Although a collector shouldn't play favorites any more than a father should, eh, sweetheart?" The last remark was addressed to the daughter, Deborah, who had come up behind Caudwell and slipped an arm around him.

Caudwell looked more like a Victorian seadog than a surgeon. He had a round red face under a shock of yellow-white hair, a hearty Santa Claus laugh, and a bluff, direct manner. Despite Lotty's vituperations, he was immensely popular with his patients. In the short time he'd been at the hospital, referrals to cardiac surgery had increased fifteen percent.

His daughter squeezed his shoulder playfully. "I know you don't play favorites with us, Dad, but you're lying to Mr. Loewenthal about your collection; come on, you know you are."

She turned to Max. "He has a piece he's so proud of he doesn't like to show it to people—he doesn't want them to see he's got vulnerable spots. But it's Christmas, Dad, relax, let people see how you feel for a change."

Max looked curiously at the surgeon, but Caudwell seemed pleased with his daughter's familiarity. The son came up and added his own jocular cajoling.

"This really is Dad's pride and joy. He stole it from Uncle Griffen when Grandfather died and kept Mother from getting her mitts on it when they split up."

Caudwell did bark out a mild reproof at that. "You'll be giving my colleagues the wrong impression of me, Steve. I didn't steal it from Grif. Told him he could have the rest of the estate if he'd leave me the Watteau and the Pietro."

"Of course he could've bought ten estates with what those two would fetch," Steve muttered to his sister over Max's head.

Deborah relinquished her father's arm to lean over Max and whisper back, "Mom, too."

Max moved away from the alarming pair to say to Caudwell, "A Pietro? You mean Pietro d'Alessandro? You have a model, or an actual sculpture?"

Caudwell gave his staccato admiral's laugh. "The real McCoy, Loewenthal. The real McCoy. An alabaster."

"An alabaster?" Max raised his eyebrows. "Surely not. I thought Pietro worked only in bronze and marble."

"Yes, yes," chuckled Caudwell, rubbing his hands together. "Everyone thinks so, but there were a few alabasters in private collections. I've had this one authenticated by experts. Come take a look at it—it'll knock your breath away. You come, too, Gioia," he barked at the immunologist. "You're Italian, you'll like to see what your ancestors were up to."

"A Pietro alabaster?" Lotty's clipped tones made Max start—he hadn't noticed her joining the little group. "I would very much like to see this piece."

"Then come along, Dr. Herschel, come along." Caudwell led them to a small hallway, exchanging genial greetings with his guests as he passed, pointing out a John William Hill miniature they might not have seen, picking up a few other people who for various reasons wanted to see his prize.

"By the way, Gioia, I was in New York last week, you know. Met an old friend of yours from Arkansas. Paul Nierman."

"Nierman?" Gioia seemed to be at a loss. "I'm afraid I don't remember him."

"Well, he remembered you pretty well. Sent you all kinds of

messages—you'll have to stop by my office on Monday and get the full strength."

Caudwell opened a door on the right side of the hall and let them into his study. It was an octagonal room carved out of the corner of the building. Windows on two sides looked out on Lake Michigan. Caudwell drew salmon drapes as he talked about the room, why he'd chosen it for his study even though the view kept his mind from his work.

Lotty ignored him and walked over to a small pedestal which stood alone against the paneling on one of the far walls. Max followed her and gazed respectfully at the statue. He had seldom seen so fine a piece outside a museum. About a foot high, it depicted a woman in classical draperies hovering in anguish over the dead body of a soldier lying at her feet. The grief in her beautiful face was so poignant that it reminded you of every sorrow you had ever faced.

"Who is it meant to be?" Max asked curiously.

"Andromache," Lotty said in a strangled voice. "Andromache mourning Hector."

Max stared at Lotty, astonished equally by her emotion and her knowledge of the figure—Lotty was totally uninterested in sculpture.

Caudwell couldn't restrain the smug smile of a collector with a true coup. "Beautiful, isn't it? How do you know the subject?"

"I should know it." Lotty's voice was husky with emotion. "My grandmother had such a Pietro. An alabaster given her great-grandfather by the Emperor Joseph the Second himself for his help in consolidating imperial ties with Poland."

She swept the statue from its stand, ignoring a gasp from Max, and turned it over. "You can see the traces of the imperial stamp here still. And the chip on Hector's foot which made the Hapsburg wish to give the statue away to begin with. How came you to have this piece? Where did you find it?"

The small group that had joined Caudwell stood silent by the entrance, shocked at Lotty's outburst. Gioia looked more horrified than any of them, but he found Lotty overwhelming at the best of times—an elephant confronted by a hostile mouse.

"I think you're allowing your emotions to carry you away, doctor." Caudwell kept his tone light, making Lotty seem more gauche by contrast. "I inherited this piece from my father, who bought it—legitimately—in Europe. Perhaps from your—grandmother, was it? But I suspect you are confused about something you may have seen in a museum as a child."

Deborah gave a high-pitched laugh and called loudly to her brother, "Dad may have stolen it from Uncle Grif, but it looks like Grandfather snatched it to begin with anyway."

"Be quiet, Deborah," Caudwell barked sternly.

His daughter paid no attention to him. She laughed again and joined her brother to look at the imperial seal on the bottom of the statue.

Lotty brushed them aside. "*I* am confused about the seal of Joseph the Second?" she hissed at Caudwell. "Or about this chip on Hector's foot? You can see the line where some Philistine filled in the missing piece. Some person who thought his touch would add value to Pietro's work. Was that you, *doctor?* Or your father?"

"Lotty." Max was at her side, gently prising the statue from her shaking hands to restore it to its pedestal. "Lotty, this is not the place or the manner to discuss such things."

Angry tears sparkled in her black eyes. "Are you doubting my word?"

Max shook his head. "I'm not doubting you. But I'm also not supporting you. I'm asking you not to talk about this matter in this way at this gathering."

"But, Max: either this man or his father is a thief!"

Caudwell strolled up to Lotty and pinched her chin. "You're working too hard, Dr. Herschel. You have too many things on your mind these days. I think the board would like to see you take a leave of absence for a few weeks, go someplace warm, get yourself relaxed. When you're this tense, you're no good to your patients. What do you say, Loewenthal?"

Max didn't say any of the things he wanted to—that Lotty was insufferable and Caudwell intolerable. He believed Lotty, believed that the piece had been her grandmother's. She knew too much about it, for one thing. And for another, a lot of artworks belonging to European Jews were now in museums or private collections around the world. It was only the most godawful coincidence that the Pietro had ended up with Caudwell's father.

But how dare she raise the matter in the way most likely to alienate everyone present? He couldn't possibly support her in such a situation. And at the same time, Caudwell's pinching her chin in that condescending way made him wish he were not chained to a courtesy that would have kept him from knocking the surgeon out even if he'd been ten years younger and ten inches taller.

"I don't think this is the place or the time to discuss such matters," he reiterated as calmly as he could. "Why don't we all cool down and get back together on Monday, eh?"

Lotty gasped involuntarily, then swept from the room without a backward glance.

Max refused to follow her. He was too angry with her to want to see her again that afternoon. When he got ready to leave the party an hour or so later, after a long conversation with Caudwell that taxed his sophisticated urbanity to the utmost, he heard with relief that Lotty was long gone. The tale of her outburst had of course spread through the gathering at something faster than the speed of sound; he wasn't up to defending her to Martha Gildersleeve who demanded an explanation of him in the elevator going down.

He went home for a solitary evening in his house in Evanston. Normally such time brought him pleasure, listening to music in his study, lying on the couch with his shoes off, reading history, letting the sounds of the lake wash over him.

Tonight, though, he could get no relief. Fury with Lotty merged into images of horror, the memories of his own disintegrated family, his search through Europe for his mother. He had never found anyone who was quite certain what became of her, although several people told him definitely of his father's suicide. And stamped over these wisps in his brain was the disturbing picture of Caudwell's children, their blond heads leaning backward at identical angles as they gleefully chanted, "Grandpa was a thief, Grandpa was a thief," while Caudwell edged his visitors out of the study.

By morning he would somehow have to reconstruct himself enough to face Lotty, to respond to the inevitable flood of calls from outraged trustees. He'd have to figure out a way of soothing Caudwell's vanity, bruised more by his children's behavior than anything Lotty had said. And find a way to keep both important doctors at Beth Israel.

Max rubbed his grey hair. Every week this job brought him less joy and more pain. Maybe it was time to step down, to let the board bring in a young MBA who would turn Beth Israel's finances around. Lotty would resign then, and it would be an end to the tension between her and Caudwell.

Max fell asleep on the couch. He awoke around five muttering, "By morning, by morning." His joints were stiff from cold, his eyes sticky with tears he'd shed unknowingly in his sleep.

But in the morning things changed. When Max got to his office he found the place buzzing, not with news of Lotty's outburst but word that Caudwell had missed his early morning surgery. Work came almost completely to a halt at noon when his children phoned to say they'd found the surgeon strangled in his own study and the Pietro Andromache missing. And on Tuesday, the police arrested Dr. Charlotte Herschel for Lewis Caudwell's murder.

III

Lotty would not speak to anyone. She was out on two hundred fifty thousand dollars' bail, the money raised by Max, but she had gone directly to her apartment on Sheffield after two nights in County Jail without stopping to thank him. She would not talk to reporters, she remained silent during all conversations with the police, and she emphatically refused to speak to the private investigator who had been her close friend for many years.

Max, too, stayed behind an impregnable shield of silence. While Lotty went on indefinite leave, turning her practice over to a series of colleagues, Max continued to go to the hospital every day. But he, too, would not speak to reporters: he wouldn't even say, "No comment." He talked to the police only after they threatened to lock him up as a material witness, and then every word had to be pried from him as if his mouth were stone and speech Excalibur. For three days V. I. Warshawski left messages which he refused to return.

On Friday, when no word came from the detective, when no reporter popped up from a nearby urinal in the men's room to try to trick him into speaking, when no more calls came from the state's attorney, Max felt a measure of relaxation as he drove home. As soon as the trial was over he would resign, retire to London. If he could only keep going until then, everything would be—not all right, but bearable.

He used the remote release for the garage door and eased his car into the small space. As he got out he realized bitterly he'd been too optimistic in thinking he'd be left in peace. He hadn't seen the woman sitting on the stoop leading from the garage to the kitchen when he drove in, only as she uncoiled herself at his approach.

"I'm glad you're home—I was beginning to freeze out here."

"How did you get into the garage, Victoria?"

The detective grinned in a way he usually found engaging. Now it seemed merely predatory. "Trade secret, Max. I know you don't want to see me, but I need to talk to you."

He unlocked the door into the kitchen. "Why not just let yourself into the house if you were cold? If your scruples permit you into the garage, why not into the house?"

She bit her lip in momentary discomfort but said lightly, "I couldn't manage my picklocks with my fingers this cold."

The detective followed him into the house. Another tall monster; five foot eight, athletic, light on her feet behind him. Maybe American mothers put growth hormones or steroids in their children's cornflakes. He'd have to ask Lotty. His mind winced at the thought.

"I've talked to the police, of course," the light alto continued behind him steadily, oblivious to his studied rudeness as he poured himself a cognac, took his shoes off, found his waiting slippers, and padded down the hall to the front door for his mail.

"I understand why they arrested Lotty—Caudwell had been doped with a whole bunch of Xanax and then strangled while he was sleeping it off. And, of course, she was back at the building Sunday night. She won't say why, but one of the tenants I.D.'d her as the woman who showed up around ten at the service entrance when he was walking his dog. She won't say if she talked to Caudwell, if he let her in, if he was still alive."

Max tried to ignore her clear voice. When that proved impossible he tried to read a journal which had come in the mail.

"And those kids, they're marvelous, aren't they? Like something out of the *Fabulous Furry Freak Brothers*. They won't talk to me but they gave a long interview to Murray Ryerson over at the *Star*.

"After Caudwell's guests left, they went to a flick at the Chestnut Street Station, had a pizza afterwards, then took themselves dancing on Division Street. So they strolled in around two in the morning— confirmed by the doorman—saw the light on in the old man's study. But they were feeling no pain and he kind of overreacted—their term—if they were buzzed, so they didn't stop in to say goodnight. It was only when they got up around noon and went in that they found him."

V. I. had followed Max from the front hallway to the door of his study as she spoke. He stood there irresolutely, not wanting his private place desecrated with her insistent, air-hammer speech, and finally went on down the hall to a little-used living room. He sat stiffly on one of the brocade armchairs and looked at her remotely when she perched on the edge of its companion.

"The weak piece in the police story is the statue," V. I. continued.

She eyed the Persian rug doubtfully and unzipped her boots, sticking them on the bricks in front of the fireplace.

"Everyone who was at the party agrees that Lotty was beside herself. By now the story has spread so far that people who weren't even in the apartment when she looked at the statue swear they heard her threaten to kill him. But if that's the case, what happened to the statue?"

Max gave a slight shrug to indicate total lack of interest in the topic.

V. I. ploughed on doggedly. "Now some people think she might have given it to a friend or a relation to keep for her until her name is cleared at the trial. And these people think it would be either her

Uncle Stefan here in Chicago, her brother Hugo in Montreal, or you. So the Mounties searched Hugo's place and are keeping an eye on his mail. And the Chicago cops are doing the same for Stefan. And I presume someone got a warrant and went through here, right?"

Max said nothing, but he felt his heart beating faster. Police in his house, searching his things? But wouldn't they have to get his permission to enter? Or would they? Victoria would know, but he couldn't bring himself to ask. She waited for a few minutes, but when he still wouldn't speak, she plunged on. He could see it was becoming an effort for her to talk, but he wouldn't help her.

"But I don't agree with those people. Because I know that Lotty is innocent. And that's why I'm here. Not like a bird of prey, as you think, using your misery for carrion. But to get you to help me. Lotty won't speak to me, and if she's that miserable I won't force her to. But surely, Max, you won't sit idly by and let her be rail-roaded for something she never did."

Max looked away from her. He was surprised to find himself holding the brandy snifter and set it carefully on a table beside him.

"Max!" Her voice was shot with astonishment. "I don't believe this. You actually think she killed Caudwell."

Max flushed a little, but she'd finally stung him into a response. "And you are God who sees all and knows she didn't?"

"I see more than you do," V. I. snapped. "I haven't known Lotty as long as you have, but I know when she's telling the truth."

"So you are God." Max bowed in heavy irony. "You see beyond the facts to the innermost souls of men and women."

He expected another outburst from the young woman, but she gazed at him steadily without speaking. It was a look sympathetic enough that Max felt embarrassed by his sarcasm and burst out with what was on his mind.

"What else am I to think? She hasn't said anything, but there's no doubt that she returned to his apartment Sunday night."

It was V. I.'s turn for sarcasm. "With a little vial of Xanax that she somehow induced him to swallow? And then strangled him for good measure? Come on, Max, you know Lotty: honesty follows her around like a cloud. If she'd killed Caudwell, she'd say something like, 'Yes, I bashed the little vermin's brains in.' Instead she's not speaking at all."

Suddenly the detective's eyes widened with incredulity. "Of course. She thinks you killed Caudwell. You're doing the only thing you can to protect her—standing mute. And she's doing the same thing. What an admirable pair of archaic knights."

"No!" Max said sharply. "It's not possible. How could she think such a thing? She carried on so wildly that it was embarrassing to be near her. I didn't want to see her or talk to her. That's why I've felt so terrible. If only I hadn't been so obstinate, if only I'd called her Sunday night. How could she think I would kill someone on her behalf when I was so angry with her?"

"Why else isn't she saying anything to anyone?" Warshawski demanded.

"Shame, maybe," Max offered. "You didn't see her on Sunday. I did. That is why I think she killed him, not because some man let her into the building."

His brown eyes screwed shut at the memory. "I have seen Lotty in the grip of anger many times, more than is pleasant to remember, really. But never, never have I seen her in this kind of—uncontrolled rage. You could not talk to her. It was impossible."

The detective didn't respond to that. Instead she said, "Tell me about the statue. I heard a couple of garbled versions from people who were at the party, but I haven't found anyone yet who was in the study when Caudwell showed it to you. Was it really her grandmother's, do you think? And how did Caudwell come to have it if it was?"

Max nodded mournfully. "Oh, yes. It was really her family's, I'm convinced of that. She could not have known in advance about the details, the flaw in the foot, the imperial seal on the bottom. As to how Caudwell got it, I did a little looking into that myself yesterday. His father was with the Army of Occupation in Germany after the war. A surgeon attached to Patton's staff. Men in such positions had endless opportunities to acquire artworks after the war."

V. I. shook her head questioningly.

"You must know something of this, Victoria. Well, maybe not. You know the Nazis helped themselves liberally to artwork belonging to Jews everywhere they occupied Europe. And not just to Jews—they plundered Eastern Europe on a grand scale. The best guess is that they stole sixteen million pieces—statues, paintings, altarpieces, tapestries, rare books. The list is beyond reckoning, really."

The detective gave a little gasp. "Sixteen million! You're joking."

"Not a joke, Victoria. I wish it were so, but it is not. The U.S. Army of Occupation took charge of as many works of art as they found in the occupied territories. In theory, they were to find the rightful owners and try to restore them. But in practice few pieces were ever traced, and many of them ended up on the black market.

"You only had to say that such-and-such a piece was worth less than five thousand dollars and you were allowed to buy it. For an officer on Patton's staff, the opportunities for fabulous acquisitions would have been endless. Caudwell said he had the statue authenticated, but of course he never bothered to establish its provenance. Anyway, how could he?" Max finished bitterly. "Lotty's family had a deed of gift from the Emperor, but that would have disappeared long since with the dispersal of their possessions."

"And you really think Lotty would have killed a man just to get this statue back? She couldn't have expected to keep it. Not if she'd killed someone to get it, I mean."

"You are so practical, Victoria. You are too analytical, sometimes, to understand why people do what they do. That was not just a statue. True, it is a priceless artwork, but you know Lotty, you know she places no value on such possessions. No, it meant her family to her, her past, her history, everything that the war destroyed forever for her. You must not imagine that because she never discusses such matters that they do not weigh on her."

V. I. flushed at Max's accusation. "You should be glad I'm analytical. It convinces me that Lotty is innocent. And whether you believe it or not I'm going to prove it."

Max lifted his shoulders slightly in a manner wholly European. "We each support Lotty according to our lights. I saw that she met her bail, and I will see that she gets expert counsel. I am not convinced that she needs you making her innermost secrets public."

V. I.'s grey eyes turned dark with a sudden flash of temper. "You're dead wrong about Lotty. I'm sure the memory of the war is a pain that can never be cured, but Lotty lives in the present, she works in hope for the future. The past does not obsess and consume her as, perhaps, it does you."

Max said nothing. His wide mouth turned in on itself in a narrow line. The detective laid a contrite hand on his arm.

"I'm sorry, Max. That was below the belt."

He forced the ghost of a smile to his mouth.

"Perhaps it's true. Perhaps it's why I love these ancient things so much. I wish I could believe you about Lotty. Ask me what you want to know. If you promise to leave as soon as I've answered and not to bother me again, I'll answer your questions."

IV

Max put in a dutiful appearance at the Michigan Avenue Presbyterian Church Monday afternoon for Lewis Caudwell's funeral. The surgeon's former wife came, flanked by her children and her husband's brother Griffen. Even after three decades in America Max found himself puzzled sometimes by the natives' behavior: since she and Caudwell were divorced, why had his ex-wife draped herself in black? She was even wearing a veiled hat reminiscent of Queen Victoria.

The children behaved in a moderately subdued fashion, but the girl was wearing a white dress shot with black lightning forks which looked as though it belonged at a disco or a resort. Maybe it was her only dress or her only dress with black in it, Max thought, trying hard to look charitably at the blonde Amazon—after all, she had been suddenly and horribly orphaned.

Even though she was a stranger both in the city and the church, Deborah had hired one of the church parlors and managed to find someone to cater coffee and light snacks. Max joined the rest of the congregation there after the service.

He felt absurd as he offered condolences to the divorced widow: did she really miss the dead man so much? She accepted his conventional words with graceful melancholy and leaned slightly against her son and daughter. They hovered near her with what struck Max as a stagey solicitude. Seen next to her daughter, Mrs. Caudwell looked so frail and undernourished that she seemed like a ghost. Or maybe it was just that her children had a hearty vitality that even a funeral couldn't quench.

Caudwell's brother Griffen stayed as close to the widow as the children would permit. The man was totally unlike the hearty seadog surgeon. Max thought if he'd met the brothers standing side by side he would never have guessed their relationship. He was tall, like his niece and nephew, but without their robustness. Caudwell had had a thick mop of yellow-white hair; Griffen's domed head was covered by thin wisps of grey. He seemed weak and nervous, and lacked Caudwell's outgoing *bonhomie*; no wonder the surgeon had found it easy to decide the disposition of their father's estate in his favor. Max wondered what Griffen had gotten in return.

Mrs. Caudwell's vague, disoriented conversation indicated that she was heavily sedated. That, too, seemed strange. A man she hadn't lived with for four years and she was so upset at his death that she could only manage the funeral on drugs? Or maybe it was the shame of coming as the divorced woman, not a true widow? But then why come at all?

To his annoyance, Max found himself wishing he could ask Victoria about it. She would have some cynical explanation—Caudwell's death meant the end of the widow's alimony and she knew she wasn't remembered in the will. Or she was having an affair with

Griffen and was afraid she would betray herself without tranquilizers. Although it was hard to imagine the uncertain Griffen as the object of a strong passion.

Since he had told Victoria he didn't want to see her again when she left on Friday, it was ridiculous of him to wonder what she was doing, whether she was really uncovering evidence that would clear Lotty. Ever since she had gone he had felt a little flicker of hope in the bottom of his stomach. He kept trying to drown it, but it wouldn't quite go away.

Lotty, of course, had not come to the funeral, but most of the rest of the Beth Israel staff was there, along with the trustees. Arthur Gioia, his giant body filling the small parlor to the bursting point, tried finding a tactful balance between honesty and courtesy with the bereaved family; he made heavy going of it.

A sable-clad Martha Gildersleeve appeared under Gioia's elbow, rather like a furry football he might have tucked away. She made bright, unseemly remarks to the bereaved family about the disposal of Caudwell's artworks.

"Of course, the famous statue is gone now. What a pity. You could have endowed a chair in his honor with the proceeds from that piece alone." She gave a high, meaningless laugh.

Max sneaked a glance at his watch, wondering how long he had to stay before leaving would be rude. His sixth sense, the perfect courtesy that governed his movements, had deserted him, leaving him subject to the gaucheries of ordinary mortals. He never peeked at his watch at functions, and at any prior funeral he would have deftly pried Martha Gildersleeve from her victim. Instead he stood helplessly by while she tortured Mrs. Caudwell and other bystanders alike.

He glanced at his watch again. Only two minutes had passed since his last look. No wonder people kept their eyes on their watches at dull meetings: they couldn't believe the clock could move so slowly.

He inched stealthily toward the door, exchanging empty remarks with the staff members and trustees he passed. Nothing negative was said about Lotty to his face, but the comments cut off at his approach added to his misery.

He was almost at the exit when two newcomers appeared. Most of the group looked at them with indifferent curiosity, but Max suddenly felt an absurd stir of elation. Victoria, looking sane and modern in a navy suit, stood in the doorway, eyebrows raised, scanning the room. At her elbow was a police sergeant Max had met with her a few times. The man was in charge of Caudwell's death, too: it was that unpleasant association that kept the name momentarily from his mind.

V. I. finally spotted Max near the door and gave him a discreet sign. He went to her at once.

"I think we may have the goods," she murmured. "Can you get everyone to go? We just want the family, Mrs. Gildersleeve, and Gioia."

"*You* may have the goods," the police sergeant growled. "I'm here unofficially and reluctantly."

"But you're here." Warshawski grinned, and Max wondered how he ever could have found the look predatory. His own spirits rose enormously at her smile. "You know in your heart of hearts that arresting Lotty was just plain dumb. And now I'm going to make you look real smart. In public, too."

Max felt his suave sophistication return with the rush of elation that an ailing diva must have when she finds her voice again. A touch here, a word there, and the guests disappeared like the hosts of Sennacherib. Meanwhile he solicitously escorted first Martha Gildersleeve, then Mrs. Caudwell to adjacent armchairs, got the brother to fetch coffee for Mrs. Gildersleeve, the daughter and son to look after the widow.

With Gioia he could be a bit more ruthless, telling him to wait because the police had something important to ask him. When the last guest had melted away, the immunologist stood nervously at the window rattling his change over and over in his pockets. The jingling suddenly was the only sound in the room. Gioia reddened and clasped his hands behind his back.

Victoria came into the room beaming like a governess with a delightful treat in store for her charges. She introduced herself to the Caudwells.

"You know Sergeant McGonnigal, I'm sure, after this last week. I'm a private investigator. Since I don't have any legal standing, you're not required to answer any questions I have. So I'm not going to ask you any questions. I'm just going to treat you to a travelogue. I wish I had slides, but you'll have to imagine the visuals while the audio track moves along."

"A private investigator!" Steve's mouth formed an exaggerated "O"; his eyes widened in amazement. "Just like Bogie."

He was speaking, as usual, to his sister. She gave her highpitched laugh and said, "We'll win first prize in the 'How I Spent My Winter Vacation' contests. Our daddy was murdered. Zowie. Then his most valuable possession was snatched. Powie. But he'd already stolen it from the Jewish doctor who killed him. Yowie! And then a P.I. to wrap it all up. Yowie! Zowie! Powie!"

"Deborah, please," Mrs. Caudwell sighed. "I know you're excited, sweetie, but not right now, okay?"

"Your children keep you young, don't they, ma'am?" Victoria said. "How can you ever feel old when your kids stay seven all their lives?"

"Oo, ow, she bites, Debbie, watch out, she bites!" Steve cried.

McGonnigal made an involuntary movement, as though restraining himself from smacking the younger man. "Ms. Warshawski is right: you are under no obligation to answer any of her questions. But you're bright people, all of you: you know I wouldn't be here if the police didn't take her ideas very seriously. So let's have a little quiet and listen to what she's got on her mind."

Victoria seated herself in an armchair near Mrs. Caudwell's. McGonnigal moved to the door and leaned against the jamb. Deborah and Steve whispered and poked each other until one or both of them shrieked. They then made their faces prim and sat with their hands folded on their laps, looking like bright-eyed choirboys.

Griffen hovered near Mrs. Caudwell. "You know you don't have to say anything, Vivian. In fact, I think you should return to your hotel and lie down. The stress of the funeral—then these strangers—"

Mrs. Caudwell's lips curled bravely below the bottom of her veil. "It's all right, Grif; if I managed to survive everything else, one more thing isn't going to do me in."

"Great." Victoria accepted a cup of coffee from Max. "Let me just sketch events for you as I saw them last week. Like everyone else in Chicago, I read about Dr. Caudwell's murder and saw it on television. Since I know a number of people attached to Beth Israel, I may have paid more attention to it than the average viewer, but I didn't get personally involved until Dr. Herschel's arrest on Tuesday."

She swallowed some coffee and set the cup on the table next to her with a small snap. "I have known Dr. Herschel for close to twenty years. It is inconceivable that she would commit such a murder, as those who know her well should have realized at once. I don't fault the police, but others should have known better: she is hot-tempered. I'm not saying killing is beyond her—I don't think it's beyond any of us. She might have taken the statue and smashed Dr. Caudwell's head in in the heat of rage. But it beggars belief to think she went home, brooded over her injustices, packed a dose of prescription tranquilizer, and headed back to the Gold Coast with murder in mind."

Max felt his cheeks turn hot at her words. He started to interject a protest but bit it back.

"Dr. Herschel refused to make a statement all week, but this afternoon, when I got back from my travels, she finally agreed to talk to me. Sergeant McGonnigal was with me. She doesn't deny that she returned to Dr. Caudwell's apartment at ten that night— she went back to apologize for her outburst and to try to plead with him to return the statue. He didn't answer when the doorman called up, and on impulse she went around to the back of the building, got in through the service entrance, and waited for some time outside the apartment door. When he neither answered the doorbell nor returned home himself, she finally went away around eleven o'clock. The children, of course, were having a night on the town."

"*She* says," Gioia interjected.

"Agreed." V. I. smiled. "I make no bones about being a partisan: I accept her version. The more so because the only reason she didn't give it a week ago was that she herself was protecting an old friend. She thought perhaps this friend had bestirred himself on her behalf and killed Caudwell to avenge deadly insults against her. It was only when I persuaded her that these suspicions were as unmerited as— well, as accusations against herself—that she agreed to talk."

Max bit his lip and busied himself with getting more coffee for the three women. Victoria waited for him to finish before continuing.

"When I finally got a detailed account of what took place at Caudwell's party, I heard about three people with an axe to grind. One always has to ask, what axe and how big a grindstone? That's what I've spent the weekend finding out. You might as well know that I've been to Little Rock and to Havelock, North Carolina."

Gioia began jingling the coins in his pockets again. Mrs. Caudwell said softly, "Grif, I am feeling a little faint. Perhaps—"

"Home you go, Mom," Steve cried out with alacrity.

"In a few minutes, Mrs. Caudwell," the sergeant said from the doorway. "Get her feet up, Warshawski."

For a moment Max was afraid that Steve or Deborah was going to attack Victoria, but McGonnigal moved over to the widow's chair and the children sat down again. Little drops of sweat dotted Griffen's balding head; Gioia's face had a greenish sheen, foliage on top of his redwood neck.

"The thing that leapt out at me," Victoria continued calmly, as though there had been no interruption, "was Caudwell's remark to Dr. Gioia. The doctor was clearly upset, but people were so focused on Lotty and the statue that they didn't pay any attention to that.

"So I went to Little Rock, Arkansas, on Saturday and found the Paul Nierman whose name Caudwell had mentioned to Gioia. Nierman lived in the same fraternity with Gioia when they were undergraduates together twenty-five years ago. And he took Dr. Gioia's anatomy and physiology exams his junior year when Gioia was in danger of academic probation, so he could stay on the football team.

"Well, that seemed unpleasant, perhaps disgraceful. But there's no question that Gioia did all his own work in medical school, passed his boards, and so on. So I didn't think the board would demand a resignation for this youthful indiscretion. The question was whether Gioia thought they would, and if he would have killed to prevent Caudwell making it public."

She paused, and the immunologist blurted out, "No. No. But Caudwell—Caudwell knew I'd opposed his appointment. He and I—our approaches to medicine were very opposite. And as soon as he said Nierman's name to me, I knew he'd found out and that he'd torment me with it forever. I—I went back to his place Sunday night to have it out with him. I was more determined than Dr. Herschel and got into his unit through the kitchen entrance; he hadn't locked that.

"I went to his study, but he was already dead. I couldn't believe it. It absolutely terrified me. I could see he'd been strangled and—well, it's no secret that I'm strong enough to have done it. I wasn't thinking straight. I just got clean away from there—I think I've been running ever since."

"You!" McGonnigal shouted. "How come we haven't heard about this before?"

"Because you insisted on focusing on Dr. Herschel," V. I. said nastily. "I knew he'd been there because the doorman told me. He would have told you if you'd asked."

"This is terrible," Mrs. Gildersleeve interjected. "I am going to talk to the board tomorrow and demand the resignations of Dr. Gioia and Dr. Herschel."

"Do," Victoria agreed cordially. "Tell them the reason you got to stay for this was because Murray Ryerson at the *Herald-Star* was doing a little checking for me here in Chicago. He found out that part of the reason you were so jealous of Caudwell's collection is that you're living terribly in debt. I won't humiliate you in public by telling people what your money has gone to, but you've had to sell your husband's art collection and you have a third mortgage on your house. A valuable statue with no documented history would have taken care of everything."

Martha Gildersleeve shrank inside her sable. "You don't know anything about this."

"Well, Murray talked to Pablo and Eduardo. . . . Yes, I won't say anything else. So anyway, Murray checked whether either Gioia or Mrs. Gildersleeve had the statue. They didn't, so—"

"You've been in my house?" Mrs. Gildersleeve shrieked.

V. I. shook her head. "Not me. Murray Ryerson." She looked

apologetically at the sergeant. "I knew you'd never get a warrant for me, since you'd made an arrest. And you'd never have got it in time, anyway."

She looked at her coffee cup, saw it was empty and put it down again. Max took it from the table and filled it for her a third time. His fingertips were itching with nervous irritation; some of the coffee landed on his trouser leg.

"I talked to Murray Saturday night from Little Rock. When he came up empty here, I headed for North Carolina. To Havelock, where Griffen and Lewis Caudwell grew up and where Mrs. Caudwell still lives. And I saw the house where Griffen lives, and talked to the doctor who treats Mrs. Caudwell, and—"

"You really are a pooper snooper, aren't you," Steve said.

"Pooper snooper, pooper snooper," Deborah chanted. "Don't get enough thrills of your own so you have to live on other people's shit."

"Yeah, the neighbors talked to me about you two." Victoria looked at them with contemptuous indulgence. "You've been a two-person wolfpack terrifying most of the people around you since you were three. But the folks in Havelock admired how you always stuck up for your mother. You thought your father got her addicted to tranquilizers and then left her high and dry. So you brought her newest version with you and were all set—you just needed to decide when to give it to him. Dr. Herschel's outburst over the statue played right into your hands. You figured your father had stolen it from your uncle to begin with—why not send it back to him and let Dr. Herschel take the rap?"

"It wasn't like that," Steve said, red spots burning in his cheeks.

"What was it like, son?" McGonnigal had moved next to him.

"Don't talk to them—they're tricking you," Deborah shrieked. "The pooper snooper and her gopher gooper."

"She—Mommy used to love us before Daddy made her take all this shit. Then she went away. We just wanted him to see what it was like. We started putting Xanax in his coffee and stuff; we wanted to see if he'd fuck up during surgery, let his life get ruined. But then he was sleeping there in the study after his stupid-ass party, and we thought we'd just let him sleep through his morning surgery. Sleep forever, you know, it was so easy, we used his own Harvard necktie. I was so fucking sick of hearing 'Early to bed, early to rise' from him. And we sent the statue to Uncle Grif. I suppose the pooper snooper found it there. He can sell it and Mother can be all right again."

"Grandpa stole it from Jews and Daddy stole it from Grif, so we thought it worked out perfectly if we stole it from Daddy," Deborah cried. She leaned her blonde head next to her brother's and shrieked with laughter.

V

Max watched the line of Lotty's legs change as she stood on tiptoe to reach a brandy snifter. Short, muscular from years of racing at top speed from one point to the next, maybe they weren't as svelte as the long legs of modern American girls, but he preferred them. He waited until her feet were securely planted before making his announcement.

"The board is bringing in Justin Hardwick for a final interview for chief of staff."

"Max!" She whirled, the Bengal fire sparkling in her eyes. "I know this Hardwick and he is another like Caudwell, looking for cost-cutting and no poverty patients. I won't have it."

"We've got you and Gioia and a dozen others bringing in so many non-paying patients that we're not going to survive another five years at the present rate. I figure it's a balancing act. We need someone who can see that the hospital survives so that you and Art can practice medicine the way you want to. And when he knows what happened to his predecessor, he'll be very careful not to stir up our resident tigress."

"Max!" She was hurt and astonished at the same time. "Oh. You're joking, I see. It's not very funny to me, you know."

"My dear, we've got to learn to laugh about it: it's the only way we'll ever be able to forgive ourselves for our terrible misjudgments." He stepped over to put an arm around her. "Now where is this remarkable surprise you promised to show me."

She shot him a look of pure mischief, Lotty on a dare as he first remembered meeting her at eighteen. His hold on her tightened and he followed her to her bedroom. In a glass case in the corner, complete with a humidity-control system, stood the Pietro Andromache.

Max looked at the beautiful, anguished face. I understand your sorrows, she seemed to say to him. I understand your grief for your mother, your family, your history, but it's all right to let go of them, to live in the present and hope for the future. It's not a betrayal.

Tears pricked his eyelids, but he demanded, "How did you get this? I was told the police had it under lock and key until lawyers decided on the disposition of Caudwell's estate."

"Victoria," Lotty said shortly. "I told her the problem and she got it for me. On the condition that I not ask how she did it. And Max, you know—*damned* well that it was not Caudwell's to dispose of."

It was Lotty's. Of course it was. Max wondered briefly how Joseph the Second had come by it to begin with. For that matter, what had Lotty's great-great-grandfather done to earn it from the emperor? Max looked into Lotty's tiger eyes and kept such reflections to himself. Instead he inspected Hector's foot where the filler had been carefully scraped away to reveal the old chip.

BILL CRENSHAW

A relative newcomer to the field, Crenshaw opened a lot of eyes when "Flicks" was nominated for and subsequently won the Edgar Award for Best Short Story of 1988.

It's the story of a cop on the trail of a fiendish and bloodthirsty serial killer. But it's more as well, because the cop is vividly drawn, and the circumstances surrounding the killings are as much a part of the story as are the killings themselves. Not a pretty sight.

Flicks

He knew it wasn't a question of if his beeper would go off.

This time Devin Corley was home, his apartment, had just opened a beer, turned on the TV, stretched out on the couch. He phoned in. Dispatcher said Majestic Theater, across town. He started the VCR, took a last pull at the beer, gave the cat fresh water, got a quick shower. Then he left. Speed was not of the essence.

He knew what he'd find. A body; Ray Tasco, his partner, taking statements, popping his gum, looking amused and surprised at once; Maggie Epps with her wedge face and her black forensic kit, diagramming the scene, scooping nameless little forensic glops into baggies; Joe Franks in a safari shirt, slung with cameras, smiling like always, always smiling, always angry. He'd give Corley grief about being away from his desk again, or being late. Corley had been away from his desk a lot. He was always late.

At the Majestic there were two uniforms in the men's john. The room was done in men's room tile, blue and white, smelled of urine, wet tobacco, stale drains, pine. Trash can on side, brown paper towels spilling out, balled up, dark with water, some with red smears. Floor around sinks wet, scattered splashes and small pools. Hints of blood in wet footprints running back and forth across the tile. In near stall somebody retching. The uniform watching the somebody was pointedly not looking at him.

"What we got?" Corley asked the uniforms.

"Got a slashing, lieutenant," said the older uniform, twenty-six maybe, Lopez maybe. Corley glanced down at the name-tag. Lopez. The younger uniform looked green at the gills. Corley didn't know him, knew he wouldn't be green long, not this kind of green. Lots of greens in Homicide, green like Greengills, green like a two-day corpse, green like Corley, like old copper.

"In here?" Corley asked.

106

Lopez snapped his head back. "In the first theater."

Corley moved to the stall. Lopez moved beside him. Greengills went to the sink and splashed water on his face.

"Who we got?" said Corley.

"Pickpocket, he says. Says he just lifted the guy's wallet. Says he didn't know he was dead."

The pickpocket turned around, face pasty, hair matted. "I didn't know, man," he said, whiney, rocking. "Jesus, I didn't know. That was blood, oh god, that was blood, man, and I didn't even feel it. My hands . . ." He grabbed for the john again. Corley turned away.

"Any of that blood his?" he asked.

"Don't think so."

The wallet was on the stainless steel shelf over the sinks. It was smeared with bloody fingerprints. Corley took out a silver pen and flipped the wallet open. "Find it in the trash can?"

"Yessir," said the younger uniform, wiping the water from his face, looking at Corley in the mirror.

"Money still in it? Credit cards?"

"Yessir."

The driver's license showed a fifty-five-year-old business type, droopy eyes, saggy chin, looking above the camera, trying to decide if he should smile for this official picture. Bussey, Tyrone Otis. Toccoa Falls, Georgia.

The pickpocket told Corley that he'd like seen this chubby dude asleep at the end of his row, which he'd seen him before with a big wad of cash in his wallet at the candy counter and seen him put the wallet inside his coat and not in his pants. Near the end of the flick when he got to the guy he kind of tripped and caught himself on the guy's seat and said sorry, excuse me, while lifting his wallet real neat, and he dropped the wallet into his popcorn box and headed right for the john to ditch the wallet and just stroll out with the plastic and the cash, but in the john his hands were bloody and the guy's wallet and his shoes, and then he heard screaming in the lobby and he ditched the wallet and tried to wash the blood off but there was too much, the more he looked, the more he saw, and somebody came in and went out, so he tried to hide. He didn't know what was happening, but he knew it was real bad.

There was a spritzing noise and thin, piney mist settled into the stall and spotted Corley's glasses. Corley tore off a little square of toilet paper and smeared the spots around on the lenses. He had the pickpocket arrested on robbery and on suspicion of murder, but he knew he wasn't the killer.

"Victim here alone?" asked Corley.

"As far as we know," said Lopez.

"Convention, maybe. Is Tasco here? Do you know Sergeant Tasco?"

Joe Franks leaned into the restroom, cameras swinging at his neck. "Hey, Corley, you in on this or not? The meat wagon's waiting. Come show me what you want."

Corley smiled. "You know what I want."

"Yeah, show me anyway so if you don't get it all, you don't blame me. Where've you been?"

"You shoot in here?"

"Yeah, I shot in here." He sounded impatient.

"You get the footprints?"

"Yeah, I got the footprints."

"Get the towels and the sink?"

"Yeah, the towels, the sink, and the stall, and the punk, and I even got a closeup of his puke, okay?"

"See, Joe," said Corley, smiling again, "you know exactly what I want."

"I hate working with you, Corley," said Franks as Corley pushed past him.

In the theater Maggie Epps was sitting on the aisle across from the body, sketchpad on her knees. "Glad you could make it, Devin," she said.

Corley fished for a snappy comeback, couldn't hook anything he hadn't said a hundred times before, said hello.

Franks showed Corley the angles he had shot. Corley asked for a couple more. The flashes illuminated the body like lightning, burned distorted images into Corley's retina.

Tasco came in, talking to somebody, squinting over his notebook. "Ray, you got the manager there?" Corley called.

"I'm the owner," the man said.

"Think you could give us some more light?"

"This is as bright as it gets, officer. This is a movie theater."

Corley turned back around. Franks snorted.

Mr. T. O. Bussey sat on the aisle in the high-backed chair, sagging left, head forward, eyes opened. Blood covered everything from his tie on down, had run under the seats toward the screen. People had tracked it back toward the lobby, footprints growing fainter up the aisle.

"You shoot that?" asked Corley.

Franks nodded. "Probably thought they were walking through cola."

Corley bent over Mr. Bussey. He put a hand on the forehead and raised the head an inch or two so that he could see the wound. "You see this?"

"Yeah. Want a shot?"

"Can I lift his head, Maggie?"

"Just watch where you plant your big feet," she said.

Corley stood behind Mr. Bussey, put his hands above the ears, and raised the head face forward, chin up. He turned his eyes away from the flashes.

"What did he get?" said Corley.

"Everything," said Maggie. "Jugular, carotid, trachea, carotid, jugular. Something real sharp. This guy never made a sound, never felt a thing. Maybe a hand in his hair jerking his head back. Nothing after that."

"From behind?" Corley lowered the head back to where he had found it.

"Left to right, curving up. You got your man in the john?"

"Don't think so. Too much blood on his shoes. He walked out in front, not behind."

"So what have you got?"

"Headache."

Maggie smiled. "It's going to get worse."

Corley smiled back. "It always does."

Corley made Greengills help bag the body. He could say that he was helping the kid get used to it, that it didn't get any better, that as bodies went this one wasn't bad, but he wasn't sure he had done it as a favor. He was afraid he'd done it to be mean.

They spent half an hour looking for the weapon. Corley didn't expect to find anything. They didn't.

He had a videotape unit brought over and sent Lopez and Greengills into the other theaters to block the parking lot exits and send the audiences through the lobby.

The owner pulled him aside and protested. Corley told him that the killer might be in another theater. The owner said something about losing the last *Deathdancer* audience and not needing any publicity hurting ticket sales and being as much a victim as that poor man. "I own nine screens in this town," he said, dragging his hand over his jaw. "I'm not responsible for this. Let's keep the profile low, okay?" There was nothing Corley could say, so he said nothing, and the owner bristled and said he had friends in this town. "I'll speak to your superior about this, Officer . . . ?"

"Corley," he said, walking away. "That's l-e-y."

The other movies ended and the audiences pushed into the lobby. Corley had them videotaped as they bunched and swayed toward the street. Two more uniforms arrived and he started them searching the other theaters for the weapon.

He left Tasco in charge and went to the station and hung around the darkroom while Franks did his printing and bitched about wasting his talent on corpses and about Corley's always wanting more shots and more prints than anybody else. Corley didn't bother to tell Franks again that it was his own fault, that Franks was the one who always waxed eloquent over his third beer and said that the camera always lied, that the image distorted as much as it revealed, that photographs were fictions. He had convinced Corley, so Corley always wanted more and more pictures, each to balance others, to offer new angles, so that reality became a sort of compromise, an average. Corley didn't say any of that again. He made the right noises at the right times, like he did when Franks said how he was going to quit as soon as he finished putting his portfolio together, as soon as he got a show somewhere.

Maybe Franks really was working on a project. Maybe he should be a real photographer. Corley didn't know. He knew Franks about as well as he could, down to a certain level, no further. He imagined that Franks knew him in about the same way. It wasn't the kind of thing they talked about.

Corley lifted a dripping print out of the fixer. "Why'd you become a cop anyway?" he said.

Franks took the print from him and put it back. It was hard to read Franks' eyes in the red light. "You're asking that like you thought there were real answers," Franks said.

Corley took the prints to his desk and did what paperwork he could. He worked until the sky got gray. By the time he stopped for doughnuts on the way home, the first edition of the *News* was on the stands. It didn't have the murder.

He thought sometimes there were real answers instead of just the same patterns and ways to deal with patterns and levels beyond which you couldn't go. He thought sometimes that there was a way to get to the next level. He thought sometimes he'd quit, do insurance fraud, something. He thought maybe he hated his job, but he didn't know that either. He had thought there was something essential about working Homicide, essential in the sense of dealing with the essences of things, a job that butted as close to the raw edge of reality as he was likely to get, and how would he do insurance after that? But whatever kind of essence he was seeing, it was mute, images beyond articulation. None of it made any sense, and he was bone-marrow tired.

The landing at his apartment was dim, and as he slid his key into the second lock, he could see the peephole darken in the apartment next door. Half past five in the morning and Gianelli was already up and prowling. Corley stood an extra second in the rectangle of light from his apartment so that Gianelli could see who he was, whoever the hell Gianelli was besides a name on a mailbox down-stairs, an eye at the peephole, the sounds of pacing footsteps, of a TV. Corley's cat sniffed at the flecks of dried blood on his shoes.

Corley tossed the paper and Franks' pictures on the desk, opened a can of smelly catfood, had a couple of doughnuts and some milk. Then he rewound the tape in the VCR and stretched out on the couch to watch the program that the call to the theater had inter-rupted. It was a cop show. At the station they laughed at cop shows. Things made sense in cop shows. He fell asleep before the first commercial.

Corley woke up with the cat in his face again. He got a hand under its middle and flicked it away, watched it twist in the air, land on all fours, sit and stretch, lick its paws. It wasn't even his cat. The apartment had come with the cat and a wall of corky tile covered with pictures of the previous occupant. The super hadn't bothered to take them down. "Throw 'em away if you want," he'd said. "What do I care?" She was pale and blonde. An actress who never made it, maybe. A model. A photographer. Corley wondered what kind of person would leave a cat and a wall covered with her own image. He still had the pictures in a box somewhere. He used the cork as a dart board, to pin up grocery lists and phone numbers. After eight months he was getting used to the cat, except when it tried to lie in his face, which it always did when he fell asleep on the couch. One of these times he was going to toss it out of the window, down to the street. Four floors down, it didn't matter if it landed on its feet or not.

He looked at his watch. Only nine thirty, but he knew he wouldn't get back to sleep. He might as well go in.

He stopped for doughnuts and coffee and the second edition. Big headline. HORROR FLICK HORROR. *Blood flowed on the screen and in the aisles last night at the Majestic Theater . . .* Great copy, he thought, great murder for the papers. Stupid murder in a stupid place. Not robbery. Not a hit, not on some salesman from upstate Georgia. Tasco would say somebody boozed, whacked, dusted. Cor-ley didn't think so. This one was weird. There was something going on here, something interesting, a new level, maybe, something new. He sat for a long time thinking.

It was going on eleven by the time he dropped the paper on his desk.

"My kids love those things," said Tasco.

"What things?"

Tasco pointed to the headline. "Horror flicks."

Corley looked at the paper. The story was covered in green felt

tip pen with questions about the case, with ideas, with an almost
unrecognizable sketch of the scene. Corley didn't remember
doodling.

There was a tapping of knuckle on glass. Captain Hupmann motioned them into his office.

"Finally," said Tasco.

"How long you been waiting?" said Corley.

"Too long."

"Sorry." He knew the captain had been waiting on him, had made
Tasco wait on him, too.

"Just go easy, okay?" Tasco said.

The captain shut the door and turned to Corley. "So where are
we on this one?"

Tasco looked at Corley. Corley shrugged.

The captain started to snap something but Tasco flipped open his
notebook. "Family notified," he said. "Victim in town for sales
convention, goes to same convention every year, never takes wife.
Concession girl remembers him because he talked funny, had an
accent she meant, and he made her put extra butter on his popcorn
twice and called her ma'am. Nobody else remembers him. Staying
at the Plaza, single room, no roommate. They don't take roll at the
meetings, so we don't know if he's been to any or if he's been seeing
the sights." Tasco looked up, popping his gum, then looked at
Corley.

"I think we've got a nut," said Corley. "Random. Maybe a one-
shot, maybe a serial."

The captain raised his eyebrows in mock surprise. "Are we taking
an interest in our work again?"

Corley shifted his weight.

"A nut," said the captain. "Ray?"

Tasco shrugged. "Seems reasonable, but we're not married to it.
Might be a user flipped out by the flick."

The captain turned back to Corley. "Why did he pick Bussey?"

Corley could picture Bussey at the convention, anonymous in the
city and the crowd, free to cuss and stay out late if he wanted, hit
the bars and the ladies, drink too much and smoke big cigars. But
Mr. Bussey hadn't gone that far. He'd just gone to a movie he
wouldn't be caught dead in at home.

"He sat in the wrong place," said Corley. "He was on the aisle.
Quick exit."

"What quick exit? This is a theater, for chrissakes. This is public.
You don't do a random in public." The captain drew his lips together. "Where do you want to go with this?" he asked finally,
looking more at Tasco than Corley.

Corley looked at Tasco before answering. He hadn't told Tasco anything. "We want to talk to the pickpocket again, the employees again. We've got some names from the audience, the paper had some more. We want them to see the tapes, see if they recognize somebody coming out of the other theaters. Ray wants to do more with Mr. Bussey's movements, see if there's some connection we don't know about."

"Okay," said the captain. "You've both got plenty of other work, but you can keep this one warm for a couple of days. Check the gangs. Maybe something there, initiation ritual, something. If it's some kind of hit, or if it's a user, it won't go far."

"I think it's a serial," said Corley.

"You mean you hope it's a serial," said the captain. "Otherwise you're not going to get him. That it?"

"Yessir," said Tasco.

"Oh, and Corley," the captain said as Corley was halfway through the door, "welcome back. Back to stay?"

They followed up with the employees and what members of the audience they could find, asked if they'd known anybody else in the theater, seen anything unusual, remembered someone walking around near the end of the movie. They showed them pictures of the pickpocket and Mr. Bussey's driver's license, the tapes of the other audiences, asked if anyone looked familiar.

Corley tried to make himself ask the questions as if they were new, as if he'd never even thought of them before. Same questions, same answers, and if you didn't listen because it all seemed the same, you missed something. Tasco always asked the questions right and was somehow not dulled by the routine, by the everlasting sameness. Tasco hunkered down and did his job, would see the waste and the stupidity of it all, say, "Jeez, why do they do that, we got to get the SOB that did this, aren't people horrible." Tasco's saving grace was that he didn't think about it. Corley didn't mean that in a mean way. It was a quality he envied, maybe even admired. Welcome back, back to stay? Sometimes he wondered why he didn't just walk away from it all.

They got Maggie to draw a seating chart and they put little pins in the squares, red for Mr. Bussey, yellow for the people they questioned, blue in seats that yellows remembered being occupied. The media played the story and boosted ratings and circulation, and more people from the audience came forward, and others who claimed to have been there but who Tasco said were probably on Mars at the time. The number of pins increased, but that was all.

"They sat all around him," said Corley, "and they didn't see anything."

"So who in this city ever sees anything?"

"Yeah, well, they should have seen something. Maybe they were watching the movie. Maybe we should see it."

They used their shields to get into the seven o'clock show. The ticket girl told them that the crowd was down, especially in *Death-dancer*. Tasco bought a big tub of popcorn and two cokes, and they sat in the middle about halfway to the screen.

The horror flicks that had scared Corley as a kid played with the dark, the uncertain, the unknown, where you might not even see the killer clearly, where you were never sure if the clicking in the night outside was the antenna wire slapping in the wind or the sound of the giant crabs moving. One thing might be another, and there was no way to tell, and you never really knew if you were safe.

But this wasn't the same. Here the only unknowns were when the next kid was going to get it and how gross it would be. A series of bright red brutalities, each more bizarre than the last, more grotesque, more unreal. Corley couldn't take it seriously. But maybe the audience could. Unless they were cops or medics, maybe this was what it was like. Corley started watching them.

They were mostly under forty, sat in couples or groups, boys close to the screen or all the way to the wall and the corners, girls in the middle, turning their heads away and looking sideways; dates close, touching, copping feels; marrieds a married distance apart. They all talked and laughed too loud. On the screen the killer stalked the victim and the audience got quiet and focused on the movie. Corley could feel muscles stiffen, tension build as the sequence drew the moment out, the moment you knew would come, was coming, came, and they screamed at the killing, and after the killing sank back spent, then started laughing nervously, talking, wisecracking at the screen, at each other. Corley watched three boys sneak up behind a row of girls and grab at their throats, the girls shrieking, leaping, the boys collapsing in laughter. A girl chanted, "Esther wet her panties," and the whole audience broke up. On the screen, the killer started stalking his next victim and the cycle began again.

"What do you think?" asked Corley, lighting a cigarette as soon as they hit the lobby. People in line for the next show stared at their faces as if trying to see if they would be scared or bored or disgusted. Corley thought they all looked hopeful somehow.

Tasco shrugged, placid as ever. "It was a horror flick."

"Was it any good?"

"Who can tell? You'll have to ask my kids."

The summer wind was warm and filled with exhaust fumes.

"You wanta come up for a beer or something?" Corley asked.

Tasco looked at his watch. "Nah, better get back. Evelyn. See you tomorrow."

Corley thought about rephrasing it, asking if he wanted to stop in for a beer somewhere, but Tasco had already made his excuse. Used to be they'd have a beer once or twice a week before Tasco started his thirty minute drive back to Evelyn and the kids and the postage-stamp yard he was so proud of, but that was before Corley had moved across town, out of his decent apartment, with the court-yard and the pool, into what he lived in now. Tasco had been to the new place once only. He'd looked around and popped his gum and looked surprised and amused and inhaled his beer and left. Corley was relieved that Tasco hadn't asked him why he'd moved. He asked himself the same thing.

After he fed the cat, Corley put on the tape of the audience leaving the other screens. At first they ignored the camera, looked away, pretended not to see it, nudged a companion, pointed discreetly. Some made faces and more people saw it, and more made faces or shot birds or mouthed, "Hi, Mom," or walked straight at the camera so that their faces filled the pictures, stuck hands or popcorn boxes in front of the lens, waved, mugged, danced, pretended to strip, to moon the camera, to kiss Corley through the TV screen.

They had taped three audiences. They acted about the same.

Before he went to bed, Corley posted the newspaper articles and Franks' pictures on the cork wall, with a shot of Mr. Bussey in the center.

The heat woke him. He lay sweating, disoriented, fingers knotted in sheets. The night light threw a yellow oval on the wall opposite, gave the room a focus, showed him right where he was. He hated the panic that came from not being sure. He took three or four deep, slow breaths.

He hadn't always had the night light. He hadn't always strapped an extra gun to his leg or carried two speedloaders in his coat pockets every time he went out. He hadn't always spent so much time in his apartment, in front of the TV, asleep in front of the TV, in bed. He tried not to think about it. He tried not to think.

It was too early to be up, too late to go back to sleep, too hot to stay in the apartment. He could make coffee and go to the roof before the sun hit the tar, could catch the breeze off the river, let the cat stalk pigeons.

While the coffee dripped he sat on the couch and looked at the pictures on the wall. In the central picture Mr. Bussey sat with head up and eyes open, like he was watching the movie, the wound like a big smile. Death in black and white. Not like the deaths in the movie. Real was more . . . something. Casual. Anticlimactic. Prosaic. Unaccompanied by soundtrack. Maybe Bussey wasn't really dead. Maybe it was just special effects. In the picture his hands held Mr. Bussey's head just above the ears. He wiped his palms on his shorts.

Mr. Gianelli's peephole darkened as Corley shut his door and the cat slid up the stairs. He was halfway to the landing when the door opened the width of the chain and Gianelli's face pressed into the crack, cheeks bulging around the wood. Over his shoulder a room was lit by a television's multi-colored glow.

"I know what you're doing, young man," Gianelli called in a rasping voice.

"Sorry if I woke you," Corley said, kept climbing, smiled. Maybe thirty-eight seemed young to Gianelli.

"You leave my antenna alone," Gianelli said. "The one on the chimney. I been seventeen years in this building. I got rights. You hear me, young man? Next time my picture goes I'm calling a cop." He slammed his door and it echoed in the stairwell like a gunshot.

Corley beat Tasco to work.

"Whoa," said Franks on his way to the coffee pot. "On time and everything. You must have figured it out."

"Figured what out?" said Corley.

Franks smiled. "That you won't get fired for being late. You want out, you got to quit."

"So who wants out?"

"Who doesn't?"

Tasco had never said anything about Corley's being late. When Tasco came in, he didn't say anything about Corley's being early.

Another homicide came in and they spent the morning and most of the afternoon down by the river and the warehouses, Tasco and Corley and Maggie and Joe and the smells of creosote and fish and gasoline. Some punk had taken a twelve-gauge to the gut, sawed-off, Maggie said, because of the spread and the powder burns, another drug hit as the new champions of free enterprise tried to corner the market. It wasn't going to get solved unless somebody rolled over. A crowd gathered at the yellow police line ribbons. Lopez and Greengills came in for crowd control. The paramedics bitched about hauling corpses. Greengills didn't seem to be bothered by the body.

It was late when they got back to the station.

"I'm going to the movie," said Corley. "I'm going to take our pickpocket. Want to come?"

"What for?"

"Like you said, maybe something in the movie freaked this guy. Maybe we can find something."

"I don't think we're going to get anywhere on this one."

"So you want to come, or not?" Tasco said no.

The pickpocket didn't want to go either. "My treat," Corley told him, not smiling.

Corley sat in Mr. Bussey's seat and told the pickpocket to reconstruct exactly what he had done, when he had done it. He got popcorn and grape soda like Bussey, put the empties into the next seat like Bussey, concentrated on the movie, tried not to see the pickpocket in the corner of his eye, tried to ignore the feeling that his back was to the door, tried to control his breathing. He hated this, hated the dark, the people around him, the long empty aisle on his left, he felt full of energy demanding use, fought to sit still. Finally on the screen the killer reached for the last survivor and the background music shrieked, and Corley slumped left and lowered his head and sat, and on the screen the girl fought off the killer, and they rescued her just in time, and they killed the killer and comforted the girl, and they discovered that the killer wasn't dead and had escaped, and then Corley felt the pickpocket fall across him, heard his "Sorry," felt the wallet slide out of his coat only because he was waiting for it. He sat slumped over while the audience filed out, giggling or groaning or silent. He sat until a nervous usher shook him and asked him to wake up.

He found the pickpocket throwing up in the men's room.

"We're just going to leave this open for a while," said the captain. "Put the river thing on warm."

Tasco nodded, popping his gum. Corley said nothing.

"Problem, Devin?"

"I'd like to stay on this a while."

"Got something to sell? New leads? Anything?"

Corley shook his head. "Not really."

"Okay, then."

They went back to their desks.

"Learn anything last night?" asked Tasco.

Corley shrugged, remembering the dark, palpable and pressing; the icy air pushing into his lungs as he sat and waited, the effort to exhale; trying to concentrate on the movie, on what might have snapped somebody; and after, trying to help the pickpocket out of the stall, embarrassed for him now, and sorry, and the pickpocket twisting his elbow out of Corley's grip and tearing in half the twenty that Corley had stuffed into his shirt pocket, bloody money maybe, something, he wouldn't have it. "Not much," he said. "Bussey must have gotten it in that last sequence, like we thought."

"Funny, isn't it, all that stuff up there on the screen, and out in the audience some dude flicks out a blade and that's that."

"Yeah," said Corley. "That's that."

Corley found himself at a movie again that night, a horror flick near the university. He sat on the aisle, last row, back to the wall. The movie looked the same as the other, felt the same, same rhythms, same victims, same bright gore. The audience was younger, more the age of the characters on the screen, and louder, maybe, but still much the same as the others, shouting at the screen, groaning, cracking jokes, laughing in the wrong places, trying to scare each other, strange responses, inappropriate somehow. They had come for the audience as much as the movie. They had come to be in a group.

He found himself the next night in another movie, on the aisle, last row, back to the wall, fingering the speedloader in his pocket, trying to remember why he was wasting his time there.

Near the end of the show, he saw a silhouette down front rise and edge toward the aisle, stop, and his guts iced as he saw it reach out its left hand and pull back someone's head, heard a scream, saw it slash across the throat with its right hand and turn and run up the aisle for the exit, coming right for him, too perfect. He braced, tightening his grips on the armrests, fought to sit, sit, as the silhouette ran toward him, then he stuck out a leg and the man went down hard and Corley was on him with his knee in the back and his gun behind the right ear. He yelled for an ambulance, ordered the man to open his fist. The man was slow. Corley brought a gun butt down on the back of his hand. The fingers opened, and something bright rolled onto the carpet. Corley stared at it for a few seconds before he saw it was a tube of lipstick.

"It's only a game, man," said a voice above him, quavering. Corley looked up. The owner of the voice was pointing with a shaking finger to the bright red lipstick slash along his throat. "Only a game."

Corley cuffed them to each other and took them in. He was not gentle with them.

The papers had fun with the story. "Off-duty Detective Nabs Lipstick Slasher," said one headline. Corley posted the stories on the corkboard.

They gave him a hard time when he got to work, asked if he'd been wounded, if the stain would come out, warned him about the chapstick chopper. He didn't let it get to him.

What got to him was how much fun the slasher and his victim had. He tried to tell Tasco about it. He'd almost lost it, he said. He'd been shaking with rage, wanted to push them around, run them in hard, give them a dose of the fear of God, but it didn't sink in. They just kept replaying it all the way into the station.

"You really didn't know for sure, did you?" the slasher had asked.

"Thought I was *gone*," said the victim. "For a second there I thought this was it." He laid his head back on the seat, his face suddenly blue fading to black as the unit passed under a street light. "Oh, wow," he said.

"Shut up," Corley had snarled. "Just shut the hell up." They had gone silent, then looked at each other and giggled.

"Drugs," said Tasco.

"They weren't looped. It was like they were, but they weren't. This guy, the victim—for all he knew it was the killer. He was scared shitless, Ray, and he loved it."

Tasco shrugged. "It's a cheap high. Love that rush, maybe. Or maybe it's like they're in the flick. Makes 'em movie stars. Everybody wants to be a movie star. Put a Walkman on your head and your *life's* a fucking movie."

"I just wish I knew what the hell was going on." Corley rocked back in his chair. "I'm going to a movie tonight. Want to come?"

Tasco stared at Corley for a second or two. "This on your own time?"

"You want to come, or not?"

"The river's on warm, remember? We're not going to get this one. It was a one shot." He paused a second. "You okay?"

Corley rocked forward. "What the hell is that supposed to mean?"

"It's not supposed to mean anything. I only wanted . . ."

"All I did was ask if you wanted to go to a flick."

"Keep your voice down. Jesus. For six months you've been a walking burnout. I've been like partnered with a zombie . . ."

"I do my job, nobody can say I don't do my job."

". . . now suddenly you're doing overtime. I'm your partner. I just want to know if you're okay, that's all."

"I'm fine," Corley snapped.

"Okay, great. I'm just asking."

Corley got up and crossed the squad room and refilled his coffee cup and sat back down. He took a sip, burned his tongue. "Yeah, well," he said, "thanks for asking. You want to come?"

Tasco shook his head. "It's going to be a long day without that."

It was a long day, but Corley made the nine o'clock at the Majestic. The ticket girl let him in on his shield again, said the numbers were up, really up. The lobby was crowded, people two deep at the candy counter, clumped around video games, whooping over electronic explosions as someone blasted something on the screen. There were no seats left at the back or on the aisle, and Corley had to sit between two people. He kept his elbows off the armrests. During the movie the audience seemed more tense, everybody wide-eyed and alert, but he caught himself with knotted muscles more than once and thought the tension maybe was in him.

The lipstick game spread like bad news, and every night Corley ran in one or two slashers for questioning, and for anger, because it wasn't a game when he saw a head snap back or heard a scream, wasn't a game when the man moving down his row or running up the aisle might have a razor tucked in his fist. The games got elaborate, became contests with teams, slashers and victims alternating roles and tallying points in the lobby between shows. Sometimes someone would slash a stranger, and Corley broke up the fights at first, but later didn't bother, didn't waste time or risk injury for a pair of idiots. He went to movies every night that week, and every night he saw more people than the night before, and felt more alert and tense, and left more exhausted. His ulcer flared like sulfur; he was smoking again.

On Friday night near the end of the movie his beeper went off and half the audience screamed and jumped and clutched in their seats, then sank back as a wave of relief swept over them and they gave themselves to laughter and curses and groans and chatter, ignoring the movie.

Corley phoned in from the lobby. They had found a body after the last show at the Astro. He had been slashed.

Corley was strangely pleased.

"Could be some frigging copycat," said Tasco the next day, yawning.

Corley wasn't sleepy. "No way," he said. "Exactly the same."

"The paper had the details."

"It's the same guy, Ray."

"Okay, okay," said Tasco, palms up. "Same guy."

The routine began again, interviews, hunting up the audience, blue and yellow pins, lack of a good witness. Tasco asked where they'd sat, what they'd seen, who they'd known. Corley asked them why they'd gone, whether they'd liked it, if they went to horror flicks often, if they'd played the assassin games. They didn't know how to answer him. He made them uncomfortable, sometimes angry, and they addressed their answers to Tasco, who looked amused and popped his gum and wrote it all down.

Corley posted the new pictures on the corkboard, and the articles and the editorials, and the movie ads. Various groups blasted the lipstick game, called for theaters to quit showing horror movies, called for theaters to close completely. Corley's theater owner wrote a guest editorial calling on readers not to be made prisoners by one maniac, not to give in to the creatures of the night. The Moviola ads promised armed guards; the Majestic dared people to come to the late show. The corkboard was covered by the end of the week, a vast montage filling the wall behind the blank television.

Tasco went with him to the movies now. There were lines at every ticket window, longer lines every night. The Moviola's security guards roamed the lobby and aisles; the Majestic installed airport metal detectors at the door; the Astro frisked its patrons, who laughed nervously, or cracked wise like Cagney or Bogart, and the guards made a big production when they found tubes of lipstick, asked if they had a license, were told it was for protection only or that they were collectors or with the FBI. They were all having a great time. The ticket girl said they gave her the creeps.

"That's two of us," Corley said.

Corley and Tasco sat on opposite sides of the theater, on the aisle, backs to the wall, linked with lapel mikes and earphones. Fewer and fewer played the lipstick game, but the audiences seemed electric and intense; Corley felt sharp and coiled, felt he could see everything, felt he was waiting for something.

After the movies, when he came home drained and sagged down on the couch, Corley found himself staring at the wall, at the picture of T.O. Bussey looking out at him from the aisle seat, his hands holding up the head, and he felt like he didn't know anything at all.

Corley turned off his electric razor and turned up the radio. An early morning DJ was interviewing a psychiatrist about the slasher. Corley knew he'd give the standard whacko profile, a quiet, polite, boy-next-door type who repressed sex and hated daddy, and that everybody who knew him would be surprised and say what a nice guy he was and how they could hardly believe it. He got his notebook to write it down so he could quote it to Tasco.

"Said he was 'quiet, withdrawn, suffers repressed sexuality and sexual expression, experiences intense emotional build-up and achieves orgasm at climax of movie and murder, cycle of build-up and release, release of life, fluids, satisfaction.' " He flipped the notebook shut.

"Jeez, I hate that," said Tasco. "I hate the hell out of that. That doesn't mean squat. That's just words. Who is he, gets paid to say crap like that? He doesn't know anything."

"I want to talk to this guy," said Corley. "I just want to sit down and talk to him, you know? I just want to buy him a drink or something and ask him what the hell is going on."

"You mean the shrink?" Tasco was squinting.

"Our guy," said Corley. "The slasher."

Tasco didn't say anything.

"He knows something," said Corley.

Tasco looked angry again. "He doesn't know anything. What are you talking about?"

Corley tried to say what he meant, couldn't find it, couldn't make it concrete. Why was it so important to get this guy, see him, find out what he looked like, why he did it, not why, exactly, but how, maybe, how in the sense of giving people a chance to maybe have their throats cut, and having them line up like it was a raffle? What would that tell him about what was driving him off the street, what kept drawing him back down, why he was carrying an extra piece, what kept him in that lousy apartment in the middle of all of this tar and pavement when he could just walk away? What did he want?

"He knows something about people," Corley said finally.

Tasco waved his hand like he was fanning flies. "What could he know? He's just a sicko . . ."

"Come on, Ray, we've seen sickoes. They don't slash in public, not like this."

Anger was in both voices now.

"Maybe they do. Maybe he just wanted to see if he could. Ever think of that? Maybe it's the thrill of offing somebody in front of a live audience. Maybe that's all."

"Yeah, that's all, and all those people out there know he's out there, too, and they can't stay away. Why can't they stay away, Tasco?"

"We can't just keep going to movies, Devin. We got lives, you know."

"We're not going get him unless we get him in the act."

"That's just stupid. That won't happen. That's a stupid thing to say."

"Watch it, sergeant."

"Oh, kiss it, Corley. Jesus."

They were silent again, avoiding each other's eyes.

"I just want to bust this guy," said Corley.

"Yeah, well," said Tasco, looking out of the window, "what I want is to go home, see my wife and kids, maybe watch a ball game." He looked back to Corley. "So, we going out again tonight or what?"

They went again that night and the next night and the next. They always sat on the aisle at opposite ends of the last row so that they could cover both rear exits. Tasco would sit through only one show; Corley sat through both. He felt better when Tasco was at the other end, when he could hear him clear his throat, or mutter something to himself, or even snore when he nodded off as he sometimes did, which amazed Corley. Corley stayed braced in his seat.

When Tasco left, Corley felt naked on the aisle, so he'd move in one seat and drape a raincoat across the aisle seat so it looked occupied, so no one would sit there. The nine o'clock show was usually a sell-out, the audience filling every seat and pressing in on him, a single vague mass in the dark at a horror flick, hiding a man with a razor, maybe even inviting him, desiring him, seeking him. After five nights Corley was ragged and jumpy.

"I'm going to sit in the projection booth," he told Tasco. "Better view."

Tasco shrugged. "End of the week and that's it, okay?"

"We'll see."

"That's got to be it, Devin."

The booth gave Corley a broader view, and gave him distance, height, a thick glass wall. At first he felt conspicuous whenever a pale face lifted his way as the audience waited for the movie to start. The manager showed him how to override the automatics and turn up the house lights, otherwise hands off. The projector looked like a giant Tommy gun sighted on the screen through a little rectangle outlined on the glass in masking tape. He had expected something more sophisticated.

Tasco was just out of sight below him, left aisle, last row, back to the wall. Through his earphone, Corley could hear the audience from Tasco's lapel mike, a general murmur, a burst of high-pitched laughter, the crying of a baby who shouldn't even be there. Corley wiped his glasses on his tie. Hundreds of people out there, could be any one of them, and what the hell were the rest of them doing out there, and what the hell was he doing up here?

The lights dimmed and the projector lit up, commercials, pre-views, the main feature. A little out-of-focus movie danced in the rectangle on the glass, blobs of color and movement bleeding out onto the masking tape; the soundtrack was thin and tinny from the booth speaker and just half a beat behind in the earphone, discon-certing. Beyond the glass, on exhibition, the audience stirred and rippled; beyond them the huge and distorted images filled the screen. He watched, and when someone stood and moved toward the aisle, he warned Tasco and felt adrenaline heat arms and legs and the figure reached the aisle and turned and walked toward restroom or candy counter, and Corley tried to relax again. It was easier to relax up here, above it all.

The movie dragged on. Corley found by staring at a central point in the audience and unfocusing his eyes, he could see all movement instantly, and everybody was moving, scratching ears and noses and scalps, lifting hands to mouths to cover coughs or to feed, rocking, putting arms around dates, leaning forward, leaning back, covering eyes with fingers. Again he saw the patterns emerge around the on-screen killings, movements ebbing as the killing neared, freezing at the death itself, melting after, and flowing across the audience again, strong and choppy, then quieter and smooth. He had to concentrate, breathe slowly and carefully, to keep himself from narrowing his vision, focusing on one person. He didn't see the movie.

A flicker in the corner of his eye, flick of light on steel. He swung eyes right, locked on movement, saw the head pulled back, the blade flicker again, realized it was happening, that he hadn't seen the killer move down the row because he was sitting right behind his victim, it was happening now, all the way across the theater from Tasco. He radioed Tasco as he turned for the stairs and punched the lights, heard Tasco yell for the man to stop, knew they were too late for the victim, but they had him now, they had him now, they had him now. He took the stairs three at a time, slipped, skidded down arms flailing, wrenched his shoulder as he tried to break the fall, then on his feet and bursting through the door behind the concession stand, drawing his pistol as he ran, putting out his left arm and vaulting over the counter, popcorn and patron flying. He stopped in front of the double doors, pistol leveled, waiting for the maniac to run into his arms.

Nobody came. Corley crouched, frozen, pistol extended in two hands, and in his left ear the theater, voices and screams and music, and Tasco maybe, Tasco shouting something, and still nobody came. He moved forward, gun still extended, and jerked open a door with his left hand.

Lights still brightening, movie running, and the screams and shouts and music in the earphone echoed, echoed in his right ear and for an instant he lost where he was. Then he heard Tasco calling him in his earphone and saw him trying to hammer his way into a knot of people below the screen, the rest of the audience in their seats, watching the movie or those down front attacking the slasher.

Corley ran down the aisle, yelling for Tasco. The earphone went dead and Tasco was gone. Corley reached the mass, started pulling people out of his way, stepping on them, pushing. Some pushed back and turned on him, and he knocked one down and another man grabbed him, and he hit the man in the face, and backed toward the wall, gun leveled. The man changed his mind, backed away. Corley called Tasco, heard nothing through the earphone. He tried to elbow his way in the crowd, started clubbing with both hands around the pistol, fighting the urge to just start pulling the trigger and have done with it. A huge man turned and started to swing; Corley watched the fist come around in slow motion, easily deflected the blow, put a knee in the solar plexus, watched the man fall like a great tree, cuffed him across the jaw as he went down, felt that he could count the pores in the potato nose. They were right beneath the speakers, the music pounding his bones. He reached for the next one in his way.

He heard a shot, saw Tasco cornered by four or five, his gun pointed toward the ceiling but lowering. The next one wouldn't be a warning shot and those guys knew it and they weren't backing off. Corley tried to shout above the music, raised his pistol and fired toward the ceiling, fired again, heard Tasco's gun answer, fired a third time, and the crowd started breaking at the edges, some hurt, some bloody. Corley tried to hold them back, grabbed at one who twisted away, and they pushed past, ignoring him, laughing or shouting, and the others were leaving their seats now, mixing with them, and some in their seats were applauding and cheering.

There were people lying all around them, some groaning, some bleeding. The slasher's victim sprawled across an aisle seat, throat opened to the stars painted on the ceiling. "Help me, Jesus," someone was saying over and over. "Jesus, help me." He heard someone calling his name, saying something. It was Tasco.

"I couldn't stop them," Tasco was saying. Corley looked down. They had used the slasher's blade, and whatever else was handy. The slasher's features were unrecognizable, the head almost severed from the body. A sudden fury flashed through Corley, and he kicked the person lying nearest to him. "Couldn't stop them," Tasco repeated, his voice trembling.

"Is this him, do you think?" asked Corley.

Tasco didn't say anything.

"Maybe Maggie can tell us," said Corley. "Maybe the M.E." He could hear the desperation in his voice.

"It could be anybody," said Tasco.

When he used the phone in the ticket office to call it all in, he heard people demanding a refund because they hadn't gotten to see the end of the movie.

Corley didn't get home until late the next afternoon. He'd made it through the last eighteen hours by thinking about the crummy little apartment high above the street, with the couch and the double locks and the television. He heard the cat yowling before he even put the key in the first lock.

He fed the cat and opened a beer, and turned on his television, but the pictures were wrong, fuzzy, filled with snow. He tried to fix the image, but nothing worked, and he grew angry. Finally he checked the roof and found his antenna bent over.

"Gianelli," he shouted, pounding, standing to one side of the door, seeing an image of Gianelli spinning in slow motion toward pavement four floors down. "Come out of there, Gianelli." No answer. He spread the name out, kicking on the door once for each syllable. *"Gi-a-nel-li!"*

"You go away now," came a voice from inside. "You go away. I'm calling the cops."

"I *am* a cop," Corley shouted, dragging out his shield and holding it to the peephole.

"You go away now," Gianelli said after a moment of silence.

Corley gave the door one last kick.

He tried to salvage the antenna, but Gianelli had done a job on it, twisting the cross-pieces, cutting the wires into a dozen pieces.

Before he went to sleep, he took down the pictures and clippings about Mr. Bussey, and he dug around until he found the pictures of the previous occupant, and he pinned them all up. He crossed the room and sat on the couch to look at them. They were all black and white, blonde and pale eyes, and he wondered if she had walked away from whatever brought her here. He thought she was very beautiful. But who could tell from pictures?

He locked the doors and cut on the night light.

STUART M. KAMINSKY

Edgar Award-winning author Stuart M. Kaminsky is perhaps best known for his Toby Peters detective series. Set in Hollywood during the thirties and forties among the rich, the famous, and the rest of the people who end up living and dying in L.A., the Peters novels would keep most authors busy enough. But Kaminsky, being an ambitious and multitalented fellow, works with a Russian detective, Inspector Porfiry Rostnikov, who has won an Edgar for his creator. Even that's not enough for our busy author, who spends what must be the rest of his waking hours teaching film and television at Florida State University.

Kaminsky doesn't have much chance to write short stories. But he does have a knack for good short fiction, as witnessed here. Featuring a famous person—not from Hollywood, but from Washington, D.C., "The Buck Stops Here" shows another side of Kaminsky, and gives former President Harry S. Truman a chance to show some of the stuff that made him one of our most surprising Presidents. This story originally appeared in *Murder in the White House*.

The Buck Stops Here

"Can you guess what this is?"

We were standing in the storage room of the Truman Library in Independence, Missouri, early in July of 1957 and the question had come from Mr. Truman himself, who was pointing at a broken wooden beam about a dozen feet long leaning against the wall.

I couldn't guess what the beam was. I was tired when I had to be alert. Hungry when I should have been undistracted and attentive. I hadn't slept since my unit officer had pulled me out of a basketball game at a YMCA in Washington, D.C., the day before.

I stood blearily looking at the beam and then over at the ex-president, who smiled at me, waiting for my answer. Truman was seventy-three years old, and although everyone from Franklin Roosevelt and President Eisenhower had referred to him as "little," the ex-president stood eye-to-eye with me, and I was slightly over 5'9". Truman wore a light suit and tie and looked dapper and alert with a white handkerchief in his breast pocket.

"Lieutenant?" Truman asked again.

"I don't know, sir," I said as he rested a hand on the beam.

"This," said Truman in his clipped Missouri twang, "is the beam from the White House that gave way under my daughter Margaret's piano. If it weren't for that piano and this beam, the major reconstruction of the White House might never have taken place. It took the fear of a piano falling on my head to get a few dollars to shore up the most important symbolic building in the United States."

"And that's why you want it in the Library," I said, looking around the room on what I hoped was the last part of the tour. I had a potential assassin to look for and some sleep to catch up on. My interest in history was not at its peak.

How had it happened? When my CO had me called out of the basketball game, I hurried down to the locker, took a fast shower, and got dressed in my sports coat, slacks, and solid blue knit tie. I was standing in front of Colonel Saint's desk within fifteen minutes of the moment he had summoned me.

Saint was drinking a cup of coffee. A matching cup stood steaming in the corner of his desk. He nodded at the steaming second cup and I smiled and took it, even though I don't drink coffee. Saint never remembered this, but that didn't bother me. What bothered me was that he had made the friendly gesture. I was being prepared for something I might not want to hear.

"Have a seat, Pevsner," Saint said, reaching a stubby finger into his cup to fish out something tiny and even darker than the amber liquid.

Saint was fully uniformed, complete with medals on his chunky chest and with his graying hair Wildrooted back and shiny.

"Thank you, sir," I said, and sat in the chrome-and-black leather chair across from him. Saint struck a pose, two hands clasped around his coffee cup. Behind him and over his head on the wall, President Eisenhower, in his five-star uniform, looked down at both of us benevolently.

"Carl Gades," Saint said, returning his finger to his coffee cup and fishing out a bit more of whatever it was that troubled him.

I didn't shake, shimmer, or show a sign when Saint looked up suddenly for my reaction. I just sipped at the bitter, hot liquid. I could see my face in the coffee. It was a bland, innocent twenty-eight-year-old face showing just what it had been trained to show: nothing.

"You know Carl Gades," Colonel Saint said, putting down the cup. "Damn coffee stinks. How can you drink it?"

I shrugged and kept drinking.

"I know Carl Gades," I said.

"You're the only member of this staff who has met him face-to-face who could identify him," the colonel said, folding his hands on his desk and looking down sourly at the coffee cup. "Kravitz wouldn't remember his mother if she wasn't wearing a name tag. Secret Service has no one who has ever seen him. They pulled your name out of the files. They can get things out of the files, off that damned microfilm, in a few hours now."

I had met Carl Gades only once and I didn't want to meet him again, but I was getting the idea that I might not have a choice. I hadn't made too many choices in my career for more than three years or, at least, that was the way it felt. I'd been drafted right out of UCLA and missed Korea by being pulled out after basic training and sent to Texas for Officers' Candidate School. After OCS I was sent to Washington for intelligence training, and a week after completing my training I was on a mission to Rome with a dyspeptic captain named Resnick. Resnick barely talked to me and barely briefed me. "Keep your eyes open," he had said, and then closed his and slept on the plane all the way to Rome.

My rapid rise in the military had been the result not of my great promise and intellect but good breeding. My father was a retired Los Angeles Police Department captain, and my uncle was an aging but still active private investigator who had handled some delicate private jobs for people in high places. Oh, yes, there was one other thing that led to my success. I was a *hawk*. I hadn't known I was a hawk. There weren't many of us, and the intelligence services probably bragged to each other about the number of hawks they had.

A hawk is an individual who takes in everything in a scene, isn't distracted by the things that draw the attention of normal people. If I'm walking down the street and hear someone scream behind me, I turn around and see not only a woman shouting at a man running down the street, but I see each crack in the street, the color of the man's socks, the woman's straggling hairs, every window on every building, and the fern sprouting yellow fronds in a fourth-floor window across the street. I see and I retain.

It's a literal photographic memory. I don't remember words or conversations, just images, images fixed that can be recalled. Unfortunately, the images sometimes come back unbidden and they don't always bear any great significance. So, for whatever it was worth, I had this gift or curse, and I was of particular value in sensitive situations where photography would be valuable but for various reasons, usually location and security, photography wouldn't be feasible.

Gades had met with Resnick and me in the Piazza Popolo. Gades had worn a wide-brimmed white hat and a white suit. He had a dark mustache and beard and was careful to keep the top of his face and eyes in the shadow of his Marcello Mastroianni hat. Gades had insisted that we meet at the statue in the center of the Piazza so that no one would be near us but the people driving madly around the Piazza.

Gades was there to trade information. We gave him a name. He gave us a name. I didn't know what either name meant. I was there to record and remember Gades, who, in broad daylight, insisted on patting us both down to be sure we weren't armed with cameras or weapons. He also informed us that he had people checking out the nearby buildings to be sure no one was lurking with a high-power telescopic-lensed camera.

Gades spoke no more than a minute in a raspy, disguised voice, and he gave his information first, confident that we wouldn't dare cross him, suggesting, in fact, that he rather enjoyed having people try to cross him so he could make examples of them and increase his value and public image.

Now, many murders—from Bombay to Kiev—later, Gades, who had become even more cautious, was back in my lap.

"No photographs of Gades," Saint said. "Son of a bitch's too careful. You're the only one who might be able to identify him. Could you?"

I pulled out the fixed picture of that day three years earlier and went over it, the split second Gades had tilted his head up and shown his deep blue eyes, the other second when he had shown a profile, the freckles on his wrist, the turn of his left ear.

"I could," I said.

"Hot damn." Saint grinned. He turned and looked up at Ike for approval, and Ike seemed to give it. "We've got them by the short ones, Lieutenant."

"Glad to hear it, sir," I'd said, finishing the coffee. "Who have we got by . . .?"

Saint leaned forward, straightened his tie, and grinned as he said, "Secret Service, FBI, all of them."

"I see," I said, "but I . . ."

"FBI got a phone conversation on a wired line," Saint said, pulling a manila folder out of his desk drawer and opening it. "Word is that Gades plans to assassinate Harry Truman. How do you like that?"

I didn't like it very much, but I was sure he didn't need me to tell him that.

"Why?" I asked.

"Revenge," whispered Colonel Saint, dramatically leaning toward me over the desk. "Gades's brother, Arthur, died in prison last month. Son of a bitch should have been executed. Tried to blow up a plane for who the hell knows why. Spent ten years in jail. Truman wouldn't let him out, turned down two appeals. At least that's the way Gades feels about it, according to the FBI. It was his only brother. Things like that make would-be assassins careless. You know what I mean?"

"Yes, sir," I said, thinking of my own brother Nate, who was in college back in California.

"People are watching Truman, but they don't know Gades," Saint went on. "Fear now is that Gades probably knows we know. FBI screwed up the whole wiretap operation. Who knows? FBI, CIA, MI, everyone and his aunt thinks Gades'll move fast. You've got a military flight to Kansas City in one hour and a half. Sergeant Ganz'll drive you. I'd like you in uniform, highly visible. Stop off at home, change, and get your ass in gear. You meet Mr. Truman in his office in Kansas City first thing in the morning. 0800 hours. Questions?"

"And I'm . . . ?" I began.

"Hawk," he said. "Spot Gades. Turn him over to the Secret Service. There'll be a couple of agents with Truman. You know Gades's reputation, and he's not likely to deviate this time. He does it himself. He does it in person. No bombs. Doesn't even like guns, though he carries one. Kills up close. Wants to scare the community. Does it, too. Kicks up his price. Let's get the bastard. Ganz has cash for you. Keep decent records this time, Pevsner."

That was it. His mouth moved from a broad smile to a thin enigma. I rose, saluted, took his return salute, and watched as Colonel Saint turned in his swivel chair, looked up at Ike and then, hands behind his head, looked out the window at the U.S. Post Office building across the street. Less than two hours later I was on an Air Force plane headed for Kansas City and drinking a Dr. Pepper handed to me by a freckle-faced airman.

We landed at the Kansas City airport on a side strip reserved for military landings. I had picked up my uniform, but I didn't have time to change into my uniform until I got on the plane. Before we landed I brushed my teeth and shaved.

Colonel Saint had given me enough money to last about a week if I was careful. If it took more, I'd have to ask. It might be a lot more. It might be forever if the FBI information was wrong or if Gades had changed his mind. I had the distinct fear that Colonel Saint wanted Gades so badly he might leave me to turn to fungus in Kansas City.

A khaki-colored Buick was waiting at the airport, and the driver, a Spec Four named Kithcart, took me to the Federal Reserve Building in downtown Kansas City, where he parked the car illegally and led me into the building where a pair of Secret Service men who identified themselves as Koster and Franklin took me to the elevator and up the stairs to Truman's office. Koster and Franklin were clean-shaven, gray-suited, about six feet tall, brown-eyed, closemouthed, and nearly bookends. I guessed they were both in their forties, but they could have been younger or older.

Truman came to the door to greet me. He shook my hand, a strong grip for an old man, and looked me straight in the eye.

"You're younger than I thought, Lieutenant," Truman said. "But so is everyone but Dean Acheson."

"Yes sir," I said.

"You know I was a captain in World War One?" he asked walking to the corner of the room, putting a white hat on his head, and picking out a black walking stick from an upright black leather container near the window.

"Yes sir," I said.

"Let's go," he said. "I'm not changing my schedule for any two-bit gangster. I'm going to the Truman Museum back home in Independence. There's a construction strike all through this area, and some of the important work has stopped on the Library. Damn shame. Everything is ready for final plastering and floorings. Stacks, shelves, and exhibit cases may not be put in for the dedication. Some carpenters and painters are on the job, but we are not on schedule. You ever been in the White House?"

Truman walked briskly past me and looked back at my face over his shoulder.

"Once, sir. I briefed President Eisenhower on a . . . a delicate mission with General Clark."

"I don't give a damn about the subject," said Truman, amiably gesturing for me to follow him through the door. "I just want to know if you're as good as they say you are. I assume you were in the President's office?"

"Yes sir," I said following him out the door. He walked quickly to the elevator flanked by the two Secret Service men.

We went down the elevator and out the building, heading over to a parking lot, where we got into a big, black Lincoln. I took in the street, the passing people, and saw nothing and no one I recognized. One of the Secret Service men sat with the driver. The other sat silently with Truman and me in the back seat.

"Microfilm," Truman said as I tried to shake off airplane weariness. "At some point, thanks to microfilm, the Truman Library will have the best collection of presidential papers anywhere. You know that, until Hoover, people simply threw away presidential papers?"

"No sir," I said, which was true.

"One exception," Truman corrected, looking over his shoulder at me. "Rutherford B. Hayes, and who the hell cares about Hayes's papers?"

"I think you do," I said.

"You are right, Lieutenant," he said. "I care about Hayes and Millard Filmore and Tyler. It's the office, Lieutenant. You put a man in the office, and it is his responsibility to fill that space with dignity. No man in his right mind would want to be President if he knew what it entails. Aside from the impossible administrative burden, he has to take all sorts of abuse from liars and demagogues. All the President is, is a glorified public relations man who spends his time flattering, kissing, and kicking people to get them to do what they are supposed to do anyway."

"I'll have to take your word on that, sir," I said, looking at the Secret Service man who scanned the road on the way to Independence and appeared to hear none of the conversation.

The trip seemed long, though Independence is only nine miles from Kansas City. When we hit Independence, we drove down Pleasant Street to the Truman Library, which clung to a knoll in the middle of thirteen landscaped acres.

"How do you like it?" Truman said as we got out of the car and the Secret Service men scanned the parking lot.

"Impressive," I said.

"Gift of the people of Independence," he said.

The Library stood on the highest point of the property, an arc-shaped building of contemporary design with an imposing portico in the middle. There weren't many windows.

We started toward the building. Truman's cane tapped on the stone path as we moved briskly, flanked by Secret Service men.

"Impressive," I repeated, hurrying to keep up with the ex-President.

"Too damned modern," he sighed. "It's got too much of that fellow in it to suit me."

"That . . ." I started.

"Frank Lloyd Wright," Truman said, picking up the pace.

I couldn't see much Frank Lloyd Wright in the building, and I was sure Wright hadn't designed the Library, but I said nothing, just scanned the building, landscape, and the workmen who unloaded a truck in the parking lot.

"Should have been Georgian," Truman said. "Neld got modern on me, and it was too far along to stop him when I realized it. I wanted it to look like Independence Hall in Philadelphia."

We strode through the doors under the portico and Truman led us past painters and repairmen who looked up at us. None of them was Gades. The ex-president opened a door and pointed through it with his cane.

"Step in," he said, "and tell me what you see."

I stepped in and found myself in the Oval Office, the same office in which I had briefed President Eisenhower two years earlier, or, at least, a near-perfect replica.

"The Oval Office," I said.

"Right," he said, motioning the Secret Service men to stay back as he joined me and closed the door. "But you're a falcon. . . ."

"Hawk," I corrected, scanning the room.

"What's wrong with the room?" he said.

"It's not what's wrong that surprises me, Mr. President," I said. "It's what's right. The mantel isn't a replica. It's the same one I saw in the White House."

Truman's laugh was a silent, pleased cackle.

"Perfect," he said, moving across the room, removing his hat, and placing his cane on the corner of his desk. On that desk near the window was a sign I knew about. It read: The Buck Stops Here. "It is original. When the White House was renovated and we moved into Blair House, I asked them to keep pieces they would normally throw out. That mantel was one of the pieces. I'll show you another."

He led me through the office and past more workmen, who he greeted by name, and led me to the storeroom where he showed me the famous beam that I failed to identify.

"Stage props of history," Truman sighed. "So, young man, what do we do now?"

I held back a yawn and stopped myself from shrugging.

"Whatever you normally do," I said. "But with me nearby and a little more caution than usual."

"I've been threatened before in my life," he said, stepping over the beam and placing his hand on a table, a nicely polished table. "That is the table on which the United Nations Charter was signed in San Francisco."

I looked at the table, but it conjured up no images. I needed sleep or rest. He showed me other items: a wax figure of himself, a rug from the Shah of Iran, a bronze figure of Andrew Jackson.

"You think he has a chance of getting me?" Truman asked soberly but without apparent fear.

"Well . . ." I began.

"Forget it," he said. "I'm not going to get a straight answer out of you on that one. I'd rather not shock Bess when I go, and I'd like to see this place finished. Never did consider myself martyr material, either. We'll just have to see what God decides to do with this one. I like to quote an epitaph on a tombstone in a cemetery in Tombstone, Arizona. 'Here lies Jack Williams. He done his damnedest.' "

"I'll do my damnedest, sir," I said.

"Almost nine," he said, looking at his watch. "Let's get back to the Oval Office."

He led the way through the storage room and back to the exhibit space, where the workmen stopped talking as we moved through and into the Oval Office.

Truman went to the desk, opened it, and pulled out a bottle.

"Situation calls for a late-morning finger or two of good bourbon, wouldn't you say, Lieutenant Pevsner?"

"Yes sir," I said with a smile, though I disliked bourbon even more than I disliked coffee, but you don't let a former President drink alone if you're invited to join him.

I took the small crystal glass he pushed toward me.

"To your powers of observation," he toasted.

I raised my glass and took a healthy sip. Truman downed his in a single shot and pursed his lips.

"That will be my only drink of the day till nightfall," he sighed.

I finished my drink and tried not to make a face.

"And now," he said. "If you want to sit, walk the grounds, browse around, I've got work to do. You are welcome to join me for lunch at noon at the house."

I thanked him and went out the door, closing it behind me as he sat behind the desk.

The Secret Service man named Koster was standing outside the office, arms folded.

I nodded to him. He nodded back, deep brown eyes scanning my uniform. For the next twenty minutes I walked around the grounds. I ran into the other Secret Service man—Franklin—who was doing the same. We didn't speak. I was trying to walk off twenty-four hours without sleep and a stiff bourbon. It wasn't working.

Just before eleven a young man came running out of the Library toward where I was standing against an oak tree trying to look alert.

"Lieutenant Pevsner?" he said.

"That's right."

"Phone call for you. Follow me."

I followed him back into the building and into a small office not far from the Oval Office. A woman sat typing in the office and a phone rested on a desk off of the receiver. I picked it up.

"Lieutenant Pevsner," I said.

"Colonel Saint," he answered.

"Nothing here that I can see yet, sir," I said.

"Look again, Lieutenant," he said. "We have definite information that Gades flew to Kansas City one week and one day ago. He's been eating steaks and waiting for a chance to get Truman."

"He's not around here," I said, looking around the office at the woman typist, who reminded me of Bulldog Turner of the Chicago Bears, and at the secretary, who looked a little like Clifton Webb.

"Some FBI crackpot has an idea. Thinks Gades will make his move today, one month to the day Gades's brother died," Saint said. "Something about the date circled in an appointment book in a hotel room Gades might have been in."

"He might be right," I said.

"The time was noted," said Saint. "Three P.M. What do you think?"

"I don't," I said.

"Find him," said Saint.

"Will do, sir," I said.

Saint hung up, and I went outside to hang around. I didn't know how to find Gades. I watched people come and go—delivery vans, a mailman. None was Gades. I was sure of that.

Noon turned the corner and Truman came sauntering out of the building with Koster and Franklin close behind, looking everywhere. Truman tilted his head back so he could see me from under his hat and motioned at me with his cane. I followed him.

"Called Bess," he said. "Told her we'd be having company. You like fried chicken?"

"Like it fine," I said, walking at his side.

We didn't take the car, which made it more difficult for the Secret Service men and me, but it was a clear, not-too-hot day and the walk helped wake me up. The walk to the gabled Victorian house on Delaware Street was probably longer than most seventy-year-olds would like to make, but Truman did it talking all the way, mostly about Andrew Jackson.

"No sign of him?" Truman asked as we went up the wooden steps. He wasn't talking about Andrew Jackson this time.

"Not yet," I said.

"Wouldn't want him to try anything around the house," he said.

"I'm watching, sir," I said with what I hoped was a reassuring smile.

"There's watching and there's watching," Truman said, pausing on the porch and looking at the two Secret Service men, who had stopped at the bottom of the steps and were casually scanning the quiet street. "Sometimes you miss what's important because it's so damned obvious that you never consider it."

"I'll keep that in mind, sir," I said.

Lunch was hot and not too spicy. Mrs. Truman served the lunch herself, but the cleaning up was done by a young woman wearing an apron and not meeting my eyes when I looked at her. The Secret Service men ate in the kitchen, though I found that Truman had invited them to join us.

"Last Secret Service fellows insisted on working shifts and getting their own food," Truman said. "These boys are less formal. Better that way. How's the chicken?"

It was fine, and I said so.

"Bess likes cooking, or so she says. Hated the White House sometimes. Plenty for her to do, but not the things she liked doing. It all happened too fast for her. One minute I was a failed Kansas farmer who couldn't keep a hat business open and in ten years I was a judge, a senator, Vice-President, and President of the United States. Hard to believe. More peas?"

I said no thanks and checked my watch. It was almost one. If Gades was going to make his move at three, he'd have to show up soon. I was considering suggesting to Truman that we stay around the house till after three, but he rose, pushed away from the table, and announced that we'd better be getting back to the Library.

Mrs. Truman, who had joined us silently for the lunch, accepted my thanks and asked her husband to come home early.

"Margaret promised to call," she said.

"Then by all means I'll be back early," he said with a smile.

The meal hadn't made me more alert. I'd eaten lightly, but it was getting late in the afternoon and the walk wasn't having the effect I'd like. The Secret Service men, as always, were silent, and Truman talked animatedly about Hubert Humphrey and the Pope's promise to send the Vatican documents on microfilm as soon as they were ready.

"Don't know what I'll do with them," Truman said, the late-afternoon sun glinting off his glasses, "but you don't turn down an offer like that."

Nothing had changed at the Library. The same workmen were there. The secretary who looked like Clifton Webb was standing at the door to the replica of the Oval Office with a sheaf of papers in his hand. Truman took his left hand out of his pocket and took the papers and hurried into his office.

Koster ran a hand through his brown hair to make sure no loose strands marred the image. He took his place in front of the door and looked stonily at me to let me know that he wasn't up for idle conversation. Franklin scanned the narrow corridor and checked the doors. He turned to us, blinked his cold blue eyes, and nodded to indicate the place was clear. Then he wandered off to watch the rear of the building. My Timex told me 1400 hours was approaching. Saint's information seemed flimsy with Bess Truman's chicken, peas, and lemonade resting heavily in my stomach and a warm Missouri sun sparkling on the grass as I stepped in front of the building.

The whole Gades business seemed dreamlike, Colonel Saint's dream. I found an oak tree in front of the Library, loosened my tie, and sat in the shade where I could get a good look at anyone approaching the building on foot or in a vehicle. Birds above me chirped away, and once in the next hour I saw a cardinal and the second mailman of the day. I checked the mailman carefully. I'd once read a story by Chesterton about a criminal who disguised himself as a mailman because mailmen seem so much a part of the landscape. But this mailman was short and pudgy and definitely not Carl Gades.

I closed my eyes and began to go over the images of the day since I had arrived. I selected, checked faces and hands, and pulled myself up and awake when the image of Truman's dining room began to fade. My eyes scanned the Library, and I listened. Only the echo of a carpenter hammering away inside.

I had a sudden feeling of nausea. I wasn't sure what caused it, but I had to stand up. My legs were trembling. Maybe it was the lack of sleep, an allergy, or too much food for lunch; but something wasn't right.

"Sometimes you miss what's important because it's so damned obvious you don't see it," Truman had said.

Chesterton's invisible mailman. He'd been standing next to me, walking at Truman's right hand, looking at the former President's back through the window of the Library in front of me. The Secret Service man, Franklin. In the morning his eyes had been brown. Less than an hour ago they had turned blue. I was sure of it. I checked the images in my memory. Confirmed. I moved down the hill, straightening my tie, and went over other images. Franklin's nose, profile. Altered. Not quite Gades, but not unlike him. Little things could take care of that. And then I checked the hands. I stopped, closed my eyes, and compared Gades's left hand with Franklin's. A tiny white scar, a blemish the size of a tack head, the pattern of the veins. I started to run and checked my Timex. It was a few minutes before three.

I could have called for Koster, but I wasn't sure if Koster was Secret Service or Gades's helpmate of the month. So I ran behind the Library where Franklin was supposed to be stationed. He wasn't there. I considered running to the window of Truman's office and telling him to get the hell out of there, but I fought down the panic and the memory of lunch. I had no weapon. I hadn't expected to need one. The damned Secret Service was supposed to supply the firepower. I ran to the wall and crept along until I got to the window. When I looked inside, my head went light and I considered diving into a migraine.

Franklin was standing in front of Truman's desk and the ex-President was looking up at him. Franklin was doing all the talking, but I couldn't hear a word. Franklin, hell, it was Gades! And he was looking at his watch. I leaned back against the wall and checked mine. If mine was accurate and his was, too, it was about three minutes to three. I hoped Gades's sense of poetic justice was operating.

I considered a leap at the window, but there were too many things that could go wrong. The window might not break or, if it did, I might be so cut up that I couldn't do anything except get myself killed along with Harry Truman. Even if I did get through the window and on my feet, I didn't think I was a hand-to-hand match for Gades. Gades liked to kill with a knife, but he was known to carry a gun. He might be impetuous, but he was no fool.

So, I hurried for the front of the Library, managing to trip once and rip the knees of my dress greens. There was no time for checking credentials. I went right for the Oval Office where Koster was standing. He looked at me, saw a panting madman with a torn uniform, knew something was up, and took a defensive position in front of the door. It was a good sign. A Gades man, knowing his boss was inside and about to commit murder, would have had his weapon out and would have put two holes in me by now.

"Hold it Lieutenant," Koster said calmly.

I stopped, looked at the door to Truman's office, and hoped that it was reasonably soundproof. What was I doing? As I stood at an impasse in front of Koster, I pulled up the image of the original White House Oval Office I'd once visited. I found the door and fixed on it as I had left the room. The door was thick and solid. I did the same for the replica Oval Office behind Koster, recalling it from the second I'd looked at the door when I'd entered the room with Truman. It was equally thick. Knowing Truman's desire for detailed authenticity, I was confident that Gades and Truman wouldn't hear us in the hall unless we shouted.

"Koster," I said, trying to control my panting. "How well do you know Franklin?"

Koster tilted his head like a curious bird.

"Come again, Lieutenant?"

"When did you meet Franklin?"

I looked at the door and considered trying to rush past him, but I didn't see how I could make it even if I were lucky enough to catch him with a knee to the groin or an elbow to the stomach.

"Three days ago," he said. "He was assigned to bolster protection for the President when word came through that there might be an attempt on his life. What's your point?"

"Did you get a call? Did he have papers?" I asked, glancing at my watch. We had less than two minutes.

"Papers, a call came through," Koster said. "We talked. He . . ."

"His eyes change color," I said.

"His eyes?"

"They were brown this morning. They're blue now. You think of any reason?"

Koster tried to remember his partner's eyes.

"Why?" he asked.

"Maybe the brown contacts bothered him. He had to take them out so he could see clearly when he killed Mr. Truman."

"Killed . . . Are you saying that Franklin is . . ."

". . . Carl Gades," I finished. "And I just saw him in there," I nodded toward the door, "with Truman."

"Let's find out," Koster said, reaching for the doorknob but keeping an eye on me. I didn't move forward. The door was locked. Koster considered knocking, thought better of it, and looked at me.

"The door's solid," I said, "but the frame is new. If we both go at it, we might be able to get it down."

"Might," he said. "Let's do it."

There wasn't much room to move. We got against the far wall and together went for the Oval Office door. Our shoulders hit together and mine went numb, but the frame splintered and we tumbled in. I went down on the floor. Koster kept his feet and took in the room.

Gades was standing next to the desk, a good fifteen feet or more from Koster. In his hand Gades held a small revolver. Truman sat behind the desk, his mouth a thin pink line.

"About thirty seconds," Gades said, aiming the weapon at us. "Then our little Mr. Truman will feel steel entering his bowels and he'll know a little of what it is like to die as my brother died."

I got to my feet shakily and stood next to Koster.

"Your brother died," Truman said, "because he was a murderer and he paid the penalty for that crime by living out what remained of his life behind bars where he belonged."

"You could have saved him," Gades spat, not taking his eyes from me and Koster.

"I made some tough decisions when I was in office," Truman said evenly. "That was not one of them."

"Shut up old man," Gades said. "Shut up and watch the clock."

I wondered how much of a chance I'd have at surviving if I made a run at Gades. Not much. I might divert him enough for Koster to get his hands on him, but Gades had killed before. He could probably take both of us out in less than a second.

"Have you ever played stud poker?" Truman asked.

"Stud poker?" Gades asked, and then laughed.

"One card in the hole, four up," Truman explained. "Everything in sight but the hole card."

"You can talk till I put the steel in your belly, old man," Gades said. "What did you have for lunch? Ah, yes. Chicken. Let's see what it looks like when it comes running out on the floor."

Gades kept his eyes on us.

"The trick," Truman said, "is to get the other fellow looking at the wrong cards. It worked with Churchill. It worked with Dewey. It worked with Stalin, and by God it'll work with you."

The next few seconds were a series of perfect images. I held them and savored them. I still have them in detail. Truman's hand had inched to the handle of the cane on his desk. He had been sitting absolutely immobile as he had talked. He had looked the old man, but in those few seconds, Harry Truman's cane swished upward under Gades's hand and Gades tried to turn the weapon in it away from us and toward Truman, who was on the rise. The gun hand went up in the air and the bullet cracked through the ceiling. Truman, now on his feet, brought the cane down with two hands on Gades's wrist. A bone broke with a sharp crack and the gun fell to the floor. Koster moved forward as Gades reacted by reaching into his jacket. The knife came out in the unbroken hand. Gades's teeth were clenched in hatred as he lunged forward over the desk. Koster was within a foot of the would-be assassin when Truman's cane cracked down on Gades's head.

Gades stagged backward, dropping the knife, and Koster hit him with a right that would have pleased Rocky Marciano.

"Little," grunted Truman, looking over the top of his glasses at the unconscious Gades on the floor. "Man doesn't know the game, he shouldn't take a drink in the dealer's parlor."

The hall was alive with people who had heard the door breaking and the gunshot. The secretary and typist and a few white-clad painters stood at the broken door trying to see what had happened.

"Show's over," said Truman. "Permanter, get that door fixed and call an ambulance. Everybody back to work."

They left reluctantly, missing Koster and me picking up the limp Gades.

"You did a fine job, Mr. President," Koster said, straightening his hair after he had secured Gades in a chair.

"Just be sure he's not playing possum," Truman said, looking up at the hole in the ceiling.

"He's not, sir," Koster said.

"Faced worse than that," Truman said looking at the unconscious Gades, "back in World War One. Hell, faced worse than that across the conference table."

"Still," I said, wearily wondering if Colonel Saint would be happy enough to pay for the new dress uniform I needed. "You took a big chance."

Truman grinned a broad campaign grin, leaned forward, and pointed to the famous sign on his desk that read:

THE BUCK STOPS HERE.

PETER LOVESEY

Lovesey has for many years been a premier writer of the historical mystery, with most of his work set in the Victorian era. Known for a number of series characters, but especially for his beloved Sergeant Cribb and Constable Thackeray, he won a Silver Dagger in 1979. Novels such as *Wobble to Death* and *The Detective Wore Silk Drawers* (don't you have to just love that title?) have done a lot to assure his place in the hearts of mystery readers on both sides of the Atlantic. So have the countless fine short stories he has penned, many of which have appeared in *Ellery Queen's Mystery Magazine*.

"The Wasp" is a poignant but forceful story, in which justice is served through a somewhat circuitous and unusual means. As always, Mr. Lovesey delivers the goods in a classy, original fashion.

The Wasp

The storm had passed, leaving a keen wind that whipped foam off the waves. Heaps of gleaming seaweed were strewn about the beach. Shells, bits of driftwood, and a few stranded jellyfish lay where the tide had deposited them. Paul Molloy, bucket in hand, was down there as he was every morning, alone and preoccupied.

His wife Gwynneth stood by the wooden steps that led off the beach through a garden of flowering trees to their property.

"Paul! Breakfast time!"

She had to shout it twice more before Paul's damaged brain registered anything. Then he turned and trudged awkwardly toward her.

The stroke last July, a few days before his sixty-first birthday, had turned him into a shambling parody of the fine man he had been. He was left with the physical coordination of a small child, except that he was slower. And dumb.

The loss of speech was the hardest for Gwynneth to bear. She hated being cut off from his thoughts. He was unable even to write, or draw pictures. She had to be content with scraps of communication. Each time he came up from the beach he handed her something he had found, a shell or a pebble. She received such gifts as graciously as she had once accepted roses.

They had said at the hospital that she ought to keep talking to him in an adult way even if he didn't appear to understand. It was a mistake to give up. So she persevered, though inevitably it sounded as if she were addressing a child.

"Darling, what a beautiful shell! Is it for me? Oh, how sweet! I'll take it up to the house and put it on the shelf with all the other treasures you found for me—except that this one must stand in the

center." She leaned forward to kiss him and made no contact with
his face. He had moved his head to look at a gull.

She helped him up the steps and they started the short, laborious
trek to the house. They had bought the land, a few miles north of
Bundaberg on the Queensland coast, ten years before Paul retired
from his Brisbane-based insurance company. As chairman, he could
have carried on for years more, but he had always promised he
would stop at sixty—before he got fat and feeble, as he used to
say. They had built themselves this handsome retirement home and
installed facilities they'd thought they would use: swimming pool,
jacuzzi, boat house, and tennis court. Only their guests used them
now.

"Come on, love, step out quick," she urged Paul, "there's beautiful bacon waiting for you." And, tirelessly trying for a spark of
interest, she added, "Cousin Haydn's still asleep by the look of it.
I don't think he'll be joining you for your walks on the beach. Not
before breakfast, anyway. Probably not at all. He doesn't care for
the sea, does he?"

Gwynneth encouraged people to stay. She missed real conversation. Cousin Haydn was on a visit from Wales. He was a distant
cousin she hadn't met before, but she didn't mind. She'd got to
know him when she'd started delving into her family history for
something to distract her. Years ago, her father had given her an
old Bible with a family tree in the front. She'd brought it up to date.
Then she had joined a family-history society and learned that a good
way of tracking down ancestors was to write to local newspapers in
the areas where they had lived. She had managed to get a letter
published in a Swansea paper and Haydn had seen it and got in
touch. He was an Evans also, and he'd done an immense amount
of research. He'd discovered a branch of his family tree that linked
up with hers, through Great-Grandfather Hugh Evans of Port
Talbot.

Paul shuffled toward the house without even looking up at the
drawn curtains.

"Mind you," Gwynneth continued, "I'm not surprised Haydn is
used to staying indoors, what with the Welsh weather *I* remember.
I expect he reads the Bible a lot, being a man of the cloth." She
checked herself for speaking the obvious again and pushed open
the kitchen door. "Come on, Paul. Just you and me for breakfast
by the look of it."

Cousin Haydn eventually appeared in time for the midmorning
coffee. On the first day after he'd arrived, he'd discarded the black

suit and dog-collar in favor of a pink T-shirt. Casual clothes made
him look several years younger—say, forty-five—but they also revealed what Gwynneth would have called a beer gut had Haydn not
been a minister.

"Feel better for your sleep?" she inquired.

"Infinitely better, thank you, Gwynneth." You couldn't mistake
him for an Australian when he opened his mouth. "And most agree-
ably refreshed by a dip in your pool."

"Oh, you had a swim?"

"Hardly a swim. I was speaking of the small circular pool."

She smiled. "The jacuzzi. Did you find the switch?"

"I was unaware that I needed to find it."

"It works the pumps that make the whirlpool effect. If you didn't
switch on, you missed something."

"Then I shall certainly repeat the adventure."

"Paul used to like it. I'm afraid of him slipping, so he doesn't get
in there now."

"Pity, if he enjoyed it."

"Perhaps I ought to take the risk. The specialist said he may begin
to bring other muscles into use that aren't affected by the stroke—
isn't that so, my darling?"

Paul gave no sign of comprehension.

"Does he understand much?" Haydn asked.

"I convince myself he does, even if he's unable to show it. If you
don't mind, I don't really care to talk about him in this way, as if
he's not one of us."

Cousin Haydn gave an understanding nod. "Let's talk about
something less depressing, then. I have good news for you,
Gwynneth."

She responded with a murmur that didn't convey much enthusiasm. Sermons in church were one thing, her kitchen was another
place altogether.

It emerged that Haydn's good news wasn't of an evangelical character. "One of the reasons for coming here—apart from following
up our fascinating correspondence—is to tell you about a mutual
ancestor, Sir Tudor Evans."

"*Sir* Tudor? We had a title in the family?"

"Back in the seventeenth century, yes."

"I don't recall seeing him on my family tree."

Haydn gave the slight smile of one who has a superior grasp
of genealogy. "Yours started in the seventeen eighties, if I recall."

"Oh, yes."

"To say that it started then is, of course, misleading. Your eighteenth-century forebears had parents, as did mine—and they in turn had parents. And so it goes back—first to Sir Tudor, and ultimately to Adam."

"Never mind Adam. Tell me about Sir Tudor." Gwynneth swung around to Paul, who was sucking the end of his thumb. "Bet you didn't know I came from titled stock, darling."

Haydn said, "A direct line. Planter Evans, they called him. He owned half of Barbados once, according to my research. Made himself a fortune in sugar cane."

"Really? A fortune. What happened to it?"

"Most of it went down with the *Gloriana* in 1683. One of the great tragedies of the sea. He'd sold the plantations to come back to the land of his fathers. He was almost home when a great storm blew up in the Bristol Channel and the ship was lost with all hands. Sir Tudor and his wife Eleanor were among those on board."

"How very sad!"

"God rest their souls, yes."

Gwynneth put her hand to her face. "I'm trying to remember. Last year was such a nightmare for us. A lot of things passed right over my head. The *Gloriana*. Isn't that the ship they found—those treasure hunters? I read about this somewhere."

"It was in all the papers," Haydn confirmed. "I have some of the cuttings with me, in my briefcase."

"I do remember. The divers were bringing up masses of stuff—coins by the bucketful, and silverware and the most exquisite jewelry. Oh, how exciting—can we make a claim?"

Cousin Haydn shook his head. "Out of the question, my dear. One would need to hire lawyers. Besides, it may be too late."

"Why?"

"As I understand it, when treasure is recovered from a wreck around the British coasts, it has to be handed over to the local receiver of wrecks or the Customs. The lawful owner then has a year and a day to make a claim. After that, the pieces are sold and the proceeds go to the salvager."

"A year and a day," said Gwynneth. "Oh, Haydn, this is too tantalizing. When did these treasure hunters start bringing up the stuff?"

"Last March."

"Eleven months! Then there's still time to make a claim. We must do it."

Haydn sighed heavily. "These things can be extremely costly."

"But we'd get it all back if we could prove our right to the treasure."

He put out his hand in a dissenting gesture. "*Your* right, my dear, not mine. Your connection is undeniable, mine is very tenuous. No, I have no personal interest here. Besides, a man of my calling cannot serve God and mammon."

"Do you really believe I have a claim?"

"The treasure hunters would dispute it, I'm sure."

"We're talking about millions of pounds, aren't we? Why should I sit back and let them take it all? I need to get hold of some lawyers—and fast."

Haydn coughed. "They charge astronomical fees."

"I know," said Gwynneth. "We can afford it—can't we, Paul?"

Paul made a blowing sound with his lips that probably had no bearing on the matter.

Gwynneth assumed so. "What is it they want—a down payment?"

"A retainer, I think is the expression."

"I can write a check tomorrow if you want. I look after all our personal finances now. There's more than enough in the deposit account. The thing is, how do I find a reliable lawyer?"

Haydn cupped his chin in his hands and looked thoughtful. "I wouldn't go to an Australian firm. Better find someone on the spot. Jones, Heap, and Jones of Cardiff are the best in Wales. I'm sure they could take on something like this."

"But is there time? We're almost into March now."

"It is rather urgent," Haydn agreed. "Look, I don't mind cutting my holiday short by a few days. If I got back to Wales at the weekend I could see them on Monday."

"I couldn't ask you to do that," said Gwynneth in a tone that betrayed the opposite.

"No trouble," said Haydn breezily.

"You're an angel. Would they accept a check in Australian pounds?"

"That might be difficult, but it's easily got around. Traveler's checks are the thing. I use them all the time. In fact, if you're serious about this—"

"Oh, yes."

"You could buy sterling traveler's checks in my name and I could pay the retainer for you."

"Would you really do that for me?"

"Anything to be of service."

She shivered with pleasure. "And now, if you've got them nearby, I'd love to have ten minutes with those press cuttings."

He left them with her, and she read them through several times during the afternoon when she was alone in her room and Paul had gone for one of his walks along the beach. Three pages cut from a color supplement had stunning pictures of the finds. She so adored the ruby necklace and the gold bracelets that she thought she would refuse to sell them. Cousin Haydn had also given her a much more detailed family tree than she had seen before. It proved beyond doubt that she was the only direct descendant of Sir Tudor Evans.

Was it all too good to be true?

One or two doubts crept into her mind later that afternoon. Presumably the treasure hunters had invested heavily in ships, divers, and equipment. They must have been confident that anything they brought up would belong to them. Maybe her claim wasn't valid under the law. She wondered also whether Cousin Haydn's research was entirely accurate. She didn't question his good faith—how could one in the circumstances?—but she knew from her own humble diggings in family history that it was all too easy to confuse one Evans with another.

On the other hand, she told herself, that's what I'm hiring the lawyers to find out. It's their business to establish whether my claim is lawful.

There was an unsettling incident toward evening. She walked down to the beach to collect Paul. The stretch where he liked to wander was never particularly crowded, even at weekends, and she soon spotted him kneeling on the sand. This time he didn't need calling. He got up, collected his bucket, and tottered toward her. Automatically she held out her hand for the gift he had chosen for her. He peered into the bucket and picked something out and placed it on her open palm.

A dead wasp.

She almost snatched her hand away and let the thing drop. She was glad she didn't, because it was obvious that he'd saved it for her and she would have hated to hurt his feelings.

She said, "Oh, a little wasp. Thank you, darling. So thoughtful. We'll take it home and put it with all my pretty pebbles and shells, shall we?"

She took a paper tissue from her pocket and folded the tiny corpse carefully between the layers.

In the house she unwrapped it and made a space on the shelf among the shells and stones. "There." She turned and smiled at Paul.

He put his thumb on the wasp and squashed it.

"Darling!"

The small act of violence shocked Gwynneth. She found herself quite stupidly reacting as if something precious had been destroyed.

"You shouldn't have done that, Paul. You gave it to me. I treasure whatever you give me. You know that."

He shuffled out of the room.

That evening over dinner she told Cousin Haydn about the incident, once again breaking her own rule and discussing Paul while he was sitting with them. "I keep wondering if he meant anything by it," she said. "It's so unlike him."

"If you want my opinion," said Haydn, "he showed some intelligence. You don't want a wasp in the house, dead or alive. As a matter of fact, I've got quite a phobia about them. It's one of the reasons I avoid the beach. You can't sit for long on any beach without being troubled by them."

"Perhaps you were stung once."

"No, I've managed to avoid them, but one of my uncles was killed by one."

"Killed by a wasp?"

"He was only forty-four at the time. It happened on the front at Aberystwyth. He was stung here, on the right temple. His face went bright red and he fell down on the shingle. My aunt ran for a doctor, but all he could do was confirm that Uncle was dead."

Clearly the tragedy had made a profound impression on Haydn. His account of the incident, spoken in simple language instead of his usual florid style, carried conviction.

"Dreadful. It must have been a rare case."

"Not so uncommon as you'd think. I tell you, Gwynneth, the wasp is one of God's creatures I studiously avoid at all times." He turned to Paul and for the first time addressed him directly, trying to end on a less grave note. "So I say more power to your thumbs, boyo."

Paul looked at him blankly.

Toward the end of the meal Haydn announced he would be leaving in the morning. "I telephoned the airport. I am advised I can get something called a standby. They say it's better before the weekend, so I'm leaving tomorrow."

"*Tomorrow?*" said Gwynneth, her voice pitched high in alarm. "But you can't. We haven't bought those traveler's checks."

"That's all right, my dear. There's a place to purchase them at the airport. All you need to do is write me a check. In fact, you could write it now in case we forget in the morning."

"How much?"

"I don't know. I'm not too conversant with the scale of fees lawyers charge these days. Are you sure you want to get involved in expense?"

"Absolutely. If I have no right to make a claim they'll let me know, won't they?"

"I'll let you know myself, my dear. How much can you spare without running up an overdraft? It's probably better for me to take more rather than less."

She wrote him a check for ten thousand Australian dollars.

"Then if you will excuse me, I'll go and pack my things and have a quiet hour before bedtime."

"Would you like an early breakfast tomorrow?"

Haydn smiled. "Early by my standards, yes. Say about eight? That gives me ample time to do something I promised myself—try the jacuzzi with the switch on. Goodnight and God bless you, my dear. And *you*, Paul, old fellow."

Gwynneth slept fitfully. At one stage in the night she noticed that Paul had his eyes open. She found his hand and gripped it tightly and talked to him as if he understood.

"I keep wondering if I've done the right thing, giving Haydn that check. It's not as if I don't trust him—I mean, you've got to trust a man of God, haven't you? I just wonder if you would have done what I did, my darling—giving him the check, I mean—and somehow I don't think so. In fact, I ask myself if you were trying to tell me something when you gave me the wasp. It was such an unusual thing for you to do. Then squashing it like that."

She must have drifted off soon after, because when she next opened her eyes the grey light of dawn was picking out the edges of the curtains. She sighed and turned toward Paul, but his side of the bed was empty. He must have gone down to the beach already.

She showered and dressed soon after, wanting to make an early start on cooking the breakfast. She would get everything ready first, she decided, and then fetch Paul from the beach before she started the cooking.

However, this was a morning of surprises.

For some unfathomable reason Paul had already come up from the beach without being called. He was seated in his usual place in the kitchen.

"Paul! You gave me quite a shock," Gwynneth told him. "What is it? Are you extra hungry this morning or something? I'll get this started presently. Would you like some bread while you're waiting? I'd better give Cousin Haydn a call first and make sure he's awake."

It crossed her mind as she went to tap on Haydn's door that Paul hadn't brought her anything from the beach. She wondered if she'd hurt his feelings by talking about the wasp as she had.

She didn't like knocking on Haydn's door in case she was interrupting his morning prayers, but it had to be done this morning in case he overslept.

He answered her call. "Thank you. Is there time for me to sample the jacuzzi?"

"Of course. Shall we say twenty minutes?"

"That should be ample."

She returned to the kitchen and made a sandwich for Paul. The bucket he always took to the beach was beside him. Without being too obvious about it, Gwynneth glanced inside to see if the customary gift of a shell or a pebble was there. It was silly, but she was feeling quite neglected.

Empty.

She said nothing about it, simply busied herself setting the table for breakfast. Presently she started heating the frying pan.

Fifteen minutes later when everything was cooked and waiting in the oven, Haydn had not appeared. "He's really enjoying that jacuzzi," she told Paul. "We'd better start, I think."

They finished.

"I'd better go and see," she said.

When she went to the door, the leg of Paul's chair was jammed against it, preventing her from opening it. "Do you mind, darling? I can't get out."

He made no move.

"Maybe you're right," Gwynneth said, always willing to assume that Paul's behavior was deliberate and intelligent. "I shouldn't fuss. It won't spoil for being left a few minutes more."

She allowed another quarter of an hour to pass. "Do you think something's happened to him? I'd better go and see, really I had. Come on, dear. Let me through."

As she took Paul by the arm and helped him to his feet, he reached out and drew her toward him, pressing his face against hers. She was surprised and delighted. He hadn't embraced her once since the stroke. She turned her face and kissed him before going to find Cousin Haydn.

Haydn was lying face down on the tile surround of the jacuzzi, which was churning noisily. He was wearing black swimming-trunks. He didn't move when she spoke his name.

"I think he may be dead," Gwynneth told the girl who took the emergency call.

The girl told her to try the kiss of life, an ambulance was on its way.

Gwynneth was still on her knees trying to breathe life into Cousin Haydn when the police arrived. They had come straight round the back of the house. "Let's have a look, lady," the sergeant said. Then, after a moment: "He's gone—no question. Who is he—your husband?"

She explained about Cousin Haydn.

"This is where you found him?"

"Well, yes. Was it an electric shock, do you think?"

"You tell me, lady. Was the jacuzzi on when you found him?"

"Yes." Gwynneth suddenly realized it was no longer running. Paul must have switched it off while she was phoning for help. She didn't want Paul brought into this. "I don't know. I may be mistaken about that."

"There could be a fault," the sergeant speculated. "We'll get it checked. Is your husband about?"

"He was." She called Paul's name. "He must have gone down to the beach. That's where he goes." She told them about the stroke.

More policemen arrived, some in plainclothes. One introduced himself as Detective Inspector Perry. He talked to Gwynneth several times in the next two hours. He went into Cousin Haydn's room and opened the suitcase he had packed for the flight home. He turned to Gwynneth and smiled.

"You say you knew this man as Haydn Evans, your cousin from Wales?"

"That's who he was."

"A distant cousin?"

Gwynneth didn't care for his grin. "I can show you the family tree if you like."

"No need for that, Mrs. Molloy. His luggage is stuffed with family trees, all as bogus as his Welsh accent. He wasn't a minister of any church or chapel. His name was Brown. Michael Herbert Brown. An English con man we've been after for months. He was getting too well known to Scotland Yard, so he came out to Queensland this summer. He's been stinging people for thousands with the treasure-hunting story. Here's your check. Lucky escape, I'd say."

They finally took the body away in an ambulance.

Detective Inspector Perry phoned late in the afternoon. "I just thought I'd let you know that your jacuzzi is safe to use, Mrs. Molloy. There's no electrical fault. I have the pathologist's report and I can tell you that Brown was not electrocuted."

"What killed him, then?"

He laughed. "Something rather appropriate. It was a sting."

Gwynneth frowned and put her hand to her throat. "A sting from a wasp?"

"In a manner of speaking." There was amusement in his voice. "Not the wasp you had in mind."

"I don't understand."

"No mystery in it, Mrs. Molloy. A sea-wasp got him. You know what a sea-wasp is?"

She knew. Everyone on the coast knew. "A jellyfish. An extremely poisonous jellyfish."

"Right, a killer."

"But the man didn't swim in the sea. He kept off the beach."

"That explains it, then."

"How?"

"He wouldn't have known about the sea-wasps. That storm washed quite a number onto the beaches. It looks as if Brown decided to take one look at the sea before he left this morning. He'd put on his swimming gear—and he must have waded in. Didn't need to go far. There were sea-wasps stranded in the shallows. You and I know how deadly they are, but I reckon an Englishman wouldn't. He got bitten, staggered back to the house, and collapsed beside the jacuzzi."

"I see." She knew it was nonsense.

"Try and remember, Mrs. Molloy. Did you see him walk down to the beach?"

"I was cooking breakfast."

"Pity. Where was your husband?"

"Paul?" She glanced over at Paul, now sitting in his usual armchair with his arms around his bucket. "He was with me in the kitchen." She was about to add that Paul had come up from the beach, but the inspector was already onto other possibilities.

"Maybe someone else saw Brown on the beach. I believe it's pretty deserted at that time."

"Yes."

"Be useful to have a witness for the inquest. All right, I heard what you said about him normally keeping off the beach, but it's a fact that he died from a sea-wasp sting. That's been established."

"I'm not questioning it."

"I ask you, Mrs. Molloy, how else could it have happened? There's only one other possibility I can think of. But how could a jellyfish get into a jacuzzi, for Christ's sake?"

LOREN D. ESTLEMAN

Widely considered one of the finest writers of hard-boiled detective fiction, Loren Estleman has won many kudos, including a Shamus Award for his Amos Walker novel, *Sugartown*, in 1985. Walker has become a very popular P.I. with a large readership, but he hasn't been Estleman's sole creation. Also adept at the Western form, Estleman is equally at home in both fields, and has worked in a variety of historical periods.

In "State of Grace," he introduces a new detective, a P.I. who lives in an apartment above a bookstore that sells, shall we say, off-color material. It shouldn't then surprise readers to discover that above Poteet resides a prostitute. The death of a priest in his upstairs neighbor's bed may echo superficially the plot line of John Gregory Dunne's *True Confessions*, but the resemblance ends there. This is a nicely turned piece that uses all the color and detail of its material to full advantage.

State of Grace

"Ralph? This is Lyla."

"Who the hell is Lyla?"

"Lyla Dane. I live in the apartment above you, for chrissake. We see each other every day."

"The hooker."

"You live over a dirty bookstore. What do you want for a neighbor, a freaking rocket scientist?"

Ralph Poteet sat up in bed and rumpled his mouse-colored hair. He fumbled the alarm clock off the night table and held it very close to his good eye. He laid it face down and scowled at the receiver in his hand. "It's two-thirty ayem."

"Thanks. My watch stopped and I knew if I called you you'd tell me what time it is. Listen, you're like a cop, right?"

"Not at two-thirty ayem."

"I'll give you a hundred dollars to come up here now."

He blew his nose on the sheet. "Ain't that supposed to be the other way around?"

"You coming up or not? You're not the only dick in town. I just called you because you're handy."

"What's the squeal?"

"I got a dead priest in my bed."

He said he was on his way and hung up. A square gin bottle slid off the blanket. He caught it before it hit the floor, but it was empty and he dropped it. He put on his Tyrolean hat with a feather in the band, found his suit pants on the floor half under the bed, and pulled them on over his pajamas. He stuck bare feet into his loafers and because it was October he pulled on his suitcoat, grunting with the effort. He was forty-three years old and forty pounds overweight. He looked for his gun just because it was 2:30 A.M., couldn't find it, and went out.

158

Lyla Dane was just five feet and ninety pounds in a pink kimono and slippers with carnations on the toes. She wore her black hair in a pageboy like Anna May Wong, but the Oriental effect fell short of her round Occidental face. "You look like crap," she told Ralph at the door.

"That's what two hours' sleep will do for you. Where's the hundred?"

"Don't you want to see the stiff first?"

"What do I look like, a pervert?"

"Yes." She opened a drawer in the telephone stand and counted a hundred in twenties and tens into his palm.

He stuck the money in a pocket and followed her through a small living room decorated by K-Mart into a smaller bedroom containing a Queen Anne bed that had cost twice as much as all the other furniture combined and took up most of the space in the room. The rest of the space was taken up by Monsignor John Breame, pastor of St. Boniface, a cathedral Ralph sometimes used to exchange pictures for money, although not so much lately because the divorce business was on the slide. He recognized the monsignor's pontifical belly under the flesh-colored satin sheet that barely covered it. The monsignor's face was purple.

"He a regular?" Ralph found a Diamond matchstick in his suitcoat pocket and stuck the end between his teeth.

"Couple of times a month. Tonight I thought he was breathing a little hard after. Then he wasn't."

"What do you want me to do?"

"Get rid of him, what else? Cops find him here the Christers'll run me out on a cross. I got a business to run."

"Cost you another hundred."

"I just gave you a hundred."

"You're lucky I don't charge by the pound. Look at that gut."

"*You* look at it. He liked the missionary position."

"What else would he?"

She got the hundred and gave it to him. He told her to leave. "Where'll I go?"

"There's beds all over town. You probably been in half of them. Or go find an all-night movie if you don't feel like working. Don't come back before dawn."

She dressed and went out after emptying the money drawer into a shoulder bag she took with her. When she was gone Ralph helped himself to a Budweiser from her refrigerator and looked up a number in the city directory and called it from the telephone in the living room. A voice like ground glass answered.

"Bishop Stoneman?" Ralph asked.

"It's three ayem," said the voice.

"Thank you. My name is Ralph Poteet. I'm a private detective. I'm sorry to have to inform you Monsignor Breame is dead."

"Mary Mother of God! What happened?"

"I'm no expert. It looks like a heart attack."

"Mary Mother of God. In bed?"

"Yeah."

"Was he—do you know if he was in a state of grace?"

"That's what I wanted to talk to you about," Ralph said.

The man Bishop Stoneman sent was tall and gaunt, with a complexion like wet pulp and colorless hair cropped down to stubble. He had on a black coat buttoned to the neck and looked like an early martyr. He said his name was Morgan. Together they wrapped the monsignor in the soiled bedding and carried him down three flights of stairs, stopping a dozen times to rest, and laid him on the backseat of a big Buick Electra parked between streetlamps. Ralph stood guard at the car while Morgan went back up for the monsignor's clothes. It was nearly 4:00 A.M. and their only witness was a skinny cat who lost interest after a few minutes and stuck one leg up in the air to lick itself.

After a long time Morgan came down and threw the bundle onto the front seat and gave Ralph an envelope containing a hundred dollars. He said he'd handle it from there. Ralph watched him drive off and went back up to bed. He was very tired and didn't wake up until the fire sirens were grinding down in front of the building. He hadn't even heard the explosion when Lyla Dane returned to her apartment at dawn.

"Go away."

"That's no way to talk to your partner," Ralph said.

"Ex-partner. You got the boot and I did, too. Now I'm giving it to you. Go away."

Dale English was a special investigator with the sheriff's department who kept his office in the City-County Building. He had a monolithic face and fierce black eyebrows like Lincoln's, creating an effect he tried to soften with pink shirts and knobby knitted ties. He and Ralph had shared a city prowl car for two years, until some evidence turned up missing from the property room. Both had been dismissed, English without prejudice because unlike the case with Ralph, none of the incriminating items had been found in English's possession.

"The boot didn't hurt you none," Ralph said.

"No, it just cost me my wife and my kid and seven years' seniority. I'd be a lieutenant now."

Ralph lowered his bulk onto the vinyl-and-aluminum chair in front of English's desk. "I wouldn't hang this on you if I could go to the city cops. Somebody's out to kill me."

"Tell whoever it is I said good luck."

"I ain't kidding."

"Me neither."

"You know that hooker got blown up this morning?"

"The gas explosion? I read about it."

"Yeah, well, it wasn't no accident. I'm betting the arson boys find a circuit breaker in the wall switch. You know what that means."

"Sure. Somebody lets himself in and turns on the gas and puts a breaker in the switch so when the guy comes home the spark blows him to hell. What was the hooker into and what was your angle?"

"It's more like who was into the hooker." Ralph told him the rest.

"This the same Monsignor Breame was found by an altar boy counting angels in his bed at the St. Boniface rectory this morning?" English asked.

"Thanks to me and this bug Morgan."

"So what do you want?"

"Hell, protection. The blowup was meant for me. Morgan thought I'd be going back to that same apartment and set it up while I was waiting for him to come down with Breame's clothes."

"Bishops don't kill people over priests that can't keep their vows in their pants."

Ralph screwed up his good eye. Its mate looked like a sour ball someone had spat out. "What world you living in? Shape the Church is in, he'd do just that to keep it quiet."

"Go away, Ralph."

"Well, pick up Morgan at least. He can't be hard to find. He looks like one of those devout creeps you see skulking around in paintings of the Crucifixion."

"I don't have jurisdiction in the city."

"That ain't why you won't do it. Hey, I told IAD you didn't have nothing to do with what went down in Property."

"It would've carried more weight if you'd submitted to a lie detector test. Mine was inconclusive." He paged through a report on his desk without looking at it. "I'll run the name Morgan and the description you gave me through the computer and see what it coughs up. There won't be anything."

"Thanks, buddy."

"You sure you didn't take pictures? It'd be your style to try and put the squeeze on a bishop."

"I thought about it, but my camera's in hock." Ralph got up. "You can get me at my place. They got the fire out before it reached my floor."

"That was lucky. Gin flames are the hardest to put out."

He was driving a brand-new red Riviera he had promised to sell for a lawyer friend who was serving two years for suborning to commit perjury, only he hadn't gotten around to it yet. He parked in a handicapped zone near his building and climbed stairs smelling of smoke and firemen's rubber boots. Inside his apartment, which was also his office, he rewound the tape on his answering machine and played back a threatening call from a loan shark named Zwingman, a reminder from a dentist's receptionist with a Nutra-Sweet voice that last month's root canal was still unpaid for, and a message from a heavy breather that he had to play back three times before deciding it was a man. He was staring toward the door, his attention on the tape, when a square of white paper slithered over the threshold.

That day he was wearing his legal gun, a short-nosed .38 Colt, in a clip on his belt, and an orphan High Standard .22 magnum derringer in an ankle holster. Drawing the Colt, he lunged and tore open the door just in time to hear the street door closing below. He swung around and crossed to the street window. Through it he saw a narrow figure in a long black coat and the back of a close-cropped head crossing against traffic to the other side. The man rounded the corner and vanished.

Ralph holstered the revolver and picked up the note. It was addressed to him in a round, shaped hand.

Mr. Poteet:

If it is not inconvenient, your presence at my home could prove to your advantage and mine.

Cordially,
Philip Stoneman,
Bishop-in-Ordinary

Clipped to it was a hundred-dollar bill.

Bishop Stoneman lived in a refurbished brownstone in a neighborhood that the city had reclaimed from slum by evicting its residents and sandblasting graffiti off the buildings. The bell was answered by a youngish bald man in a dark suit and clerical collar who introduced himself as Brother Edwards and directed Ralph to a curving staircase, then retired to be seen no more. Ralph didn't hear Morgan climbing behind him until something hard probed his right kidney. A hand patted him down and removed the Colt from its clip. "End of the hall."

The bishop was a tall old man, nearly as thin as Morgan, with iron-gray hair and a face that fell away to the white shackle of his collar. He rose from behind a redwood desk to greet his visitor in an old-fashioned black frock that made him look like a crow. The room was large and square and smelled of leather from the books on the built-in shelves and pipe tobacco. Morgan entered behind Ralph and closed the door.

"Thank you for coming, Mr. Poteet. Please sit down."

"Thank Ben Franklin." But he settled into a deep leather chair that gripped his buttocks like a big hand in a soft glove.

"I'm grateful for this chance to thank you in person," Stoneman said, sitting in his big swivel. "I'm very disappointed in Monsignor Breame. I'd hoped that he would take my place at the head of the diocese."

"You bucking for cardinal?"

He smiled. "I suppose you've shown yourself worthy of confidence. Yes, His Holiness has offered me the red hat. The appointment will be announced next month."

"That why you tried to croak me? I guess your right bower cashing in in a hooker's bed would look bad in Rome."

One corner of the desk supported a silver tray containing two long-stemmed glasses and a cut-crystal decanter half full of ruby liquid. Stoneman removed the stopper and filled both glasses. "This is an excellent Madeira. I confess that the austere life allows me two mild vices. The other is tobacco."

"What are we celebrating?" Ralph didn't pick up his glass.

"Your new appointment as chief of diocesan security. The position pays well and the hours are regular."

"In return for which I forget about Monsignor Breame?"

"And entrust all related material to me. You took pictures, of course." Stoneman sipped from his glass.

Ralph lifted his. "I'd be pretty stupid not to, considering what happened to Lyla Dane."

"I heard about the tragedy. That child's soul could have been saved."

"You should've thought about that before your boy Morgan croaked her." Ralph gulped off half his wine. It tasted bitter.

The bishop laid a bony hand atop an ancient ornate Bible on the desk. His guest thought he was about to swear his innocence. "This belonged to St. Thomas. More, not Aquinas. I have a weakness for religious antiques."

"Thought you only had two vices." The air in the room stirred slightly. Ralph turned to see who had entered, but his vision was thickening. Morgan was a shimmering shadow. The glass dropped from Ralph's hand. He bent to retrieve it and came up with the derringer. Stoneman's shout echoed. Ralph fired twice at the shadow and pitched headfirst into its depths.

He awoke feeling pretty much the way he did most mornings, with his head throbbing and his stomach turning over. He wanted to turn over with it, but he was stretched out on a hard, flat surface with his ankles strapped down and his arms tied above his head. He was looking up at water-stained tile. His joints ached.

"The sedative was in the stem of your glass," Stoneman was saying. He was out of Ralph's sight and Ralph had the impression he'd been talking for a while. "You've been out for two hours. The unpleasant effect is temporary, rather like a hangover."

"Did I get him?" Ralph's tongue moved sluggishly.

"No, you missed rather badly. It required persuasion to get Morgan to carry you down here to the basement instead of killing you on the spot. He was quite upset."

Ralph squirmed. There was something familiar about the position he was tied in. For some reason he thought of Mrs. Thornton, his ninth-grade American Lit. teacher. *What is the significance of Poe's "Pit and the Pendulum" to the transcendentalist movement?* His organs shriveled.

"Another antique," said the bishop. "The Inquisition did not end when General Lasalle entered Madrid, but went on for several years in the provinces. This particular rack was still in use after Torquemada's death. The gears are original. The wheel is new, and of course I had to replace the ropes. Morgan?"

A shoe scraped the floor and a spoked shadow fluttered across Ralph's vision. His arms tightened. He gasped.

"That's enough. We don't want to put Mr. Poteet back under." To Ralph: "Morgan just returned from your apartment. He found neither pictures nor film nor even a camera. Where are they?"

"I was lying. I didn't take no pictures."

"Morgan."

Ralph shrieked.

"Enough! His Holiness is sensitive about scandal, Mr. Poteet. I won't have Monsignor Breame's indiscretions bar me from the Vatican. Who is keeping the pictures for you?"

"There ain't no pictures, honest."

"Morgan!"

A socket started to slip. Ralph screamed and blubbered.

"Enough!" Stoneman's fallen-away face moved into Ralph's vision. His eyes were fanatic. "A few more turns will sever your spine. You could be spoon-fed for the rest of your life. Do you think that after failing to kill you in that apartment I would hesitate to cripple you? Where are the pictures?"

"I didn't take none!"

"Morgan!"

"No!" It ended in a howl. His armpits were on fire. The ropes creaked.

"Police! Don't move!"

The bishop's face jerked away. The spoked shadow fluttered. The tension went out of Ralph's arms suddenly, and relief poured into his joints. A shot flattened the air. Two more answered it. Something struck the bench Ralph was lying on and drove a splinter into his back. He thought at first he was shot, but the pain was nothing; he'd just been through worse. He squirmed onto his hip and saw Morgan, one black-clad arm stained and glistening, leveling a heavy automatic at a target behind Ralph's back. Scrambling out of the line of fire, Ralph jerked his bound hands and the rack's wheel, six feet in diameter with handles bristling from it like a ship's helm, spun around. One of the handles slapped the gun from Morgan's hand. Something cracked past Ralph's left ear and Morgan fell back against the tile wall and slid down it. The shooting stopped.

Ralph wriggled onto his other hip. A man he didn't know in a houndstooth coat with a revolver in his hand had Bishop Stoneman spread-eagled against a wall and was groping in his robes for weapons. Dale English came off the stairs with the Luger he had been carrying since Ralph was his partner. He bent over Morgan on the floor, then straightened and holstered the gun. He looked at Ralph. "I guess you're okay."

"I am if you got a pocketknife."

"Arson boys found the circuit breaker in the wall switch just like you said." He cut Ralph's arms free and sawed through the straps on his ankles. "When you didn't answer your telephone I went to your place and found Stoneman's note."

"He confessed to the hooker's murder."

"I know. I heard him."

"How the hell long were you listening?"

"We had to have enough to pin him to it, didn't we?"

"You son of a bitch. You just wanted to hear me holler."

"Couldn't help it. You sure got lungs."

"I got to go to the toilet."

"Stick around after," English said. "I need a statement to hand to the city boys. They won't like County sticking its face in this."

Ralph hobbled upstairs. When he was through in the bathroom he found his hat and coat and headed out. At the front door he turned around and went back into the bishop's study, where he hoisted Thomas More's Bible under one arm. He knew a bookseller who would probably give him at least a hundred for it.

JOAN HESS

Joan Hess has written a number of nifty mysteries, including two series. Carole Mallory, the owner of a small mystery bookstore, has some fascinating adventures, as does Hess's other major protagonist, a female sheriff, whose books are written under a pseudonym.

Neither series quite prepares one for the following offbeat, unique story. Suffice it to say that not everything is exactly as it seems; perhaps one should say that not everyone in this little gem sees things the same way, with murderous results.

Death of
a Romance Writer

The young woman hesitated at the top of the great curving staircase, grumbling rather rudely to herself as she gazed at the scene below. "Hell's bells!" she muttered under her breath. "Doesn't she like anything besides waltzes? A little New Wave rock, or at least jazz?"

In the grand ballroom ladies dressed in pastel gowns swept across the floor under the benevolent eyes of elegant gentlemen in black waistcoats and ruffled shirts. A stringed orchestra labored its way through the familiar melodies with grim concentration. Servants moved inconspicuously along the walls of the vast room, their expressions studiously blank. The same old thing, down to the canapes and sweet sherry.

Gathering up her skirt with pale, delicately tapered fingers, the woman forced herself to move down the stairs. Her heart-shaped mouth was curled slightly, and her deep jade eyes flittered across the crowd without curiosity. He would make an appearance in a few minutes, she reminded herself glumly, but perhaps she could have a bit of fun in the meantime. The fun would certainly end when he appeared—whoever he was.

"Lady Althea!" gushed a shrill, nasal voice from the shadows behind her. "I was so hoping to see you this evening. The ball is absolutely delightful."

Lady Althea, the woman repeated to herself. A silly name, as usual, invoking images of moonlit gardens and scented breezes. Why not a simple "Kate" or "Jane"? Oh, no. It was always "Desiree" or "Bianca," as if her bland personality must be disguised by alluring nomenclature.

The dowager tottered out of the shadows on tiny feet. In her seventies (hundreds, Althea sniffed to herself), the woman's face was a mesh of tiny lines, and her faded blue eyes glittered with malevolence. Her thin white hair was decorated with a handful of dusty plumes, one of which threatened to sweep across her hawkish nose with every twitch of the woman's head.

"Who're you?" Althea demanded bluntly.

The dowager raised a painted eyebrow. "I am your mother-in-law's dearest friend, Lady Althea. You had tea only yesterday at my summer home. Your first introduction to society, I believe. I'm amazed that it has slipped your mind."

"Yeah, sorry." Althea moved away from the woman's rancid breath and fluttery hands. Surely these people could be induced to brush their teeth, she thought testily. They didn't, of course. As far as she could tell, they had no bodily functions whatsoever. A few bouts of the vapors, a shoulder slashed by a duelling sword, a mysterious scar across the cheek. But nothing mundane to interrupt the flow of their lives.

Ignoring the woman's frown, Althea stood on her toes to peer around the room. He wasn't here yet. Good. Now, if she could only liven up the music and get these nameless people to loosen up a little bit, the evening might provide some amusement. A ball could be a ball, but it seldom was.

The dowager was not ready to allow Althea to escape. "Your dear mother-in-law has told me of your tragic history, and I must tell you how much I admire your courage," she hissed. Little drops of spittle landed on Althea's cheek, like a fine mist of acid rain.

"Sure, thanks," Althea said. "I'm a plucky sort, I understand. Personally, I'd rather watch television or read a confession magazine, but I never get the chance."

"Television? What might that be, my dear girl?"

Althea shook her head. "Never mind. Hey, which one of these ladies" (dames, broads) "is my mother-in-law? The one with the chicken beak or that fat slug in the corner?"

"Lady Althea! I must tell you that I am somewhat shocked by your manner," the dowager gasped. Her hand fluttered to her mouth. "I was led to believe you had been raised most properly in a convent; that you were of gentle birth and delicate nature."

"Is that so? I guess I'd better behave," Althea said dryly. She tucked a stray curl of her raven black hair into place, and checked the row of tiny seed pearl buttons on her elbow-length gloves. Now that, she told herself sternly, was the accepted and expected behavior. She glanced at the dowager.

"So which one is my mother-in-law?"

"Your mother-in-law is there," the dowager said, gesturing with a molting fan toward a grim-visaged woman sitting on a straight-backed chair. "But where is your dear husband, Lady Althea? I had such hopes of speaking to him."

"Beats me," Althea said. So she was already married, she thought with a sigh. These rapid shifts were disconcerting. Dear husband, huh! Gawd, he was probably a bodice ripper like the rest of them. And she had decided to wear her new gown—genuine silk and just the right color for her eyes. Perhaps there was enough time to change into something more expendable.

Frowning, Althea glanced across the coiffed heads of the guests to study her mother-in-law. A real loser, with a profile that ought to be illegal. Translucent blue complexion, hooded eyes, mouth tighter than a miser's purse. But the woman did have a smidgen of charm—all found in the garish diamond broach on her chest. From across the room, Althea could see the brilliance of the stone, and even the dull glow of the gold setting. Now *that* was charming.

Leaving the dowager puffing resentfully at the bottom of the stair-case, Althea began to thread her way between the dancers. Despite her intention of finding the punchbowl, she found herself curtsying in front of her mother-in-law. Damn.

"Althea, dear child," the woman said frostily. She extended a limp white hand, as though she expected Althea to clasp it to her bosom—or kiss it, for God's sake!

Althea eyed it warily. At last she touched it timidly, then snatched her hand away and hid it behind her back. "Good evening," she said, swallowing a sour taste in the back of her throat. The diamond broach. It would keep her in penthouses and champagne for the rest of her life, if only . . .

"Excrutia, this child is charming!" the dowager said, shoving Althea aside. "But where is your son? Dear Jared must be eager to present his charming bride to his friends . . ."

Jared, huh. Althea brushed a black curl off her eyebrow as she checked the crowd. She was destined to be stuck with an elegant moniker, and so was he. Once, she remembered with a faint sigh, she had particularly liked a chap named Sam—but of course he had become a Derek. Sam had had bulging biceps and a busted nose, but it hadn't kept him from stirring up a bit of inventiveness between the covers. Derek, on the other hand, had spent hours gazing into her eyes and murmuring (bleating) endearments that were supposed to sweep her off her feet. Sam's approach was brisker—and a hell of a lot more interesting.

The mother-in-law was snivelling down her nose. "Where is my son, Althea? Have you already managed to . . . distract him from his duties as host?"

Althea thought of several snappy remarks but again found herself in an awkward curtsy. "No, ma'am. I haven't seen him since—"

Since what? It was impossible to keep track of the convoluted framework. Since he rescued her? Married her? Raped her? Jared would never do such a thing, she amended sourly. No doubt he had kept her from being raped by one of the marauding highwaymen that accosted virgins. Considering Jared, it might have been more fun to be accosted . . .

"Well, Althea," the mother-in-law snorted in a well-bred voice, "you must feel most fortunate to have snared my son. He is, after all, the owner of this charming manor and of all the land from here to the cliffs. And you, a penniless orphan, destined to become a scullery maid—had not heaven intervened on your behalf."

Sam's mother was a cheery drunkard who was still producing babies on an annual basis. This one had probably produced Jared by virgin birth. Forget that; birth was messy. Jared had no doubt simply appeared one day, lisping French and nibbling cucumber sandwiches under his nanny's approving smile.

Althea swallowed an angry response. Fluttering her thick lashes, she murmured, "Yes, ma'am, I was most fortunate to have met your son. When my father died, leaving me a penniless orphan at the mercies of my unscrupulous uncle, I feared for my life." Melodrama, pure and nauseating. Why couldn't she have been a barmaid? A bit of slap and giggle in the shadows behind the stables, a feather bed to keep warm for a guy like Sam. But instead she had to hang around with the aristocracy. Snivellers and snorters, bah!

But there was no point in worrying about this Jared fellow. Maybe he was a Sam in disguise. Maybe chickens had lips, and the moon was made of green cheese. Maybe it was time to start expecting the Easter bunny to show up with a bunch of purple eggs.

The mother-in-law person stood up imperiously and held a lace handkerchief to her nose. "I am going into the garden for a bit of fresh air," she announced. "Send Jared to me when he appears, Althea. I must speak to him; it is of the greatest importance."

Hmmm? Had the old bat noticed her repeated glances at the diamond broach? If she were to tattle to this Jared person, Althea might find herself scrubbing pots after all. It seemed prudent to assume the dutiful role.

"Please don't take a chill, Lady Excrutia," Althea said in a solicitous whine. "Shall I fetch a shawl for you from your dressing room? Allow me to bring it to you in the garden."

The dowager with the plumes beamed approvingly at Althea's meek posture. "Charming child, just charming. But look, here's Jared!"

Oh, hell. Althea tried to forget about the promised encounter in

the garden—for a few minutes anyway. Forcing herself into a sem-
blance of pleased surprise, she lifted her eyes to meet those of the
unknown Jared.

Oh, my God, she thought with a scowl. Another arrogant one.
There went another bodice, ripped into shreds. Endless lovemaking,
with nothing but simmering frustration as the result. And those
granite gray eyes boring into her, for God's sake! It was more than
anyone should have to bear . . . it really was.

"Damnedest thing I've ever seen!" The lieutenant leaned against
the kitchen counter, watching the body being wheeled out of the
tiny office. For the first time in his career even the paramedics were
subdued.

The two men waited for the medical examiner to finish wiping
the inky smudges off his hands, then crowded into the room. The
desk was cluttered with notebooks, chewed pencil stubs, and an
overflowing ashtray. A lipstick-stained coffee cup lay on the floor
in a dried brown puddle. A typewriter hummed softly, and with a
snort the second of the plainclothes detectives leaned over to switch
it off.

"How'd you discover the body?" the medical examiner asked.
Like Lady Macbeth, he seemed obsessed with the invisible marks
on his hands, rubbing them against each other nervously.

"The woman in the next apartment called the super. It seems the
woman who lived here was a writer, and the neighbor was used to
the sound of the typewriter clattering all day long. She told the super
the last couple of days there was no sound, and it was driving her
crazy," the first detective said.

The second snorted again. "If I lived next door to one of these
writers, and had to listen to that noise all day, I might have strangled
the broad myself. As it is, I have to listen to my wife screaming at
the kids every night and—"

"Damnedest thing," the first repeated, shaking his head. "In
twenty-nine years on the force, I've seen a lot of weird things—but
I've never seen anyone strangled with a typewriter ribbon."

The medical examiner laughed. "As good as a wire or a rope,
but a hell of a lot messier. All you have to do now is find someone
with ink-stained hands."

The second detective was reading the titles of the paperback books
on a shelf above the desk. "Look at this, Carl. Do you know what
the victim wrote? Romance novels, by damn! You know the things:
Sweet Moonlight, The Towering Passion of Lady Bianca, etc., etc."

"My wife reads that stuff," the first admitted. He shook his head.
"I dunno why, though. Gimme a good ball game on television and

a six-pack to keep me cool. That's my idea of romance—me, Budweiser, and the Yankees."

The medical examiner raised his hand in a farewell gesture. "I'll get back to you in a day or two, Carl. Don't waste your time reading the victim's books—unless you think the intellectuals of the world conspired to do her in!" Chuckling to himself, he left the two detectives exchanging glances.

"Naw, Carl," the second said, "don't get your hopes up. It was a prowler or something. Let's go talk to the doorman and the elevator operator."

The first sighed, thinking of the tedious interviews that would prove necessary, the trivial gossip that the neighbors would feel obliged to share, the dinner he would not have a chance to eat that night.

"Too bad it wasn't a suicide," he grumbled. "My wife always makes meatballs on Mondays and then goes bowling with a bunch of the girls. Good game on tonight."

"Then we'd have our note," the second added, pointing at a piece of paper sticking out of the typewriter. "But nobody, not even dippy romance writers, can strangle themselves. My money's on the neighbor; she's probably half-deaf from the noise. She just couldn't stand the sound of the typewriter any longer and went berserk. I would've."

"She's eighty-three," the first one said. He leaned over to read the manuscript page, then straightened up. "My wife will get a kick out of this, you know. Yours will, too. All women think this stuff is great—all the damned moonlight and wine and deep soulful stares! It spoils them for the real world, Marv."

"Yeah, my wife wanted me to take her out to dinner for her birthday. Hell, the babysitter drives a damn Mercedes! I can't see spending half a week's salary on fancy food."

"So what'd you do?" Carl asked as they went out the door of the office and started for the living room.

The one named Marv shrugged his shoulders. "I brought home a real nice pizza."

Lady Althea wrapped her arms around Sam's stocky waist and snuggled against him, ignoring the black smudges on his back from her previous caresses. For a long time, the horse's rhythmic clops were the only sound on the road. The moon illuminated the trees on either side of them with a silver haze, and the light breeze had an earthy redolence. At last the horse and its two riders were gone into the darkness, although a faint giggle seemed to linger in the air.

Back at the cold and lifeless manor house, the ball was over. The nameless gentility had disappeared, the orchestra vanished, the vast room as quiet as a tomb. In the center of the room lay a body. Two arrogant eyes stared at the darkened chandelier, unblinking and glazed with faint surprise. Blood had long since coagulated on the gash across his neck.

There was more blood in the garden. The figure there had the same surprised expression, and a similar slash across the neck. The bosom no longer heaved, although it had the appearance of a mountain range arising from the manicured lawn. The surface of this alpine region was smooth, except for a tiny rip in its surface where a broach had been removed hastily and without regard for the crinoline fabric.

His majesty's guards remained puzzled by the scene for a few weeks, then dismissed it from their minds. One or two of the younger ones sometimes mentioned it over pints of ale in the new roadhouse, but the older officers usually ignored them. The barmaid, always full of throaty laughter and ready for a frolic, kept them more amused on the feather beds upstairs.

MAX ALLAN COLLINS

Collins, the author of the Shamus Award-winning first novel *True Detective*, has been hot ever since that 1983 debut, with novels and stories about Nathan Heller, a P.I. who after leaving the force set up shop in the corrupt Chicago of the 1930s.

Perhaps it's his sensitivity to the strangeness in people that has made him so popular. No matter why, he shows the strength of his gift here in a story based upon a true incident. The names have, of course, been changed, and considerable time has passed since the sad, odd events that gave rise to "Marble Mildred."

Marble Mildred

In June 1936, Chicago was in the midst of the Great Depression and a sweltering summer, and I was in the midst of Chicago. Specifically, on this Tuesday afternoon, the ninth to be exact, I was sitting on a sofa in the minuscule lobby of the Van Buren Hotel. The sofa had seen better days, and so had the hotel. The Van Buren was no flophouse, merely a moderately rundown residential hotel just west of the El tracks, near the LaSalle Street Station.

Divorce work wasn't the bread and butter of the A-1 Detective Agency, but we didn't turn it away. I use the editorial "we," but actually there was only one of us, me, Nathan Heller, "president" of the firm. And despite my high-flown title, I was just a down-at-the-heels dick reading a racing form in a seedy hotel's seedy lobby, waiting to see if a certain husband showed up in the company of another woman.

Another woman, that is, than the one he was married to; the dumpy, dusky dame who'd come to my office yesterday.

"I'm not as good-looking as I was fourteen years ago," she'd said, coyly, her voice honeyed by a Southern drawl, "but I'm a darn sight younger looking than *some* women I know."

"You're a very handsome woman, Mrs. Bolton," I said, smiling, figuring she was fifty if she was a day, "and I'm sure there's nothing to your suspicions."

She had been a looker once, but she'd run to fat, and her badly hennaed hair and overdone makeup were no help; nor was the raccoon stole she wore over a faded floral print housedress. The stole looked a bit ratty and in any case was hardly called for in this weather.

"Mr. Heller, they are more than suspicions. My husband is a successful businessman, with an office in the financial district. He is easy prey to gold diggers."

176

The strained formality of her tone made the raccoon stole make sense, somehow.

"This isn't the first time you've suspected him of infidelity."

"Unfortunately, no."

"Are you hoping for reconciliation, or has a lawyer advised you to establish grounds for divorce?"

"At this point," she said, calmly, the Southern drawl making her words seem more casual than they were, "I wish only to know. Can you understand that, Mr. Heller?"

"Certainly. I'm afraid I'll need some details . . ."

She had them. Though they lived in Hyde Park, a quiet, quietly well-off residential area, Bolton was keeping a room at the Van Buren Hotel, a few blocks down the street from the very office in which we sat. Mrs. Bolton believed that he went to the hotel on assignations while pretending to leave town on business trips.

"How did you happen to find that out?" I asked her.

"His secretary told me," she said, with a crinkly little smile, proud of herself.

"Are you sure you need a detective? You seem to be doing pretty well on your own . . ."

The smile disappeared and she seemed quite serious now, digging into her big black purse and coming back with a folded wad of cash. She thrust it across the desk toward me, as if daring me to take it.

I don't take dares, but I do take money. And there was plenty of it: a hundred in tens and fives.

"My rate's ten dollars a day and expenses," I said, reluctantly, the notion of refusing money going against the grain. "A thirty-dollar retainer would be plenty . . ."

She nodded curtly. "I'd prefer you accept that. But it's all I can afford, remember; when it's gone, it's gone."

I wrote her out a receipt and told her I hoped to refund some of the money, though of course I hoped the opposite, and that I hoped to be able to dispel her fears about her husband's fidelity, though there was little hope of that, either. Hope was in short supply in Chicago, these days.

Right now, she said, Joe was supposedly on a business trip; but the secretary had called to confide in Mrs. Bolton that her husband had been in the office all day.

I had to ask the usual questions. She gave me a complete description (and a photo she'd had foresight to bring), his business address, working hours, a list of places he was known to frequent.

And, so, I had staked out the hotel yesterday, starting late afternoon. I didn't start in the lobby. The hotel was a walk-up, the lobby on the second floor; the first floor leased out to a saloon, in the window of which I sat nursing beers and watching people stroll by. One of them, finally, was Joseph Bolton, a tall, nattily attired businessman about ten years his wife's junior; he was pleasant looking, but with his wire-rimmed glasses and receding brown hair was no Robert Taylor.

Nor was he enjoying feminine company, unless said company was already up in the hotel room before I'd arrived on the scene. I followed him up the stairs to the glorified landing of a lobby, where I paused at the desk while he went on up the next flight of stairs (there were no elevators in the Van Buren) and, after buying a newspaper from the desk clerk, went up to his floor, the third of the four-story hotel, and watched from around a corner as he entered his room.

Back down in the lobby, I approached the desk clerk, an older guy with rheumy eyes and a blue bow tie. I offered him a buck for the name of the guest in Room 3C.

"Bolton," he said.

"You're kidding," I said. "Let me see the register." I hadn't bothered coming in earlier to bribe a look because I figured Bolton would be here under an assumed name.

"What it's worth to you?" he asked.

"I already paid," I said, and turned his register around and looked in it. Joseph Bolton it was. Using his own goddamn name. That was a first.

"Any women?" I asked.

"Not that I know of," he said.

"Regular customer?"

"He's been living here a couple months."

"Living here? He's here every night?"

"I dunno. He pays his six bits a day, is all I know. I don't tuck him in."

I gave the guy half a buck to let me rent his threadbare sofa. Sat for another couple of hours and followed two women upstairs. Both seemed to be hookers; neither stopped at Bolton's room.

At a little after eight, Bolton left the hotel and I followed him over to Adams Street, to the Berghoff, the best German restaurant for the money in the Loop. What the hell—I hadn't eaten yet either. We both dined alone.

That night I phoned Mrs. Bolton with my report, such as it was.

"He has a woman in his room," she insisted.

"It's possible," I allowed.

"Stay on the job," she said, and hung up.

I stayed on the job. That is, the next afternoon I returned to the Van Buren Hotel, or anyway to the saloon underneath it, and drank beers and watched the world go by. Now and then the world would go up the hotel stairs. Men I ignored; women that looked like hookers I ignored. One woman, who showed up around four-thirty, I did not ignore.

She was as slender and attractive a woman as Mildred Bolton was not, though she was only a few years younger. And her wardrobe was considerably more stylish than my client's—high-collared white dress with a bright colorful figured print, white gloves, white shoes, a felt hat with a wide turned-down brim.

She did not look like the sort of woman who would be stopping in at the Van Buren Hotel, but stop in she did.

So did I. I trailed her up to the third floor, where she was met at the door of Bolton's room by a male figure. I just got a glimpse of the guy, but he didn't seem to be Bolton. She went inside.

I used a pay phone in the saloon downstairs and called Mrs. Bolton in Hyde Park.

"I can be there in forty minutes," she said.

"What are you talking about?"

"I want to catch them together. I'm going to claw that hussy's eyes out."

"Mrs. Bolton, you don't want to do that . . ."

"I most certainly do. You can go home, Mr. Heller. You've done your job, and nicely."

And she had hung up.

I'd mentioned to her that the man in her husband's room did not seem to be her husband, but that apparently didn't matter. Now I had a choice: I could walk back up to my office and write Mrs. Bolton out a check refunding seventy of her hundred dollars, goddamnit (ten bucks a day, ten bucks expenses—she'd pay for my bribes and beers).

Or I could do the Christian thing and wait around and try to defuse this thing before it got even uglier.

I decided to do the latter. Not because it was the Christian thing—I wasn't a Christian, after all—but because I might be able to convince Mrs. Bolton she needed a few more days' work out of me, to figure out what was really going on here. It seemed to me she could use a little more substantial information, if a divorce was to come out of this. It also seemed to me I could use the money.

I don't know how she arrived—whether by El or streetcar or bus or auto—but as fast as she was walking, it could've been on foot. She was red in the face, eyes hard and round as marbles, fists churning as she strode, her head floating above the incongruous raccoon stole.

I hopped off my bar stool and caught her at the sidewalk.

"Don't go in there, Mrs. Bolton," I said, taking her arm gently.

She swung it away from me, held her head back and, short as she was, looked down at me, nostrils flared. I felt like a matador who dropped his cape.

"You've been discharged for the day, Mr. Heller," she said.

"You still need my help. You're not going about this the right way."

With indignation she began, "My husband . . ."

"Your husband isn't in there. He doesn't even get off work till six."

She swallowed. The redness of her face seemed to fade some; I was quieting her down.

Then fucking fate stepped in, in the form of that swanky dame in the felt hat, who picked that very moment to come strolling out of the Van Buren Hotel like it was the goddamn Palmer House. On her arm was a young man, perhaps eighteen, perhaps twenty, in a cream-color seersucker suit and a gold tie, with a pale complexion and sky-blue eyes and corn-silk blond hair. He and the woman on his arm shared the same sensitive mouth.

"Whore!" somebody shouted.

Who else? My client.

I put my hand over my face and shook my head and wished I was dead, or at least in my office.

"Degenerate!" Mrs. Bolton sang out. She rushed toward the slender woman, who reared back, properly horrified. The young man gripped the woman's arm tightly; whether to protect her or himself, it wasn't quite clear.

Well, the sidewalks were filled with people who'd gotten off work, heading for the El or the LaSalle Street Station, so we had an audience. Yes we did.

And Mrs. Bolton was standing nose to nose with the startled woman, saying defiantly, "I am *Mrs.* Bolton—you've been up to see my husband!"

"Why, Mrs. Bolton," the woman said, backing away as best she could. "Your husband is not in his room."

"Liar!"

"If he were in the room, I wouldn't have been in there myself, I assure you."

"Lying whore . . ."

"Okay," I said, wading in, taking Mrs. Bolton by the arm, less gently this time, "that's enough."

"Don't talk to my mother that way," the young man said to Mrs. Bolton.

"I'll talk to her any way I like, you little degenerate."

And the young man slapped my client. It was a loud, ringing slap, and drew blood from one corner of her wide mouth.

I pointed a finger at the kid's nose. "That wasn't nice. Back away."

My client's eyes were glittering; she was smiling, a blood-flecked smile that wasn't the sanest thing I ever saw. Despite the gleeful expression, she began to scream things at the couple: "Whore! Degenerate!"

"Oh Christ," I said, wishing I'd listened to my old man and finished college.

We were encircled by a crowd who watched all this with bemused interest, some people smiling, others frowning, others frankly amazed. In the street the clop-clop of an approaching mounted police officer, interrupted in the pursuit of parking violators, cut through the din. A tall, lanky officer, he climbed off his mount and pushed through the crowd.

"What's going on here?" he asked.

"This little degenerate hit me," my client said, wearing her bloody mouth and her righteous indignation like medals, and she grabbed the kid by the tie and yanked the poor son of a bitch by it, jerking him silly.

It made me laugh. It was amusing only in a sick way, but I was sick enough to appreciate it.

"That'll be all of that," the officer said. "Now what happened here?"

I filled him in, in a general way, while my client interrupted with occasional non sequiturs; the mother and son just stood there looking chagrined about being the center of attention for perhaps a score of onlookers.

"I want that dirty little brute arrested," Mrs. Bolton said, through an off-white picket fence of clenched teeth. "I'm a victim of assault!"

The poor shaken kid was hardly a brute, and he was cleaner than most, but he admitted having struck her, when the officer asked him.

"I'm going to have to take you in, son," the officer said.

The boy looked like he might cry. Head bowed, he shrugged and his mother, eyes brimming with tears herself, hugged him.

The officer went to a call box and summoned a squad car and soon the boy was sent away, the mother waiting pitifully at the curb as the car pulled off, the boy's pale face looking back, a sad cameo in the window.

I was at my client's side.

"Let me help you get home, Mrs. Bolton," I said, taking her arm again.

She smiled tightly, patronizingly, withdrew her arm. "I'm fine,

Mr. Heller. I can take care of myself. I thank you for your assistance."

And she rolled like a tank through what remained of the crowd, toward the El station.

I stood there a while, trying to gather my wits; it would have taken a better detective than yours truly to find them, however, so, finally, I approached the shattered woman who still stood at the curb. The crowd was gone. So was the mounted officer. All that remained were a few horse apples and me.

"I'm sorry about all that," I told her.

She looked at me, her face smooth, her eyes sad; they were a darker blue than her son's. "What's your role in this?"

"I'm an investigator. Mrs. Bolton suspects her husband of infidelity."

She laughed harshly—a very harsh laugh for such a refined woman. "My understanding is that Mrs. Bolton has suspected that for some fourteen years—and without foundation. But at this point, it would seem moot, one would think."

"Moot? What are you talking about?"

"The Boltons have been separated for months. Mr. Bolton is suing her for divorce."

"What? Since when?"

"Why, since January."

"Then Bolton *does* live at the Van Buren Hotel, here?"

"Yes. My brother and I have known Mr. Bolton for years. My son Charles came up to Chicago recently, to find work, and Joe—Mr. Bolton—is helping him find a job."

"You're, uh, not from Chicago?"

"I live in Woodstock. I'm a widow. Have you any other questions?"

"Excuse me, ma'am. I'm sorry about this. Really. My client misled me about a few things." I tipped my hat to her.

She warmed up a bit; gave me a smile. Tentative, but a smile. "Your apology is accepted, mister . . . ?"

"Heller," I said. "Nathan. And your name?"

"Marie Winston," she said, and extended her gloved hand.

I grasped it, smiled.

"Well," I said, shrugged, smiled, tipped my hat again, and headed back for my office.

It wasn't the first time a client had lied to me, and it sure wouldn't be the last. But I'd never been lied to in quite this way. For one thing, I wasn't sure Mildred Bolton knew she *was* lying. This lady clearly did not have all her marbles.

I put the hundred bucks in the bank and the matter out of my mind, until I received a phone call, on the afternoon of June 14.

"This is Marie Winston, Mr. Heller. Do you remember me?"

At first, frankly, I didn't; but I said, "Certainly. What can I do for you, Mrs. Winston?"

"That . . . incident out in front of the Van Buren Hotel last Wednesday, which you witnessed . . ."

"Oh yes. What about it?"

"Mrs. Bolton has insisted on pressing charges. I wonder if you could appear in police court tomorrow morning, and explain what happened?"

"Well . . ."

"Mr. Heller, I would greatly appreciate it."

I don't like turning down attractive women, even on the telephone; but there was more to it than that: the emotion in her voice got to me.

"Well, sure," I said.

So the next morning I headed over to the south Loop police court and spoke my piece. I kept to the facts, which I felt would pretty much exonerate all concerned. The circumstances were, as they say, extenuating.

Mildred Bolton, who glared at me as if I'd betrayed her, approached the bench and spoke of the young man's "unprovoked assault." She claimed to be suffering physically and mentally from the blow she'd received. The latter, at least, was believable. Her eyes were round and wild as she answered the judge's questions.

When the judge fined young Winston one hundred dollars, Mrs. Bolton stood in her place in the gallery and began to clap. Loudly. The judge looked at her, too startled to rap his gavel and demand order; then she flounced out of the courtroom very girlishly, tossing her raccoon stole over her shoulder, exulting in her victory.

An embarrassed silence fell across the room. And it's hard to embarrass hookers, a brace of which were awaiting their turn at the docket.

Then the judge pounded his gavel and said, "The court vacates this young man's fine."

Winston, who'd been hangdog throughout the proceedings, brightened like his switch had been turned on. He pumped his lawyer's hand and turned to his mother, seated behind him just beyond the railing, and they hugged.

On the way out Marie Winston, smiling gently, touched my arm and said, "Thank you very much, Mr. Heller."

"I don't think I made much difference."

"I think you did. The judge vacated the fine, after all."

"Hell, I had nothing to do with that. Mildred was your star witness."

"In a way I guess she was."

"I notice her husband wasn't here."

Son Charles spoke up. "No, he's at work. He . . . well, he thought it was better he not be here. We figured *that woman* would be here, after all."

" 'That woman' is sick."

"In the head," Charles said bitterly.

"That's right. You or I could be sick that way, too. Somebody ought to help her."

Marie Winston, straining to find some compassion for Mildred Bolton, said, "Who would you suggest?"

"Damnit," I said, "the husband. He's been with her fourteen years. She didn't get this way overnight. The way I see it, he's got a responsibility to get her some goddamn *help* before he dumps her by the side of the road."

Mrs. Winston smiled at that, some compassion coming through after all. "You have a very modern point of view, Mr. Heller."

"Not really. I'm not even used to talkies yet. Anyway, I'll see you, Mrs. Winston. Charles."

And I left the graystone building and climbed in my '32 Auburn and drove back to my office. I parked in the alley, in my space, and walked over to the Berghoff for lunch. I think I hoped to find Bolton there. But he wasn't.

I went back to the office and puttered a while; I had a pile of retail credit-risk checks to whittle away at.

Hell with it, I thought, and walked over to Bolton's office building, a narrow, fifteen-story, white granite structure just behind the Federal Reserve on West Jackson, next to the El. Bolton was doing all right—better than me, certainly—but as a broker he was in the financial district only by a hair. No doubt he was a relatively small-time insurance broker, making twenty or twenty-five grand a year. Big money by my standards, but a lot of guys over at the Board of Trade spilled more than that.

There was no lobby really, just a wide hall between facing rows of shops—newsstand, travel agency, cigar store. The uniformed elevator operator, a skinny, pockmarked guy about my age, was waiting for a passenger. I was it.

"Tenth floor," I told him, and he took me up.

He was pulling open the cage doors when we heard the air crack, three times.

"What the hell was that?" he said.

"It wasn't a car backfiring," I said. "You better stay here."

I moved cautiously out into the hall. The elevators came up a central shaft, with a squared-off "c" of offices all about. I glanced quickly at the names on the pebbled glass in the wood-partition walls, and finally lit upon BOLTON AND SCHMIDT, INSURANCE BROKERS. I swallowed and moved cautiously in that direction as the door flew open and a young woman flew out—a dark-haired dish of maybe twenty with wide eyes and a face drained of blood, her silk stockings flashing as she rushed my way.

She fell into my arms and I said, "Are you wounded?"

"No," she swallowed, "but somebody is."

The poor kid was gasping for air; I hauled her toward the bank of elevators. Even under the strain, I was enjoying the feel and smell of her.

"You wouldn't be Joseph Bolton's secretary, by any chance?" I asked, helping her onto the elevator.

She nodded, eyes still huge.

"Take her down," I told the operator.

And I headed back for that office. I was nearly there when I met Joseph Bolton, as he lurched down the hall. He had a gun in his hand. His light brown suitcoat was splotched with blood in several places; so was his right arm. He wasn't wearing his eyeglasses, which made his face seem naked somehow. His expression seemed at once frightened, pained, and sorrowful.

He staggered toward me like a child taking its first steps, and I held my arms out to him like daddy. But they were more likely his last steps: he fell to the marble floor and began to writhe, tracing abstract designs in his own blood on the smooth surface.

I moved toward him and he pointed the gun at me, a little .32 revolver. "Stay away! Stay away!"

"Okay, bud, okay," I said.

I heard someone laughing.

A woman.

I looked up and in the office doorway, feet planted like a giant surveying a puny world, was dumpy little Mildred, in her floral housedress and raccoon stole. Her mug was split in a big goofy smile.

"Don't pay any attention to him, Mr. Heller," she said, lightly. "He's just faking."

"He's shot to shit, lady!" I said.

Keeping their distance out of respect and fear were various tenth-floor tenants, standing near their various offices, as if witnessing some strange performance.

"Keep her away from me!" Bolton managed to shout. His mouth

was bubbling with blood. His body moved slowly across the marble floor like a slug, leaving a slimy red trail.

I moved to Mrs. Bolton, stood between her and Bolton. "You just take it easy . . ."

Mrs. Bolton, giggling, peeked out from in back of me. "Look at him, fooling everybody."

"You behave," I told her. Then I called out to a businessman of about fifty near the elevators. I asked him if there were any doctors in the building, and he said yes, and I said then for Christsake go get one.

"Why don't you get up and stop faking?" she said teasingly to her fallen husband, the Southern drawl dripping off her words. She craned her neck around me to see him, like she couldn't bear to miss a moment of the show.

"Keep her away! Keep her away!"

Bolton continued to writhe like a wounded snake, but he kept clutching that gun, and wouldn't let anyone near him. He would cry out that he couldn't breathe, beating his legs against the floor, but he seemed always conscious of his wife's presence. He would move his head so as to keep my body between him and her round cold glittering eyes.

"Don't you mind Joe, Mr. Heller. He's just putting on an act."

If so, I had a hunch it was his final performance.

And now he began to scream in pain.

I approached him and he looked at me with tears in his eyes, eyes that bore the confusion of a child in pain, and he relented, allowed me to come close, handed me the gun, like he was offering a gift. I accepted it, by the nose of the thing, and dropped it in my pocket.

"Did you shoot yourself, Mr. Bolton?" I asked him.

"Keep that woman away from me," he managed, lips bloody.

"He's not really hurt," his wife said, mincingly, from the office doorway.

"Did your wife shoot you?"

"Just keep her away . . ."

Two people in white came rushing toward us—a doctor and a nurse—and I stepped aside, but the doctor, a middle-aged, rather heavyset man with glasses, asked if I'd give him a hand. I said sure and pitched in.

Bolton was a big man, nearly two hundred pounds I'd say, and pretty much dead weight; we staggered toward the elevator like drunks. Like Bolton himself had staggered toward me, actually. The nurse tagged along.

So did Mrs. Bolton.

The nurse, young, blond, slender, did her best to keep Mrs. Bolton out of the elevator, but Mrs. Bolton pushed her way through like a fullback. The doctor and I, bracing Bolton, couldn't help the young nurse.

Bolton, barely conscious, said, "Please . . . please, keep her away."

"Now, now," Mrs. Bolton said, the violence of her entry into the elevator forgotten (by her), standing almost primly, hands folded over the big black purse, "everything will be all right, dear. You'll see."

Bolton began to moan; the pain it suggested wasn't entirely physical.

On the thirteenth floor, a second doctor met us and took my place hauling Bolton, and I went ahead and opened the door onto a waiting room where patients, having witnessed the doctor and nurse race madly out of the office, were milling about expectantly. The nurse guided the doctors and their burden down a hall into an X-ray room. The nurse shut the door on them and faced Mrs. Bolton with a firm look.

"I'm sorry, Mrs. Bolton, you'll have to wait."

"Is that so?" she said.

"Mrs. Bolton," I said, touching her arm.

She glared at me. "Who invited you?"

I resisted the urge to say, *you did, you fucking cow*, and just stood back while she moved up and down the narrow corridor between the offices and examining rooms, searching for a door that would lead her to her beloved husband. She trundled up and down, grunting, talking to herself, and the nurse looked at me helplessly.

"She *is* the wife," I said, with a facial shrug.

The nurse sighed heavily and went to a door adjacent to the X-ray room and called out to Mrs. Bolton; Mrs. Bolton whirled and looked at her fiercely.

"You can view your husband's treatment from in here," the nurse said.

Mrs. Bolton smiled in tight triumph and drove her taxicab of a body into the room. I followed her. Don't ask me why.

A wide glass panel looked in on the X-ray room. Mrs. Bolton climbed onto an examination table, got up on her knees, and watched the flurry of activity beyond the glass, as her husband lay on a table being attended by the pair of frantic doctors.

"Did you shoot him, Mrs. Bolton?" I asked her.

She frowned but did not look at me. "Are *you* still here?"

"You lied to me, Mrs. Bolton."

"No, I didn't. And I didn't shoot him, either."

"What happened in there?"

"I never touched that gun." She was moving her head side to side, like somebody in the bleachers trying to see past the person sitting in front.

"Did your husband shoot himself?"

She made a childishly smug face. "Joe's just faking to get everybody's sympathy. He's not really hurt."

The door opened behind me and I turned to see a police officer step in.

The officer frowned at us, and shook his head as if to say "Oh, no." It was an understandable response: it was the same cop, the mounted officer, who'd come upon the disturbance outside the Van Buren Hotel. Not surprising, really—this part of the Loop was his beat, or anyway his horse's.

He crooked his finger for me to step out in the hall and I did.

"I heard a murder was being committed up on the tenth floor of 166," he explained, meaning 166 West Jackson. "Do you know what happened? Did you see it?"

I told him what I knew, which for somebody on the scene was damned little.

"Did she do it?" the officer asked.

"The gun was in the husband's hand," I shrugged. "Speaking of which . . ."

And I took the little revolver out of my pocket, holding the gun by its nose again.

"What make is this?" the officer said, taking it.

"I don't recognize it."

He read off the side: "Narizmande Eibar Spair. Thirty-two caliber."

"It got the job done."

He held the gun so that his hand avoided the grip; tried to break it open, but couldn't.

"What's wrong with this thing?" he said.

"The trigger's been snapped on empty shells, I'd say. After six slugs were gone, the shooter kept shooting. Just once around wouldn't drive the shells into the barrel like that."

"Judas," the officer said.

The X-ray room's door opened and the doctor I'd shared the elevator and Bolton's dead weight with stepped into the hall, bloody and bowed.

"He's dead," the doctor said, wearily. "Choked to death on his own blood, poor bastard."

I said nothing; just glanced at the cop, who shrugged.

"The wife's in there," I said, pointing.

But I was pointing to Mrs. Bolton, who had stepped out into the hall. She was smiling pleasantly.

She said, "You're not going to frighten me about Joe. He's a great big man and as strong as a horse. Of course, I begin to think he ought to go to the hospital this time—for a while."

"Mrs. Bolton," the doctor said, flatly, with no sympathy whatsoever, "your husband is dead."

Like a spiteful brat, she stuck out her tongue. "Liar," she said.

The doctor sighed, turned to the cop. "Shall I call the morgue, or would you like the honor?"

"You should make the call, Doctor," the officer said.

Mrs. Bolton moved slowly toward the door to the X-ray room, from which the other doctor, his smock blood-spattered, emerged. She seemed to lose her footing, then, and I took her arm yet again. This time she accepted the help. I walked her into the room and she approached the body, stroked its brow with stubby fingers.

"I can't believe he'd go," she said.

From behind me, the doctor said, "He's dead, Mrs. Bolton. Please leave the room."

Still stroking her late husband's brow, she said, "He feels cold. So cold."

She kissed his cheek.

Then she smiled down at the body and patted its head, as one might a sleeping child, and said, "He's got a beautiful head, hasn't he?"

The officer stepped into the room and said, "You'd better come along with me, Mrs. Bolton. Captain Stege wants to talk to you."

"You're making a terrible mistake. I didn't shoot him."

He took her arm; she assumed a regal posture. He asked her if she would like him to notify any relatives or friends.

"I have no relatives or friends," she said, proudly. "I never had anybody or wanted anybody except Joe."

A crowd was waiting on the street. Damn near a mob, and at the forefront were the newshounds, legmen and cameramen alike. Cameras were clicking away as Davis of the *News* and a couple of others blocked the car waiting at the curb to take Mrs. Bolton to the Homicide Bureau. The mounted cop, with her in tow, brushed them and their questions aside and soon the car, with her in it, was inching into the late afternoon traffic. The reporters and photogs began flagging cabs to take quick pursuit, but snide, boyish Davis lingered to ask me a question.

"What were you doing here, Heller?"

"Getting a hangnail looked at up at the doctor's office."

"Fuck, Heller, you got blood all over you!"

I shrugged, lifted my middle finger. "Hell of a hangnail."

He smirked and I smirked and pushed through the crowd and hoofed it back to my office.

I was sitting at my desk, about an hour later, when the phone rang.

"Get your ass over here!"

"Captain Stege?"

"No, Walter Winchell. You were an eyewitness to a homicide, Heller! Get your ass over here!"

The phone clicked in my ear and I shrugged to nobody and got my hat and went over to the First District Station, entering off Eleventh. It was a new, modern, nondescript high rise; if this was the future, who needed it.

In Stege's clean little office, from behind his desk, the clean little cop looked out his black-rimmed, round-lensed glasses at me and said, "Did you see her do it?"

"I told the officer at the scene all about it, Captain."

"You didn't make a statement."

"Get a stenographer in here and I will."

He did and I did.

That seemed to cool the stocky little cop down. He and I had been adversaries once, though were getting along better these days. But there was still a strain.

Thought gripped his doughy, owlish countenance. "How do you read it, Heller?"

"I don't know. He had the gun. Maybe it was suicide."

"Everybody in that building agrees with you. Bolton's been having a lot of trouble with his better half. They think she drove him to suicide, finally. But there's a hitch."

"Yeah?"

"Suicides don't usually shoot themselves five times, two of 'em in the back."

I had to give him that.

"You think she's nuts?" Stege asked.

"Nuttier than a fruitcake."

"Maybe. But that was murder—premeditated."

"Oh, I doubt that, Captain. Don't you know a crime of passion when you see it? Doesn't the unwritten law apply to women as well as men?"

"The answer to your question is yes to the first, and no to the second. You want to see something?"

"Sure."

From his desk he handed me a small slip of paper.

It was a receipt for a gun sold on June 11 by the Hammond Loan Company of Hammond, Indiana, to a Mrs. Sarah Weston.

"That was in her purse," Stege said, smugly. "Along with a powder puff, a hanky, and some prayer leaflets."

"And you think Sarah Weston is just a name Mrs. Bolton used to buy the .32 from the pawn shop?"

"Certainly. And that slip—found in a narrow side pocket in the lining of her purse—proves premeditation."

"Does it, Captain?" I said, smiling, standing, hat in hand. "It seems to me premeditation would have warned her to get *rid* of that receipt. But then, what do I know? I'm not a cop." From the doorway I said, "Just a detective."

And I left him there to mull that over.

In the corridor, on my way out, Sam Backus buttonholed me.

"Got a minute for a pal, Nate?"

"Sam, if we were pals, I'd see you someplace besides court."

Sam was with the Public Defender's office, and I'd bumped into him from time to time, dating back to my cop days. He was a conscientious and skillful attorney who, in better times, might have had a lucrative private practice; in times like these, he was glad to have a job. Sam's sharp features and receding hairline gave the smallish man a ferretlike appearance; he was similarly intense, too.

"My client says she employed you to do some work for her," he said, in a rush. "She'd like you to continue—"

"Wait a minute, wait a minute—your client? Not Mrs. Mildred Bolton?"

"Yes."

"She's poison. You're on your own."

"She tells me you were given a hundred-dollar retainer."

"Well, that's true, but I figured I earned it."

"She figures you owe her some work, or some dough."

"Sam, she lied to me. She misrepresented herself and her intentions." I was walking out the building and he was staying right with me.

"She's a disturbed individual. And she's maintaining she didn't kill her husband."

"They got her cold." I told him about Stege's evidence.

"It could've been planted," he said, meaning the receipt. "Look, Bolton's secretary was up there, and Mrs. Bolton says he and the girl—an Angela something, sounds like 'who-you'—were having an affair."

"I thought the affair was supposed to be with Marie Winston."

"Her, too. Bolton must've been a real ladies' man. And the Winston woman was up there at that office this afternoon, too, before the shooting."

"Was she there during the shooting, though?"

"I don't know. I need to find out. The Public Defender's office doesn't have an investigative staff, you know that, Nate. And I can't afford to hire anybody, and I don't have the time to do the legwork myself. You owe her some days. Deliver."

He had a point.

I gathered some names from Sam, and the next morning I began to interview the participants.

"An affair with Joe?" Angela Houyoux said. "Why, that's nonsense."

We were in the outer office of BOLTON AND SCHMIDT. She'd given me the nickel tour of the place: one outer office, and two inner ones, the one to the south having been Bolton's. The crime scene told me nothing. Angela, the sweet-smelling dark-haired beauty who'd tumbled into my arms and the elevator yesterday, did.

"I was rather shaken by Mrs. Bolton's behavior at first—and his. But then it became rather routine to come to the office and find the glass in the door broken, or Mr. Bolton with his hands cut from taking a knife away from Mrs. Bolton. After a few weeks, I grew quite accustomed to having dictation interrupted while Mr. and Mrs. Bolton scuffled and fought and yelled. Lately they argued about Mrs. Winston a lot."

"How was your relationship with Mrs. Bolton?"

"Spotty, I guess you'd call it. Sometimes she'd seem to think I was interested in her husband. Other times she'd confide in me like a sister. I never said much to her. I'd just shrug my shoulders or just look at her kind of sympathetic. I had the feeling she didn't have anybody else to talk to about this. She'd cry and say her husband was unfaithful—I didn't dare point out they'd been separated for a year and that Mr. Bolton had filed for divorce and all. One time . . . well, maybe I shouldn't say it."

"Say it."

"One time she said she 'just might kill' her husband. She said they never convict a woman for murder in Cook County."

Others in the building at West Jackson told similar tales. Bolton's business partner, Schmidt, wondered why Bolton bothered to get an injunction to keep his wife out of the office, but then refused to mail her her temporary alimony, giving her a reason to come to the office all the time.

"He would dole out the money, two or three dollars at a time," Schmidt said. "He could have paid her what she had coming for a month, or at least a week—Joe made decent money. It would've got rid of her. Why parcel it out?"

The elevator operator I'd met yesterday had a particularly wild yarn.

"Yesterday, early afternoon, Mr. Bolton got on at the ninth floor. He seemed in an awful hurry and said, 'Shoot me up to eleven.' I had a signal to stop at ten, so I made the stop and Mrs. Bolton came charging aboard. Mr. Bolton was right next to me. He kind of hid behind me and said, 'For God's sake, she'll kill us both!' I sort of forced the door closed on her, and she stood there in the corridor and raised her fist and said, 'Goddamnit, I'll fix you!' I guess she meant Bolton, not me."

"Apparently."

"Anyway, I took him up to eleven and he kind of sighed and as he got off he said, 'It's just hell, isn't it?' I said it was a damn shame he couldn't do anything about it."

"This was yesterday."

"Yes, sir. Not long before he was killed."

"Did it occur to you, at the time, it might lead to that?"

"No, sir. It was pretty typical, actually. I helped him escape from her before. And I kept her from getting on the elevator downstairs, sometimes. After all, he had an injunction to keep her from 'molesting him at his place of business,' he said."

Even the heavyset doctor up on thirteen found time for me.

"I think they were *both* sick," he said, rather bitterly I thought.

"What do you mean, Doctor?"

"I mean that I've administered more first aid to that man than a battlefield physician. That woman has beaten her husband, cut him with a knife, with a razor, created commotions and scenes with such regularity that the patrol wagon coming for Mildred is a commonplace occurrence on West Jackson."

"How well did you know Bolton?"

"We were friendly. God knows I spent enough time with him, patching him up. He should've been a much more successful man than he was, you know. She drove him out of one job and another. I never understood him."

"Oh?"

"Well, they live, or lived, in Hyde Park. That's a university neighborhood. Fairly refined, very intellectual, really."

"Was Bolton a scholar?"

"He had bookish interests. He liked having the University of Chicago handy. Now why would a man of his sensibilities endure a violent harridan like Mildred Bolton?"

"In my trade, Doc," I said, "we call that a mystery."

I talked to more people. I talked to a pretty blond legal secretary named Peggy O'Reilly who, in 1933, had been employed by Ocean Accident and Guarantee Company. Joseph Bolton, Jr., had been a business associate there.

"His desk was four feet from mine," she said. "But I never went out with him. There was no social contact whatsoever, but Mrs. Bolton didn't believe that. She came into the office and accused me of—well, called me a 'dirty hussy,' if you must know. I asked her to step out into the hall where we wouldn't attract so much attention, and she did—and proceeded to tear my clothes off me. She tore the clothes off my body, scratched my neck, my face, kicked me, it was horrible. The attention it attracted . . . oh, dear. Several hundred people witnessed the sight—two nice men pulled her off of me. I was badly bruised and out of the office a week. When I came back, Mr. Bolton had been discharged."

A pattern was forming here, one I'd seen before; but usually it was the wife who was battered and yet somehow endured and even encouraged the twisted union. Only Bolton was a battered husband, a strapping man who never turned physically on his abusing wife; his only punishment had been to withhold that money from her, dole it out a few bucks at a time. That was the only satisfaction, the only revenge, he'd been able to extract.

At the Van Buren Hotel I knocked on the door of what had been Bolton's room. 3C.

Young Charles Winston answered. He looked terrible. Pale as milk, only not near as healthy. Eyes bloodshot. He was in a T-shirt and boxer shorts. The other times I'd seen him he'd been fully and even nattily attired.

"Put some clothes on," I said. "We have to talk."

In the saloon below the hotel we did that very thing.

"Joe was a great guy," he said, eyes brimming with tears. He would have cried into his beer, only he was having a mixed drink. I was picking up the tab, so Mildred Bolton was buying it.

"Is your mother still in town?"

He looked up with sharp curiosity. "No. She's back in Woodstock. Why?"

"She was up at the office shortly before Bolton was killed."

"I know. I was there, too."

"Oh?" Now, that was news.

"We went right over, after the hearing."

"To tell him how it came out?"

"Yes, and to thank him. You see, after that incident out in front, last Wednesday, when they took me off to jail, Mother went to see Joe. They met at the Twelfth Street Bus Depot. She asked him if he would take care of my bail—she could have had her brother do it, in the morning, but I'd have had to spend the night in jail first." He smiled fondly. "Joe went right over to the police station with the money and got me out."

"That was white of him."

"Sure was. Then we met Mother over at the taproom of the Auditorium Hotel."

Very posh digs; interesting place for folks who lived at the Van Buren to be hanging out.

"Unfortunately, I'd taken time to stop back at the hotel to pick up some packages my mother had left behind. Mrs. Bolton must've been waiting here for me. She followed me to the Auditorium taproom, where she attacked me with her fists, and told the crowd in no uncertain terms, and in a voice to wake the dead, that my mother was"—he shook his head—" 'nothing but a whore' and such. Finally the management ejected her."

"Was your mother in love with Joe?"

He looked at me sharply. "Of course not. They were friendly. That's the extent of it."

"When did you and your mother leave Bolton's office?"

"Yesterday? About one-thirty. Mrs. Bolton was announced as being in the outer office, and we just got the hell out."

"Neither of you lingered."

"No. Are you going to talk to my mother?"

"Probably."

"I wish you wouldn't," he said glumly.

I drank my beer, studying the kid.

"Maybe I won't have to," I said, smiled at him, patted his shoulder, and left.

I met with public defender Backus in a small interrogation room at the First District Station.

"Your client is guilty," I said.

I was sitting. He was standing. Pacing.

"The secretary was in the outer office at all times," I said. "In view of other witnesses. The Winstons left around one-thirty. They were seen leaving by the elevator operator on duty."

"One of them could have sneaked back up the stairs . . ."

"I don't think so. Anyway, this meeting ends my participation, other than a report I'll type up for you. I've used up the hundred."

From my notes I read off summaries of the various interviews I'd conducted. He finally sat, sweat beading his brow, eyes slitted behind the glasses.

"She says she didn't do it," he said.

"She says a lot of things. I think you can get her off, anyway."

He smirked. "Are you a lawyer now?"

"No. Just a guy who's been in the thick of this bizarre fucking case since day one."

"I bow to your experience if not expertise."

"You can plead her insane, Sam."

"A very tough defense to pull off, and besides, she won't hear of it. She wants no psychiatrists, no alienists involved."

"You can still get her off."

"How in hell?"

I let some air out. "I'm going to have to talk to her before I say any more. It's going to have to be up to her."

"You can't tell me?"

"You're not my client."

Mildred Bolton was.

And she was ushered into the interrogation room by a matron who then waited outside the door. She wore the same floral print dress, but the raccoon stole was gone. She smiled faintly upon seeing me, sat across from me.

"You been having fun with the press, Mildred, haven't you?"

"I sure have. They call me 'Marble Mildred.' They think I'm cold."

"They think it's unusual for a widow to joke about her dead husband."

"They're silly people. They asked me the name of my attorney and I said, 'Horsefeathers.' " She laughed. That struck her very funny; she was proud of herself over that witty remark.

"I'm glad you can find something to smile about."

"I'm getting hundreds of letters, you know. Fan mail! They say, 'You should have killed him whether you did or not.' I'm not the only woman wronged in Chicago, you know."

"They've got you dead bang, Mildred. I've seen some of the evidence. I've talked to the witnesses."

"Did you talk to Mrs. Winston? It was her fault, you know. Her and that . . . that boy."

"You went to see Joe after the boy was fined in court."

"Yes! I called him and told him that the little degenerate had been convicted and fined. Then I asked Joe, did he have any money, because I didn't have anything to eat, and he said yes. So I went to the office and when I got there he tried to give me a check for ten dollars. I said, 'I guess you're going to pay that boy's fine and that's why you haven't any money for me.' He said, 'That's all you're going to get.' And I said, 'Do you mean for a whole *week*? To pay rent out of and eat on?' He said, 'Yes, that's all you get.' "

"He was punishing you."

"I suppose. We argued for about an hour and then he said he had business on another floor—that boy's lawyer is on the ninth floor, you know—and I followed him, chased him to the elevator, but he got away. I went back and said to Miss Houyoux, 'He ran away from me.' I waited in his office and in about an hour he came back. I said, 'Joe, I have been your wife for fourteen years and I think I deserve more respect and better treatment than that.' He just leaned back in his chair so cocky and said, 'You know what you are?' And then he said it."

"Said it?"

She swallowed; for the first time, those marble eyes filled with tears. "He said, 'You're just a dirty old bitch.' Then he said it again. Then I said, 'Just a dirty old bitch for fourteen years?' And I pointed the gun at him."

"Where was it?"

"It was on his desk where I put it. It was in a blue box I carried in with me."

"What did you do with it, Mildred?"

"The box?"

"The gun."

"Oh. That. I fired it at him."

I gave her a handkerchief and she dabbed her eyes with it.

"How many times did you fire the gun, Mildred?"

"I don't know. He fell over in his chair and then he got up and came toward me and he said, 'Give me that gun, give me that gun.' I said, 'No, I'm going to finish myself now. Let go of me because my hand is on the trigger!' " Her teeth were clenched. "He struggled with me, and his glasses got knocked off, but he got the gun from my hand and he went out in the hall with it. I followed him, but then I turned and went back in his office. I was going to jump out of the window, but I heard him scream in the hall and I ran to him. The gun was lying beside him and I reached for it, but he reached and got it first. I went back in the office."

"Why?"

"To jump out the window, I told you. But I just couldn't leave him. I started to go back out and when I opened the door some people were around. You were one of them, Mr. Heller."

"Where did you get that gun, Mildred?"

"At a pawn shop in Hammond, Indiana."

"To kill Joe?"

"To kill myself."

"But you didn't."

"I'm sorry I didn't. I had plenty of time to do it at home, but I wanted to do it in his office. I wanted to embarrass him."

"He was shot in the back, Mildred. Twice."

"I don't know about that. Maybe his body turned when I was firing. I don't know. I don't remember."

"You know that the prosecution will not buy your suicide claims."

"They are *not* claims!"

"I know they aren't. But they won't buy them. They'll tell the judge and the jury that all your talk of suicide is just a clever excuse to get around planning Joe's murder. In other words, that you premeditated the killing and supplied yourself with a gun—and a reason for having a gun."

"I don't know about those things."

"Would you like to walk away from this?"

"Well, of course. I'm not crazy."

Right.

"You can, I think. But it's going to be hard on you. They're going to paint you as a shrew. As a brutal woman who battered her husband. They'll suggest that Bolton was too much of a gentleman for his own good, that he should have struck back at you, physically."

She giggled. "He wasn't such a gentleman."

"Really?"

"He wasn't what you think at all. Not at all."

"What do you mean, Mildred?"

"We were married for fourteen years before he tried to get rid of me. That's a long time."

"It sure is. What is it about your husband that we're getting wrong?"

"I haven't said."

"I know that. Tell me."

"I won't tell you. I've never told a living soul. I never will."

"I think you should. I think you need to."

"I won't. I won't now. I won't ever."

"There were no other women, were there, Mildred?"

"There were countless women, countless!"

"Like Marie Winston."

"She was the worst!"

"What about her son?"

"That little . . ." She stopped herself.

"That little degenerate? That's what you seem to always call him."

She nodded, pursing her thin wide lips.

"Joe was living in a fleabag hotel," I said. "A guy with *his* money. Why?"

"It was close to his work."

"Relatively. I think it had to do with who he was living with. A young man."

"A lot of men room together."

"There were no other women, were there, Mildred? Your husband used you to hide behind, didn't he, for many years."

She was crying now. The marble woman was crying now. "I loved him. I loved him."

"I know you did. And I don't know when you discovered it. Maybe you never did, really. Maybe you just suspected, and couldn't bring yourself to admit it. Then, after he left you, after he moved out of the house, you finally decided to find out, really find out. You hired me, springing for a hundred precious bucks you'd scrimped and saved, knowing I might find things out you'd want kept quiet. Knowing I might confirm the suspicions that drove you bughouse for years."

"Stop it . . . please stop it . . ."

"Your refined husband who liked to be near a college campus. You knew there were affairs. And there were. But not with women."

She stood, squeezing my hanky in one fist. "I don't have to listen to this!"

"You do if you want to be a free woman. The unwritten law doesn't seem to apply to women as equally as it does to men. But if you tell the truth about your husband—about just who it was he was seeing behind your back—I guarantee you no jury will convict you."

Her mouth was trembling.

I stood. "It's up to you, Mildred."

"Are you going to tell Mr. Backus?"

"No. You're my client. I'll respect your wishes."

"I wish you would just go. Just go, Mr. Heller."

I went.

I told Backus nothing except that I would suggest he introduce expert testimony from an alienist. He didn't. His client wouldn't hear of it.

The papers continued to have a great time with Marble Mildred. She got to know the boys of the press, became bosom buddies with the sob sisters, warned cameramen not to take a profile pic or she'd break their lens, shouted greetings and wisecracks to one and all. She laughed and talked; being on trial for murder was a lark to her.

Of course, as the trial wore on, she grew less boisterous, even became sullen at times. On the stand she told her story more or less straight, but minus any hint her husband was bent. The prosecution, as I had told her they would, ridiculed her statement that she'd bought the .32 to do herself in. The prosecutor extolled "motherhood and wifehood," but expressed "the utmost comtempt for

Mildred Bolton." She was described as "dirt," "filth," "vicious," and more. She was sentenced to die in the electric chair.

She didn't want an appeal, a new trial.

"As far as I am concerned," she told the stunned judge, "I am perfectly satisfied with things as they now stand."

But Cook County was squeamish about electrocuting a woman; just half an hour before the execution was to take place, hair shaved above one ear, wearing special females-only electrocution shorts, Mildred was spared by Governor Horner.

Mildred, who'd been strangely blissful in contemplation of her electrocution, was less pleased with her new sentence of 199 years. Nonetheless she was a model prisoner, until August 29, 1943, when she was found slumped in her cell, wrists slashed. She had managed to smuggle some scissors in. It took her hours to die. Sitting in the darkness, waiting for the blood to empty out of her.

She left a note, stuck to one wall:

To whom it may concern. In the event of my death do not notify anybody or try to get in touch with family or friends. I wish to die as I have lived, completely alone.

What she said was true, but I wondered if I was the only person alive who knew that it hadn't been by choice.

AUTHOR'S NOTE: I wish to acknowledge the true-crime article "Joseph Bolton, the Almost Indestructible Husband" by Nellise Child. Also helpful was the Mildred Bolton entry in *Find the Woman* by Jay Robert Nash. And my thanks to my research associate George Hagenauer. Most names in the preceding fact-based story have been changed or at least altered (exceptions include the Boltons and Captain Stege); fact, speculation, and fiction are freely mixed therein.

F. PAUL WILSON

F. Paul Wilson has made a name for himself by writing well-received, intriguing tales that fall into several different genre pigeonholes. His first published books were science fiction adventures that appeared in the middle of the 1970s, but his career began to take off when *The Keep*, a compulsively readable horror/fantasy novel set in central Europe during World War II, was published in 1980. Since then he has become one of the hottest horror writers around, not that his work is accurately to be classified as horror. All his work tends to defy the genre classifications that are placed on it, as witnessed by his latest page-turner, *Black Wind*, a horror/fantasy/international thriller set mostly in Japan during World War II.

"Faces," first published in *Night Visions IV*, could be considered horror; some of the punch the story carries is due to a graphically horrific description of the details of a murder. But what makes "Faces" one of our picks for best mystery and suspense of the year is the way it depicts a cop on the trail of a serial killer, and the personal story behind the headlines.

Faces

Bite her face off.

No pain. Her dead already. Kill her quick like others. Not want make pain. Not her fault.

The boyfriend groan but not move. Face way on ground now. Got from behind. Got quick. Never see. He can live.

Girl look me after the boyfriend go down. Gasp first. When see face start scream. Two claws not cut short rip her throat before sound get loud.

Her sick-scared look just like all others. Hate that look. Hate it terrible.

Sorry, girl. Not your fault.

Chew her face skin. Chew all. Chew hard and swallow. Warm wet redness make sickish but chew and chew. Must eat face. Must get all down. Keep down.

Leave the eyes.

The boyfriend groan again. Move arm. Must leave quick. Take last look blood and teeth and stare-eyes that once pretty girlface.

Sorry, girl. Not your fault.

Got go. Get way hurry. First take money. Girl money. Take the boyfriend wallet, also too. Always take money. Need money.

Go now. Not too far. Climb wall of near building. Find dark spot where can see and not be seen. Where can wait. Soon the Detective Harrison arrive.

In downbelow can see the boyfriend roll over. Get to knees. Sway. See him look the girlfriend.

The boyfriend scream terrible. Bad to hear. Make so sad. Make cry.

Kevin Harrison heard Jacobi's voice on the other end of the line and wanted to be sick.

"Don't say it," he groaned.

"Sorry," said Jacobi. "It's another one."

"Where?"

"West Forty-ninth, right near—"

"I'll find it." All he had to do was look for the flashing red lights. "I'm on my way. Shouldn't take me too long to get in from Monroe at this hour."

"We've got all night, lieutenant." Unsaid but well understood was an admonishing, *You're the one who wants to live on Long Island.*

Beside him in the bed, Martha spoke from deep in her pillow as he hung up.

"Not another one?"

"Yeah."

"Oh, God! When is it going to stop?"

"When I catch the guy."

Her hand touched his arm, gently. "I know all this responsibility's not easy. I'm here when you need me."

"I know." He leaned over and kissed her. "Thanks."

He left the warm bed and skipped the shower. No time for that. A fresh shirt, yesterday's rumpled suit, a tie shoved into his pocket, and he was off into the winter night.

With his secure little ranch house falling away behind him, Harrison felt naked and vulnerable out here in the dark. As he headed south on Glen Cove Road toward the LIE, he realized that Martha and the kids were all that were holding him together these days. His family had become an island of sanity and stability in a world gone mad.

Everything else was in flux. For reasons he still could not comprehend, he had volunteered to head up the search for this killer. Now his whole future in the department had come to hinge on his success in finding him.

The papers had named the maniac "the Facelift Killer." As apt a name as the tabloids could want, but Harrison resented it. The moniker was callous, trivializing the mutilations perpetrated on the victims. But it had caught on with the public and they were stuck with it, especially with all the ink the story was getting.

Six killings, one a week for six weeks in a row, and eight million people in a panic. Then, for almost two weeks, the city had gone without a new slaying.

Until tonight.

Harrison's stomach pitched and rolled at the thought of having to look at one of those corpses again.

* * *

"That's enough," Harrison said, averting his eyes from the faceless thing.

The raw, gouged, bloody flesh, the exposed muscle and bone were bad enough, but it was the eyes—those naked, lidless, staring eyes were the worst.

"This makes seven," Jacobi said at his side. Squat, dark, jowly, the sergeant was chewing a big wad of gum, noisily, aggressively, as if he had a grudge against it.

"I can count. Anything new?"

"Nah. Same m.o. as ever—throat slashed, money stolen, face gnawed off."

Harrison shuddered. He had come in as Special Investigator after the third Facelift killing. He had inspected the first three via coroner's photos. Those had been awful. But nothing could match the effect of the real thing up close and still warm and oozing. This was the fourth fresh victim he had seen. There was no getting used to this kind of mutilation, no matter how many he saw. Jacobi put on a good show, but Harrison sensed the revulsion under the sergeant's armor.

And yet . . .

Beneath all the horror, Harrison sensed something. There was anger here, sick anger and hatred of spectacular proportions. But beyond that, something else, an indefinable something that had drawn him to this case. Whatever it was, that something called to him, and still held him captive.

If he could identify it, maybe he could solve this case and wrap it up. And save his ass.

If he did solve it, it would be all on his own. Because he wasn't getting much help from Jacobi, and even less from his assigned staff. He knew what they all thought—that he had taken the job as a glory grab, a shortcut to the top. Sure, they wanted to see this thing wrapped up, too, but they weren't shedding any tears over the shit he was taking in the press and on TV and from City Hall.

Their attitude was clear: *If you want the spotlight, Harrison, you gotta take the heat that goes with it*.

They were right, of course. He could have been working on a quieter case, like where all the winos were disappearing to. He'd chosen this instead. But he wasn't after the spotlight, dammit! It was this case—something about this case!

He suddenly realized that there was no one around him. The body had been carted off, Jacobi had wandered back to his car. He had been left standing alone at the far end of the alley.

And yet not alone.

Someone was watching him. He could feel it. The realization sent

a little chill—one completely unrelated to the cold February wind—
trickling down his back. A quick glance around showed no one
paying him the slightest bit of attention. He looked up.

There!

Somewhere in the darkness above, someone was watching him.
Probably from the roof. He could sense the piercing scrutiny and it
made him a little weak. That was no ghoulish neighborhood voyeur,
up there. That was the Facelift Killer.

He had to get to Jacobi, have him seal off the building. But he
couldn't act spooked. He had to act calm, casual.

See the Detective Harrison's eyes. See from way up in dark. Tall-
thin. Hair brown. Nice eyes. Soft brown eyes. Not hard like many-
many eyes. Look here. Even from here see eyes make wide. Him
know it me.

Watch the Detective Harrison turn slow. Walk slow. Tell inside
him want to run. Must leave here. Leave quick.

Bend low. Run cross roof. Jump to next. And next. Again
till most block away. Then down wall. Wrap scarf round head.
Hide bad-face. Hunch inside big-big coat. Walk through lighted
spots.

Hate light. Hate crowds. Theatres here. Movies and plays. Like
them. Some night sneak in and see. See one with man in mask.
Hang from wall behind big drapes. Make cry.

Wish there mask for me.

Follow street long way to river. See many lights across river. Far
past there is place where grew. Never want go back to there. Never.

Catch back of truck. Ride home.

Home. Bright bulb hang ceiling. Not care. The Old Jessi waiting.
The Jessi friend. Only friend. The Jessi's eyes not see. Ever. When
the Jessi look me, her face not wear sick-scared look. Hate that
look.

Come in kitchen window. The Jessi's face wrinkle-black. Smile
when hear me come. TV on. Always on. The Jessi can not watch.
Say it company for her.

"You're so late tonight."

"Hard work. Get moneys tonight."

Feel sick. Want cry. Hate kill. Wish stop.

"That's nice. Are you going to put it in the drawer?"

"Doing now."

Empty wallets. Put money in slots. Ones first slot. Fives next slot.
Then tens and twenties. So the Jessi can pay when boy bring foods.
Sometimes eat stolen foods. Mostly the Jessi call for foods.

The Old Jessi hardly walk. Good. Do not want her go out. Bad peoples round here. Many. Hurt one who not see. One bad man try hurt Jessi once. Push through door. Thought only the blind Old Jessi live here.

Lucky the Jessi not alone that day.

Not lucky bad man. Hit the Jessi. Laugh hard. Then look me. Get sick-scared look. Hate that look. Kill him quick. Put in tub. Bleed there. Bad man friend come soon after. Kill him also too. Late at night take both dead bad men out. Go through window. Carry down wall. Throw in river.

No bad men come again. Ever.

"I've been waiting all night for my bath. Do you think you can help me a little?"

Always help. But the Old Jessi always ask. The Jessi very polite.

Sponge the Old Jessi back in tub. Rinse her hair. Think of the Detective Harrison. His kind eyes. Must talk him. Want stop this. Stop now. Maybe will understand. Will. Can feel.

Seven grisly murders in eight weeks.

Kevin Harrison studied a photo of the latest victim, taken before she was mutilated. A nice eight by ten glossy furnished by her agent. A real beauty. A dancer with Broadway dreams.

He tossed the photo aside and pulled the stack of files toward him. The remnants of six lives in this pile. Somewhere within had to be an answer, the thread that linked each of them to the Facelift Killer.

But what if there was no common link? What if all the killings were at random, linked only by the fact that they were beautiful? Seven deaths, all over the city. All with their faces gnawed off. *Gnawed.*

He flipped through the victims one by one and studied their photos. He had begun to feel he knew each one of them personally:

Mary Detrick, 20, a junior at N.Y.U., killed in Washington Square Park on January 5. She was the first.

Mia Chandler, 25, a secretary at Merrill Lynch, killed January 13 in Battery Park.

Ellen Beasley, 22, a photographer's assistant, killed in an alley in Chelsea on January 22.

Hazel Hauge, 30, artist agent, killed in her Soho loft on January 27.

Elisabeth Paine, 28, housewife, killed on February 2 while jogging late in Central Park.

Joan Perrin, 25, a model from Brooklyn, pulled from her car while stopped at a light on the Upper East Side on February 8.

He picked up the eight by ten again. And the last: Liza Lee, 21,

Dancer. Lived across the river in Jersey City. Ducked into an alley for a toot with her boyfriend tonight and never came out.

Three blondes, three brunettes, one redhead. Some stacked, some on the flat side. All caucs except for Perrin. All lookers. But besides that, how in the world could these women be linked? They came from all over town, and they met their respective ends all over town. What could—

"Well, you sure hit the bullseye about that roof!" Jacobi said as he burst into the office.

Harrison straightened in his chair. "What did you find?"

"Blood."

"Whose?"

"The victim's."

"No prints? No hairs? No fibers?"

"We're working on it. But how'd you figure to check the roof top?"

"Lucky guess."

Harrison didn't want to provide Jacobi with more grist for the departmental gossip mill by mentioning his feeling of being watched from up there.

But the killer *had* been watching, hadn't he?

"Any prelims from pathology?"

Jacobi shrugged and stuffed three sticks of gum into his mouth. Then he tried to talk.

"Same as ever. Money gone, throat ripped open by a pair of sharp pointed instruments, not knives, the bite marks on the face are the usual: the teeth that made them aren't human, but the saliva is."

The "non-human" teeth part—more teeth, bigger and sharper than found in any human mouth—had baffled them all from the start. Early on someone remembered a horror novel or movie where the killer used some weird sort of false teeth to bite his victims. That had sent them off on a wild goose chase to all the dental labs looking for records of bizarre bite prostheses. No dice. No one had seen or even heard of teeth that could gnaw off a person's face.

Harrison shuddered. What could explain wounds like that? What were they dealing with here?

The irritating pops, snaps, and cracks of Jacobi's gum filled the office.

"I liked you better when you smoked."

Jacobi's reply was cut off by the phone. The sergeant picked it up.

"Detective Harrison's office!" he said, listened a moment, then, with his hand over the mouthpiece, passed the receiver to Harrison. "Some fairy wants to shpeak to you," he said with an evil grin.

"Fairy?"

"Hey," he said, getting up and walking toward the door. "I don't mind. I'm a liberal kinda guy, y'know?"

Harrison shook his head with disgust. Jacobi was getting less likeable every day.

"Hello. Harrison here."

"Shorry dishturb you, Detective Harrishon."

The voice was soft, pitched somewhere between a man's and a woman's, and sounded as if the speaker had half a mouthful of saliva. Harrison had never heard anything like it. Who could be—?

And then it struck him: It was three a.m. Only a handful of people knew he was here.

"Do I know you?"

"No. Watch you tonight. You almosht shee me in dark."

That same chill from earlier tonight ran down Harrison's back again.

"Are . . . are you who I think you are?"

There was a pause, then one soft word, more sobbed than spoken: "Yesh."

If the reply had been cocky, something along the line of *And just who do you think I am?* Harrison would have looked for much more in the way of corroboration. But that single word, and the soul deep heartbreak that propelled it, banished all doubt.

My God! He looked around frantically. No one in sight. Where the fuck was Jacobi now when he needed him? This was the Facelift Killer! He needed a trace!

Got to keep him on the line!

"I have to ask you something to be sure you are who you say you are."

"Yesh?"

"Do you take anything from the victims—I mean, besides their faces?"

"Money. Take money."

This is him! The department had withheld the money part from the papers. Only the real Facelift Killer could know!

"Can I ask you something else?"

"Yesh."

Harrison was asking this one for himself.

"What do you do with the faces?"

He had to know. The question drove him crazy at night. He dreamed about those faces. Did the killer tack them on the wall, or press them in a book, or freeze them, or did he wear them around the house like that Leatherface character from that chainsaw movie?

On the other end of the line he sensed sudden agitation and panic: "No! Can not shay! Can *not!*"

"Okay, okay. Take it easy."

"You will help shtop?"

"Oh, yes! Oh, God, yes, I'll help you stop!" He prayed his genuine heartfelt desire to end this was coming through. "I'll help you any way I can!"

There was a long pause, then:

"You hate? Hate me?"

Harrison didn't trust himself to answer that right away. He searched his feelings quickly, but carefully.

"No," he said finally. "I think you have done some awful, horrible things but, strangely enough, I don't hate you."

And that was true. Why didn't he hate this murdering maniac? Oh, he wanted to stop him more than anything in the world, and wouldn't hesitate to shoot him dead if the situation required it, but there was no personal hatred for the Facelift Killer.

What is it in you that speaks to me? he wondered.

"Shank you," said the voice, couched once more in a sob.

And then the killer hung up.

Harrison shouted into the dead phone, banged it on his desk, but the line was dead.

"What the hell's the matter with you?" Jacobi said from the office door.

"That so-called 'fairy' on the phone was the Facelift Killer, you idiot! We could have had a trace if you'd stuck around!"

"Bullshit!"

"He knew about taking the money!"

"So why'd he talk like that? That's a dumb-ass way to try to disguise your voice."

And then it suddenly hit Harrison like a sucker punch to the gut. He swallowed hard and said:

"Jacobi, how do you think your voice would sound if you had a jaw crammed full of teeth much larger and sharper than the kind found in the typical human mouth?"

Harrison took genuine pleasure in the way Jacobi's face blanched slowly to yellow-white.

He didn't get home again until after seven the following night. The whole department had been in an uproar all day. This was the first break they had had in the case. It wasn't much, but contact had been made. That was the important part. And although Harrison had done nothing he could think of to deserve any credit, he

had accepted the commissioner's compliments and encouragement
on the phone shortly before he had left the office tonight.

But what was most important to Harrison was the evidence from
the call—*Damn!* he wished it had been taped—that the killer wanted
to stop. They didn't have one more goddamn clue tonight than they'd
had yesterday, but the call offered hope that soon there might be
an end to this horror.

Martha had dinner waiting. The kids were scrubbed and pajamaed
and waiting for their goodnight kiss. He gave them each a hug and
poured himself a stiff scotch while Martha put them in the sack.

"Do you feel as tired as you look?" she said as she returned from
the bedroom wing.

She was a big woman with bright blue eyes and natural dark blond
hair. Harrison toasted her with his glass.

"The expression 'dead on his feet' has taken on a whole new
meaning for me."

She kissed him, then they sat down to eat.

He had spoken to Martha a couple of times since he had left the
house twenty hours ago. She knew about the phone call from
the Facelift Killer, about the new hope in the department about the
case, but he was glad she didn't bring it up now. He was sick of
talking about it. Instead, he sat in front of his cooling meatloaf and
wrestled with the images that had been nibbling at the edges of his
consciousness all day.

"What are you daydreaming about?" Martha said.

Without thinking, Harrison said, "Annie."

"Annie who?"

"My sister."

Martha put her fork down. "Your sister? Kevin, you don't have
a sister."

"Not any more. But I did."

Her expression was alarmed now. "Kevin, are you all right? I've
known your family for ten years. Your mother has never once mentioned—"

"We don't talk about Annie, Mar. We try not to even think about
her. She died when she was five."

"Oh. I'm sorry."

"Don't be. Annie was . . . deformed. Terribly deformed. She
never really had a chance."

Open trunk from inside. Get out. The Detective Harrison's house
here. Cold night. Cold feel good. Trunk air make sick, dizzy.

Light here. Hurry round side of house.

Darker here. No one see. Look in window. Dark but see good.

Two little ones there. Sleeping. Move away. Not want them cry.

Go more round. The Detective Harrison with lady. Sit table near window. Must be wife. Pretty but not oh-so-beauty. Not have mom-face. Not like ones who die.

Watch behind tree. Hungry. They not eat food. Talk-talk-talk. Can not hear.

The Detective Harrison do most talk. Kind face. Kind eyes. Some terrible sad there. Hides. Him understands. Heard in phone voice. Understands. Him one can stop kills.

Spent day watch the Detective Harrison car. All day watch at police house. Saw him come-go many times. Soon dark, open trunk with claw. Ride with him. Ride long. Wonder what town this?

The Detective Harrison look this way. Stare like last night. Must not see me! Must *not*!

Harrison stopped in mid-sentence and stared out the window as his skin prickled.

That *watched* feeling again.

It was the same as last night. Something was out in the backyard watching them. He strained to see through the wooded darkness outside the window but saw only shadows within shadows.

But something was *there!* He could feel it!

He got up and turned on the outside spotlights, hoping, *praying* that the backyard would be empty.

It was.

He smiled to hide his relief and glanced at Martha.

"Thought that raccoon was back."

He left the spots on and settled back into his place at the table. But the thoughts racing through his mind made eating unthinkable.

What if that maniac had followed him out here? What if the call had been a ploy to get him off-guard so the Facelift Killer could do to Martha what he had done to the other women?

My God . . .

First thing tomorrow morning he was going to call the local alarm boys and put in a security system. Cost be damned, he had to have it. Immediately!

As for tonight . . .

Tonight he'd keep the .38 under the pillow.

Run away. Run low and fast. Get bushes before light come. Must stay way now. Not come back.

The Detective Harrison *feel* me. Know when watched. Him the one, sure.

Walk in dark, in woods. See back many houses. Come park. Feel strange. See this park before. Can not be—

Then know.

Monroe! This Monroe! Born here! Live here! Hate Monroe! Monroe bad place, bad people! House, home, old home near here! There! Cross park! Old home! New color but same house.

Hate house!

Sit on froze park grass. Cry. Why Monroe? Do not want be in Monroe. The Mom gone. The Sissy gone. The Jimmy very gone. House here.

Dry tears. Watch old home long time till light go out. Wait more. Go to windows. See new folks inside. The Mom took the Sissy and go. Where? Don't know.

Go to back. Push cellar window. Crawl in. See good in dark. New folks make nice cellar. Wood on walls. Rug on floor. No chain.

Sit floor. Remember . . .

Remember hanging on wall. Look little window near ceiling. Watch kids play in park cross street. Want go with kids. Want play there with kids. Want have friends.

But the Mom won't let. Never leave basement. Too strong. Break everything. Have TV. Broke it. Have toys. Broke them. Stay in basement. Chain round waist hold to center pole. Can not leave.

Remember terrible bad things happen.

Run. Run way Monroe. Never come back.

Till now.

Now back. Still hate house! Want hurt house. See cigarettes. With matches. Light all. Burn now!

Watch rug burn. Chair burn. So hot. Run back to cold park. Watch house burn. See new folks run out. Trucks come throw water. House burn and burn.

Glad but tears come anyway.

Hate house. Now house gone. Hate Monroe.

Wonder where the Mom and the Sissy live now.

Leave Monroe for new home and the Old Jessi.

The second call came the next day. And this time they were ready for it. The tape recorders were set, the computers were waiting to begin the tracing protocol. As soon as Harrison recognized the voice, he gave the signal. On the other side of the desk, Jacobi put on a headset and people started running in all directions. Off to the races.

"I'm glad you called," Harrison said. "I've been thinking about you."

"You undershtand?" said the soft voice.

"I'm not sure."

"Musht help shtop."

"I will! I will! Tell me how!"

"Not know."

There was a pause. Harrison wasn't sure what to say next. He didn't want to push, but he had to keep him on the line.

"Did you . . . hurt anyone last night?"

"No. Shaw houshes. Your houshe. Your wife."

Harrison's blood froze. Last night—in the back yard. That had been the Facelift Killer in the dark. He looked up and saw genuine concern in Jacobi's eyes. He forced himself to speak.

"You were at my house? Why didn't you talk to me?"

"No-no! Can not let shee! Run way your house. Go mine!"

"*Yours?* You live in Monroe?"

"No! Hate Monroe! Once lived. Gone long! Burn old houshe. Never go back!"

This could be important. Harrison phrased the next question carefully.

"You burned your old house? When was that?"

If he could just get a date, a year . . .

"Lasht night."

"*Last night?*" Harrison remembered hearing the sirens and fire horns in the early morning darkness.

"Yesh! Hate houshe!"

And then the line went dead.

He looked at Jacobi who had picked up another line.

"Did we get the trace?"

"Waiting to hear. Christ, he sounds retarded, doesn't he?"

Retarded. The word sent ripples across the surface of his brain. Non-human teeth . . . Monroe . . . retarded . . . a picture was forming in the settling sediment, a picture he felt he should avoid.

"Maybe he is."

"You'd think that would make him easy to—"

Jacobi stopped, listened to the receiver, then shook his head disgustedly.

"What?"

"Got as far as the Lower East Side. He was probably calling from somewhere in one of the projects. If we'd had another thirty seconds—"

"We've got something better than a trace to some lousy pay phone," Harrison said. "We've got his old address!" He picked up his suit coat and headed for the door.

"Where we goin'?"

"Not 'we.' Me. I'm going out to Monroe."

* * *

Once he reached the town, it took Harrison less than an hour to find the Facelift Killer's last name.

He first checked with the Monroe Fire Department to find the address of last night's house fire. Then he went down to the brick fronted Town Hall and found the lot and block number. After that it was easy to look up its history of ownership. Mr. and Mrs. Elwood Scott were the current owners of the land and the charred shell of a three-bedroom ranch that sat upon it.

There had only been one other set of owners: Mr. and Mrs. Thomas Baker. He had lived most of his life in Monroe but knew nothing about the Baker family. But he knew where to find out: Captain Jeremy Hall, Chief of Police in the Incorporated Village of Monroe.

Captain Hall hadn't changed much over the years. Still had a big belly, long sideburns, and hair cut bristly short on the sides. That was the "in" look these days, but Hall had been wearing his hair like that for at least thirty years. If not for his Bronx accent, he could have played a redneck sheriff in any one of those southern chain gang movies.

After pleasantries and local-boy-leaves-home-to-become-big-city-cop-and-now-comes-to-question-small-town-cop banter, they got down to business.

"The Bakers from North Park Drive?" Hall said after he had noisily sucked the top layer off his steaming coffee. "Who could forget them? There was the mother, divorced, I believe, and the three kids—two girls and the boy."

Harrison pulled out his note pad. "The boy's name—what was it?"

"Tommy, I believe. Yeah—Tommy. I'm sure of it."

"He's the one I want."

Hall's eyes narrowed. "He is, is he? You're working on that Facelift case aren't you?"

"Right."

"And you think Tommy Baker might be your man?"

"It's a possibility. What do you know about him?"

"I know he's dead."

Harrison froze. "Dead? That can't be!"

"It sure as hell *can* be!" Without rising from his seat, he shouted through his office door. "Murph! Pull out that old file on the Baker case! Nineteen eighty-four, I believe!"

"Eighty-four?" Harrison said. He and Martha had been living in Queens then. They hadn't moved back to Monroe yet.

"Right. A real messy affair. Tommy Baker was thirteen years old when he bought it. And he bought it. *Believe* me, he bought it!"

Harrison sat in glum silence, watching his whole theory go up in smoke.

The Old Jessi sleeps. Stand by mirror near tub. Only mirror have. No like them. The Jessi not need one.

Stare face. Bad face. Teeth, teeth, teeth. And hair. Arms too thin, too long. Claws. None have claws like my. None have face like my.

Face not better. Ate pretty faces but face still same. Still cause sick-scared look. Just like at home.

Remember home. Do not want but thoughts will not go.

Faces.

The Sissy get the Mom-face. Beauty face. The Tommy get the Dad-face. Not see the Dad. Never come home anymore. Who my face? Never see where come. Where my face come? My hands come?

Remember home cellar. Hate home! Hate cellar more! Pull on chain round waist. Pull and pull. Want out. Want play. *Please*. No one let.

One day when the Mom and the Sissy go, the Tommy bring friends. Come down cellar. Bunch on stairs. Stare. First time see sick-scared look. Not understand.

Friends! Play! Throw ball them. They run. Come back with rocks and sticks. Still sick-scared look. Throw me, hit me.

Make cry. Make the Tommy laugh.

Whenever the Mom and the Sissy go, the Tommy come with boys and sticks. Poke and hit. Hurt. Little hurt on skin. Big hurt inside. Sick-scared look hurt most of all. Hate look. Hate hurt. Hate them.

Most hate the Tommy.

One night chain breaks. Wait on wall for the Tommy. Hurt him. Hurt the Tommy outside. Hurt the Tommy inside. Know because pull inside outside. The Tommy quiet. Quiet, wet, red. The Mom and the Sissy get sick-scared look and scream.

Hate that look. Run way. Hide. Never come back. Till last night.

Cry more now. Cry quiet. In tub. So the Jessi not hear.

Harrison flipped through the slim file on the Tommy Baker murder.

"This is it?"

"We didn't need to collect much paper," Captain Hall said. "I mean, the mother and sister were witnesses. There's some photos in that manila envelope at the back."

Harrison pulled it free and slipped out some large black and whites. His stomach lurched immediately.

"My *God!*"

"Yeah, he was a mess. Gutted by his older sister."

"His *sister?*"

"Yeah. Apparently she was some sort of freak of nature."

Harrison felt the floor tilt under him, felt as if he were going to slide off the chair.

"Freak?" he said, hoping Hall wouldn't notice the tremor in his voice. "What did she look like?"

"Never saw her. She took off after she killed the brother. No one's seen hide nor hair of her since. But there's a picture of the rest of the family in there."

Harrison shuffled through the file until he came to a large color family portrait. He held it up. Four people: two adults seated in chairs; a boy and a girl, about ten and eight, kneeling on the floor in front of them. A perfectly normal American family. Four smiling faces.

But where's your oldest child. Where's your big sister? Where did you hide that fifth face while posing for this?

"What was her name? The one who's not here?"

"Not sure. Carla, maybe? Look at the front sheet under *Suspect.*"

Harrison did: Carla Baker—called 'Carly,' " he said.

Hall grinned. "Right. Carly. Not bad for a guy getting ready for retirement."

Harrison didn't answer. An ineluctable sadness filled him as he stared at the incomplete family portrait.

Carly Baker . . . poor Carly . . . where did they hide you away? In the cellar? Locked in the attic? How did your brother treat you? Bad enough to deserve killing?

Probably.

"No pictures of Carly, I suppose."

"Not a one."

That figures.

"How about a description?"

"The mother gave us one but it sounded so weird, we threw it out. I mean, the girl sounded like she was half spider or something!" He drained his cup. "Then later on I got into a discussion with Doc Alberts about it. He told me he was doing deliveries back about the time this kid was born. Said they had a whole rash of monsters, all delivered within a few weeks of each other."

The room started to tilt under Harrison again.

"Early December, 1968, by chance?"

"Yeah! How'd you know?"

He felt queasy. "Lucky guess."

"Huh. Anyway, Doc Alberts said they kept it quiet while they looked into a cause, but that little group of freaks—'cluster,' he called them—was all there was. They figured that a bunch of mothers had been exposed to something nine months before, but whatever it had been was long gone. No monsters since. I understand most of them died shortly after birth, anyway."

"Not all of them."

"Not that it matters," Hall said, getting up and pouring himself a refill from the coffee pot. "Someday someone will find her skeleton, probably somewhere out in Haskins' marshes."

"Maybe." *But I wouldn't count on it.* He held up the file. "Can I get a xerox of this?"

"You mean the Facelift Killer is a twenty-year-old girl?"

Martha's face clearly registered her disbelief.

"Not just any girl. A freak. Someone so deformed she really doesn't look human. Completely uneducated and probably mentally retarded to boot."

Harrison hadn't returned to Manhattan. Instead, he'd headed straight for home, less than a mile from Town Hall. He knew the kids were at school and that Martha would be there alone. That was what he had wanted. He needed to talk this out with someone a lot more sensitive than Jacobi.

Besides, what he had learned from Captain Hall and the Baker file had dredged up the most painful memories of his life.

"A monster," Martha said.

"Yeah. Born one on the outside, *made* one on the inside. But there's another child monster I want to talk about. Not Carly Baker. Annie . . . Ann Harrison."

Martha gasped. "That sister you told me about last night?"

Harrison nodded. He knew this was going to hurt, but he had to do it, had to get it out. He was going to explode into a thousand twitching bloody pieces if he didn't.

"I was nine when she was born. December 2, 1968—a week after Carly Baker. Seven pounds, four ounces of horror. She looked more fish than human."

His sister's image was imprinted on the rear wall of his brain. And it should have been after all those hours he had spent studying her loathsome face. Only her eyes looked human. The rest of her was awful. A lipless mouth, flattened nose, sloping forehead, fingers and toes fused so that they looked more like flippers than hands and feet, a bloated body covered with shiny skin that was a dusky gray-blue. The doctors said she was that color because her heart was bad, had a defect that caused mixing of blue blood and red blood.

A repulsed nine-year-old Kevin Harrison had dubbed her The Tuna—but never within earshot of his parents.

"She wasn't supposed to live long. A few months, they said, and she'd be dead. But she didn't die. Annie lived on and on. One year. Two. My father and the doctors tried to get my mother to put her into some sort of institution, but Mom wouldn't hear of it. She kept Annie in the third bedroom and talked to her and cooed over her and cleaned up her shit and just hung over her all the time. *All* the time, Martha!"

Martha gripped his hand and nodded for him to go on.

"After a while, it got so there was nothing else in Mom's life. She wouldn't leave Annie. Family trips became a thing of the past. Christ, if she and Dad went out to a movie, *I* had to stay with Annie. No babysitter was trustworthy enough. Our whole lives seemed to center around that freak in the back bedroom. And me? I was forgotten.

"After a while I began to hate my sister."

"Kevin, you don't have to—"

"Yes, I do! I've got to tell you how it was! By the time I was fourteen—just about Tommy Baker's age when he bought it—I thought I was going to go crazy. I was getting all B's in school but did that matter? Hell, no! 'Annie rolled halfway over today. Isn't that wonderful?' " Big deal! She was five years old, for Christ sake! I was starting point guard on the high school junior varsity basketball team as a goddamn freshman, but did anyone come to my games? Hell no!

"I tell you, Martha, after five years of caring for Annie, our house was a powderkeg. Looking back now I can see it was my mother's fault for becoming so obsessed. But back then, at age fourteen, I blamed it all on Annie. I really hated her for being born a freak."

He paused before going on. This was the really hard part.

"One night, when my dad had managed to drag my mother out to some company banquet that he had to attend, I was left alone to babysit Annie. On those rare occasions, my mother would always tell me to keep Annie company—you know, read her stories and such. But I never did. I'd let her lie back there alone with our old black and white TV while I sat in the living room watching the family set. This time, however, I went into her room."

He remembered the sight of her, lying there with the covers half way up her fat little tuna body that couldn't have been much more than a yard in length. It was winter, like now, and his mother had dressed her in a flannel nightshirt. The coarse hair that grew off the back of her head had been wound into two braids and fastened with pink bows.

"Annie's eyes brightened as I came into the room. She had never spoken. Couldn't, it seemed. Her face could do virtually nothing in the way of expression, and her flipper-like arms weren't good for much, either. You had to read her eyes, and that wasn't easy. None of us knew how much of a brain Annie had, or how much she understood of what was going on around her. My mother said she was bright, but I think Mom was a little whacko on the subject of Annie.

"Anyway, I stood over her crib and started shouting at her. She quivered at the sound. I called her every dirty name in the book. And as I said each one, I poked her with my fingers—not enough to leave a bruise, but enough to let out some of the violence in me. I called her a lousy goddamn tunafish with feet. I told her how much I hated her and how I wished she had never been born. I told her everybody hated her and the only thing she was good for was a freak show. Then I said, 'I wish you were dead! Why don't you die? You were supposed to die years ago! Why don't you do everyone a favor and do it now!'

"When I ran out of breath, she looked at me with those big eyes of hers and I could see the tears in them and I knew she had understood me. She rolled over and faced the wall. I ran from the room.

"I cried myself to sleep that night. I'd thought I'd feel good telling her off, but all I kept seeing in my mind's eye was this fourteen-year-old bully shouting at a helpless five-year-old. I felt awful. I promised myself that the first opportunity I had to be alone with her the next day I'd apologize, tell her I really didn't mean the hateful things I'd said, promise to read to her and be her best friend, anything to make it up to her.

"I awoke the next morning to the sound of my mother screaming. Annie was dead."

"Oh, my God!" Martha said, her fingers digging into his arm.

"Naturally, I blamed myself."

"But you said she had a heart defect!"

"Yeah. I know. And the autopsy showed that's what killed her—her heart finally gave out. But I've never been able to get it out of my head that my words were what made her heart give up. Sounds sappy and melodramatic, I know, but I've always felt that she was just hanging on to life by the slimmest margin and that I pushed her over the edge."

"Kevin, you shouldn't have to carry that around with you! Nobody should!"

The old grief and guilt were like a slowly expanding balloon in his chest. It was getting hard to breathe.

"In my coolest, calmest, most dispassionate moments I convince myself that it was all a terrible coincidence, that she would have died that night anyway and that I had nothing to do with it."

"That's probably true, so—"

"But that doesn't change the fact that the last memory of her life was of her big brother—the guy she probably thought was the neatest kid on earth, who could run and play basketball, one of the three human beings who made up her whole world, who should have been her champion, her defender against a world that could only greet her with revulsion and rejection—standing over her crib telling her how much he hated her and how he wished she was dead!"

He felt the sobs begin to quake in his chest. He hadn't cried in over a dozen years and he had no intention of allowing himself to start now, but there didn't seem to be any stopping it. It was like running down hill at top speed—if he tried to stop before he reached bottom, he'd go head over heels and break his neck.

"Kevin, you were only fourteen," Martha said soothingly.

"Yeah, I know. But if I could go back in time for just a few seconds, I'd go back to that night and rap that rotten hateful fourteen-year-old in the mouth before he got a chance to say a single word. But I can't. I can't even say I'm sorry to Annie! I never got a chance to take it back, Martha! I never got a chance to make it up to her!"

And then he was blubbering like a goddamn wimp, letting loose half a lifetime's worth of grief and guilt, and Martha's arms were around him and she was telling him everything would be all right, all right, all right . . .

The Detective Harrison understand. Can tell. Want to go kill another face now. Must not. The Detective Harrison not like. Must stop. The Detective Harrison help stop.

Stop for good.

Best way. Only one way stop for good. Not jail. No chain, no little window. Not ever again. Never!

Only one way stop for good. The Detective Harrison will know. Will understand. Will do.

Must call. Call now. Before dark. Before pretty faces come out in night.

Harrison had pulled himself together by the time the kids came home from school. He felt strangely buoyant inside, like he'd been purged in some way. Maybe all those shrinks were right after all: sharing old hurts did help.

He played with the kids for a while, then went into the kitchen to see if Martha needed any help with slicing and dicing. He felt as close to her now as he ever had.

"You okay?" she said with a smile.

"Fine."

She had just started slicing a red pepper for the salad. He took over for her.

"Have you decided what to do?" she asked.

He had been thinking about it a lot, and had come to a decision.

"Well, I've got to inform the department about Carly Baker, but I'm going to keep her out of the papers for a while."

"Why? I'd think if she's that freakish looking, the publicity might turn up someone who's seen her."

"Possibly it will come to that. But this case is sensational enough without tabloids like the *Post* and *The Light* turning it into a circus. Besides, I'm afraid of panic leading to some poor deformed innocent getting lynched. I think I can bring her in. She *wants* to come in."

"You're sure of that?"

"She so much as told me so. Besides, I can sense it in her." He saw Martha giving him a dubious look. "I'm serious. We're somehow connected, like there's an invisible wire between us. Maybe it's because the same thing that deformed her and those other kids deformed Annie, too. And Annie was my sister. Maybe that link is why I volunteered for this case in the first place."

He finished slicing the pepper, then moved on to the mushrooms.

"And after I bring her in, I'm going to track down her mother and start prying into what went on in Monroe in February and March of sixty-eight to cause that so-called 'cluster' of freaks nine months later."

He would do that for Annie. It would be his way of saying good-bye and I'm sorry to his sister.

"But why does she take their faces?" Martha said.

"I don't know. Maybe because theirs were beautiful and hers is no doubt hideous."

"But what does she *do* with them?"

"Who knows? I'm not all that sure I *want* to know. But right now—"

The phone rang. Even before he picked it up, he had an inkling of who it was. The first sibilant syllable left no doubt.

"Ish thish the Detective Harrishon?"

"Yes."

Harrison stretched the coiled cord around the corner from the kitchen into the dining room, out of Martha's hearing.

"Will you shtop me tonight?"

"You want to give yourself up?"

"Yesh. Pleashe, yesh."

"Can you meet me at the precinct house?"

"No!"

"Okay! Okay!" God, he didn't want to spook her now. "Where? Anywhere you say."

"Jusht you."

"All right."

"Midnight. Plashe where lasht fashe took. Bring gun but not more cop."

"All right."

He was automatically agreeing to everything. He'd work out the details later.

"You undershtand, Detective Harrishon?"

"Oh, Carly, Carly, I understand more than you know!"

There was a sharp intake of breath and then silence at the other end of the line. Finally:

"You know Carly?"

"Yes, Carly. I know you." The sadness welled up in him again and it was all he could do to keep his voice from breaking. "I had a sister like you once. And you . . . you had a brother like me."

"Yesh," said that soft, breathy voice. "You undershtand. Come tonight, Detective Harrishon."

The line went dead.

Wait in shadows. The Detective Harrison will come. Will bring lots cop. Always see on TV show. Always bring lots. Protect him. Many guns.

No need. Only one gun. The Detective Harrison's gun. Him's will shoot. Stop kills. Stop forever.

The Detective Harrison must do. No one else. The Carly can not. Must be the Detective Harrison. Smart. Know the Carly. Understand.

After stop, no more ugly Carly. No more sick-scared look. Bad face will go way. Forever and ever.

Harrison had decided to go it alone.

Not completely alone. He had a van waiting a block and a half away on Seventh Avenue and a walkie-talkie clipped to his belt, but he hadn't told anyone who he was meeting or why. He knew if he did, they'd swarm all over the area and scare Carly off completely. So he had told Jacobi he was meeting an informant and that the van was just a safety measure.

He was on his own here and wanted it that way. Carly Baker

wanted to surrender to him and him alone. He understood that. It was part of that strange tenuous bond between them. No one else would do. After he had cuffed her, he would call in the wagon.

After that he would be a hero for a while. He didn't want to be a hero. All he wanted was to end this thing, end the nightmare for the city and for poor Carly Baker. She'd get help, the kind she needed, and he'd use the publicity to springboard an investigation into what had made Annie and Carly and the others in their 'cluster' what they were.

It's all going to work out fine, he told himself as he entered the alley.

He walked half its length and stood in the darkness. The brick walls of the buildings on either side soared up into the night. The ceaseless roar of the city echoed dimly behind him. The alley itself was quiet—no sound, no movement. He took out his flashlight and flicked it on.

"Carly?"

No answer.

"Carly Baker—are you here?"

More silence, then, ahead to his left, the sound of a garbage can scraping along the stony floor of the alley. He swung the light that way, and gasped.

A looming figure stood a dozen feet in front of him. It could only be Carly Baker. She stood easily as tall as he—a good six foot two—and looked like a homeless street person, one of those animated rag-piles that live on subway grates in the winter. Her head was wrapped in a dirty scarf, leaving only her glittery dark eyes showing. The rest of her was muffled in a huge, shapeless overcoat, baggy old polyester slacks with dragging cuffs, and torn sneakers.

"Where the Detective Harrishon's gun?" said the voice.

Harrison's mouth was dry but he managed to get his tongue working.

"In its holster."

"Take out. Pleashe."

Harrison didn't argue with her. The grip of his heavy Chief Special felt damn good in his hand.

The figure spread its arms; within the folds of her coat those arms seem to bend the wrong way. And were those black hooked claws protruding from the cuffs of the sleeves?

She said, "Shoot."

Harrison gaped in shock.

The Detective Harrison not shoot. Eyes wide. Hands with gun and light shake.

Say again: "Shoot!"

"Carly, no! I'm not here to kill you. I'm here to take you in, just as we agreed."

"*No!*"

Wrong! The Detective Harrison not understand! Must shoot the Carly! Kill the Carly!

"Not jail! Shoot! Shtop the kills! Shtop the Carly!"

"No! I can get you help, Carly. Really, I can! You'll go to a place where no one will hurt you. You'll get medicine to make you feel better!"

Thought him understand! Not understand! Move closer. Put claw out. Him back way. Back to wall.

"Shoot! Kill! Now!"

"No, Annie, please!"

"Not Annie! Carly! Carly!"

"Right. Carly! Don't make me do this!"

Only inches way now. Still not shoot. Other cops hiding not shoot. Why not protect?

"*Shoot!*" Pull scarf off face. Point claw at face. "End! End! *Pleashe!*"

The Detective Harrison face go white. Mouth hang open. Say, "Oh, my *God!*"

Get sick-scared look. Hate that look! Thought him understand! Say he know the Carly! Not! Stop look! *Stop!*

Not think. Claw go out. Rip throat of the Detective Harrison. Blood fly just like others.

No-No-No! Not want hurt!

The Detective Harrison gurgle. Drop gun and light. Fall. Stare.

Wait other cops shoot. Please kill the Carly. Wait.

No shoot. Then know. No cops. Only the poor Detective Harrison. Cry for the Detective Harrison. Then run. Run and climb. Up and down. Back to new home with the Old Jessi.

The Jessi glad hear Carly come. The Jessi try talk. Carly go sit tub. Close door. Cry for the Detective Harrison. Cry long time. Break mirror million piece. Not see face again. Not ever. Never.

The Jessi say, "Carly, I want my bath. Will you scrub my back?"

Stop cry. Do the Old Jessi's black back. Comb the Jessi's hair.

Feel very sad. None ever comb the Carly's hair. Ever.

JAMES M. REASONER

James M. Reasoner, whose Texas P.I. Cody has earned him a loyal following, is a writer to watch. His taut, compassionate style serves his fast-moving, well-balanced plots well, giving vivid life to his characters, male and female.

In this tense, ironic story, readers are taken through a detour into the somewhat strange world of those paranoid fanatics known as "survivalists." An unusual and satisfying story of sudden violence and greed, "The Safest Place in the World," first appeared in *An Eye for Justice*, the third annual Private Eye Writers of America anthology. Incidentally, Mr. Reasoner is married to another fine writer, Shamus and Anthony Award winner L. J. Washburn.

The Safest Place
in the World

The eye squinting at me over the sights of the automatic weapon was pale gray and insane. One burst would just about cut me in half.

The things a private eye gets into for his clients . . .

It began simply enough. All I would have to do, Connie Lamb had said, was make friends with her ex-husband Roy. Roy had legal custody of their son Jeremy, and Connie wanted to get the boy back before Roy turned him into a killer.

She was pretty upset when she came into my office on Camp Bowie Boulevard, on the west side of Fort Worth on the edge of the museum district. Sensing that just being in a private investigator's office was adding to her nervousness, I took her a couple of doors down the street to an ice cream place and calmed her down over a couple of bowls of Fudge Ripple. It was summer, after all, and what could be more soothing than a bowl of good ice cream?

"Roy didn't have any trouble getting custody," Connie said. "He did find me in bed with another man, after all. And I don't have the greatest background in the world." Her spoon rattled against the bowl as she put it down. "Before I was married I did a lot of drugs and got busted for it a few times. I just thank God I didn't mess up my chromosomes and stuff. Jeremy was always a healthy little kid."

His mother was pretty healthy, too, I thought. She was a tall brunette, her hair cut fairly short, and though she had to be in her early thirties she looked ten years younger than that. Her figure was striking, to say the least, especially in tight blue jeans and a sleeveless jersey top. I told myself sternly that I should not be thinking semi-lecherous thoughts about a potential client in distress.

"Roy's lawyer brought all of that up, of course," she was saying.

"I never had a chance. And naturally he made Roy sound like Ward Cleaver or somebody. It was disgusting." She looked out the window toward the traffic passing by on Camp Bowie, but I don't think she was seeing the cars. "I never had a chance. He's a goddamned *accountant*, after all."

I waited a moment, then asked, "How old is Jeremy now?"

"He's twelve. Roy's had him since he was nine. I guess Roy thought he wasn't old enough to brainwash until now."

"Brainwash is a strong word," I pointed out. "I suppose all parents try to mold their children in one way or another."

"He's taking Jeremy with him to that camp on weekends! He's taking him out there and teaching him how to kill!"

The ice cream parlor was doing brisk business on a hot afternoon like that one, and several people turned to look at our table. Connie's voice wasn't loud, but it carried a lot of intensity. I said, "Take it easy. I can understand you wanting to get your son back. Maybe I can help you."

"You can. If you can just get proof that Roy's getting Jeremy involved with all that paramilitary crap, I'm sure any judge would give him back to me."

I had an image in my mind of a twelve-year-old in fatigues and helmet, carrying an M-16. Maybe she had a point. A lot of judges I knew wouldn't look kindly on that sort of parental influence. If she could prove that she had cleaned up her act and wasn't sleeping around or doing drugs, she could stand a good chance of regaining custody.

"Tell me more about Roy," I said.

It was a common enough picture: Roy Lamb was an accountant, as she had told me, and worked at the livestock exchange for one of the cattle companies headquartered there. During the week he fit the stereotypical mild-mannered image of his profession. It was only on the weekends that he became a raving gun-nut, to hear her tell it. He and some friends of his gathered out in the boonies in Wise County, northwest of Fort Worth, and shot off their rifles and machine guns, practiced military maneuvers, and generally prepared themselves to survive once the godless Communists came in and took over the United States.

"He thinks he's going to be a damned guerrilla fighter," Connie said bitterly. "Either that, or the Russians will drop the bomb and he'll be a survivalist. He's got his basement stocked with all kinds of survival gear and food, and he's talking about buying a place out in the country and building an underground bunker. Then he'll move all the stuff out there. I tell you, Mr. Cody, it's kind of scary."

"Was your husband like that before you married him?"

Connie shook her head. "It started about five years ago. I put up with it for a couple of years, thinking that maybe Roy would grow out of it. It was almost like he was a little kid playing soldier. But he never changed. I was going to divorce him, but well, he kind of got the goods on me first, if you know what I mean."

I knew what she meant, all right. And I wasn't sure that Jeremy Lamb wouldn't be just as well off with his father as with her. That wasn't my decision to make, though. My job was just to gather evidence and turn it over to her. After that it was all up to her and her ex-husband and the judicial system.

"Will you take the case?" she asked, staring pitifully across the empty ice cream bowl at me.

"I'll look into it for you," I told her. I quoted her my daily rate and she nodded and reached for her purse.

"I'll give you a check," she said.

"Let's walk back down to the office. We'll fill out a contract, and you can give me a retainer then."

Back in the office, the business taken care of, she stood up and extended a hand to me. I shook it, still vaguely uncomfortable after all these years about shaking hands with women, and told her I'd call her when I had something to report. She had already given me Roy Lamb's address and phone number and told me where he worked. All that information was written down in my notebook. We were through for now, and I should have been ready to go to work.

Her hand was cool and soft, though, and as she smiled at me across the desk and said, "I know this will all work out," I knew distinctly that I didn't want her to go yet. I wanted to come up with some reason for her to stay a little longer, so that I could talk to her and look into her dark brown eyes.

I kept my mouth shut and let out a sigh of relief when the door shut behind her. The appeal she had been oozing had probably been totally unconscious on her part, but I knew one thing.

I was too damned old for that sort of stuff.

Cowtown, the city where the West begins. That's what they used to call Fort Worth. Still do, in the Chamber of Commerce brochures. And the name is authentic enough. The Old West is still alive in the spirit of the town, even after the influx of Yankees during the seventies and eighties. The livestock industry has been a vital part of the economy for over a hundred years.

But in some parts of town, Fort Worth is the city where the Hype begins.

I sat in a restaurant in the Stockyards area and watched the tourists in newly bought Stetsons as they gawked at longhorns mounted on the walls and sat on bar stools shaped like saddles. I was in a booth next to the wall, drinking dark beer and waiting for Roy Lamb.

The livestock exchange building was only a few blocks away, and Connie had told me that Roy often had lunch here. The day before I had followed the same routine, but he hadn't shown up.

Today he did. He came in about ten minutes after noon, wearing a suit and carrying a small briefcase. He was alone, so maybe he planned on getting a little work done while he ate. He was a little over six feet, with the beginnings of a paunch. His light brown hair was carefully styled and brushed, and the horned-rim glasses he wore were just the right touch with the conservative gray suit. Just like Connie had described him. He looked honest. I might have even trusted him with my money.

Of course, his honesty wasn't what was in question.

He cooperated by sitting at one of the tables between the bar and the wall, where he would have a good view of the booth where I was waiting. He set his briefcase down on the red-and-white-checked tablecloth and sprung it open, taking out a sheaf of papers. A waitress came over, and he ordered quickly, without consulting a menu.

I picked up one of the magazines I had brought with me and opened it up, holding it so that the cover was visible. I sipped my beer and began reading an article about combat shotguns and how they were perfect weapons for defending your family when it came time to ensure their survival.

I didn't look at Roy Lamb as I read.

I made it through that article and a couple of others on how to build a radiation detector from items you could find in an ordinary kitchen or some such, while Roy Lamb ate a chef's salad and drank a glass of iced tea. It looked like he wasn't going to pay any attention to me, and I was starting to wonder how many days I might have to do this.

But then he put his papers back in the briefcase, closed it, stood up. His eyes lit on the cover of the magazine, and he smiled.

A couple of steps brought him over beside my booth, and he said, "Say, I hate to bother you, but isn't that the new issue?"

I looked over the top of the magazine, keeping my face neutral, and said, "What? Oh, the magazine. Yeah, I just picked it up."

"I subscribe. My copy must be late this month. Hell of a magazine, isn't it?"

I laid the magazine down on the table, keeping my place with a finger. "Sure is," I agreed. "Lots of good information. We'd be better off if more people knew what was going on in the world."

"That's the truth," he said emphatically. He stuck out his hand. "Roy Lamb."

I shook hands and told him my name, then gestured at the other magazines on the seat beside me. "You read these, too?"

He leaned over slightly so that he could see their titles. "You bet. They're good magazines."

I nodded to the seat on the other side of the table. "You're welcome to look at these if you want. They're all new issues, and I'm just killing time waiting for a guy."

"Well . . ." Roy looked at his watch, and for a second I thought he was going to say that he had to get back to work. But then he said, "I don't have to get back right away. I got some work done while I was eating, so I think I can justify taking a few minutes off."

The few minutes turned out to be almost half an hour. He sat across from me and let me buy him another glass of iced tea, though he turned down my offer of a beer. We hit it off right away, flipping through the magazines and making comments on the articles. I'm no weapons expert, but you can't be in my line of work and not know something about guns, so I was able to keep up with what he was saying and add some remarks of my own. Anyway, Roy did most of the talking.

He was everything that Connie had told me he was. On the surface, a normal, likeable guy, but his interest in guns bordered on passion. And his politics followed right along with the philosophies of the magazines. It all came down to us versus the Russians and us versus the subversive elements in our own country who wanted to bring us down. Of course, it was always possible that a great natural disaster, like the shifting of the earth's magnetic poles, would come along first and plunge the world into chaos, beating World War III to the punch.

Whatever catastrophe happened, it was going to be up to the average man to be prepared to defend himself and his family. To *survive* . . .

And I couldn't say, even to myself, that he was necessarily wrong. Something about his attitude made me a little uncomfortable, though. It was like he was anxious for something to happen, so that he could demonstrate just how well prepared he was.

You can make friends in a hurry if you get a man to talking about his hobby. By the time Roy had to get back to the livestock exchange building we were buddies, at least in his eyes. I told him I had lunch there frequently, and he said that he did, too. Even as I said, "Maybe we'll run into each other again," I knew damn well that we would.

That was a Tuesday. By Thursday night, when Connie Lamb

called me wanting to know how things were progressing, I had had lunch with Roy twice more. He had told me about his son and the breakup of his marriage, and I had heard all about how Connie cheated on him, neglecting him and Jeremy to run around with men she met in bars. As I talked to Connie on the phone, I could hear talking and laughter and hard-driving music in the background, and I thought it was safe to assume she wasn't home studying her Sunday-school lesson.

None of my business.

I assured her that the job was going well. I had dropped a few hints already about wishing I could find a group in the area who thought the way I did, and Roy had said noncommittally that he had heard of such a group. I was sure that he was just checking with the leaders to make sure it was all right before he told me about it.

"Be sure you let me know what happens. They'll be going out to their camp this weekend. I'm certain of that. They always do."

"I'll keep you advised," I told her.

She partially covered the phone and yelled at somebody to hold on, that she was almost through, then said, "Thanks again, Mr. Cody. You don't know how much this means to me."

I told her she was welcome and hung up. I was earning my money on this one.

At lunch the next day, Roy was excited. Maybe it was the prospect of the weekend, maybe it was the fact that he was going to recruit a new member for his group.

"I spoke to some friends of mine," he told me, "some guys I go out in the field to train with. They said I could bring you with me this weekend."

"You're talking about organized survival training?" I asked.

"That's right. We rent a place out in the country, an old farm with about two hundred acres of land. It makes a great staging area."

"Military maneuvers?" I kept my voice down.

Roy nodded. "We've got a target range and an obstacle course and plenty of room for war games. It's quite a setup."

"Who runs it?"

"The commander is a man named Brian Hayes. He was a Green Beret colonel in 'Nam. Great guy. He's an expert in everything from demolitions to unarmed combat."

"Sounds great," I said enthusiastically. "What do I have to do to join?"

"Well, one of the troop has to sponsor you, but that's no problem. I'll be your sponsor. You come out this weekend and take part, and we see if you fit into the group. If you do, that's all there is to it.

If for some reason you don't like it, well, there's no hard feelings. There are just a couple of things."

"Like what?"

"It'll cost you a couple hundred dollars."

"For a weekend?" I tried to sound suitably put out.

"It's worth it, Cody. The group furnishes all the uniforms and equipment."

"Including weapons?"

He nodded. "If you don't have your own. A lot of the guys already have their own armaments."

"Well, that sounds a little more reasonable, if the fee covers all that. What's the other thing?"

"Just a little background info on you, mainly your place of employment."

I was ready for that question, even though it hadn't come up so far in our conversations. A friend of mine who worked at one of the downtown banks was prepared to tell anybody who asked that I was part of their security force. I told Roy the same thing, and he nodded happily. He would pass it along to someone higher up in the group, probably this Brian Hayes who ran the thing. If the checking up didn't go too deep—and I had a feeling it wouldn't—my story would be accepted, and so would I.

"How do I get to the place?" I asked.

"I can come by and pick you up," Roy said. "That is, if you don't mind riding up with me."

"Not at all. That sounds fine."

"That'll give you a chance to meet my son Jeremy. He'll be going with us."

I smiled. "After all you've told me, I'm looking forward to meeting him."

"Yeah, he's a great kid. Twelve years old. Just the right age to start teaching him how to be a real man."

"Damn right," I said.

He left first, heading back to his office. I stayed where I was for a long time, drinking beer and watching the tourists soak up the phony Western culture.

Jeremy was fairly tall for his age, with a touch of the gangliness that went with being twelve. His hair was blond and short, and his face had a scattering of freckles. He shook hands with me and said he was glad to meet me, and I did the same.

"Didn't I tell you he was a great kid?" Roy asked, parental pride strong in his voice.

Jeremy rode in the backseat of Roy's Volvo. Roy drove northwest out of Fort Worth toward Decatur. It was a typical summer Saturday, already hot enough to make you sweat if you were outside more than a minute. The sky was high and clear, the air almost bone-dry.

Just the kind of day to go out in the country and play war.

Roy talked quite a bit, obviously excited at the prospect of training over the weekend. He already had his camouflage fatigues on, as did Jeremy, and I could see that the mental image I had had of the boy as I talked to his mother a few days before hadn't been far wrong. There was something ridiculous about the whole situation.

"How many members do you have?" I asked Roy as we drove through a little town called Alvord. There was a nudist colony nearby, I remembered, where one of my more embarrassing cases had taken me.

"We have forty in the group right now," Roy replied, "but it's growing all the time. Small but vital, that's us."

Forty members at two hundred dollars a head. That was eight thousand dollars every weekend. Not a bad business. It sounded like ex-colonel Brian Hayes might be cleaning up.

Jeremy hadn't said much. I half-turned in the seat and asked him, "You enjoy the training, Jeremy?"

"You bet," he said. "Dad's teaching me how to shoot, and Colonel Hayes has already taught us how to kill an enemy with our bare hands, three different ways!"

There was a disturbing amount of enthusiasm in his voice, and suddenly Connie Lamb's barhopping didn't sound so much like a bad influence.

Roy said, "It's important to be prepared for the dangerous times that are coming, of course, but you'll see that one of the best things about the camp is that you can put all the mundane little details of your everyday life in perspective. For instance, I've been working on a deal for my bosses all week that's been a real killer. They're buying a big herd up in Jack County, and I've been putting the figures together for them. You wouldn't believe how many details there are to consider in a hundred-thousand-dollar deal, especially when it's a cash sale. But I can put all that behind me while I'm training this weekend."

He rattled on some more, but I didn't pay much attention. As far as I could tell, Jeremy was healthy and well cared for, at least physically. Roy and I had never talked about how much money he made, but he had to be doing all right to afford four hundred dollars every weekend for the two of them to go out to the camp. I knew he loved the boy, and Jeremy seemed to like him. I could see why a judge had given custody to Roy in the divorce action.

If it wasn't for all the paramilitary survivalism, I would have said that Jeremy would be a lot better off staying right where he was.

But I just couldn't reconcile that thinking with teaching a twelve-year-old three different ways to kill with his bare hands.

Roy turned off the highway onto an asphalt-topped county road and followed that for several miles, then turned again onto a dirt road. After a mile or so, I noticed that the land to the left of the road was now fenced. A high chain-link fence, in fact, that looked like it should have been topped with barbed wire but wasn't.

"That must be the place," I said, nodding toward the fenced-off property.

Roy glanced at me. "How did you know?"

"Lucky guess." I shrugged. "Figured you'd want your privacy. That's why the fence is there, isn't it?"

"Survival training is serious business," he said solemnly. "We don't want any of the locals blundering in and getting hurt. We get enough bad publicity."

"Boy, that's the truth." I made my voice sound bitter. "Damned newspaper and TV reporters never get things right. They always make things sound worse than they are."

"You are absolutely right, Cody. I've got a feeling you and the colonel are going to get along just fine. You'll be a regular in the group before you know it."

There was an open gate in the fence a little farther on. Roy turned in there. I was a little surprised there was no guard on the gate, but I thought I saw movement in a clump of oaks nearby. A hidden guard? That was a possibility.

The narrow driveway led through more trees, across a little dry wash, and up a hill. The old farmhouse sat among trees at the top of the hill. There were a couple dozen cars parked around on the grass.

The farmhouse looked like it had been there a long time, but it had been restored. Either that, or it had been cared for with great diligence. The wooden siding on its walls appeared newly white-washed. The trim was painted dark brown. There were two floors, and a big porch ran the entire width of the house. A small group of men sat there in rocking chairs, waiting for something.

The something must have been us, because the men stood up and came to the edge of the porch to greet us. In the lead was a man in his forties, tall and athletic, with sandy hair and a heavy mous-tache. He wore dark, aviator-style sunglasses. The other men were a little younger, but they were cut from the same mold. A couple had short, neat beards. All of them wore fatigues and looked like they had probably been born in them.

The leader snapped a casual salute, which Roy and Jeremy returned crisply. He said, "Mornin', Mr. Lamb, Jeremy. This the new man you told me about?"

"That's right, Colonel," Roy said. He quickly introduced us, and the leader turned out to be Brian Hayes, as I had suspected. His handshake was hard, almost painful, and I let myself wince a little bit.

"Glad to meet you, Mr. Cody," Hayes said. "It's always a pleasure to meet another man who believes in good old-fashioned American values."

"Nothing wrong with being a good old-fashioned American," I said.

"Of course there's nothing wrong with that. You have the fee for the weekend, I believe?"

I pulled out my wallet, gave him nine twenties and two tens. He took the bills and passed them on to one of the other men. A slight smile tugged at his lips. "We'll get you all set up," he told me. "Roy, why don't you and Jeremy go on down to the staging area after you draw your weapons from the armory. The rest of us will be down shortly, and we can get underway."

Hayes and one of the other men took me into the house while the rest of them marched off somewhere. The place was well appointed, especially the huge dining room which had been made by knocking out some walls and combining rooms. It was paneled in dark wood, with animal heads mounted on the walls, along with a collection of antique weapons. The long table was massive, made of thick slabs of wood. There was something about it that reminded me of an ancient mead hall, where the Viking warriors could gather and carouse after a hard day of pillaging.

In the back part of the house was another large room lined with metal lockers that would have looked right at home in any junior high. I was told that I could leave my clothes and personal possessions there.

They outfitted me with a set of fatigues. I felt silly, but I tried not to let that show. Get into the spirit of things, that's what I had to do. Get in there and play soldier with the rest of them.

I got the feeling that Hayes and his cadre weren't playing, though.

The armory was behind the house and had been a barn at one time. One of the men who had been on the porch was waiting there for us. He issued me an M-16. I checked the magazine. Empty.

"You'll be issued ammo for target practice later," Hayes told me. He picked up a bulky weapon that looked more like a kid's toy. "For maneuvers, we use these. They fire paint balls. I'm sure you've heard of them."

I had. They were a standard part of all these civilian war games. I had to admit, though, I was a little surprised they didn't use regular weapons and blanks. The atmosphere around the place was serious, almost grim.

Almost like it was the real thing, and not just play.

I was starting to get a bad feeling about this setup. I told myself I'd seen too many hokey TV shows that used paramilitary groups as villains, read too many action novels in that same vein. But something sure as hell wasn't right.

We went down the hill to the staging area.

Nearly all the group must have been in attendance that weekend, because there were at least thirty-five men waiting for the training to get underway. I saw a few teenagers, but no one else as young as Jeremy. And there were no women there, either. That made sense, though. To their way of thinking, it was part of a man's duty to protect defenseless females.

The men were all shapes and sizes, but they had one thing in common. With the exception of Hayes and his lieutenants, all of them looked out of place in the camouflage fatigues. They were trying hard to look like hardened survivalists, but something about them just didn't cut it. They looked like accountants and merchants and computer salesmen wearing funny outfits. I watched them as one of Hayes's subordinates put us through several drills, and though the members of the troop tried hard and made the right moves, there was more than a touch of clumsiness about them.

Maybe in a year or so, these guys might shape up and become good civilian soldiers. Maybe. Until then, they were no threat to godless Communists or anybody but themselves.

And Hayes and his men never stopped praising them and telling them what good fighting men they were turning into.

It was a scam, all right, I decided as I went through the drills and workouts with the rest of them. I was willing to bet that Hayes owned this place and that most of the eight thousand bucks a week went right into his pocket. He and his buddies, probably all of them combat vets from the same unit, had set up this deal to bilk a bunch of average guys who wanted to play at being commandos and guerrilla fighters. Not a bad idea, and obviously successful.

The most interesting part was that I couldn't see one damn thing illegal about it.

Nobody had hired me to get the goods on ex-colonel Brian Hayes, though. I could testify in court that Roy Lamb was taking his son to a survival training camp where he was being taught how to kill some hypothetical "enemy." That was the extent of my job.

In the meantime, though, I was stuck out here for the rest of the weekend.

Late Saturday morning, unarmed combat training came up on the schedule. So far, I had managed to blend in with the other guys, but now Hayes surprised me by calling my name. "You're a newcomer here, Mr. Cody," he said with a tight little smile, "so I'm sure you won't mind if we see just what you can do."

I shrugged my shoulders. "You're in charge, Colonel."

He nodded. "That's right, mister." He gestured at one of his men. "You and Lieutenant Starnes here can put on a demonstration for us."

Starnes was a whipcord-thin man of medium height, quite likely fast and mean. He grinned at me and stepped forward.

I wiped sweat off my forehead. Starnes was eight or ten years younger than me and quite a bit lighter. But I didn't want to back down. Stupid male pride, maybe.

I grinned right back at him and handed my empty M-16 to Roy Lamb, who was standing nearby. "Sure, be glad to," I said.

"Be careful, Cody," Roy whispered to me. "Starnes is good."

I just nodded and turned back to face the lieutenant.

"You can start it off, mister," he rasped at me.

I didn't wait any longer. I swung a roundhouse punch, telegraphing it badly.

He twisted and let my fist go by, then lashed out and chopped me in the side. Pain shot through me. I tried to turn around and block the next blow, but it slipped past my guard and drove into my belly. Air puffed out of my lungs, leaving me gasping.

I saw the arrogant grin on Starnes's face as he moved in for the kill. So far, I hadn't put up much of a fight.

That was the way I had intended for it to go. I wanted to look just as clumsy and ineffectual as the rest of the troop. But Starnes had hurt me, and he had enjoyed it. I forgot what I had planned and let my instincts take over.

The punch he aimed at my jaw found only air.

Instead of letting him polish me off, I drove inside, putting my shoulder into his belly and bulling him backward. His balance went and he fell, and I landed right on top of him. I brought my right elbow up under his chin, knocking his head back so that it bounced off the hard ground. His throat was wide open, and I could have crushed his larynx and left him there to suffocate slowly.

My brain started functioning again just in time, and I slipped awkwardly off his body, making it look like I lost my balance. He hit me savagely in the kidney, and the groan I let out was genuine. I rolled away as he tried to stomp me in the head.

Then two of the other lieutenants had hold of his arms, dragging him back, and Hayes was stepping forward with a grin on his face. "You see what happens when you lose your temper, men," he called out. "Cody had an advantage for a moment, but he lost it because he wasn't in control of his anger. You have to channel your emotion, make it work for you, rather than letting it take control of you."

I knew it was bullshit, and maybe he did, too. The only one who had lost control was Starnes.

I got up and brushed myself off, retrieving my rifle from Roy Lamb. Hayes went on with the training schedule, and the little incident between me and Starnes was quickly forgotten.

Almost forgotten. There was an ache in my side that kept reminding me when I moved wrong.

Lunch in the big dining room was simple fare, light because of the heat. We got a short rest period after we ate, and then it was back to work. In the middle of the afternoon, I got a chance to talk to Jeremy alone, as both of us took a five-minute break under the shade of an oak tree.

"You enjoy this kind of stuff, Jeremy?" I asked him.

"Sure." He shrugged. "It's fun, shooting and fighting and things like that. It's important, too. Besides, it gives me a chance to spend more time with my dad."

"What do you do during the week? Don't you go to ball games or anything like that?" My old-fashioned attitudes were cropping up again, but I couldn't help it.

Jeremy shook his head. "I have to spend a lot of my time studying, you know. And Dad's always busy with his work, or with things like checking our food supply and replenishing it."

I looked away from him and grimaced. He sure as hell didn't sound much like a kid. I glanced back at him and asked, "Studying? You going to summer school or something?"

"No, sir. My dad gives me books and articles to read on survival preparedness and then quizzes me on them."

"We've got to be ready for whatever comes," Roy Lamb said from behind us.

I glanced up, wondering how much of the conversation he had overheard and whether he thought I was meddling. "You're sure right," I agreed with him. "Can't be too prepared."

He gave me a funny look anyway.

I was starting to wonder if it would be possible to get out of here tonight. My job was done, and I didn't see any point in prolonging it.

Hayes called us back into formation, and that ended my speculation for the moment.

I was sore by the time the day was over. As the sun finally set, Hayes gathered the whole group together and made a little speech to get our minds off our aching muscles.

"You'll read articles and hear people talk about where the safest place to be is in case of war, nuclear or otherwise. Well, I don't care if they say Australia or Idaho or Timbuktu." His voice rose in stirring tones. "The safest place in the world is the place a man is willing to defend with his life! Remember that the next time you look around your home."

It was effective rhetoric, and as we went in to supper, I could see the smiles on the faces of the men. They believed in what they were doing and in what they were hearing. Maybe, in the long run, it didn't really matter that Hayes was taking them for a ride.

Maybe they were getting their money's worth in heroic dreams alone.

Our time was our own after supper, so I decided to take a walk around the farm. There was no particular reason for it, just something to do to kill time. I didn't feel like sitting in the makeshift barracks on the second floor of the farmhouse and joining in one of the ongoing poker games.

I had showered and put my own clothes back on, and I suppose in the back of my mind was the thought that I could hike back to the highway and catch a ride back to Fort Worth, leaving this phony training camp behind me.

That was before I spotted the helicopter, though.

It was parked about a hundred yards away from the house in a little clearing in the trees. I hadn't spotted it earlier because it was covered with camo netting. I wouldn't have seen it now if I hadn't nearly run into one of the landing skids.

"What the hell?" I muttered.

There was nothing unusual in a helicopter, of course. It was a good-sized chopper, a four-man job, and that was about all I could tell about it under its camouflage. I couldn't help but wonder why it was hidden. Nobody had said anything about using a helicopter in our training, but maybe we just hadn't gotten to that yet.

The man behind me was good. I barely heard him in time to dodge the knife he tried to put in my back.

I went down, scissoring with my feet and catching his left leg at the knee. He stumbled and fell, but he held on to the knife and came back up onto his feet at the same time I did.

"This time I'll kill you, you son of a bitch!" Starnes hissed at me.

I held up my hands, palm out. "Wait a minute, Starnes!" I said quickly. "I was just taking a walk. No need to get upset."

"Don't give me that crap! What are you, a cop? You're sure as hell not one of those lard-ass toy soldiers!"

I shook my head. "I don't know what you're talking about."

"You could have had me this morning. You could have killed me, and you know it! The colonel told me to keep an eye on you."

So my bad feelings had been from more than the mild swindle Hayes was working on his "recruits." Starnes wanted me dead, and there had to be a reason for that.

"You'd better drop that knife, mister," I said coldly. "I'm from Military Intelligence, and we know all about your operation here."

He laughed.

It had been worth a try. Not much of one, maybe, but a try.

Starnes came at me, fast and vicious.

There was enough moonlight so that we weren't fighting in darkness, but it was still a desperate struggle among shadows. I blocked his first thrust and tried to get a hand on his wrist, but he was too slippery. He squirmed away and lashed at me back-handed. The point of the knife ripped my shirt and laid a shallow scratch across my stomach.

He was out of position for a split second, though. I kicked, burying the toe of my boot in his groin. He gave a strangled scream and hacked at me with the knife as I drove in on him. I knocked the blade aside and caught him flush on the jaw with a punch, putting all of my weight behind the blow. He went down hard and stayed down. I clutched my throbbing hand and hoped I hadn't broken a knuckle.

I hadn't, I decided after a few moments. Starnes was unconscious but alive. He'd probably be out a good while. The longer the better, as far as I was concerned. My shirt was wet with the blood leaking from the wound he had given me, and I didn't feel one damn bit guilty about kicking him in the balls.

There was a possibility that Starnes was just crazy and had decided to kill me because he thought I had shown him up that morning. I didn't think so, though. My gut told me that Hayes had given him the orders to kill if I got too close to something I shouldn't.

I suddenly wanted to get back to that armory and get my hands on a gun.

The armory was locked, so I had to give up that idea. Given time, I might have been able to pick the heavy padlock on the door, but I didn't think I had that much time. I circled around the house instead, finding a lighted window on the first floor. I was glad that the simulated hardships of survival training meant that there were no air conditioners in the place. The glass was up, and I could hear everything that Hayes and a couple of his men were saying inside.

"They're all accounted for except that Cody," one of the lieutenants said. "Everybody else is upstairs."

"I sent Starnes to keep an eye on Cody," Hayes told him. "He should be back soon."

"You think Cody's a cop?"

"It's possible," Hayes admitted. "More than likely, though, he's just a nosy bastard. He never should have taken Ed down like that in the unarmed combat drill. Ed'll kill him if he's got the least excuse."

"We don't need that," another voice said.

"We can handle it," Hayes assured him. "There are plenty of places on this farm where an unmarked grave will never be found. I grew up here, remember."

That confirmed one of my guesses. This was Hayes's place.

I heard the rattle of papers. "All right," Hayes went on, his voice stern now like he was conducting an operations briefing. In a way, I guess he was. "Here are the details of the deal. The meeting is at the main ranch house at eleven o'clock next Wednesday. Lamb's bosses will arrive right at eleven, and they'll have the cash with them. We land right behind their car, blocking them in. We waste them, take the briefcase with the money, and we're gone. Less than a minute on the ground if everything goes according to plan, and we'll practice enough Monday and Tuesday so that it *will* go according to plan. Once we're airborne again, we put napalm into the house so that there won't be any witnesses left. Any questions?"

"Sounds good, Colonel," one of the other men said. "Lamb doesn't suspect anything?"

"Hell, no," Hayes snorted. "I'm his trusted commanding officer. He thought I was sympathizing with him when he was bitching about setting up this cattle sale."

"Just like all the others," a man said, chuckling.

"Right. Just like all the others."

And they had thought that I was a security officer at a bank, with access to all sorts of information about money transfers and things like that. I wondered suddenly what kinds of jobs the other "troops" had. I was willing to bet that a lot of them involved money.

Targets for armed robberies from the sky, carried out with military precision.

I remembered hearing about a couple of heists like that over the last year or so, and as far as I knew, the men who had been responsible for them had never been caught. It wasn't the kind of deal you could pull all the time, but two or three jobs a year, if they were big enough, would make all this phony survival training worthwhile. Plus they were taking in the fees from the suckers who were unwittingly helping them.

This had gotten a lot more grim than just a custody hassle.

"Don't move, you son of a bitch!" a voice grated behind me.

Slowly, I turned my head, not wanting to alarm him. Starnes had come to sooner than I had hoped, and he had gotten a gun from somewhere. This wasn't an army-surplus M-16, though, but a full-sized Ingram MAC-10. And as I said, the eye squinting at me over the sights was pale gray and insane.

I stood as still as possible, trying not to even breathe.

"I oughta blow you away," Starnes rasped. "Now get inside, and keep your damn mouth shut!"

I walked slowly away from the window, Starnes right behind me, prodding me every few steps with the hard barrel of the Ingram.

I was getting mad again. I forced it down. There was no way in hell I could spin around and disarm him before he could squeeze off a burst.

We went up onto the porch and inside the house; the screen door slammed behind us. Starnes marched me down the hall toward the room where Hayes and the others had been having their meeting. They all jerked their heads around and stared when Starnes shoved me through the door.

"He was listening outside the window," Starnes said, "and he found the helicopter."

Hayes's face was tightly drawn as he looked at me. He had finally taken off the sunglasses, and I could see that his eyes were blue.

"All right," he said after a moment. "Take care of him, Starnes." There was no mercy on his face or in his voice, and the other men looked the same.

Starnes caught my collar and hustled me back outside.

I wasn't going to just stand still and let him kill me. Even if it was futile, I had to do *something*. I waited, trying to control my fear and anger, waited for the best moment.

It never came.

"I'm going to enjoy this," Starnes growled, pushing me into the woods behind the house, toward the chopper. "You been askin' for it, you goddamn smart ass."

"Cody!" a voice yelled behind us. "Hit the dirt!"

I reacted instinctively, doing like the voice said, diving to the ground as Starnes spun around and looked for a target. We both spotted him at the same time, standing about twenty yards away, a rifle in his hands. Starnes fired as I launched myself toward him.

I hit his knees as the Ingram ripped off a burst. He went down and I was all over him, clubbing my hands together and driving them into the back of his head. His face smashed into the ground, and I grabbed his hair and lifted him back up and slammed him down again several times. It wasn't until I rolled his limp body over and saw the blood and the distorted features that I saw the rough chunk of rock on the ground. The stains on the rock were dark in the moonlight.

I picked up the Ingram and ran over to where Roy Lamb writhed on the ground, his legs blown out from under him by the heavy slugs. The empty M-16 lay on the grass beside him.

Roy was crying almost silently. I knelt beside him, and he opened his eyes, focusing on me after a few seconds. "Cody . . . ," he gasped. "Saw you and . . . Starnes . . . from the window . . . thought something was wrong . . ."

"You were right," I told him. "He was going to kill me."

"Wh-why . . .?"

"Too long a story," I told him. "Hayes and the others, they're the bad guys, Roy. They're the real enemy. I've got to stop them, so I'll have to leave you here for a little while." I didn't like the way he was bleeding, but there was nothing I could do about extensive wounds like he had suffered.

"Jeremy . . . he's back there . . ."

"I'll get him out," I promised. "And then I'll come back for you."

His hand caught my arm, dug in painfully. "I . . . I'm sorry . . ."

"You saved my life, Roy. It's not your fault—"

I broke off. He was unconscious, his hand slipping off my arm.

I went back toward the house at a run, the Ingram cradled in my arms. I had fired one once, with a cop friend of mine at the police firing range, but I wasn't real confident about handling it. Maybe I wouldn't have to do any more shooting.

As I neared the porch, a shape came out of the shadows, and Hayes called to me, "Is that you, Starnes?"

I brought the Ingram up. "Hold it, Hayes!"

He went for the pistol holstered on his hip, and I knew it wasn't loaded with blanks. I hesitated, and he had the .45 all the way out of the holster before I pressed the trigger of the machine gun.

The recoil threatened to push the muzzle up. I held it down, squeezing off short bursts that chewed up the porch of the old house. Hayes grunted and folded up, the pistol falling from his hands and bouncing down the steps to the ground.

His men came boiling out of the house, but so did the trainees. I covered all of them with the Ingram and yelled for nobody to move. I spotted Jeremy in the crowd on the porch and called out to him. "Your dad's in the woods, Jeremy," I told him. "He's been hurt."

He came off the porch and ran past me while I kept the rest of
them under the gun. I backed off, then turned and hurried into the
darkness after Jeremy.

There was plenty of confusion behind me, and I expected Hayes's
men to be after me in a matter of minutes. Moving Roy Lamb might
not be a good idea, but I didn't see that I had any choice.

I found Jeremy beside him. I pulled the kid to his feet and shoved
the Ingram into his hand. "You've fired a gun before," I told him.
"Just be careful." Then I bent to pick up Roy, who was still out
cold. I had in mind that we'd head for the helicopter. I didn't think
they'd risk shooting it up.

I heard car doors slamming, the roar of engines. Headlights lanced
through the woods, then turned and went away, and all I could see
was the red glow of taillights as the cars raced toward the highway.

They were pulling out.

All of them.

I figured it was a trap, but with Hayes dead, the others must have
thought it made more sense to cut and run. With everything that
had happened, there would be no chance of continuing with the
survival camp scheme.

I would have liked to wait until morning before catfooting back
up to the house, but with Roy badly injured, there wasn't that much
time. I found that I was worried for nothing. The place was deserted,
and the phone still worked. I got hold of the operator and started
yelling for help as loud as I could.

Then I went back into the woods to wait with Jeremy and his
father.

"What do you mean you won't testify?" Connie Lamb asked me,
her voice rising stridently. "It's not bad enough that the damn reporters are making out that Roy's a hero, and now you say you
won't tell the truth!"

"The truth is your husband saved my life," I told her flatly. "He's
going to be in a wheelchair the rest of his life as it is. I'm not going
to help take his son away from him."

She leaned over the desk in my office, glaring at me. "He wouldn't
have gotten shot if he hadn't been out there at that camp with those
other lunatics!"

"You may have a point there," I admitted. "But he went up
against one of those lunatics armed only with an empty rifle he was
using to practice field-stripping methods. And he saved my life."

"You keep coming back to that!"

"It is pretty important to me," I said.

"I'll have you subpoenaed."

I shrugged. "Go to it. But it won't look good, having to haul me into court. And once I'm on the stand, I'll have to offer my testimony that Roy saved my life and helped capture a band of ruthless criminals. That won't help your case, either."

She stared at me for a long moment, then turned and stalked out of the office. Even after all that had happened, I couldn't help but admire the rear view.

The rest of Hayes's men had been rounded up, and a few of the recruits had even come forward to tell the cops about the operation of the camp. It was going to be a nice mess before it was all cleaned up, but I had a feeling when the investigation was over, there would be several military-flavored robberies cleared up.

As for me, I was back in Fort Worth, definitely not a safe place. Less than ten miles from my office was Carswell Air Force Base, with its long-range bombers that made it a prime target for a Russian attack. Not to mention the damage that would be done to the agriculture and oil industries if the city was suddenly vaporized by the godless Communists. The safest place in the world? Not here.

Besides, my office rent was due in a few days and Connie Lamb had decided not to pay me the rest of the money she owed me. Unless another case came along in a hurry, I was going to be in trouble.

I locked the door and went across the street to commune with the spirits of Remington and Russell. Then, maybe, a bowl of ice cream . . . ?

Simon Brett

In less than two decades, Simon Brett has amassed an impressive mystery *oevre*, with novels such as *Cast, In Order of Disappearance*, and *Not Dead, Only Resting*. Though he writes, as he says himself, solely to entertain, his work is more than mere entertainment, having considerable heart and substance. A producer in radio and television in England for over ten years, he's doing quite well these days with Charles Paris, his middle-aged and somewhat unsuccessful actor-who-solves-crimes.

Here Mr. Brett, without the benefit of Mr. Paris, tells a poignant story about a tough-minded woman who won't accept the death of her brother without knowing all the circumstances surrounding it. The result of her determination to discover the truth can't bring her brother back to life, but she does ultimately bring meaning to his tragic end.

An Unmentionable Death

Harriet Chailey rang the doorbell of Number 73, Drefford Road. It was a large Edwardian house in that part of the city where property prices had rocketed in the last decade. Through the open doors of the garage she could see the discreet chromium gleam of a vintage Bentley.

Two undergraduates, propped on their bicycles in the street behind her, indulged in the common delusion of their age that the whole world wanted to hear what they had to say. They talked loudly of a party that evening, anatomising its probable guest list. The banter was comfortingly familiar. It seemed such a short time ago that she had been in the town to visit Dickie, Dickie before he took his degree, before he started his research. Dickie had talked just like that in those days, in the days before he became obsessed by his subject, in the days when there had been room in his life for something other than work.

But that had been more than five years ago. And now, as she had had to remind herself so many times in the last three days, Dickie was dead.

She felt again the surge of guilt. She should have kept more closely in touch with her younger brother after their parents died. But it had become decreasingly easy to do so. Of latter years it had been almost impossible to get Dickie talking about anything outside his subject. That subject—some detail of Old French syntax—was so obscure that people incautious enough to enquire about it condemned themselves to a half-hour lecture.

Mind you, Dickie had been good at it. A world expert. Invited to conferences all over the globe—Tokyo, San Francisco, even Paris—to give lectures about the subject. Apparently highly respected in academic circles. But, for the average member of the public—that is, for anyone with interests outside that particular crux

248

of Old French syntax—there were no two ways about it, Dickie's obsession had turned him into a bore.

Though maybe, Harriet thought wryly, he wasn't alone in that. A family failing . . . ? She knew she was equally single-minded about her own work at the British Embassy in Rome. Get her on to her special subject and perhaps the effect wasn't so very different . . .

If only they had both relaxed sometimes. Let up for a while. Thought about other things. Taken time to bridge their eight-year age difference, time to get to know each other.

It was too late now for such hopes.

The door of 73 Drefford Road opened to reveal a man in his fifties. He was tweed-suited and round-faced, with white hair worn almost rakishly long. He looked at her quizzically, unsurprised by a visit from a stranger but with no idea as to who she might be.

'Good afternoon. I'm Harriet Chailey,' she announced in her startlingly deep, almost masculine voice.

His face instantly composed itself into an expression of compassion.

'I'm so dreadfully sorry about what happened. Do come in.' He ushered her across a tall hallway, heavy with dark wood, into a sitting room of subsided leather chairs and piles of overspilling files, rather like the staff room of a prep school. Naive paintings of South American origin hung on the walls, between framed photographs of vintage Bentley rallies.

'My name's Michael Brewer. I was Richard's . . . well, landlord I suppose I have to say, but I hope his friend, too. Do sit down.'

'Thank you.'

'Could I get you a cup of tea? Or coffee if you'd rather . . . ?'

'No, thank you. I've only just finished lunch.'

'Ah.' He perched diffidently on the arm of a sofa. 'I don't know if Richard ever mentioned me to you in his letters or . . . ?'

'No. No, we didn't correspond that much, I'm afraid. Rather lost touch over the last few years.'

'Yes. Well, of course. Otherwise I'd have known you were his next-of-kin and wouldn't have dreamed of making the arrangements so quickly or . . .'

He petered out, embarrassed, and then, although Harriet had made no accusation, returned to his own defence.

'I feel dreadful. It's just that he'd never mentioned having any family while he was living here. No one in college seemed to know much about his background. He kept himself to himself.'

'Yes.'

'And since very few people came to visit him here—and those who did were . . . well, didn't seem to be close friends . . . To put it bluntly, it seemed as though I was the nearest to a friend he had, so when it came to funeral arrangements, I thought the quicker everything was sorted out, the better.'

Harriet nodded firmly. 'I am very grateful to you.'

'Take my word for it, please, Miss Chailey, that, had I had any idea that Richard had a sister, I wouldn't have—'

'Of course not. Don't worry. It's just unfortunate. One of those things.'

'Yes.'

But Michael Brewer didn't look fully comforted. His expression remained anxious, and Harriet felt she should try to put him at his ease. After all, the man had done more than many would have done in the circumstances.

'I really *am* very grateful to you, Mr. Brewer. At least somebody saw to it that my brother had a proper funeral.'

'Yes.' He shrugged. 'Well, it was the least I could do.'

'Hm. Was it in the college chapel?'

'The funeral?'

'Yes.'

Michael Brewer looked embarrassed. 'No. No.'

'Oh.' Some instinct restrained Harriet from pursuing this. 'I would like to see Dickie's—Richard's—grave, Mr Brewer. You know, I mean, pay my last respects, as it were . . .'

His embarrassment grew. 'I'm sorry. Your brother's funeral was at a crematorium and . . .'

'Ah.' Somehow this was the greatest shock. When the news had come through to the Embassy three days before, she had been knocked sideways, but she had clung on to the image of Dickie's body, the thought that, even though he was dead, there was something of him left. But now she knew even that perverse comfort to be illusory.

Firmly, remembering her diplomatic training, she shifted the conversation away from this emotive area. 'Are you connected with the university yourself, Mr Brewer?'

'I used to teach a certain amount,' he acknowledged. 'But, as you have probably read in the press, there have been a lot of cutbacks in education recently. I'm afraid three years ago I was found to be "surplus to requirements".'

'Oh, I'm sorry,' she said formally. 'What was your subject?'

'Spanish.'

Harriet gestured to the walls. 'Hence the paintings?'

'Yes. I still go to South America most summers.'

'Really? I was posted to Bogotá for a while some years back.'

'Ah?'

'I'm in the Foreign Office,' she explained.

He nodded. 'I don't know Bogotá well. Only ever spent a few days there.'

'Oh.'

The small talk was slowing to a standstill. There was no point in further evasion. 'Mr Brewer,' asked Harriet with characteristic directness, 'how did my brother die?'

'Erm . . .'

'I mean, what did he die of?'

The man's embarrassment was now painful to witness. 'I think,' he said eventually, 'it said "Pneumonia" on the death certificate. But you'd have to ask his doctor if you want the full details.'

Dr Hart, like his surgery, was a bit run-down and seedy. He and his sports jacket looked tired, as if they had both seen enough of sick-beds and symptoms. He had a full waiting room of coughers and complainers and students with psychosomatic essay crises. The way he kept glancing at his watch left Harriet in no doubt that she had been squeezed in on sufferance.

'Your brother first came to see me about three months ago, I suppose. Complaining of gastric trouble. Diarrhoea, occasional vomiting, he said. I prescribed for him, but he didn't seem to get better. Came in a couple more times, still no improvement. Towards the end I went and saw him at the house. But by then the pneumonia had set in and . . .'

The doctor shrugged. Another case ended as all cases will eventually end. The only difference was with this one the end had come a little earlier than might have been expected.

'But surely he should have gone into hospital?' Harriet protested.

Dr Hart nodded wearily. 'I tried to persuade him to go in when he came to the surgery. I wanted some tests done. But he didn't want to know about it. Said he hadn't got the time . . .'

'Had to get on with his work . . .'

'Yes. That was it. And by the last time I saw him, I'm afraid he was beyond tests.' The doctor sighed. 'I'm sorry, Miss Chailey, but if a patient's determined *not* to look after himself, there's not a lot we doctors can do about it.'

'No. And there wasn't a post-mortem?'

'There was no need. I had seen your brother just before he died. It wasn't a case of a sudden, unexplained illness.'

'No.' Harriet was silent for a moment. 'Dr Hart, what do you think made him ill?'

The reply was brusque almost to the point of rudeness. 'Self-neglect. As I said, he didn't look after himself. God knows what he

ate or when he ate it. I think Mr Brewer tried to make him eat the
occasional proper meal, but most of the time . . . He just let himself
go, I'm afraid. And under those circumstances, he would be prey
to any infection that came along. He had so weakened himself by
the end that the slightest chill could have turned to pneumonia.
Your brother led a rather eccentric life, Miss Chailey.' Another,
undisguised, look at the watch. 'And now, if you'll excuse me . . .'

Harriet rose from her chair. At the door she stopped.

'You are telling me everything you know, Dr Hart, aren't you?'

'Yes,' he replied gruffly, turning his attention to the pile of notes
on his desk. 'Of course I am.'

'It just seems so sad,' Harriet said, pausing in her removal of
books from shelves and looking across the chaos of paper covering
her late brother's room, 'that Dickie never got married. I'm sure if
he'd had someone else to think about, he wouldn't have got so
immersed in his work. I mean, no wife would have let him get *that*
immersed, would she?'

'No,' Michael Brewer concurred gently.

'You didn't see any evidence of girl friends? I mean, no one came
round on a regular basis . . . ?'

'Very few people on any sort of basis.'

'No. It seems as if my brother was completely sexless.'

Michael Brewer grunted agreement.

Harriet sighed. 'I know there are people like that. But as a child
he was always lively . . . sociable. He must have been dreadfully
lonely.'

'I honestly don't think he was,' said Michael Brewer, offering
what comfort he could. 'I think his work so absorbed him that he
didn't really notice whether he was with people or on his own.'

'Hm. It's strange. Somehow, now, the work itself just seems ir-
relevant.' She picked another book off the shelf. 'I mean, I can't
even understand the titles of these—God knows what I'd make of
the contents. No doubt they're worth quite a lot, but certainly not
to the average man in the street.'

'No.'

'Do you think there'd be any chance of getting rid of them through
the university? I mean, one of the libraries . . . someone working
in the same field . . . ?'

'I'm sure that'd be possible. Would you like me to handle it, Miss
Chailey?'

'Well, if you wouldn't mind, I'd be extremely grateful.'

'No problem. Would you be hoping to make some money from
the sale?'

'Oh, goodness, no. Just so long as they go somewhere where they're appreciated.'

'Of course.'

She looked round the room with a kind of hopelessness. 'He didn't really have much, did he? I mean, all these files and books and journals, yes, but not much personal stuff.'

'No. Obviously there are his clothes and . . . Do you want to check through all those?'

'No, no. I'll give them to Oxfam or . . .'

'Would you like me to organise that, too?'

'Well, it does seem rather an imposition . . .'

'Not at all. I'm on the spot. It's quite easy for me. And you said you had to get back to Rome . . .'

'Yes, I told them it would only be a few days. Compassionate leave.'

The thought of all the work piling up in her office came to her with sudden urgency. And the Ambassador was giving that party on Saturday. There's no way they'd get it all organised properly without her. Hm, there was a good flight the following afternoon. . . .

'Look, you leave it all with me,' Michael Brewer said soothingly. 'If you're sure there's nothing you want . . . ?'

'Well, I'd better keep looking. There might be some old family photographs or . . .'

'Stay as long as you like. It's no problem.'

'Thanks.'

Harriet yawned, and sneaked a look at her watch. Nearly eight o'clock. Been a long couple of days. Still, she should really keep checking through. There might be something, some memory to keep open the book of her brother's life.

But the thought of the next afternoon's flight had lodged in her mind. Just another half-hour here, she thought with a hint of guilt, and then back to the hotel. Quick dinner, early night and train to London in the morning. There was nothing for her here.

'Mr Brewer,' she asked diffidently, 'about Dickie's illness . . .'

The man stiffened. 'Yes . . . ?'

'How long was he actually bedridden at the end?'

'I suppose about three weeks.'

'And was he eating properly then?'

'Well, I tried to make him, but he wasn't interested. And when he did eat something, he had difficulty keeping it down.'

'It was very good of you to look after him.'

Michael Brewer shrugged. 'Only sorry I wasn't more effective.'

'And he kept on working?'

'Yes. Right to the end. I tried to persuade him to stop, to go into the hospital, but . . . he was very strong-willed.'

'Yes.'

The doorbell rang. With a muttered 'Excuse me', Michael Brewer went downstairs. He left the door open, and Harriet could hear the conversation from the hall.

First, Michael Brewer's urbane 'Good evening.'

Then an unexpected voice. Young, rough, slightly furtive.

'Oh, hello. I was given this address by a friend.'

'Really?'

'Friend called Rod.'

'Oh?' Apparently the name meant nothing to Michael Brewer.

'He said this was the place to come to. . . . Said there was someone here who—'

'I'm sorry. You've been misinformed. I think you have the wrong address. There's no one here who can help you.'

Intrigued by the conversation, Harriet had been drawn to the doorway of Dickie's room. Through the banisters she could see the visitor at the front door. A boy in his late teens, spiked black punk hair, torn denim jeans and jacket. A haunted face, an air of twitchiness, but, as well, a kind of insolence.

As she looked, Michael Brewer closed the front door. Harriet went back hastily into the room and, to look busy, knelt down by a pile of files at the foot of a bookcase. She tugged to dislodge them, and released a pile of glossy magazines from under the files.

She opened one.

In spite of her occasionally spinsterish manner, Harriet Chailey's experience of life had been broader than might be supposed. She recognised pornography when she saw it.

But she had never seen pornography like this before. There were no female bodies in the pictures. They were all men.

She reached further under the bookcase and pulled out a thin cigar box. Lifting the lid revealed a couple of plastic syringes, some blood-stained bandages and a small polythene bag with dregs of white powder at the bottom.

'Ah.'

She turned to see Michael Brewer framed in the doorway. His face was a mask of pity.

'I'm sorry,' he said. 'I thought I'd got rid of all that stuff. I was hoping you wouldn't have to find out about it.'

'What?' asked Harriet, bewildered. 'Do you mean that Dickie died from a drug overdose?'

'No,' Michael Brewer replied sadly. 'No. That wasn't it.'

* * *

'I still find it hard to believe,' said Harriet. 'I mean, from what I remember of Dickie . . .'

'You said you hadn't seen him for a long time . . .' Michael Brewer's voice was gentle and compassionate.

'True.'

'And you said it seemed odd that there was no sexual dimension to his life . . .'

'Yes . . .'

'No, I'm sorry. From the time he moved in, there was no question about it.'

'Oh.'

'Boys used to call here. Ask any of the neighbours. Young men calling late at night. For your brother.'

'I see.' A thought struck her. 'You mean . . . was that young man this evening . . . ?'

Michael Brewer nodded. 'I'm sorry. I really didn't want you to find out about it.'

'Better I should know.'

'Why? Why do you say that? I'd have thought you'd got enough to come to terms with—just having heard your brother's died—without *this*.'

'No. I want to find out as much as I can about him. I regret I didn't get to know him better while he was alive. Now I just want to find out everything about Dickie.'

'Ah.'

'Maybe it's my way of coping with the bereavement.'

'Maybe . . . ' Michael Brewer shook his head sorrowfully. 'I think you may just be making more pain for yourself.'

'Perhaps I need the pain. As a kind of expiation. Punishment for not having got to know him while he was alive.'

Michael Brewer nodded, accepting this interpretation.

'Why didn't Dr Hart tell me?'

'We discussed it, Miss Chailey. We both felt the less people who knew, the better.'

'That was not very professional of him, as a doctor.'

'Perhaps not. But as a human being . . . well, it was at least compassionate.'

'Yes.' Harriet looked at her watch. 'He wouldn't still be at the surgery, would he?'

'No.'

'Do you have his home phone number?'

'Yes,' said Michael Brewer, with a rueful nod.

* * *

'Are you saying you didn't make the diagnosis straight away?'

'All right, I am, yes.' Dr Hart's voice was testy. He was annoyed enough at being rung at home; and now to have his professional expertise questioned was even more annoying. 'Look, Miss Chailey, have you any idea how many patients I see in a day? I get them all through—pensioners with arthritis, menopausal women, students with God knows what problems. Sex, depression, drugs—have you any idea of the scale of the drugs problem in this university? And it just gets worse and worse, because the pushers never seem to get caught—or as soon as one is caught, another two appear to take his place.

'Well, as a result of all this, there's not a lot of time, you know. So, on the whole, as a doctor, you go for the obvious. Someone comes in complaining of diarrhoea, you tend to prescribe something for diarrhoea. Look, for God's sake, until just before he died, I didn't even know your brother was homosexual.'

'Nor did I.'

'No. Well, there you are. You grew up with him and didn't know. I met him for what . . . three . . . four ten-minute consultations? So how am I expected to know every detail of his life?'

'I see your point. I mean the drugs thing . . . that's the biggest shock to me. He used to be so anti-drugs. Really priggish about it. Still, I suppose I'm talking about a long time ago.'

'People change.'

'Yes. Did you know about his drug habit?'

'Again, not till the end, no. If I had known, I might have been able to do something about it.'

'Did Michael Brewer tell you?'

'No. God, he tried to keep it from me. He did everything to try and stop me from finding out.'

'Why?'

'Because he was a good friend to your brother.'

'He wasn't more than that, was he?'

'What do you mean?'

Michael Brewer had left Harriet discreetly alone in his study to make the phone call, so she felt she could risk this line of questioning. 'Well,' she continued, 'we've established that Dickie was gay . . .'

'No. Absolutely not. I'm certain Michael isn't. No, he's just that rarity in this day and age—a good man. He found himself in the situation of having a sick man on his hands, and he just did his best to look after that sick man.'

'But if Michael didn't tell you, how did you find out about the drugs?'

'I . . . came across some stuff in your brother's room. Syringes, what have you . . .' Just as I did, thought Harriet, as the doctor went on, 'Michael Brewer wasn't even there at the time.'

'Did you talk to Dickie about it?'

'No. He was too far gone with the pneumonia by then. Virtually unconscious.'

'But surely that was the time to get him into hospital?'

'Look, Miss Chailey, your brother was going to die. There was nothing I could do about it, nothing anyone could do about it at that stage. I agreed with Michael Brewer that it would be more compassionate to let him die in his own surroundings than in the exposed anonymity of a hospital ward.'

'And was another consideration the fact that you didn't want your failure to be known to the hospital doctors?'

'Failure? What do you mean, Miss Chailey?'

'I mean your failure to diagnose earlier what was really wrong with Dickie.'

There was a silence from the other end of the line. Then, grudgingly, Dr Hart conceded, 'All right. Yes. I should have been alert to it, and I wasn't. As I say, so many people come through the surgery. With some types you're immediately suspicious. You spot them as high-risk the minute they walk in. But with someone like your brother . . . who seemed so . . . well, eccentric, yes, but otherwise quite ordinary . . . I mean, the last person you would associate with either homosexuality or drugs.'

'True,' Harriet agreed. 'And it was because you didn't want your mistake shown up that you signed the death certificate with "Pneumonia" and—?'

'Pneumonia was what he died of,' Dr Hart objected.

'All right, that was what he died of, but it wasn't what killed him.'

'You're splitting hairs.'

'No, I'm not.' Harriet pressed on relentlessly. 'And for the same reason you were happy to see the funeral arrangements made as quickly as possible? Happy that he should be cremated? To destroy the evidence of your blunder?'

'All right. If that's how you choose to put it, yes.'

There was a silence after this admission. Then the doctor came again to his own defence. 'Listen, Miss Chailey, I don't feel particularly proud of how I've behaved over this. But AIDS is a new disease, it's currently an incurable disease, about which your average GP—and I've never claimed to be more than your average GP—knows very little. Now, if a known drug addict—or one of the local rent boys—comes into my surgery complaining of diarrhoea or weight loss . . . all right, I'm on my guard. With someone like your brother . . .' he repeated, 'when he comes in with something that could be caused by food poisoning or one of any number of viruses, well . . .'

'Yes.' Harriet sighed. Through her anger and frustration, she couldn't help seeing the doctor's point of view. 'And how do you suppose my brother contracted it?' she asked dully.

'Take your pick. Given his promiscuous active homosexuality . . . given the fact that he'd been to a conference in San Francisco within the last year . . . given the drug habit . . . given all the facts I didn't know about him until just before he died . . . he was a prime target.'

'Yes.' Harriet felt empty and listless. 'Well, thank you, Doctor, for telling me the truth.'

'I'm sorry I didn't tell you first time round, but . . . Quite honestly, I really didn't think it was necessary for you to know something that could only cause you pain.'

'Thanks for the thought.'

The doctor cleared his throat at the other end of the line. 'If it's any comfort to you, Miss Chailey,' he said, 'you've made me feel an incompetent old fool.'

Harriet wasn't hungry when she got back to her hotel that night. The quick dinner she had been promising herself had lost its appeal. So had the early night. The revelations of the evening had made sleep a very distant possibility.

Even the next day's flight to Rome had become remote and unimportant. The Ambassador's party on Saturday had lost its urgency. It would still happen somehow, whether she was there or not.

The fact that her brother had died of AIDS made everything else seem trivial.

She had found almost nothing of personal relevance in his room. Just his keys. Still, she noticed with a pang as she put them in her handbag, that they were attached to the brass Italian key ring she had given him for a birthday in the days when they still remembered each other's birthdays.

Ironically, the only other items she had brought from 73 Drefford Road were the gay magazines and the box of drug equipment. In a perverse way, as if it made any difference at this stage of her brother's life (or rather death), she felt she should remove this incriminating evidence from his room.

She glanced through the magazines, not disgusted or intrigued by their contents, just bewildered. And bewildered at the sidelights they offered on her brother's life. How little she had known him.

The magazines, she noticed, went in sequence. Published every month. Dickie's collection covered the last six months. Maybe there had once been other back-numbers. Michael Brewer had implied that he had checked through the room to remove all the evidence of homosexuality he could find. He had presumably only missed this lot because they were jammed under the files.

Abstractedly, trying to control and organise her thoughts, Harriet placed the magazines in order. She put down the oldest first. Six months ago, five months, four months, three months, two months. Then the latest.

She looked at the cover of the most recent magazine and felt a sudden dryness in her mouth. Oh my God, she thought.

The taxi driver seemed confused by her request.

'It's not that I don't know where to take you,' he said. 'It's just you don't seem the sort to want to go there.'

'I know where I want to go,' said Harriet, firmness as ever further deepening her husky voice.

This seemed to explain things for the taxi driver. 'Oh,' he said to her considerable amusement, 'I get it. You're one of them trans-sexuals, aren't you?'

It was a small pub behind the bus station. Small and run-down. Outside motor bikes clustered like insects round a rotten fruit.

Harriet's determination was so strong that she didn't stop to think how incongruous her smart Italian coat must look amidst the studded leather and frayed denim of the interior. As she ordered a red wine, she was unaware of the quizzical eyebrows of the ear-ringed and heavily moustached barman, or of the open amazement and mut-tered comments of the other drinkers.

She looked eagerly round the bar. There were a few other women, though their livid, streak-dyed hair and black vampire make-up gave them the look of another species from her own. But most of the occupants of the bar were male. Young men with blonded hair and haggard eyes, shrieking jokey insults at each other. Thickset men in heavy leathers. Older men in furtive raincoats.

She tried to imagine Dickie in this environment. She tried to picture the young man she remembered from her childhood leaning twitchily against the bar like these other men, but her mind could not encompass the image.

And then she saw it.

A familiar, haunted face. Pained and putty-coloured under black spiked hair. The boy sat alone, uninterested in the half of beer in his hand. His eyes darted anxiously around the bar.

Harriet Chailey moved across to sit beside him. He gave no sign of having noticed her.

She touched his arm. He recoiled as if she'd burnt him, and the sunken, paranoid eyes found hers.

'What do you want?' he hissed.

'I want to talk to you.'

'I haven't done nothing wrong. I haven't got nothing on me.'

Their dialogue was attracting attention from the drinkers around them, who seemed to bristle and move almost imperceptibly closer. The atmosphere was not friendly.

'I just want to talk,' Harriet persisted, again placing a gentle hand on the boy's denim sleeve.

This time he sprang to his feet, and a flicker of menace went through the watching crowd.

'I'll pay you,' said Harriet.

The hollow eyes turned back to her.

'Money?'

She nodded.

'How much?'

'Twenty pounds.'

The boy nodded, and sat back down again. As he did so, he flicked a message with his head to the protective crowd around him. They relaxed and returned to their drinks.

'What do you want to know?' he asked truculently.

'I want to know about Seventy-three Drefford Road,' said Harriet.

Michael Brewer came back from the shops the next morning and let himself in through the front door of 73 Drefford Road. As he closed it, he was shocked to hear a deep female voice from the top of the stairs.

'Good morning.'

He spun round to face her. 'Miss Chailey.'

'I apologise for letting myself in. I had Dickie's keys.'

'Of course. I must confess to being somewhat surprised to see you. I understood that you were catching a plane back to Rome this afternoon.'

'That was my intention, yes.'

'And can I ask what made you change your mind?'

'If you come up to Dickie's room, I'll tell you.'

'Very well.' Michael Brewer nodded slowly. 'Will you just allow me to put my shopping in the kitchen?'

'Of course.'

'Can I offer you a cup of coffee or anything of the sort?'

'No, thank you.'

Harriet was sitting in an armchair in front of the bathroom door when Michael Brewer entered his late tenant's room. 'Now,' he asked amiably, apparently unperturbed by her trespass, 'what is this? Is there something else of Richard's you want to look for? Or something you've found and want to show me . . . ?'

'This is the only thing I want to show you.' She indicated the latest edition of the gay magazine on the table beside her.

'Oh?'

'But time enough for that. Do sit down.'

'Thank you,' said Michael Brewer, acting on the invitation.

'I'm sorry. It's ridiculous my offering you a chair in your own house.'

He shrugged to indicate that he was unworried by this social solecism. 'Well, now . . . ?' He raised a quizzical eyebrow.

'I just wanted to say how much care you put into looking after Dickie, and . . .'

He made a gesture of self-depreciation. 'The least I could do.'

'Yes. How soon did you realise what was actually wrong with him?'

'I didn't have any suspicions until near the end. I should have thought of it earlier. You know, knowing the life he led. I mean, when he started getting recurrent diarrhoea . . .'

'Losing weight . . .'

'Yes. And also getting this sort of skin infection. . . . I should have put two and two together. . . . But I'm afraid I didn't. Until it was too late.'

'Do you think Dickie himself knew what was wrong with him?'

'No, I'm sure he had no idea. Right up to the end. I certainly didn't say anything about it to him. I wanted to spare him as much pain as I could.'

'That was very thoughtful.'

'Well . . . Anyway, Richard didn't really think about his health. For him being ill was just an inconvenience. . . .'

'Something that kept him from the dissection of Old French syntax?'

'Precisely.'

'It was unfortunate, Mr Brewer, that Dr Hart didn't spot what was really wrong with Dickie.'

'Yes. Perhaps it was.'

'Didn't you feel that you should share your suspicions with him the minute you realised what it was?'

'I did think about that, yes. But, quite honestly—and this may have been very wrong of me—by the time I realised what was happening, which was very near the end, I thought it better to keep quiet. I mean, the point is, with AIDS, there is no cure. Richard was under a death sentence from the moment he contracted the dreadful thing. And, given a choice between having a load of tests, being labelled as a plague victim, being hospitalised—and the alternative, which was dying with a degree of dignity . . .'

'And in ignorance . . .'

'Yes. Well, I'm afraid I chose the second course.'

'Hm.' Harriet looked pensive. 'It's a strange disease, AIDS. Nobody yet knows much about it.'

'No. That's what makes it so terrifying.'

'Yes. There have even been cases of pathologists refusing to do post-mortems on AIDS victims.'

'So I've heard.'

'And I dare say ordinary doctors aren't immune from that kind of fear. They're only human, after all. I dare say some of them would rather not investigate an AIDS patient too closely.'

'Maybe not.'

'And be quite happy if the victim's body is disposed of as soon as possible without too many questions asked.'

'I suppose that could happen, yes.'

'The other strange thing is that a lot of the symptoms—at least the early symptoms—could be mistaken for all kinds of other ailments.'

'So I believe.'

'Did you know, for instance,' said Harriet suddenly, 'that systematic poisoning could produce a lot of the same symptoms as AIDS?'

There was a half-beat pause before Michael Brewer replied, 'No. No, I didn't.'

'Arsenic, for instance.'

'Really?'

'Oh yes. Diarrhoea . . . vomiting . . . weight-loss certainly, because the victim can't keep anything down . . . discoloration of the skin . . . dermatitis—all classic symptoms of arsenic poisoning. So long as the case wasn't investigated too closely, it would be quite easy to confuse the symptoms.'

'Oh.' Michael Brewer smiled urbanely. 'What a mine of information you are, Miss Chailey. I'm sure you're very good at Trivial Pursuit.'

'Thank you. Yes, I'm not bad at it.'

'But, of course, I believe that nowadays it is extremely difficult to obtain arsenic in this country, so I can't imagine that the confusion you describe would be very likely ever to occur in real life.'

'No. No. Mind you, in other countries arsenic is still relatively easy to obtain.'

'Really? Another Trivial Pursuit answer?'

'No. All I'm saying is that smuggling arsenic into this country would be quite as easy as—perhaps even easier than—smuggling in other illegal substances.'

Michael Brewer was icily silent. When he finally spoke, there was a new cold detachment in his voice. 'May I ask precisely what you're saying, Miss Chailey?'

'What I'm saying is that there is a lot of drug abuse in this city. In the university and with the local youngsters. . . .'

'So I've heard.'

'And the young people must get their supplies from some-where . . .'

'Presumably.'

'One of their sources is this address. Seventy-three Drefford Road.'

'What?' His face was suddenly pale. 'Where did you hear that from?'

'A young addict.'

'You can't believe what they say!'

'I believed this one. He was the boy who came round here last night.'

'He wasn't looking for drugs. He was—'

Harriet overruled him. 'The boy was looking for drugs. He told me. Oh, you played it very cleverly, yes. You made it seem as if he was a rent boy coming round looking for Dickie. But he wasn't. He was after drugs. Just like all the other late-night visitors to this house.'

'But your brother—'

'My brother wasn't homosexual.'

'Look, I know it's hard for you to believe that a member of your family—'

'You can stop all that, Mr Brewer. There's no point in trying to maintain that pretence any longer. I know what's been going on here.'

'Oh?' The voice was icier than ever.

'You've been smuggling in drugs from South America for some years. I don't know how long, but certainly since you lost your job.'

'What do you mean?'

'Come on, Mr Brewer. Vintage Bentleys are an expensive hobby. You need a fairly healthy income from somewhere to keep that going.'

'But I—'

'Good little system you had worked out. All ticking over fine. Until Dickie found out what you were up to. He'd always hated drugs, hated what they did to people, and I think he must have threatened to expose what you were doing.'

'You don't know what you're talking about.'

'Yes I do,' said Harriet implacably. 'You fobbed Dickie off for a while . . . maybe said you'd stop dealing, maybe said you'd confess voluntarily . . . somehow you bought time. But my brother remained a threat . . . until you saw a way of getting rid of him—a way which would never be investigated too closely. You started systematically to poison him, and at the same time worked out how to make it appear that he was in a high-risk category for catching AIDS.'

Michael Brewer was calmer now. Once again he had control of himself. He rubbed his chin reflectively. 'Say that what you're suggesting was true . . . what was it that started you thinking that way?'

'Two things,' Harriet replied firmly. 'First,'—she pointed at it—'this magazine.'

'What about it?'

'Good idea, getting the magazines. I think you built up the collection privately, then slipped them into this room towards the end, when Dickie was too ill to notice what was going on. You hid them, but you didn't hide them too well. Hid them just badly enough, in fact, so that Dr Hart couldn't fail to find them. Just as I couldn't fail to find them yesterday.'

'You have no proof of that.'

'But I think I do. Circumstantial evidence, at least.'

'Oh?'

'You see, this one . . .'—again she indicated the magazine on the table—'was only published a fortnight ago . . .'

'But—'

'And by then Dickie was far too ill to get out of bed—let alone go out and buy magazines.'

'Ah.' Michael Brewer nodded ruefully, acknowledging his carelessness. 'You mentioned two things . . .?' He was now almost diffident in his casualness.

'The other thing was the drugs.'

'Oh?'

'That made me suspicious. It seemed like overkill. All right, we all know by now—no one could help knowing from all the publicity campaigns—that AIDS can be contracted by promiscuous homosexual activity or by drug addicts sharing needles. One or other would have been good enough to start people wondering about the nature of Dickie's illness. To build him up as both a promiscuous gay *and* an intravenous drug abuser seemed excessive. It also started me thinking that perhaps you had access to drugs yourself.'

'Ah!' Michael Brewer bowed his head contritely. 'Yes, I agree that was maybe a bit over the top.'

'You realise,' said Harriet, 'that what you've just said is tantamount to an admission that you did kill my brother?'

'Yes.' He smiled grimly. 'Yes, I realise that.' Slowly, he started to loosen his tie. 'And you must realise why I am not afraid to make that admission to you.'

'The admission that you killed Dickie?'

'Yes. I killed him. And I can tell you that in complete confidence, because, I'm afraid, Miss Chailey, there is no chance that you are going to leave this house alive.'

He tugged savagely at one end of his tie, which came loose and flicked out across the room like a whip.

'You're going to kill me too?'

'You've left me no alternative. Just as your brother left me no alternative. I had to kill him, I'm afraid. Self-protection. It's dog-eat-dog out there, you know.'

'I know,' said Harriet. 'I do work for the British Foreign Office, after all.'

Michael Brewer smiled condescendingly as he started to wind the ends of the tie around his hands. 'Always worth trying a little joke, isn't it? Playing for time. Won't work, but worth trying.'

'Strangling,' observed Harriet, 'won't be nearly such a good murder as the other one. Not nearly so ingenious. And all that dreadful business of getting rid of the body to cope with.'

'Needs must when the devil drives, my dear.' Michael Brewer moved slowly towards her. 'And, though I appreciate your concern, don't worry, I'll think of something.'

'What's more,' Harriet went on gamely, 'I don't think even Dr Hart will sign a death certificate describing a strangling as "natural causes".'

'NO, HE BLOODY WELL WON'T!'

The new voice took them both by surprise, as the bathroom door was flung open and Dr Hart crashed into the room.

Michael Brewer gazed at the apparition with his mouth open. It closed with a snap as Dr Hart's fist caught him on the point of the jaw. The murderer crumpled backwards in a heap, and offered no resistance as the doctor plunged a syringe into his wrist.

'That'll keep him quiet till the police come.'

'Good heavens,' said Harriet.

Dr Hart looked slightly sheepish. 'I'm sorry. I'm not normally a violent man, but I'm afraid, with drugs, I just see red. When I hit him I was hitting all the pushers in the world. When I think of the wreckage of young lives which I've seen pass through my surgery . . .'

'Yes. Are you sure it was all recorded?'

'Certain.' He went back into the bathroom and emerged with a cassette recorder. He spooled it back some way and pressed the 'Play' button. Michael Brewer's confession was reassuringly repeated.

Harriet looked wistfully around the room. 'I'll never forgive myself,' she said, 'for not getting to know Dickie better, but at least now I'll know that what I remember of him was what he was really like.'

'Yes.' Dr Hart looked at her. 'Thank you for asking me to help.'

'There was no one else I could ask.'

'No. Still, at least I feel I've done something. I told you how you made me feel last night. . . .'

'Yes.'

'Well, at least this morning I feel less of an incompetent old fool.' He gave her a weary grin. 'Marginally less, anyway.'

ROBERT BARNARD

It hasn't been that long since Barnard first appeared on the scene. Within just a few years of his first published novel, Barnard was recognized as a master of traditional mysteries. Novels such as *Death of an Old Goat, Death on the High C's*, and others have made him a favorite, though, and his best-known protagonist, Perry Trethowan, has made quite a name for himself. Barnard himself is a professor of literature and a serious literary critic. His fiction tends to have a light, ironic touch that makes death perhaps inevitable but never dull. And he's won a number of awards to prove it.

"More Final Than Divorce" doesn't disappoint. Winner recently of the first Agatha Award for best domestic mystery short story, it awaits you presently. We won't delay nor spoil your impending pleasure with undue explanation.

More Final Than Divorce

Gerry Porter had no desire to murder his wife. He would much have preferred simply to trade her in for a new model. But Gerry was a businessman, and he knew how to do his sums. He totted up the value of his butchery business, of their house and two cars, of the time-share villa in Spain. He knew it was no longer a question simply of paying her a pittance as alimony—that the judge would award his wife a substantial proportion of the marital estate. Every way he looked at it it was impossible for him to keep his business, a roof over his head, and a new wife. He sighed. It would have to be something more final than divorce. It would have to be murder. Personally, he told himself, he blamed these feminists. It it hadn't been for these new divorce laws Sandra would be alive today.

Well, actually Sandra *was* alive today. That was of course the problem. He didn't think Sandra had any suspicions about the newer model, but the moment she did she'd tell her friends, and therein would lie the main danger. For Gerry was determined that the police should not hear about the newer model, because he had no intention that Sandra's death should be treated as a case of murder. Everyone knew who the first suspect was when a wife or husband was murdered. No, Sandra was not going to be murdered. Sandra was going to have an accident. Or commit suicide.

Gerry went about it in a methodical way. There were always plenty of newspapers around in his butcher's shop as wrapping, and between customers he studied them avidly. Plenty of people did die by accident, and the inquests on them were reported in the local rag. Gerry began classifying them in his mind into road accidents, domestic accidents, and accidents at work. The last category was out, since Sandra did not go to work. The first category was large, and encompassed many different kinds of death in or under motor vehicles. Gerry did notice how many people seemed to die on holiday abroad, and he toyed with the idea of getting some Spaniard to run into her or run her down on some particularly dangerous stretch of Iberian road. But the thought of being in the power of some greasy wop (Gerry was neither a liberal nor a tolerant thinker) made him go off the idea. And the more he read about the advances in forensic science, the less inclined he felt to tamper with his wife's car.

But the more he thought about it, the same objection seemed to apply to domestic accidents. People did electrocute themselves; some even, apparently (God, what ignorant bastards people were!) perched electric fires on the ends of their baths. But the Porters had central heating, and Gerry doubted his ability to render their high-speed kettle lethal in a way that would fool Forensics.

Gerry was sent off on to another tack entirely one evening when he passed the living-room while his wife was having coffee with a friend, and heard her say:

"Oh God, the Change! There's times I've wondered whether I'd ever get through it."

Gerry was a heavy man, with heavy footsteps, and he could not stop to hear any more. Sandra in fact went on to say that luckily she now seemed to be over the worst. Gerry had gone on to the front door, and out to the garage, and a little idea was jigging around in his mind. Gone were thoughts of accidents with car exhaust fumes, of pushing Sandra under an underground train. Suicide while the balance of her mind was disturbed. Or, to be more precise, the balance of her body.

With no plan as yet firmly formulated, he nevertheless began laying the ground next evening in the pub.

"You're thoughtful, Gerry," said Sam Eagleton to him, as he sat over his second pint. And indeed he was. It was quite a strain. Because Gerry was usually the life and soul of the Cock and Pheasant, with a steady stream of salacious, off-colour or racist jokes.

"Aye. It's the wife. She's a bit under the weather . . ." After a pause, occupied with a gaze into the brown depths of his beer mug, he added: "It's the Change. It's a rotten thing to have to go through. It does things to a woman. We can count ourselves lucky we don't have anything like it."

It was a most un-Gerry-like topic of conversation. Sam Eagleton thought it a bit off to mention it at all, and not good form, as it was understood at the Cock and Pheasant. He said: "Aye, it's a bad business," and changed the subject.

They got used, in the Cock and Pheasant and other places that Gerry Porter frequented, to the topic of The Change over the next few weeks. It was supplemented by other causes of worry and distress to Sandra, for Gerry had decided that her suicide would be the result of a cumulative burden of miseries, of myriad worries that finally became too much to bear.

"The wife's mother is in a bad way," he would say. "Senile. It's a terrible burden on Sandra."

Gerry's mother-in-law was in a home, and he had in the past made ribald jokes about her increasingly erratic behaviour. Now, apparently, all he could see was the distress that it must cause his wife.

"Gerry's gone all serious on us," said his friend Paul Tutin when he had gone out one evening, still long-faced.

There were other problems and vicissitudes in the Porter household that were tediously canvassed. Sandra's attempts to get O-Level English, one of the things she studied at one of her many evening classes, had hitherto been the subject of innumerable sexist jokes about the thickness of women. Now all they heard was what a terrible grief it was to her. "But she shouldn't be trying to get it now," he would say. "Not while she's going through the Change." They had no children to cause them worry, but nephews and nieces were press-ganged into service, and a brother of Sandra's who was serving a jail sentence was represented as an agonizing worry. But in the end it all came back to the Change.

"It does something to some women," Gerry would say. "You've no idea. Sometimes I wonder if it's the same woman I married. She says that every morning she dreads waking up."

One afternoon, while she was shopping in Darlington, Sandra dropped into the Cherry Tree Tea Shop, and was glad to see two of her old friends sitting in the window. They waved her over to their table.

"Hello, Sandra, how *are* you?" Mary Eagleton hailed.

"Fine," said Sandra, sitting down. "Just fine."

"Oh good. I *am* glad. Gerry was telling Sam the other night that the good old menopause was getting you down."

"A lot Gerry knows about it."

"When are you taking your O-Level again?" asked Mary, over the cream cakes.

"Next week!" said Sandra, roaring with laughter. "And I haven't opened a book since I failed last time. I bet the examiners are sharpening their pencils and licking their lips over the thought of giving me bottom grades."

"How's your mother?" asked Brenda Tutin.

"Great! Completely gaga. Doesn't even know me when I go in, so I've stopped going. It's a great relief."

"Gerry says you're very upset about it," said Brenda.

Sandra raised her eyebrows.

"What *exactly* has Gerry been saying?" she asked.

Things went on pretty much as normal in the next few weeks. Sandra took up yet another evening class—cake-decorating, of all things—and so they saw very little of each other, except at breakfast. Gerry insisted on the full menu with trimmings at breakfast-time— porridge, egg and bacon with sausage and tomato, two or three slices of toast and marmalade. He said it set him up for the day. Sandra, who had been to diet classes and keep fit classes, found cooking it rather nauseating, but she didn't have to watch him eat it, because he propped up his *Sun* newspaper against the coffee pot, and devoured its edifying contents along with the bacon and sausage.

He was back from the pub (or from the newer model) more often in the evening now when she got back from her classes. He was even rather considerate, something he had not been for many years, not since the first week of their honeymoon. When she flopped down in the armchair ("Everything seems to tire her now," he said in the pub) he offered her a vodka and tonic, and was even prepared to make her a mug of Ovaltine. Sometimes she accepted, sometimes she did not. It was certainly pleasant to have him actually doing something for her in the kitchen ("She's been desperate for sleep," Gerry planned to tell the police. "She's been trying everything.")

The crunch came nearly six months after Gerry had first made his decision. Sandra got back from evening classes and was *exhausted,* she said.

"Vodka and tonic, darling?" Gerry asked.

"That *would* be nice, Smoochie," she said, using a pet name they had almost abandoned.

When he brought it over Sandra noticed that he was not smelling of beer. She snuggled up on to the sofa in front of the roaring gas fire.

"This is the life!" she said.

Gerry was watching her as she tasted her drink, though ostensibly he was at the sideboard, getting one for himself. She gave no sign that it tasted any different, and he breathed out. She swung her feet up on the sofa, and took another sip or two of the vodka and tonic.

"Funny," she said. "I feel famished."

"Let me get you something."

"Would you, Smoochie? Just a few biscuits, and a bit of cheese."

When he got back the vodka and tonic was half drunk. Sandra ate the biscuits and cheese ravenously.

"I don't know why cake-decoration should be so *gruelling*," she said, taking a good swig at her drink. "I could almost settle down to sleep here in front of the fire."

"Why don't you?" Gerry said, sitting down by the head of the sofa and running his fingers through her hair. Sandra downed the rest of her drink.

"Lovely not to have the television on," she said, her voice seeming to come from far away. Her head dropped on to the arm of the sofa, her eyes closed. Soon Gerry heard gentle snores.

He jumped up and looked at his watch. It was just after ten. He could aim at the 10.45 or the 10.55. Both were expresses, and both were usually on time. He put in his pocket a little bottle of prepared vodka and sleeping draught ("She had it with her drink. I thought she wanted to sleep; I didn't realize she wanted it to deaden the pain," he would tell the police). He intended to force it down her throat if she should show signs of waking up. Then he went out into the drive and opened both doors of his wife's little Fiat (his own Range-Rover always had the garage). Then he went back into the sitting-room, took his wife gently in his arms, and carried her through the front door and out to the car. He laid her gently in the front passenger seat, and got in beside her.

The drive to the bridge was uneventful, though Gerry was bathed in sweat by the end of it. They met no more than three or four cars going in the other direction. After only ten minutes they turned into the narrow road, scarcely more than a track, which led to the railway bridge. His heart banged with relief as he parked Sandra's car under a clump of trees.

He looked at his watch. Ten minutes to go before the 10.45 went by, if it was on time. He looked at his wife. She was breathing deeply, her head lolling to one side. The Sovipol he had got from the doctor ("*She* can't sleep, Doctor, and that means *I* don't sleep, and it's affecting the business . . .") was working like a dream. He got out of the car, leant back in, and with a butcher's strength he lifted Sandra across into the driver's seat. He wiped the steering-wheel, then put her fingers on it in two or three different positions. Then he let them fall, and pressed the little bottle of vodka and Sovipol into them.

"I was already in bed," he would tell the police. "I'd had a hard day. I was knackered. I did hear her driving off, but I thought she must have left something behind at her class. She's been getting very forgetful, since the Change started . . ."

Time to get her on to the bridge. It was an old one, dating from the time when this neglected track was an important road. He took her in his arms and carried her—almost tenderly—the hundred yards there. No sound of a train yet. He laid her in a sitting position by the bridge and then straightened. God—he could do with a fag. But would that be wise? No—there in the distance was the regular hum of the diesel: the Intercity 125 from King's Cross to Leeds. He waited a moment. It wouldn't be here for a minute or two yet. Thank God he hadn't needed to force the contents of the bottle down her. His nerves as it was were stretched beyond bearing by the tension. He wanted to wet himself. Then, as the noise of the train grew nearer, he stretched down to the comatose figure by the bridge. He put his hands under the body.

And immediately he felt an open palm smash suddenly into his face. In a moment it was he who was on his back across the parapet of the bridge. Suddenly it was his wife who had strong hands on his shoulders, his wife who was pushing, pushing. Dimly he heard her voice.

"They were karate classes, Smoochie. Karate classes."

Then she dropped him into the path of the oncoming express.

The police were extremely sympathetic. It was child's play to them to unravel the details of Gerry's plan. They talked to his friends and heard about his change of character in his pub sessions, the conversations that had prepared the way. They found his dolly-bird in a little flat in central Darlington (though she said she would never have married him, not in a million years). They found the railway timetables in his study, analysed the earth in the pot plant into which Sandra Porter had poured most of her drink. ("It tasted so off. I thought he'd given me gin by mistake, which I hate, and I didn't want to offend him.") They talked to the neighbour who had passed them on the road and seen that it was Gerry driving, talked to the poacher who had seen Gerry park the car and seen him press Sandra's hands to the steering-wheel. *Those* prints wouldn't have deceived a rookie constable into thinking that they were those of a woman actually driving a car. No, Gerry Porter would never have got away with it, even if he had succeeded in killing his wife.

Sandra was quite affecting. She had drunk about a quarter of her drink, she said, but had filled the glass up with tonic water so he shouldn't know. ("He could be awfully touchy," she said.) What she had drunk had sent her soundly to sleep. When she began to awake she was in the car, in the driving seat, and her husband was pressing her hands to the steering-wheel. She was confused and terrified. How had she got here? What was going on? She had feigned sleep until she had heard the train, her husband had lifted her up, and then she—terrified—had used the techniques she had learnt at self-defence classes. ("The police are always recommending that we do them, and with the number of ghastly rapes we've had around here . . .")

Only Inspector Potter of the South Yorkshire C.I.D. had doubts.

"Why weren't there more signs of struggle?" he asked. "Why did she make no attempt to immobilize him rather than kill him? Why did she take up karate classes, mid-term, after he'd started laying the ground in his pubs? Why did she take such care, driving to the Darlington Police Station, not to disturb the fake prints?"

"She *had* to kill him," said his Super. "Otherwise he'd have been stalking her through the woods. She was practically out of her mind."

"Yet she was careful not to disturb those prints . . . Oh, I grant you there's no point in nagging away at it. It's an academic exercise. We'd never secure a conviction, not even for manslaughter. Never in a million years."

But the doubts remained in his mind. He noticed that a few days after the inquest and funeral, Porter's Family Butchery was open again for business. He noted that Sandra ran it very efficiently, with the help of a stalwart chap, fifteen years her junior, whom he heard she had met at karate class. When, a year after Gerry's death, he saw in the paper that she had married him, he showed the announcement to the Super.

"We'd never have got a conviction," he repeated. "But she did it very nicely, didn't she? Got her freedom, her boyfriend, *and* the whole of the property. Beats a divorce settlement any time! He handed himself to her on a plate, did Gerry Porter. On a ruddy plate!"

JOE R. LANSDALE

Joe R. Lansdale writes in a number of modes, ranging from the lovely Western novel *The Magic Wagon* to the viciously horrific novel *The Nightrunners*, and into the taut, knife's-edge suspense novel *Waltz of Shadows*. He does all these things very effectively, making many writers wring their hands and tear out their hair trying to figure out how he switches gears so effortlessly. We have no answers, unfortunately, but we do have a fine example of his talent, one of the more violent suspense stories to have appeared in 1988. Mr. Lansdale, who is personally a most gentle and personable man, has a way with stories like this one, which appeared previously in *Grue* magazine.

The God of the Razor

(For Ray Puechner and Ardath Mayhar)

Richards arrived at the house about eight. The moon was full and it was a very bright night, in spite of occasional cloud cover; bright enough that he could get a good look at the place. It was just as the owner had described it. Run down. Old. And very ugly.

The style was sort of gothic, sort of plantation, sort of cracker box. Like maybe the architect had been unable to decide on a game plan, or had been drunkenly in love with impossible angles.

Digging the key loaned him from his pocket, he hoped this would turn out worth the trip. More than once his search for antiques had turned into a wild goose chase. At this time, it was really a long shot. The owner, a sick old man named Klein, hadn't been inside the house in twenty years. A lot of things could happen to antiques in that time, even if the place was locked and boarded up. Theft. Insects. Rats. Leaks. Any one of those, or a combination of, could turn the finest of furniture into rubble and sawdust in no time. But it was worth the gamble. On occasion, his luck had been phenomenal.

As a thick, dark cloud rolled across the moon, Richards, guided by his flashlight, mounted the rickety porch, squeaked the screen and groaned the door open.

Inside, he flashed the light around. Dust and darkness seemed to crawl in there until the cloud passed and lunar light fell through the boarded windows in a speckled and slatted design akin to camouflaged netting. In places, Richards could see that the wallpaper had fallen from the wall in big sheets that dangled halfway down to the floor like the dropping branches of weeping willows.

To his left was a wide, spiraling staircase, and following its ascent with his light, he could see there were places where the railing hung brokenly askew.

Directly across from this was a door. A narrow, recessed one. As there was nothing in the present room to command his attention, he decided to begin his investigation there. It was as good a place as any.

Using his flashlight to bat his way through a skin of cobwebs, he went over to the door and opened it. Cold air embraced him, brought with it a sour smell, like a freezer full of ruined meat. It was almost enough to turn Richards' stomach, and for a moment he started to close the door and forget it. But an image of wall to wall antiques clustered in the shadows came to mind, and he pushed forward, determined. If he were going to go to all the trouble to get the key and drive way out here in search of old furniture to buy, then he ought to make sure he had a good look, smell or no smell.

Using his flash, and helped by the moonlight, he could tell that he had discovered a basement. The steps leading down into it looked aged and precarious, and the floor appeared oddly glass-like in the beam of his light.

So he could examine every nook and cranny of the basement, Richards decided to descend the stairs. He put one foot carefully on the first step, and slowly settled his weight on it. Nothing collapsed. He went down three more steps, cautiously, and though they moaned and squeaked, they held.

When Richards reached the sixth step, for some reason he could not define, he felt oddly uncomfortable, had a chill. It was as if someone with ice-cold water in their kidneys had taken a piss down the back of his coat collar.

Now he could see that the floor was not glassy at all. In fact, the floor was not visible. The reason it had looked glassy from above was because it was flooded with water. From the overall size of the basement, Richards determined that the water was most likely six or seven feet deep. Maybe more.

There was movement at the edge of Richards' flashlight beam, and he followed it. A huge rat was swimming away from him, pushing something before it; an old partially-deflated volleyball perhaps. He could not tell for sure. Nor could he decide if the rat was trying to mount the object or bite it.

And he didn't care. Two things that gave him the willies were rats and water, and here were both. To make it worse, the rats were the biggest he'd ever seen, and the water was the dirtiest imaginable. It looked to have a lot of oil and sludge mixed in with it, as well as being stagnant.

It grew darker, and Richards realized the moon had been hazed by a cloud again. He let that be his signal. There was nothing more to see here, so he turned and started up. Stopped. The very large shape of a man filled the doorway.

Richards jerked the light up, saw that the shadows had been playing tricks on him. The man was not as large as he'd first thought. And he wasn't wearing a hat. He had been certain before that he was, but he could see now that he was mistaken. The fellow was bareheaded, and his features, though youthful, were undistinguished; any character he might have had seemed to retreat into the flesh of his face or find sanctuary within the dark folds of his shaggy hair. As he lowered the light, Richards thought he saw the wink of braces on the young man's teeth.

"Basements aren't worth a damn in this part of the country," the young man said. "Must have been some Yankees come down here and built this. Someone who didn't know about the water table, the weather and all."

"I didn't know anyone else was here," Richards said. "Klein send you?"

"Don't know a Klein."

"He owns the place. Loaned me a key."

The young man was silent a moment. "Did you know the moon is behind a cloud? A cloud across the moon can change the entire face of the night. Change it the way some people change their clothes, their moods, their expressions."

Richards shifted uncomfortably.

"You know," the young man said. "I couldn't shave this morning."

"Beg pardon?"

"When I tried to put a blade in my razor, I saw that it had an eye on it, and it was blinking at me, very fast. Like this . . . oh, you can't see from down there can you? Well, it was very fast. I dropped it and it slid along the sink, dove off on the floor, crawled up the side of the bathtub and got in the soap dish. It closed its eye then, but it started mewing like a kitten wanting milk. Ooooowwwwaaa, Oooowwwaa, was more the way it sounded really, but it reminded me of a kitten. I knew what it wanted, of course. What it always wants. What all the sharp things want.

"Knowing what it wanted made me sick and I threw up in the toilet. Vomited up a razor blade. It was so fat it might have been pregnant. Its eye was blinking at me as I flushed it. When it was gone the blade in the soap dish started to sing high and silly-like.

"The blade I vomited, I know how it got inside of me." The young man raised his fingers to his throat. "There was a little red mark right here this morning, and it was starting to scab over. One or two of them always find a way in. Sometimes it's nails that get in me. They used to come in through the soles of my feet while I slept, but I stopped that pretty good by wearing my shoes to bed."

In spite of the cool of the basement, Richards had started to sweat. He considered the possibility of rushing the guy or just trying to push past him, but dismissed it. The stairs might be too weak for sudden movement, and maybe the fruitcake might just have his say and go on his way.

"It really doesn't matter how hard I try to trick them," the young man continued, "they always win out in the end. Always."

"I think I'll come up now," Richards said, trying very hard to sound casual.

The young man flexed his legs. The stairs shook and squealed in protest. Richards nearly toppled backwards into the water.

"Hey!" Richards yelled.

"Bad shape," the young man said. "Need a lot of work. Rebuilt entirely would be the ticket."

Richards regained both his balance and his composure. He couldn't decide if he was angry or scared, but he wasn't about to move. Going up he had rotten stairs and Mr. Looney Tunes. Behind him he had the rats and water. The proverbial rock and a hard place.

"Maybe it's going to cloud up and rain," the young man said. "What do you think? Will it rain tonight?"

"I don't know," Richards managed.

"Lot of dark clouds floating about. Maybe they're rain clouds. Did I tell you about the God of the Razor? I really meant to. He rules the sharp things. He's the god of those who live by the blade. He was my friend Donny's god. Did you know he was Jack the Ripper's god?"

The young man dipped his hand into his coat pocket, pulled it out quickly and whipped his arm across his body twice, very fast. Richards caught a glimpse of something long and metal in his hand. Even the cloud-veiled moonlight managed to give it a dull, silver spark.

Richards put the light on him again. The young man was holding the object in front of him, as if he wished it to be examined. It was an impossibly large straight razor.

"I got this from Donny," the young man said. "He got it in an old shop somewhere. Gladewater, I think. It comes from a barber kit, and the kit originally came from England. Says so in the case. You should see the handle on this baby. Ivory. With a lot of little designs and symbols carved into it. Donny looked the symbols up. They're geometric patterns used for calling up a demon. Know what else? Jack the Ripper was no surgeon. He was a barber. I know, because Donny got the razor and started having these visions where Jack the Ripper and the God of the Razor came to talk to him. They explained what the razor was for. Donny said the reason they could talk to him was because he tried to shave with the razor and cut himself. The blood on the blade, and those symbols on the handle, they opened the gate. Opened it so the God of the Razor could come and live inside Donny's head. The Ripper told him that the metal in the blade goes all the way back to a sacrificial altar the Druids used."

The young man stopped talking, dropped the blade to his side. He looked over his shoulder. "That cloud is very dark . . . slow moving. I sort of bet on rain." He turned back to Richards. "Did I ask you if you thought it would rain tonight?"

Richards found he couldn't say a word. It was as if his tongue had turned to cork in his mouth. The young man didn't seem to notice or care.

"After Donny had the visions, he just talked and talked about this house. We used to play here when we were kids. Had the boards on the back window rigged so they'd slide like a trap door. They're still that way . . . Donny used to say this house had angles that sharpened the dull edges of your mind. I know what he means now. It is comfortable, don't you think?"

Richards, who was anything but comfortable, said nothing. Just stood very still, sweating, fearing, listening, aiming the light.

"Donny said the angles were honed best during the full moon. I didn't know what he was talking about then. I didn't understand about the sacrifices. Maybe you know about them? Been all over the papers and on the TV. The Decapitator they called him.

"It was Donny doing it, and from the way he started acting, talking about the God of the Razor, Jack the Ripper, this old house and its angles, I got suspicious. He got so he wouldn't even come around near or during a full moon, and when the moon started waning, he was different. Peaceful. I followed him a few times, but didn't have any luck. He drove to the Safeway, left his car there and walked. He was as quick and sneaky as a cat. He'd lose me right off. But then I got to figuring . . . him talking about this old house and all . . . and one full moon I came here and waited for him, and he showed up. You know what he was doing? He was bringing the heads here, tossing them down there in the water like those South American Indians used to toss bodies and stuff in sacrificial pools . . . It's the angles of the house, you see."

Richards had that sensation like ice-cold piss down his collar again, and suddenly he knew what that swimming rat had been pursuing, and what it was trying to do.

"He threw all seven heads down there, I figure," the young man said. "I saw him toss one." He pointed with the razor. "He was standing about where you are now when he did it. When he turned and saw me, he ran up after me. I froze, couldn't move a muscle. Every step he took, closer he got to me, the stranger he looked . . . he slashed me with the razor, across the chest, real deep. I fell down and he stood over me, the razor cocked," the young man cocked the razor to show Richards. "I think I screamed. But he didn't cut me again. It was like the rest of him was warring with the razor in his hand. He stood up, and walking stiff as one of those wind-up toy soldiers and went back down the stairs, stood about where you are now, looked up at me, and drew that razor across his throat so hard and deep he damn near cut his head off. He fell back in the water there, sunk like an anvil. The razor landed on the last step.

"Wasn't any use; I tried to get him out of there, but he was gone, like he'd never been. I couldn't see a ripple. But the razor was lying there and I could hear it. Hear it sucking up that blood like a kid sucking the sweet out of a sucker. Pretty soon there wasn't a drop of blood on it . . . I picked it up . . . so shiny, so damned shiny. I came upstairs, passed out on the floor from the loss of blood.

"At first I thought I was dreaming, or maybe delirious, because I was lying at the end of this dark alley between these trashcans with my back against the wall. There were legs sticking out of these trashcans, like tossed mannikins. Only they weren't mannikins. There were razor blades and nails sticking out of the soles of the feet and blood was running down the ankles and legs, swirling so that they looked like giant peppermint sticks. Then I heard a noise like someone trying to dribble a medicine ball across a hardwood floor. **Plop, plop, plop**. And then I saw the God of the Razor.

"First there's nothing in front of me but stewing shadows, and the next instant he's there. Tall and black—not Negro—but black like obsidian rock. Had eyes like smashed windshield glass and teeth like polished stickpins. Was wearing a top hat with this shiny band made out of chrome razor blades. His coat and pants looked like they were made out of human flesh, and sticking out of the pockets of his coat were gnawed fingers, like after dinner treats. And he had this big old turnip pocket watch dangling out of his pants pocket on a strand of gut. The watch swung between his legs as he walked. And that plopping sound, know what that was? His shoes. He had these tiny, tiny feet and they were fitted right into the mouths of these human heads. One of the heads was a woman's and it dragged long black hair behind it when the God walked.

"Kept telling myself to wake up. But I couldn't. The God pulled this chair out of nowhere—it was made out of leg bones and the seat looked like scraps of flesh and hunks of hair—and he sat down, crossed his legs and dangled one of those ragged-head shoes in my face. Next thing he does is whip this ventriloquist dummy out of the air, and it looked like Donny, and was dressed like Donny had been last time I'd seen him, down there on the stair. The God put the dummy on his knee and Donny opened his eyes and spoke. 'Hey, buddy boy,' he said, 'how goes it? What do you think of the razor's bite? You see, pal, if you don't die from it, it's like a vampire's bite. Get my drift? You got to keep passing it on. The sharp things will tell you when, and if you don't want to do it, they'll bother you until you do, or you slice yourself bad enough to come over here on the Darkside with me and Jack and the others. Well, got to go back now, join the gang. Be talking with you real soon, moving into your head.'

"Then he just sort of went limp on the God's knee, and the God took off his hat and he had this zipper running along the middle of his bald head. A goddamned zipper! He pulled it open. Smoke and fire and noises like screaming and car wrecks happening came out of there. He picked up the Donny dummy, which was real small now, and tossed him into the hole in his head way you'd toss a treat into a Great Dane's mouth. Then he zipped up again and put on his hat. Never said a word. But he leaned forward and held his turnip watch so I could see it. The watch hands were skeleton fingers, and there was a face in there, pressing its nose in little smudged circles against the glass, and though I couldn't hear it, the face had its mouth open and it was screaming, **and that face was mine**. Then the God and the alley and the legs in the trashcans were gone. And so was the cut on my chest. Healed completely. Not even a mark.

"I left out of there and didn't tell a soul. And Donny, just like he said, came to live in my head, and the razor started singing to me nights, probably a song sort of like those sirens sang for that Ulysses fellow. And come near and on the full moon, the blades act up, mew and get inside of me. Then I know what I need to do . . . I did it tonight. Maybe if it had rained I wouldn't have had to do it . . . but it was clear enough for me to be busy."

The young man stopped talking, turned, stepped inside the house, out of sight. Richards sighed, but his relief was short-lived. The young man returned and came down a couple of steps. In one hand, by the long blonde hair, he was holding a teenaged girl's head. The other clutched the razor.

The cloud veil fell away from the moon, and it became quite bright.

The young man, with a flick of his wrist, tossed the head at Richards, striking him in the chest, causing him to drop the light. The head bounced between Richard's legs and into the water with a flat splash.

"Listen . . ." Richards started, but anything he might have said aged, died and turned to dust in his mouth.

Fully outlined in the moonlight, the young man started down the steps, holding the razor before him like a battle flag.

Richards blinked. For a moment it looked as if the guy were wearing a . . . He was wearing a hat. A tall, black one with a shiny, metal band. And he was much larger now, and between his lips was the shimmer of wet, silver teeth like thirty-two polished stickpins.

Plop, plop came the sound of his feet on the steps, and in the lower and deeper shadows of the stairs, it looked as if the young man had not only grown in size and found a hat, but had darkened his face and stomped his feet into pumpkins . . . But one of the pumpkins streamed long, dark hair.

Plop, plop . . . Richards screamed and the sound of it rebounded against the basement walls like a superball.

Shattered starlight eyes beneath the hat. A Cheshire smile of argentine needles in a carbon face. A big dark hand holding the razor, whipping it back and forth like a lion's talon snatching at warm, soft prey.

Swish, swish, swish.

Richard's scream was dying in his throat, if not in the echoing basement, when the razor flashed for him. He avoided it by stepping briskly backwards. His foot went underwater, but found a step there. Momentarily. The rotting wood gave way, twisted his ankle, sent him plunging into the cold, foul wetness.

Just before his eyes, like portholes on a sinking ship, were covered by the liquid darkness, he saw the God of the Razor—now manifest in all his horrid form—lift a splitting-head shoe and step into the water after him.

Richards torqued his body, swam long, hard strokes, coasted bottom; his hand touched something cold and clammy down there and a piece of it came away in his fingers.

Flipping it from him with a fan of his hand, he fought his way to the surface and broke water as the blonde girl's head bobbed in front of him, two rat passengers aboard, gnawing viciously at the eye sockets.

Suddenly, the girl's head rose, perched on the crown of the tall hat of the God of the Razor, then it tumbled off, rats and all, into the greasy water.

Now there was the jet face of the God of the Razor and his mouth was open and the teeth blinked briefly before the lips drew tight, and the other hand, like an eggplant sprouting fingers, clutched Richards' coat collar and plucked him forward, and Richards—the charnel breath of the God in his face, the sight of the lips slashing wide to once again reveal brilliant dental grill work—went as limp as a pelt. And the God raised the razor to strike.

And the moon tumbled behind a thick, dark cloud.

White face, shaggy hair, no hat, a fading glint of silver teeth . . . the young man holding the razor, clutching Richards' coat collar.

The juice back in his heart, Richards knocked the man's hand free, and the guy went under. Came up thrashing. Went under again. And when he rose this time, the razor was frantically flaying the air.

"Can't swim," he bellowed, "can't—" Under he went, and this time he did not come up. But Richards felt something touch his foot from below. He kicked out savagely, dog paddling wildly all the while. Then the touch was gone and the sloshing water went immediately calm.

Richards swam toward the broken stairway, tried to ignore the blonde head that lurched by, now manned by a four-rat crew. He got hold of the loose, dangling stair rail and began to pull himself up. The old board screeched on its loosening nail, but held until Richards gained a hand on the door ledge, then it gave way with a groan and went to join the rest of the rotting lumber, the heads, the bodies, the faded stigmata of the God of the Razor.

Pulling himself up, Richards crawled into the room on his hands and knees, rolled over on his back . . . and something flashed between his legs . . . It was the razor. It was stuck to the bottom of his shoe . . . That had been the touch he had felt from below; the young guy still trying to cut him, or perhaps accidentally striking him during his desperate thrashings to regain the surface.

Sitting up, Richards took hold of the ivory handle and freed the blade. He got to his feet and stumbled toward the door. His ankle and foot hurt like hell where the step had given way beneath him, hurt so badly he could hardly walk.

Then he felt the sticky, warm wetness oozing out of his foot to join the cold water in his shoe, and he knew that he had been cut by the razor.

But then he wasn't thinking anymore. He wasn't hurting anymore. The moon rolled out from behind a cloud like a colorless eye and he just stood there looking at his shadow on the lawn. The shadow of an impossibly large man wearing a top hat and balls on his feet, holding a monstrous razor in his hand.

DEAN R. KOONTZ

Dean R. Koontz admits to having been writing professionally for about thirty years. We suspect that he may have been doing it longer, but there's no incriminating evidence available to prove it. He was once a writer of science fiction, or speculative fiction as it was called in the 1960s. In the last few years he has garnered critical praise and a large audience, both of which are long overdue recognitions of his major talent. His work is always suspenseful, and his concerns are with great issues and deal with the real lives of people we care very much about.

"Twilight of the Dawn" is a haunting tale not of crime, but nonetheless of suspense. It deals with a realm of experience where death is a matter of spiritual debate.

Twilight of the Dawn

"Sometimes you can be the biggest jackass who ever lived," my wife said the night I took Santa Claus away from my son.

We were in bed, but she was clearly not in the mood for either sleep or romance.

Her voice was sharp, scornful. "What a terrible thing to do to a little boy."

"He's seven years old—"

"He's a little boy," Ellen said harshly, though we rarely spoke to each other in anger. For the most part ours was a happy, peaceful marriage.

We lay in silence. The drapes were drawn back from the French doors that opened onto the second-floor balcony, so the bedroom was limned by ash-pale moonlight. Even in that dim glow, even though Ellen was cloaked in blankets, her anger was apparent in the tense, angular position in which she was pretending to seek sleep.

Finally she said, "Pete, you used a sledgehammer to shatter a little boy's fragile fantasy, a *harmless* fantasy, all because of your obsession—"

"It wasn't harmless," I said patiently. "And I don't have an obsession—"

"Yes, you do," she said.

"I simply believe in rational—"

"Oh, shut up," she said.

"Won't you even talk to me about it?"

"No. It's pointless."

I sighed. "I love you, Ellen."

She was silent a long while,

Wind soughed in the eaves, an ancient voice.

In the boughs of one of the backyard cherry trees, an owl hooted.

At last Ellen said, "I love you, too, but sometimes I want to kick your ass."

I was angry with her because I felt that she was not being fair, that she was allowing her least admirable emotions to overrule her reason. Now, many years later, I would give anything to hear her say that she wanted to kick my ass, and I'd bend over with a smile.

From the cradle, my son Benny was taught that God did not exist under any name or in any form, and that religion was the refuge of weak-minded people who did not have the courage to face the universe on its own terms. I would not permit Benny to be baptised, for in my view that ceremony was a primitive initiation rite by which the child would be inducted into a cult of ignorance and irrationalism.

Ellen—my wife and Benny's mother—had been raised as a Methodist and still was stained (as I saw it) by lingering traces of faith. She called herself an agnostic, unable to go further and join me in the camp of the atheists. I loved her so much that I was able to tolerate her equivocation on the subject. However I had nothing but scorn for others who could not face the fact that the universe was godless and that human existence was nothing more than a biological accident.

I despised all those who bent their knees to humble themselves before an imaginary lord of creation, all the Methodists and Lutherans and Catholics and Baptists and Mormons and Jews and others. They claimed many labels but in essence shared the same sick delusion.

My greatest loathing was reserved, however, for those who had once been clean of the disease of religion, rational men and women like me who had slipped off the path of reason and fallen into the chasm of superstition. They were surrendering their most precious possessions—their independent spirit, self-reliance, intellectual integrity—in return for half-baked, dreamy promises of an afterlife with togas and harp music. I was more disgusted by the rejection of their previously treasured secular enlightenment than I would have been to hear some old friend confess that he had suddenly developed an all-consuming obsession for canine sex and had divorced his wife in favor of a German Shepherd bitch.

Hal Sheen, my partner with whom I had founded Fallon and Sheen Design, had been as proud of his atheism too. In college we were best friends, and together we were a formidable team of debaters whenever the subject of religion arose; inevitably, anyone harboring a belief in a supreme being, anyone daring to disagree with our view of the universe as a place of uncaring forces, any of *that* ilk was

sorry to have met us, for we stripped away his pretensions to adulthood and revealed him for the idiot child he was. Indeed we often
didn't even wait for the subject of religion to arise but skillfully
baited fellow students who, to our certain knowledge, were
believers.

Later, with degrees in architecture, neither of us wished to work
for anyone but ourselves, so we formed a company. We dreamed
of creating brawny yet elegant, functional yet beautiful buildings
that would astonish—and win the undiluted admiration of—not only
the world but of our fellow professionals. And with brains, talent,
and dogged determination, we began to attain some of our goals
while we were still very young men. Fallon and Sheen Design, a
wunderkind company, was the focus of a revolution in design that
excited university students as well as long-time professionals.

The most important aspect of our tremendous success was that
our atheism lay at the core of it, for we consciously set out to create
a new architecture that owed nothing to religious inspiration. Most
laymen are not aware that virtually all the structures around them,
including those resulting from modern schools of design, incorporate
architectural details originally developed to subtly reinforce the rule
of God and the place of religion in life. For instance vaulted ceilings,
first used in churches and cathedrals, were originally meant to draw
the gaze upward and to induce, by indirection, contemplation of
heaven and its rewards. Underpitch vaults, barrel vaults, grain
vaults, fan vaults, quadripartite and sexpartite and tierceron vaults
are more than mere arches; they were conceived as agents of religion, quiet advertisements for Him and His authority. From the
start Hal and I were determined that no vaulted ceilings, no spires,
no arched windows or doors, no slightest design element born of
religion would be incorporated into a Fallon and Sheen building. In
reaction we strove to direct the eye earthward and, by a thousand
devices, to remind those who passed through our structures that
they were born of the earth, not children of any god but merely
more intellectually advanced cousins of apes.

Hal's reconversion to the Roman Catholicism of his childhood
was, therefore, a shock to me. At the age of thirty-seven, when he
was at the top of his profession, when by his singular success he had
proven the supremacy of unoppressed, rational man over imagined
divinities, he returned with apparent joy to the confessional, humbled himself at the communion rail, dampened his forehead and
breast with so-called holy water, and thereby rejected the intellectual
foundation on which his entire adult life, to that point, had been
based.

The horror of it chilled my heart, my marrow.

For taking Hal Sheen from me, I despised religion more than ever. I redoubled my efforts to eliminate any wisp of religious thought or superstition from my son's life, and I was fiercely determined that Benny would never be stolen from me by incense-burning, bell-ringing, hymn-singing, self-deluded, mush-brained fools. When he proved to be a voracious reader from an early age, I carefully chose books for him, directing him away from works that even indirectly portrayed religion as an acceptable part of life, firmly steering him to strictly secular material that would not encourage unhealthy fantasies. When I saw that he was fascinated by vampires, ghosts, and the entire panoply of traditional monsters that seem to intrigue all children, I strenuously discouraged that interest, mocked it, and taught him the virtue and pleasure of rising above such childish things. Oh, I did not deny him the enjoyment of a good scare, for there's nothing religious in that. Benny was permitted to savor the fear induced by books about killer robots, movies about the Frankenstein monster, and other threats that were the work of man. It was only monsters of satanic origin that I censored from his books and films, for belief in things satanic is merely another facet of religion, the flip side of God worship.

I allowed him Santa Claus until he was seven, though I had a lot of misgivings about that indulgence. The Santa Claus legend includes a Christian element, of course. Good *Saint* Nick and all that. But Ellen was insistent that Benny would not be denied that fantasy. I reluctantly agreed that it was probably harmless, but only as long as we scrupulously observed the holiday as a secular event having nothing to do with the birth of Jesus. To us Christmas was a celebration of the family and a healthy indulgence in materialism.

In the back yard of our big house in Buck's County, Pennsylvania, grew a pair of enormous, long-lived cherry trees, under the branches of which Benny and I often sat in the milder seasons, playing checkers or card games. Beneath those boughs, which already had lost most of their leaves to the tugging hands of autumn, on an unusually warm day in early October of his seventh year, as we were playing Uncle Wiggly, Benny asked if I thought Santa was going to bring him lots of stuff that year. I said it was too early to be thinking about Santa, and he said that *all* the kids were thinking about Santa and were starting to compose want lists already. Then he said, "Daddy, how's Santa *know* we've been good or bad. He can't watch all us kids all the time, can he? Do our guardian angels talk to him and tattle on us, or what?"

"Guardian angels?" I said, startled and displeased. "What do you know about guardian angels?"

"Well, they're supposed to watch over us, help us when we're in trouble, right? So I thought maybe they also talk to Santa Claus."

Only months after Benny was born, I had joined with like-minded parents in our community to establish a private school guided by the principals of secular humanism, where even the slightest religious thought would be kept out of the curriculum; in fact our intention was to insure that, as our children matured, they would be taught history, literature, sociology, and ethics from an anti-clerical viewpoint. Benny had attended our preschool and, by that October of which I write, was in second-grade of the elementary division, where his classmates came from families guided by the same rational principals as our own. I was surprised to hear that in such an environment he was still subjected to religious propagandizing.

"Who told you about guardian angels?"

"Some kids."

"They believe in these angels?"

"Sure. I guess."

"Why?"

"They saw it on TV."

"They did, huh?"

"It was a show you won't let me watch. *Highway to Heaven.*"

"And just because they saw it on TV they think it's true?"

Benny shrugged and moved his game piece five spaces along the Uncle Wiggly board.

I believed then that popular culture—especially television—was the bane of all men and women of reason and good will, not least of all because it promoted a wide variety of religious superstitions and, by its saturation of every aspect of our lives, was inescapable and powerfully influential. Books and movies like *The Exorcist* and television programs like *Highway to Heaven* could frustrate even the most diligent parent's attempts to raise his child in an atmosphere of untainted rationality.

The unseasonably warm October breeze was not strong enough to disturb the game cards, but it gently ruffled Benny's fine brown hair. Wind-mussed, sitting on a pillow on his redwood chair in order to be at table level, he was so small and vulnerable. Loving him, wanting the best possible life for him, I grew angrier by the second; my anger was directed not at Benny but at those who, intellectually and emotionally stunted by their twisted philosophy, would propagandize an innocent child.

"Benny," I said, "listen, there are no guardian angels. They don't exist. It's all an ugly lie told by people who want to make you believe that you aren't responsible for your own successes in life. They want you to believe that the bad things in life are the result of your sins and *are* your fault, but that all the good things come from the grace

of God. It's a way to control you. That's what all religion is—a tool
to control and oppress you."

He blinked at me. "Grace who?"

It was my turn to blink. "What?"

"Who's Grace? You mean Mrs. Grace Keever at the toy shop?
What tool will she use to press me with?" He giggled. "Will I be
all mashed flat and on a hanger when they're done? Daddy, you're
silly."

He was only a seven-year-old boy, after all, and I was solemnly
discussing the oppressive nature of religious belief as if we were two
intellectuals drinking espresso in a coffee house. Blushing at the
realization of my own capacity for foolishness, I pushed aside the
Uncle Wiggly board and struggled harder to make him understand
why believing in such nonsense as guardian angels was not merely
innocent fun but was a step toward intellectual and emotional en-
slavement of a particularly pernicious sort. When he seemed alter-
nately bored, confused, embarrassed, and utterly baffled—but never
for a moment even slightly enlightened—I grew frustrated, and at
last (I am now ashamed to admit this) I made my point by taking
Santa Claus away from him.

Suddenly it seemed clear to me that by allowing him to indulge
in the Santa myth, I'd laid the groundwork for the very irrationality
that I was determined to prevent him from adopting. How could I
have been so misguided as to believe that Christmas could be celebrated entirely in a secular spirit, without giving credence to the
religious tradition that was, after all, the genesis of the holiday. Now
I saw that erecting a Christmas tree in our home and exchanging
gifts, by association with such other Christmas paraphernalia as
manger scenes on church lawns and trumpet-tooting plastic angels
in department-store decorations, had generated in Benny an assumption that the spiritual aspect of the celebration had as much
validity as the materialistic aspect, which made him fertile ground
for tales of guardian angels and all the other rot about sin and
salvation.

Under the boughs of the cherry trees, in an October breeze that
was blowing us slowly toward another Christmas, I told Benny the
truth about Santa Claus, explained that the gifts came from his
mother and me. He protested that he had evidence of Santa's reality:
the cookies and milk that he always left out for the jolly fat man
and that were unfailingly consumed. I convinced him that Santa's
sweet tooth was in fact my own and that the milk—which I don't
like—was always poured down the drain. Methodically, relentlessly—but with what I thought was kindness and love—I stripped
from him all of the so-called magic of Christmas and left him in no

doubt that the Santa stuff had been a well-meant but mistaken deception.

He listened with no further protest, and when I was finished he claimed to be sleepy and in need of a nap. He rubbed his eyes and yawned elaborately. He had no more interest in Uncle Wiggly and went straight into the house and up to his room.

The last thing I said to him there beneath the cherry trees was that strong, well-balanced people have no need of imaginary friends like Santa Claus and guardian angels. "All we can count on is ourselves, our friends, and our families, Benny. If we want something in life, we can't get it by asking Santa Claus and certainly not by praying for it. We get it only by earning it—or by benefitting from the generosity of friends or relatives. There's no reason ever to *wish* for or pray for anything."

Three years later, when Benny was in the hospital and dying of bone cancer, I understood for the first time why other people felt a need to believe in God and to seek comfort in prayer. Our lives are touched by some tragedies so enormous and so difficult to bear that the temptation to seek mystical answers to the cruelty of the world is powerful indeed.

Even if we can accept that our own deaths are final and that no souls survive the decomposition of our flesh, we often can't endure the idea that our *children*, when stricken in youth, are also doomed to pass from this world into no other. Children are special, so how can it be that they too will be wiped out as completely as if they had never existed? I have seen atheists, despising religion and incapable of praying for themselves, suddenly invoke the name of God in behalf of their own seriously ill children—then realize, sometimes with embarrassment but often with regret, that their philosophy denies them the foolishness of petitioning for divine intercession.

When Benny was afflicted with bone cancer, I was not shaken from my convictions; not once during the ordeal did I put principles aside and turn blubberingly to God. I was stalwart, steadfast, stoical, and determined to bear the burden by myself, though there were times when the weight bowed my head and when the very bones of my shoulders felt as if they would splinter and collapse under a mountain of grief.

That day in October of Benny's seventh year, as I sat beneath the cherry trees and watched him return to the house to nap, I did not know how severely my principles and self-reliance would be tested in the days to come. I was proud of having freed my son of his Christ-related fantasies about Santa Claus, and I was pompously certain that the day would come when Benny, grown to adulthood,

would eventually thank me for the rigorously rational upbringing
that he had received.

When Hal Sheen told me that he had returned to the fold of the
Catholic church, I thought he was setting me up for a joke. We were
having an after-work cocktail at a hotel bar near our offices, and I
was under the impression that the purpose of our meeting was to
celebrate some grand commission that Hal had won for us. "I've
got news for you," he had said cryptically that morning. "Let's meet
at the Regency for a drink at six o'clock." But instead of telling me
that we had been chosen to design a building that would add another
chapter to the legend of Fallon and Sheen, he told me that after
more than a year of quiet debate with himself, he had shed his
atheism as if it were a moldy cocoon and had flown forth into the
realm of faith once more. I laughed, waiting for the punch line, and
he smiled, and in his smile there was something—perhaps pity for
me—that instantly convinced me that he was serious.

I argued quietly, then not so quietly. I scorned his claim to have
rediscovered God, and I tried to shame him for his surrender of
intellectual dignity.

"I've decided a man can be both an intellectual and a practicing
Christian or Jew or Buddhist," Hal said with annoying self-
possession.

"Impossible!" I said, striking our table with one fist to emphasize
my rejection of that muddle-headed contention. Our cocktail glasses
rattled, and an unused ashtray nearly fell on the floor, which caused
other patrons to look our way.

"Look at Malcolm Muggeridge," Hal said. "Or C. S. Lewis. Isaac
Singer. Christians and a Jew—*and* undisputed intellectuals."

"Listen to you!" I said, appalled. "On how many occasions have
other people raised those names—and others—when we were arguing the intellectual supremacy of atheism, and you joined me in
proving what fools the Muggeridges, Lewises, and Singers of this
world really are."

He shrugged. "I was wrong."

"Just like that?"

"No, not just like that. Give me some credit, Pete. I've spent a
year reading, thinking . . . I've actively resisted the urge to return
to the faith, and yet I've been won over."

"By whom? What propagandizing priest or—"

"No one won me over. It's been entirely an inner debate, Pete.
No one but me has known that I've been wavering on this tightrope."

"Then what started you wavering?"

"Well, for a couple of years now, my life has been empty. . . ."

"Empty? You're young and healthy. You're married to a smart and beautiful woman. You're at the top of your profession, admired by one and all for the freshness and vigor of your architectural vision, and you're wealthy! You call that an empty life?"

He nodded. "Empty. But I couldn't figure out why. Just like you, I added up all that I've got, and it seemed like I should be the most fulfilled man on the face of the earth. But I felt hollow, and each new project we approached had less interest for me. Gradually I realized that all I'd built and that all I might build in the days to come was not going to satisfy me because the achievements were not lasting. Oh, sure, one of our buildings might stand for two hundred years, but a couple of centuries are but a grain of sand falling in the hourglass of Time. Structures of stone and steel and glass are not enduring monuments; they're not, as we once thought, testimonies to the singular genius of mankind. Rather the opposite: they're reminders that even our mightiest structures are fragile, that our greatest achievements can be quickly erased by earthquakes, wars, tidal waves, or simply by the slow gnawing of a thousand years of sun and wind and rain. So what's the point?"

"The point," I reminded him angrily, "is that by erecting those structures, by creating better and more beautiful buildings, we are improving the lives of our fellow men and encouraging others to reach toward higher goals of their own, and then together all of us are making a better future for the whole human species."

"Yes, but to what end?" he pressed. "If there's no afterlife, if each individual's existence ends entirely in the grave, then the *collective* fate of the species is precisely that of the individual: death, emptiness, blackness, nothingness. Nothing can come from nothing. You can't claim a noble, higher purpose for the species as a whole when you allow no higher purpose for the individual spirit." He raised one hand to halt my response. "I know, I know. You've arguments against that statement. I've supported you in them through countless debates on the subject. But I can't support you any more, Pete. I think there *is* some purpose to life besides just living, and if I didn't think so then I would leave the business and spend the rest of my life having fun, enjoying the precious finite number of days left to me. However, now that I believe there is something called a soul and that it survives the body, I can go on working at Fallon and Sheen because it's my destiny to do so, which means the achievements there are meaningful. I hope you'll be able to accept this. I'm not going to proselytise. This is the first and last time you'll hear me mention religion because I'll respect your right *not* to believe. I'm sure we can go on as before."

But we could not.

I felt that religion was a hateful degenerative sickness of the mind, and I was thereafter uncomfortable in Hal's presence. I still pretended that we were close, that nothing had changed between us, but I felt that he was not the same man he had been.

Besides, Hal's new faith inevitably began to infect his fine architectural vision. Vaulted ceilings and arched windows began to appear in his designs, and everywhere his new buildings encouraged the eye and mind to look up and regard the heavens. This change of direction was welcomed by certain clients and even praised by critics in prestigious journals, but I could not abide it because I knew he was regressing from the man-centered architecture that had been our claim to originality. Fourteen months after his embrace of the Roman Catholic Church, I sold out my share of the company to him and set up my own organization free of his influence.

"Hal," I told him the last time I saw him, "even when you claimed to be atheist, you evidently never understood that the nothingness at the end of life isn't to be feared or raged against. Either accept it regretfully as a fact of life . . . or welcome it."

Personally, I welcomed it, because not having to concern myself about my fate in the afterlife was liberating. Being a nonbeliever, I could concentrate entirely on winning the rewards of *this* world, the one and only world.

The night of the day that I took Santa Claus away from Benny, the night Ellen told me that she wanted to kick me in the ass, as we lay in our moonlit bedroom on opposite sides of the large four-poster bed, she also said, "Pete, you've told me all about your childhood, and of course I've met your folks, so I have a good idea what it must've been like to be raised in that crackpot atmosphere. I can understand why you'd react against their religious fanaticism by embracing atheism. But sometimes . . . you get carried away. You aren't happy to just *be* an atheist; you're so eager to impose your philosophy on everyone else, no matter the cost, that sometimes you behave very much like your own parents . . . except instead of selling God, you're selling godlessness."

I raised up on the bed and looked at her blanket-shrouded form. I couldn't see her face; she was turned away from me. "That's just plain nasty, Ellen."

"It's true."

"I'm nothing like my parents. Nothing like them. I don't *beat* atheism into Benny the way they tried to beat God into me."

"What you did to him today was as bad as beating him."

"Ellen, all kids learn the truth about Santa Claus eventually, some of them even sooner than Benny did."

She turned toward me, and suddenly I could see her face just well enough to discern the anger in it but, unfortunately, not well enough to glimpse the love that I knew was also there. She said, "Sure, they all learn the truth about Santa Claus, but they don't have the fantasy ripped away from them by their own fathers, damn it!"

"I didn't *rip* it away. I reasoned him out of it."

"He's not a college boy on a debating team," she said. "You can't reason with a seven-year-old. They're all emotion at that age, all heart. Pete, he came into the house today after you were done with him, and he went up to his room, and an hour later when I went up there he was still crying."

"Okay, okay," I said. "I feel like a shit."

"Good. You should."

"And I'll admit that I could have handled it better, been more tactful about it."

She turned away from me again and said nothing.

"But I didn't do anything wrong." I said. "I mean, it was a real mistake to think we could celebrate Christmas in a strictly secular way. Innocent fantasies can lead to some that aren't so innocent."

"Oh, shut up," she said again. "Shut up and go to sleep before I forget I love you."

The trucker who killed Ellen was trying to make more money to buy a boat. He was a fisherman whose passion was trolling; to afford the boat he had to take on more work. He was using amphetamines to stay awake. The truck was a Peterbilt, the biggest one they make. Ellen was driving her blue BMW. They hit head on, and though she apparently tried to take evasive action, she never had a chance.

Benny was devastated. I put all work aside and stayed home with him the entire month of July. He needed a lot of hugging, reassuring, and some gentle guidance toward acceptance of the tragedy. I was in bad shape too, for Ellen had been more than my wife and lover: she had been my toughest critic, my greatest champion, my best friend, and my only confidant. At night, alone in the bedroom we had shared, I put my face against the pillow upon which she had slept, breathed in the faintly lingering scent of her, and wept; I couldn't bear to wash the pillowcase for weeks. But in front of Benny, I managed for the most part to maintain control of myself and provide him with the example of strength that he so terribly needed.

There was no funeral. Ellen was cremated, and her ashes were dispersed at sea.

A month later, on the first Sunday in August, when we had begun to move grudgingly and sadly toward acceptance, forty or fifty friends and relatives came to the house, and we held a quiet memorial service for Ellen, a purely secular service with not even the slightest thread of religious content. We gathered on the patio near the pool, and half a dozen friends stepped forward to tell amusing stories about Ellen and to explain what an impact she'd had on their lives.

I kept Benny at my side throughout the service, for I wanted him to see that his mother had been loved by others, too, and that her existence had made a difference in more lives than his and mine. He was only eight years old, but he seemed to take from the service the very comfort that I had hoped it would give him. Hearing his mother praised, he was unable to hold back his tears, but now there was something more than grief in his face and eyes: now he was also proud of her, amused by some of the practical jokes that she had played on friends and that they now recounted, and intrigued to hear about aspects of her that had theretofore been invisible to him. In time these new emotions were certain to dilute his grief and help him adjust to his loss.

The day following the memorial service, I rose late. When I went looking for Benny, I found him beneath one of the cherry trees in the back yard. He sat with his knees drawn up against his chest and his arms around his legs, staring at the far side of the broad valley on one slope of which we lived, but he seemed to be looking at something still more distant.

I sat beside him. "How you doin'?"

"Okay," he said.

For a while neither of us spoke. Overhead the leaves of the tree rustled softly. The dazzling white-pink blossoms of spring were long gone, of course, and the branches were bedecked with fruit not yet quite ripe. The day was hot, but the tree threw plentiful, cool shade.

At last he said, "Daddy?"

"Hmmmm?"

"If it's all right with you . . ."

"What?"

"I know what you say . . ."

"What I say about what?"

"About there being no heaven or angels or anything like that."

"It's not just what I say, Benny. It's true."

"Well . . . just the same, if it's all right with you, I'm going to picture Mommy in heaven, wings and everything."

I knew he was still in a fragile emotional condition even a month after her death and that he would need many more months if not years to regain his full equilibrium, so I did not rush to respond with one of my usual arguments about the foolishness of religious faith. I was silent for a moment, then said, "Well, let me think about that for a couple minutes, okay?"

We sat side by side, staring across the valley, and I know that neither of us was seeing the landscape before us. I was seeing Ellen as she had been on the Fourth of July the previous summer, wearing white shorts and a yellow blouse, tossing a Frisbee with me and Benny, radiant, laughing, laughing. I don't know what poor Benny was seeing, though I suspect his mind was brimming with gaudy images of heaven complete with haloed angels and golden steps spiraling up to a golden throne.

"She can't just end," he said after a while. "She was too nice to j-j-just end. She's got to be . . . somewhere."

"But that's just it, Benny. She *is* somewhere. Your mother goes on in you. You've got her genes, for one thing. You don't know what genes are, but you've got them: her hair, her eyes . . . And because she was a good person who taught you the right values, you'll grow up to be a good person, as well, and you'll have kids of your own some day, and your mother will go on in them and in *their* children. Your mother still lives in our memories, too, and in the memories of her friends. Because she was kind to so many people, those people were shaped to some small degree by her kindness; they'll now and then remember her, and because of her they might be kinder to people, and that kindness goes on and on."

He listened solemnly, although I suspected that the concepts of immortality through bloodline and impersonal immortality through one's moral relationships with other people were beyond his grasp. I tried to think of a way to restate it so a child could understand.

But he said, "Nope. Not good enough. It's nice that lots of people are gonna remember her. But it's not good enough. *She* has to be somewhere. Not just her memory. *She* has to go on . . . so if it's all right with you, I'm gonna figure she's in heaven."

"No, it's not all right, Benny." I put an arm around him. "The healthy thing to do, son, is to face up to unpleasant truths—"

He shook his head. "She's all right, Daddy. She didn't just end. She's somewhere now. I know she is. And she's happy."

"Benny—"

He stood, looked up into the trees, and said, "We have cherries to eat soon?"

"Benny, let's not change the subject. We—"

"Can we drive into town for lunch at Mrs. Foster's restaurant—burgers and fries and Cokes and then a cherry sundae?"

"Benny—"

"Can we, can we?"

"All right. But—"

"I get to drive!" he shouted and ran off toward the garage, giggling at his joke.

During the next year Benny's stubborn refusal to let his mother go was at first frustrating, then annoying, and finally intensely aggravating. He talked to her nearly every night as he lay in bed, waiting for sleep to come, and he seemed confident that she could hear him. Often, after I tucked him in and kissed him goodnight and left the room, he slipped out from under the covers, knelt beside the bed, and prayed that his mother was happy and safe where she had gone.

Twice I accidentally heard him. On other occasions I stood quietly in the hall after leaving his room, and when he thought I had gone downstairs, he humbled himself before God, though he could know nothing more of God than what he had illicitly learned from television shows or other pop culture that I had been unable to monitor.

I was determined to wait him out, certain that his childish faith would expire naturally when he realized that God would never answer him. As the days passed without a miraculous sign assuring him that his mother's soul had survived death, Benny would begin to understand that all he had been taught about religion was true, and he eventually would return quietly to the realm of reason where I had made—and was patiently saving—a place for him. I did not want to tell him I knew of his praying, did not want to force the issue because I knew that in reaction to a too heavy-handed exercise of parental authority, he might cling even longer to his irrational dream of life everlasting.

But after four months, when his nightly conversations with his dead mother and with God did not cease, I could no longer tolerate even whispered prayers in my house, for though I seldom heard them, I *knew* they were being said, and knowing was somehow as maddening as hearing every word of them. I confronted him. I reasoned with him at great length on many occasions. I argued, pleaded. I tried the classic carrot-and-stick approach: I punished him for the expression of any religious sentiment; and I rewarded him for the slightest antireligious statement, even if he made it unthinkingly or even if it was only my *interpretation* of what he'd said that was antireligious. He received few rewards and much punishment. I did not spank him or in any way physically abuse him; that much, at least, is to my credit; I did not attempt to beat God out of him the way my parents had tried to beat Him *into* me.

I took Benny to Dr. Gerton, a psychiatrist, when everything else had failed. "He's having difficulty accepting his mother's death," I told Gerton. "He's just not . . . coping. I'm worried about him.

After three sessions with Benny over a period of two weeks, Dr. Gerton called to say he no longer needed to see Benny. "He's going to be all right, Mr. Fallon. You've no need to worry about him."

"But you're wrong," I insisted. "He needs analysis. He's still not . . . coping."

"Mr. Fallon, you've said that before, but I've never been able to get a clear explanation of what behavior strikes you as evidence of his inability to cope. What's he *doing* that worries you so?"

"He's praying," I said. "He prays to God to keep his mother safe and happy. And he talks to his mother as if he's sure she hears him, talks to her *every* night."

"Oh, Mr. Fallon, if that's all that's been bothering you, I can assure you there's no need to worry. Talking to his mother, praying for her, all that's perfectly ordinary and—"

"Every night!" I repeated.

"Ten times a day would be all right. Really, there's nothing un-healthy about it. Talking to God about his mother and talking to his mother in heaven . . . it's just a psychological mechanism by which he can slowly adjust to the fact that she's no longer actually here on earth with him. It's perfectly ordinary."

I'm afraid I shouted: "It's not perfectly ordinary in *this* house, Dr. Gerton. We're atheists!"

He was silent for a moment, then sighed. "Mr. Fallon, you've got to remember that your son is more than your son—he's a person in his own right. A *little* person but a person nonetheless. You can't think of him as property or as an unformed mind to be molded—"

"I have the utmost respect for the individual, Dr. Fallon. Much more respect than do the hymn-singers who value their fellow men less than they do their imaginary master in the sky."

His silence lasted longer than before. Finally he said, "All right. Then surely you realize there's no guarantee the son will be the same person in every respect as the father. He'll have ideas and desires of his own. And ideas about religion might be one area in which the disagreement between you will widen over the years rather than narrow. This might not be *only* a psychological mechanism that he's using to adapt to his mother's death; it might also turn out to be the start of lifelong faith. At least you have to be prepared for the possibility."

"I won't have it," I said firmly.

His third silence was the longest of all. Then: "Mr. Fallon, I have no need to see Benny again. There's nothing I can do for him because there's nothing he really needs from me. But perhaps you should consider some counseling for yourself."

I hung up on him.

* * *

For the next six months Benny infuriated and frustrated me by clinging to his fantasy of heaven. Perhaps he no longer spoke to his mother every evening, and perhaps sometimes he even forgot to say his prayers, but his stubborn faith could not be shaken. When I spoke of atheism, when I made a scornful joke about God, when I tried to reason with him, he would only say, "No, Daddy, you're wrong," or "No, Daddy, that's not the way it is," and he would either walk away from me or try to change the subject. Or he would do something even more infuriating: he would say, "No, Daddy, you're wrong," and then he would throw his small arms around me, hug me very tight, and tell me that he loved me, and at these moments there was a too-apparent sadness about him that included an element of pity, as if he was afraid for me and felt that *I* needed guidance and reassurance. Nothing made me angrier than that. He was nine years old, not an ancient guru! As punishment for his willful disregard of my wishes, I took away his television privileges for days—and sometimes weeks—at a time, forbid him to have dessert after dinner, and once refused to allow him to play with his friends for an entire month. Nothing worked.

Religion, the disease that had turned my parents into stern and solemn strangers, the disease that had made my childhood a nightmare, the very sickness that had stolen my best friend, Hal Sheen, from me when I least expected to lose him, *religion* had now wormed its way into my house again. It had contaminated my son, the only important person left in my life. No, it wasn't any particular religion that had a grip on Benny. He didn't have any formal theological education, so his concepts of God and heaven were thoroughly nondenominational, vaguely Christian, yes, but only vaguely. It was religion without structure, without dogma or doctrine, religion based entirely on childish sentiment; therefore some might say that it was not really religion at all, and that I should not have worried about it. But I knew Dr. Gerton's observation was true: this childish faith might be the seed from which a true religious conviction would grow in later years. The virus of religion was loose in my house, and I was dismayed, distraught, and perhaps even somewhat deranged by my failure to find a cure for it.

To me, this was the essence of horror. It wasn't the acute horror of a bomb blast or plane crash, mercifully brief, but a chronic horror that went on day after day, week after week.

I was sure that the worst of all possible troubles had befallen me and that I was in the darkest time of my life.

Then Benny got bone cancer.

* * *

Nearly two years after his mother died, on a blustery day in later February, we were in the park by the river, flying a kite. When Benny ran with the control stick, paying out string, he fell down. Not just once. Not twice. Repeatedly. When I asked what was wrong, he said he had a sore muscle in his right leg: "Must've twisted it when the guys and I were climbing trees yesterday."

He favored the leg for a couple of days, and when I suggested he ought to see a doctor, he said he was feeling better.

A week later he was in the hospital, undergoing tests, and in another two days, the diagnosis was confirmed: bone cancer. It was too widespread for surgery. His physicians instituted an immediate program of radium treatments and chemotherapy.

Benny lost his hair, lost weight. He grew so pale that each morning I was afraid to look at him because I had the crazy idea that if he got any paler he would begin to turn transparent and, when he was finally as clear as glass, would shatter in front of my eyes.

After five weeks he took a sudden turn for the better and was, though not in remission, at least well enough to come home. The radium and chemotherapy were continued on an outpatient basis.

I think now that he improved not due to the radium or cytotoxic agents or drugs but simply because he wanted to see the cherry trees in bloom one last time. His temporary turn for the better was an act of sheer will, a triumph of mind over body.

Except for one day when a sprinkle of rain fell, he sat in a chair under the blossom-laden boughs, enjoying the spring greening of the valley and delighting in the antics of the squirrels that came out of the nearby woods to frolic on our lawn. He sat not in one of the redwood lawn chairs but in a big, comfortably padded easy chair that I brought out from the house, his legs propped on a hassock, for he was thin and fragile; a harder chair would have bruised him horribly.

We played card games and Chinese checkers, but usually he was too tired to concentrate on a game for long, so mostly we just sat there, relaxing. We talked of days past, of the many good times he'd had in his ten short years, and of his mother. But we sat in silence a lot, too. It was never an awkward silence; sometimes melancholy, yes, but never awkward.

Neither of us spoke of God or guardian angels or heaven. I know he had not lost his belief that his mother had survived the death of her body in some form and that she had gone on to a better place. But he said nothing more of that and did not discuss his own hopes for the afterlife. I believe he avoided the subject out of respect for me and because he wanted no friction between us during those last days.

I will always be grateful to him for not putting me to the test. I am afraid that I'd have tried to force him to embrace rationalism even in his last days, thereby making a bigger jackass of myself than usual.

After only nine days at home, he suffered a relapse and returned to the hospital. I booked him into a semi-private room with two beds: he took one, and I took the other.

Cancer cells had migrated to his liver, and a tumor was found there. After surgery he improved for a few days, was almost buoyant, but then sank again.

Cancer was found in his lymphatic system, in his spleen, tumors everywhere.

His condition improved, declined, improved, and declined again. However each improvement was less encouraging than the one before it, while each decline was steeper.

I was rich, intelligent, and talented. I was famous in my field. But I could do nothing to save my son. I had never felt so small, so powerless.

At least I could be strong for Benny. In his presence I tried to be cheerful. I did not let him see me cry, but I wept quietly at night, curled in the fetal position, reduced to the helplessness of a child, while he lay in troubled, drug-induced slumber on the other side of the room. During the day, when he was away for therapy or tests or surgery, I sat at the window, staring out, seeing nothing.

As if some alchemical spell had been cast, the world became gray, entirely gray. I was aware of no color in anything; I might have been living in an old black-and-white movie. Shadows became more stark and sharp-edged. The air itself seemed gray, as though contaminated by a toxic mist so fine that it could not be seen, only sensed. Voices were fuzzy, the audial equivalent of gray. The few times that I switched on the TV or the radio, the music seemed to have no melody that I could discern. My interior world was as gray as the physical world around me, and the unseen but acutely sensed mist that fouled the outer world had penetrated to my core.

Even in the depths of that despair, I did not step off the path of reason, did not turn to God for help or condemn God for torturing an innocent child. I did not consider seeking the counsel of clergymen or the help of faith healers.

I endured.

If I had slipped and sought solace in superstition, no one could have blamed me. In little more than two years, I'd had a falling out with my only close friend, had lost my wife in a traffic accident, and had seen my son succumb to cancer. Occasionally you hear about people with bad runs of luck like that, or you read about them in the papers, and strangely enough they usually talk about how they were brought to God by their suffering and how they found peace in faith. Reading about them always makes you sad and stirs your compassion, and you can even forgive them their witless religious sentimentality. Of course, you always quickly put them out of your mind because you know that a similar chain of tragedies could befall you, and such a realization does not bear contemplation. Now I not only had to contemplate it but *live* it, and in the living I did not bend my principles.

I faced the void and accepted it.

After putting up a surprisingly long, valiant, painful struggle against the virulent cancer that was eating him alive, Benny finally died on a night in August. They had rushed him into the intensive care unit two days before, and I had been permitted to sit with him only fifteen minutes every second hour. On that last night, however, they allowed me to come in from the ICU lounge and stay beside his bed for several hours because they knew he did not have long.

An intravenous drip pierced his left arm. An aspirator was inserted in his nose. He was hooked up to an EKG machine that traced his heart activity in green light on a bedside monitor, and each beat was marked by a soft beep. The lines and the beeps frequently became erratic for as much as three or four minutes at a time.

I held his hand. I smoothed the sweat-damp hair away from his brow. I pulled the covers up to his neck when he was seized by chills and lowered them when the chills gave way to fevers.

Benny slipped in and out of consciousness. Even when awake he was not always alert or coherent.

"Daddy?"

"Yes, Benny?"

"Is that you?"

"It's me."

"Where am I?"

"In bed. Safe. I'm here, Benny."

"Is supper ready?"

"Not yet."

"I'd like burgers and fries."

"That's what we're having."

"Where're my shoes?"

"You don't need shoes tonight, Benny."

"Thought we were going for a walk."

"Not tonight."

"Oh."

Then he sighed and slipped away again.

Rain was falling outside. Drops pattered against the ICU windows and streamed down the panes. The storm contributed to the gray mood that had claimed the world.

Once, near midnight, Benny woke and was lucid. He knew exactly where he was, who I was, and what was happening. He turned his head toward me and smiled. He tried to rise up on one arm, but he was too weak even to lift his head.

I got out of my chair, stood at the side of his bed, held his hand, and said, "All these wires . . . I think they're going to replace a few of your parts with robot stuff."

"I'll be okay," he said in a faint, tremulous voice that was strangely, movingly confident.

"You want a chip of ice to suck on?"

"No. What I want . . ."

"What? Anything you want, Benny."

"I'm scared, Daddy . . ."

My throat grew tight, and I was afraid that I was going to lose the composure that I had strived so hard to hold onto during the long weeks of his illness. I swallowed and said, "Don't be scared, Benny. I'm with you. Don't—"

"No," he said, interrupting me. "I'm not scared . . . for me. I'm afraid . . . for you."

I thought he was delirious again, and I didn't know what to say.

But he was not delirious, and with his next few words he made himself painfully clear: "I want us all . . . to be together again . . . like we were before Mommy died . . . together again someday. But I'm afraid that you . . . won't . . . find us."

The rest is agonizing to recall. I was indeed so obsessed with holding fast to my atheism that I could not bring myself to tell my son a harmless lie that would make his last minutes easier. If only I had promised to believe, had told him that I would seek him in the next world, he would have gone to his rest more happily. Ellen was right when she called it an obsession. I merely held Benny's hand tighter, blinked back tears, and smiled at him.

He said, "If you don't believe you can find us . . . then maybe you won't find us."

"It's all right, Benny," I said soothingly. I kissed him on the forehead, on his left cheek, and for a moment I put my face against his and held him as best I could, trying to compensate with affection for the promise of faith that I refused to give.

"Daddy . . . if only . . . you'd look for us?"

"You'll be okay, Benny."

". . . just *look* for us . . ."

"I love you, Benny. I love you with all my heart."

". . . if you look for us . . . you'll find us . . ."

"I love you, I love you, Benny."

". . . don't look . . . won't find . . ."

"Benny, Benny. . . ."

The gray ICU light fell on the gray sheets and on the gray face of my son.

The gray rain streamed down the gray window.

He died while I held him.

Abruptly color came back into the world. Far too much color, too intense, overwhelming. The light brown of Benny's staring, sightless eyes was the purest, most penetrating, most beautiful brown that I had ever seen. The ICU walls were a pale blue that made me feel as if they were not made of plaster but of water, and as if I was about to be drowned in a turbulent sea. The sour-apple green of the EKG monitor screen blazed bright, searing my eyes. The watery blue walls flowed toward me. I heard running footsteps as nurses and interns responded to the lack of telemetry data from their small patient, but before they arrived I was swept away by a blue tide, carried into deep blue currents.

I shut down my company. I withdrew from negotiations for new commissions. I arranged for those commissions already undertaken to be transferred as quickly as possible to other design firms of which I approved and with which my clients felt comfortable. I pink-slipped my employees, though with generous severance pay, and helped them to find new jobs where possible.

I converted my wealth into treasury certificates and conservative savings instruments, investments that required no monitoring. The temptation to sell the house was great, but after considerable thought I merely closed it up and hired a part-time caretaker to look after it in my absence.

Years later than Hal Sheen, I had reached his conclusion that no monuments of man were worth the effort it took to erect them. Even the greatest edifices of stone and steel were pathetic vanities, of no consequence in the long run. When viewed in the context of the vast, cold universe in which trillions of stars blazed down on tens of trillions of planets, even the pyramids were as fragile as origami sculptures. In the dark light of death and entropy, even heroic effort and acts of genius appeared foolish.

Yet relationships with family and friends were no more enduring than humanity's fragile monuments of stone. I had once told Benny that we lived on in memory, in the genetic trace, in the kindness that our own kindnesses encouraged in others. But those things now seemed as insubstantial as shapes of smoke in a brisk wind.

Unlike Hal Sheen, however, I did not seek comfort in religion. No blows were hard enough to crack my obsession.

I had thought that religious mania was the worst horror of all, but now I had found one that was worse: the horror of an atheist who, unable to believe in God, is suddenly also unable to believe in the value of human struggle and courage, and is therefore unable to find meaning in anything whatsoever, neither in beauty nor in pleasure nor in the smallest act of kindness.

I spent that autumn in Bermuda. I bought a Cheoy Lee sixty-six-foot sport yacht, a sleek and powerful boat, and learned how to handle it. Alone, I ran the Caribbean, sampling island after island. Sometimes I dawdled along at quarter-throttle for days at a time, in sync with the lazy rhythms of Caribbean life. But then suddenly I would be overcome with the frantic need to move, to stop wasting time, and I would press forward, engines screaming, slamming across the waves with reckless abandon, as if it mattered whether I got anywhere by any particular time.

When I tired of the Caribbean, I went to Brazil, but Rio held interest for only a few days. I became a rich drifter, moving from one first-class hotel to another in one far-flung city after another: Hong Kong, Singapore, Istanbul, Paris, Athens, Cairo, New York, Las Vegas, Acapulco, Tokyo, San Francisco. I was looking for something that would give meaning to life, though the search was conducted with the certain knowledge that I would not find what I sought.

For a few days I thought I could devote my life to gambling. In the random fall of cards, in the spin of roulette wheels, I glimpsed the strange, wild shape of fate. By committing myself to swimming in that deep river of randomness, I thought I might be in harmony with the pointlessness and disorder of the universe and therefore at peace. In less than a week I won and lost fortunes, and at last I walked away from the gaming tables with a hundred-thousand-dollar loss. That was only a tiny fraction of the millions on which I could draw, but in those few days I learned that even immersion in the chaos of random chance provided no escape from an awareness of the finite nature of life and of all things human.

In the spring I went home to die. I'm not sure if I meant to kill myself. Or, having lost the will to live, perhaps I believed that I could just lie down in a familiar place and succumb to death without needing to lift my hand against myself. But although I did not know how death would be attained, I was certain death was my goal.

The house in Buck's County was filled with painful memories of Ellen and Benny, and when I went into the kitchen and looked out the window at the cherry trees in the back yard, my heart ached as if pinched in a vise. The trees were ablaze with thousands of pink and white blossoms.

Benny had loved the cherry trees when they were at their radiant best, and the sight of their blossoms sharpened my memories of Benny so well that I felt I had been stabbed. For a while I leaned against the kitchen counter, unable to breathe, then gasped painfully for breath, then wept.

In time I went out and stood beneath the trees, looking up at the beautifully decorated branches. Benny had been dead almost nine months, but the trees he had loved were still thriving, and in some way I could not quite grasp, their continued existence meant that at least a part of Benny was still alive. I struggled to understand that crazy idea—

—and suddenly the cherry blossoms fell. Not just a few. Not just hundreds. Within one minute every blossom on both trees dropped to the ground. I turned around, around, startled and confused, and the whirling white flowers were as thick as snowflakes in a blizzard. I had never seen anything like it. Cherry blossoms just don't fall by the thousands, simultaneously, on a windless day.

When the phenomenon ended I plucked blossoms off my shoulders and out of my hair. I examined them closely. They were not withered or seared or marked by any sign of tree disease.

I looked up at the branches.

Not one blossom remained on either tree.

My heart was hammering.

Around my feet, drifts of cherry blossoms began to stir in a mild breeze that sprang up from the west.

"No," I said, so frightened that I could not even admit to myself what I was saying no *to*.

I turned from the trees and ran to the house. As I went, the last of the cherry blossoms blew off my hair and clothes.

In the library, however, as I took a bottle of Jack Daniels from the bar cabinet, I realized that I was still clutching blossoms in my hand. I threw them down on the floor and scrubbed my palm on my pants as if I had been handling something foul.

I went to the bedroom with the Jack Daniels and drank myself unconscious, refusing to face up to the reason why I needed to drink at all. I told myself that it had nothing to do with the cherry trees, that I was drinking only because I needed to escape the misery of the past few years.

Mine was a diamond-hard obsession.

I slept for eleven hours and woke with a hangover. I took two aspirin, stood in the shower under very hot water for fifteen minutes, under a cold spray for one minute, toweled vigorously, took two more aspirins, and went into the kitchen to make coffee.

Through the window above the sink, I saw the cherry trees ablaze with pink and white blossoms.

Hallucination, I thought with relief. Yesterday's blizzard of blossoms was just hallucination.

I ran outside for a closer look at the trees. I saw that only a few pink-white petals were scattered on the lush grass beneath the boughs, no more than would have blown off in the mild spring breeze.

Relieved but also curiously disappointed, I returned to the kitchen. The coffee had brewed. As I poured a cupful, I remembered the blossoms that I had cast aside in the library.

I drank two cups of fine Columbian before I had the nerve to go to the library. The blossoms were there: a wad of crushed petals that had yellowed and acquired brown edges during the night. I picked them up, closed my hand around them.

All right, I told myself shakily, you don't have to believe in Christ or in God the Father or in some bodiless Holy Spirit.

Religion is a disease.

No, no, you don't have to believe in any of the silly rituals, in the dogma and doctrine. In fact you don't have to believe in *God* to believe in an afterlife.

Irrational, unreasonable.

No, wait, think about it: Isn't it possible that life after death is perfectly natural, not a divine gift but a simple fact of nature? The caterpillar lives one life, then transforms itself to live again as a butterfly. So, damn it, isn't it conceivable that our bodies are the caterpillar stage and that our spirits take flight into another existence when the bodies are no longer of use to us? The human metamorphosis may just be a transformation of a higher order than that of the caterpillar.

Slowly, with dread and yet hope, I walked through the house, out the back door, up the sloped yard to the cherry trees. I stood beneath their flowery boughs and opened my hand to reveal the blossoms I had saved from yesterday.

"Benny?" I said wonderingly.

The blossomfall began again. From both trees, the pink and white petals dropped in profusion, spinning lazily to the grass, catching in my hair and on my clothes.

I turned, breathless, gasping. "Benny? Benny?"

In a minute the ground was covered with a white mantle, and again not one small bloom remained on the trees.

I laughed. It was a nervous laugh that might degenerate into a mad cackle. I was not in control of myself.

Not quite sure why I was speaking aloud, I said, "I'm scared. Oh, shit, am I scared."

The blossoms began to drift up from the ground. Not just a few of them. All of them. They rose back toward the branches that had shed them only moments ago. It was a blizzard in reverse. The soft petals brushed against my face.

I was laughing again, laughing uncontrollably, but my fear was fading rapidly, and this was good laughter.

Within another minute, the trees were cloaked in pink and white as before, and all was still.

I sensed that Benny was not within the tree, that this phenomenon did not conform to pagan belief any more than it did to traditional Christianity. But he was *somewhere*. He was not gone forever. He was out there somewhere, and when my time came to go where he and Ellen had gone, I only needed to believe that they could be found, and then I would surely find them.

The sound of an obsession cracking could probably be heard all the way to China.

A scrap of writing by H. G. Wells came into my mind. I had always admired Well's work, but nothing he had written had ever seemed so true as that which I recalled while standing under the cherry trees: "The past is but the beginning of a beginning, and all that is and has been is but the twilight of the dawn." He was writing about history, of course, and about the long future that awaited mankind, but those words seemed to apply, as well, to death and to the mysterious rebirth that followed it. A man might live a hundred years, yet his long life is but the twilight of the dawn.

"Benny," I said. "Oh, Benny."

But no more blossoms fell, and through the years that followed I received no more signs. Nor did I need them.

From that day forward, I knew that death was not the end and that I would be rejoined with Ellen and Benny on the other side.

And what of God? Does He exist? I don't know. Although I have believed in an afterlife of some kind for ten years now, I have not become a churchgoer. But if, upon my death, I cross into that other plane and find Him waiting for me, I will not be entirely surprised, and I will return to His arms as gratefully and happily as I will return to Ellen's and to Benny's.

SUE GRAFTON

With a Shamus Award and three Anthony Awards in two years, Sue Grafton and her unique brand of contemporary P.I. story have been well appreciated. Her Kinsey Millhone novels, alphabetized, including the Shamus Award-winning *"B" IS FOR BURGLAR* and the twice-honored *"C" IS FOR CORPSE*, rank her with the top writers of crime in the eighties.

"Non Sung Smoke" is a terrific example of how she captures the modern idiom in a taut, suspenseful story fueled by idiosyncratic characters with really bad timing. If the name Grafton sounds familiar in another context, it could be because her father C. W. Grafton was a fine mystery writer in the 1940s. Her own name is also gaining a different distinction, as the president of the Private Eye Writers of America.

Non Sung Smoke

The day was an odd one, brooding and chill, sunlight alternating with an erratic wind that was being pushed toward California in advance of a tropical storm called Bo. It was late September in Santa Teresa. Instead of the usual Indian summer, we were caught up in vague presentiments of the long, gray winter to come. I found myself pulling sweaters out of my bottom drawer and I went to the office smelling of mothballs and last year's cologne.

I spent the morning caught up in routine paperwork which usually leaves me feeling productive, but this was the end of a dull week and I was so bored I would have taken on just about anything. The young woman showed up just before lunch, announcing herself with a tentative tap on my office door. She couldn't have been more than twenty, with a sultry, pornographic face and a tumble of long dark hair. She was wearing an outfit that suggested she hadn't gone home the night before unless, of course, she simply favored low-cut sequined cocktail dresses at noon. Her spike heels were a dyed-to-match green and her legs were bare. She moved over to my desk with an air of uncertainty, like someone just learning to roller skate.

"Hi, how are you? Have a seat," I said.

She sank into a chair. "Thanks. I'm Mona Starling. I guess you're Kinsey Millhone, huh."

"Yes, that's right."

"Are you really a private detective?"

"Licensed and bonded," I said.

"Are you single?"

I did a combination nod and shrug which I hoped would cover two divorces and my current happily *un*married state.

"Great," she said, "then you'll understand. God, I can't believe I'm really doing this. I've never hired a detective, but I don't know what else to do."

312

"What's going on?"

She blushed, maybe from nervousness, maybe from embarrassment, but the heightened coloring only made her green eyes more vivid. She shifted in her seat, the sequins on her dress winking merrily. Something about her posture made me down-grade her age. She looked barely old enough to drive.

"I hope you don't think this is dumb. I . . . uh, ran into this guy last night and we really hit it off. He told me his name was Gage. I don't know if that's true or not. Sometimes guys make up names, you know, like if they're married or maybe not sure they want to see you again. Anyway, we had a terrific time, only he left without telling me how to get in touch. I was just wondering how much it might cost to find out who he is."

"How do you know he won't get in touch with you?"

"Well, he might. I mean, I'll give him a couple of days of course. All I'm asking for is his name and address. Just in case."

"I take it you'll want his phone number, too."

She laughed uneasily. "Well, yeah."

"What if he doesn't want to renew the acquaintance?"

"Oh, I wouldn't bother him if he felt that way. I know it looks like a pickup, but it really wasn't. For me, at any rate. I don't want him to think it was casual on my part."

"I take it you were . . . ah, *intimate*," I said.

"Un-uh, we just balled, but it was incredible and I'd really like to see him again."

Reluctantly, I pulled out a legal pad and made a note. "Where'd you meet this man?"

"I ran into him at Mooter's. He talked like he hung out there a lot. The music was so loud we were having to shout, so after a while we went to the bar next door where it was quiet. We talked for hours. I know what you're going to say. Like why don't I let well enough alone or something, but I just can't."

"Why not go back to Mooter's and ask around?"

"Well, I would, but I, uh, have this boyfriend who's really jealous and he'd figure it out. If I even look at another guy, he has this incredible ESP reaction. He's spooky sometimes."

"How'd you get away with it last night?"

"He was working, so I was on my own," she said. "Say you'll help me, okay? Please? I've been cruising around all night looking for his car. He lives somewhere in Montebello, I'm almost sure."

"I can probably find him, Mona, but my services aren't cheap."

"I don't care," she said. "That's fine. I have money. Just tell me how much."

I debated briefly and finally asked her for fifty bucks. I didn't have the heart to charge my usual rates. I didn't really want her business, but it was better than typing up file notes for the case I'd just done. She put a fifty-dollar bill on my desk and I wrote out a receipt, bypassing my standard contract. As young as she was, I wasn't sure it'd be binding anyway.

I jotted down a description of the man named Gage. He sounded like every stud on the prowl I've ever seen. Early thirties, five foot ten, good build, dark hair, dark moustache, great smile, and a dimple in his chin. I was prepared to keep writing, but that was the extent of it. For all of their alleged hours of conversation, she knew precious little about him. I quizzed her at length about hobbies, interests, what sort of work he did. The only real information she could give me was that he drove an old silver Jaguar which is where they "got it on" (her parlance, not mine) the first time. The second time was at her place. After that, he apparently disappeared like a puff of smoke. Real soul mates, these two. I didn't want to tell her what an old story it was. In Santa Teresa, the eligible men are so much in demand they can do anything they want. I took her address and telephone number and said I'd get back to her. As soon as she left, I picked up my handbag and car keys. I had a few personal errands to run and figured I'd tuck her business in when I was finished with my own.

Mooter's is one of a number of bars on the Santa Teresa singles' circuit. By night, it's crowded and impossibly noisy. Happy Hour features well drinks for fifty cents and the bartender rings a gong for every five-dollar tip. The tables are small, jammed together around a dance floor the size of a boxing ring. The walls are covered with caricatures of celebrities, possibly purchased from some other bar, as they seem to be signed and dedicated to someone named Stan whom nobody's ever heard of. An ex-husband of mine played jazz piano there once upon a time, but I hadn't been in for years.

I arrived that afternoon at two, just in time to watch the place being opened up. Two men, day drinkers by the look of them, edged in ahead of me and took up what I surmised were habitual perches at one end of the bar. They were exchanging the kind of pleasantries that suggest daily contact of no particular depth. The man who let us in apparently doubled as bartender and bouncer. He was in his thirties, with curly blond hair, and a T-shirt reading BOUNCER stretched across an impressively muscular chest. His arms were so big I thought he might rip his sleeves out when he flexed.

I found an empty stool at the far end of the bar and waited while he made a couple of martinis for the two men who'd come in with me. A waitress appeared for work, taking off her coat as she moved through the bar to the kitchen area.

The bartender then ambled in my direction with an inquiring look.

"I'll have a wine spritzer," I said.

A skinny guy with a guitar case came into the bar behind me. When the bartender saw him, he grinned. "Hey, how's it goin'? How's Fresno?"

They shook hands and the guy took a stool two down from mine. "Hot. And dull, but Mary Jane's was fine. We really packed 'em in."

"Smirnoff on the rocks?"

"Nah, not today. Gimme a beer instead. Bud'll do."

The bartender pulled one for him and set his drink on the bar at the same time I got mine. I wondered what it must be like to hang out all day in saloons, nursing beers, shooting the shit with idlers and ne'er-do-wells. The waitress came out of the kitchen, tying an apron around her waist. She took a sandwich order from the guys at the far end of the bar. The other fellow and I both declined when she asked if we were interested in lunch. She began to busy herself with napkins and flatware.

The bartender caught my eye. "You want to run a tab?"

I shook my head. "This is fine," I said. "I'm trying to get in touch with a guy who was in here last night."

"Good luck. The place was a zoo."

"Apparently, he's a regular. I thought you might identify him from a description."

"What's he done?"

"Not a thing. From what I was told, he picked up a young lady and ran out on her afterward. She wants to get in touch with him, that's all."

He stood and looked at me. "You're a private detective."

"That's right."

He and the other fellow exchanged a look.

The fellow said, "Help the woman. This is great."

The bartender shrugged. "Sure, why not? What's he look like?"

The waitress paused, listening in on the conversation with interest.

I mentioned the first name and description Mona'd given me. "The only other thing I know about him is he drives an old silver Jaguar."

"Gage Vesca," the other fellow said promptly.

The bartender said, "Yeah, that's him."

"You know how I might get in touch?"

The other fellow shook his head and the bartender shrugged. "All

I know is he's a jerk. The guy's got a vanity license plate reads STALYUN if that tells you anything. Besides that, he just got married a couple months back. He's bad news. Better warn your client. He'll screw anything that moves."

"I'll pass the word. Thanks." I put a five-dollar bill on the bar and hopped down off the stool, leaving the spritzer untouched.

"Hey, who's the babe?" the bartender asked.

"Can't tell you that," I said, as I picked up my bag.

The waitress spoke up. "Well, I know which one she's talking about. That girl in the green-sequined dress."

I went back to my office and checked the telephone book. No listing for Vescas of any kind. Information didn't have him either, so I put in a call to a friend of mine at the DMV who plugged the license plate into the computer. The name Gage Vesca came up, with an address in Montebello. I used my crisscross directory for a match and came up with the phone number, which I dialed just to see if it was good. As soon as the maid said "Vesca residence," I hung up.

I put in a call to Mona Starling and gave her what I had, including the warning about his marital status and his character references which were poor. She didn't seem to care. After that, I figured if she pursued him, it was her lookout . . . and his. She thanked me profusely before she rang off, relief audible in her voice.

That was Saturday.

Monday morning, I opened my front door, picked up the paper, and caught the headlines about Gage Vesca's death.

"Shit!"

He'd been shot in the head at close range sometime between two and six A.M. on Sunday, then crammed into the trunk of his Jaguar and left in the long-term parking lot at the airport. Maybe somebody hoped the body wouldn't be discovered for days. Time enough to set up an alibi or pull a disappearing act. As it was, the hood had popped open and a passerby had spotted him. My hands were starting to shake. What kind of chump had I been?

I tried Mona Starling's number and got a busy signal. I threw some clothes on, grabbed my car keys, and headed over to the Frontage Road address she'd given me. As I chirped to a stop out front, a Yellow cab pulled away from the curb with a lone passenger. I checked the house number. A duplex. I figured the odds were even that I'd just watched Mona split. She must have seen the headlines about the same time I did.

I took off again, craning for sight of the taxi somewhere ahead. Beyond the next intersection, there was a freeway on-ramp. I caught a flash of yellow and pursued it. By keeping my foot to the floor and judiciously changing lanes, I managed to slide in right behind the taxi as it took the airport exit. By the time the cab deposited Mona at the curb out in front, I was squealing into the short-term lot with the parking ticket held between my teeth. I shoved it in my handbag and ran.

The airport at Santa Teresa only has five gates, and it didn't take much detecting to figure out which one was correct. United was announcing a final boarding call for a flight to San Francisco. I used the fifty bucks Mona'd paid me to snag a seat and a boarding pass from a startled reservations clerk and then I headed for the gate. I had no luggage and nothing on me to set off the security alarm as I whipped through. I flashed my ticket, opened the double doors, and raced across the tarmac for the plane, taking the portable boarding stairs two at a time. The flight attendant pulled the door shut behind me. I was in.

I spotted Mona eight rows back in a window seat on the left-hand side, her face turned away from me. This time she was wearing jeans and an oversized shirt. The aisle seat was occupied, but the middle was empty. The plane was still sitting on the runway, engines revving, as I bumped across some guy's knees, saying, " 'scuse me, pardon me," and popped in beside Ms. Starling. She turned a blanched face toward me and a little cry escaped. "What are you doing here?"

"See if you can guess."

"I didn't do it," she whispered hoarsely.

"Yeah, right. I bet. That's probably why you got on a plane the minute the story broke," I said.

"That's *not* what happened."

"The hell it's not!"

The man on my left leaned forward and looked at us quizzically.

"The fellow she picked up Friday night got killed," I said, conversationally. I pointed my index finger at my head like a gun and fired. He decided to mind his own business, which suited me. Mona got to her feet and tried to squeeze past. All I had to do was extend my knees and she was trapped. Other people were taking an interest by now. She did a quick survey of the situation, rolled her eyes, and sat down again. "Let's get off the plane. I'll explain in a minute. Just don't make a scene," she said, the color high in her cheeks.

"Hey, let's not cause you any embarrassment," I said. "A man was murdered. That's all we're talking about."

"I know he's dead," she hissed, "but I'm innocent. I swear to God."

We got up together and bumped and thumped across the man's

knees, heading down the aisle toward the door. The flight attendant
was peeved, but she let us deplane.

We went upstairs to the airport bar and found a little table at the
rear. When the waitress came, I shook my head, but Mona ordered
a Pink Squirrel. The waitress had questions about her age, but I
had to question her taste. A Pink Squirrel? Mona had pulled her
wallet out and the waitress scrutinized her California driver's license,
checking Mona's face against the stamp-sized color photograph,
apparently satisfied at the match. As she passed the wallet back to
Mona, I snagged it and peeked at the license myself. She was twenty-
one by a month. The address was the same one she'd given me. The
waitress disappeared and Mona snatched her wallet, shoving it down
in her purse again.

"What was that for?" she said sulkily.

"Just checking. You want to tell me what's going on?"

She picked up a packet of airport matches and began to bend the
cover back and forth. "I lied to you."

"This comes as no surprise," I said. "What's the truth?"

"Well, I did pick him up, but we didn't screw. I just told you that
because I couldn't think of any other reason I'd want his home
address."

"Why *did* you want it?"

She broke off eye contact. "He stole something and I had to get
it back."

I stared at her. "Let me take a flyer," I said. "It had to be
something illegal or you'd have told me about it right up front. Or
reported it to the cops. So it must be dope. Was it coke or
grass?"

She was wide-eyed. "Grass, but how did you know?"

"Just tell me the rest," I replied with a shake of my head. I love
the young. They're always amazed that we know anything.

Mona glanced up to my right.

The waitress was approaching with her tray. She set an airport
cocktail napkin on the table and placed the Pink Squirrel on it.
"That'll be three-fifty."

Mona took five ones from her billfold and waved her off. She
sipped at the drink and shivered. The concoction was the same pink
as bubble gum, which made me shiver a bit as well. She licked her
lips. "My boyfriend got a lid of this really incredible grass. 'Non
Sung Smoke' it's called, from the town of Non Sung in Thailand."

"Never heard of it," I said. "Not that I'm any connoisseur."

"Well, me neither, but he paid like two thousand dollars for it
and he'd only smoked one joint. The guy he got it from said half a

hit would put you away so we weren't going to smoke it every day. Just special occasions."

"Pretty high-class stuff at those rates."

"The best."

"And you told Gage."

"Well, yeah," she said reluctantly. "We met and we started talking. He said he needed to score some pot so I mentioned it. I wasn't going to sell him ours. I just thought he might try it and then if he was interested, maybe we could get some for him. When we got to my place, I went in the john while he rolled a joint, and when I came out, he was gone and so was the dope. I had to take a cab back to Mooter's to pick up my car. I was in such a panic. I knew if Jerry found out he'd have a fit!"

"He's your boyfriend?"

"Right," she said, looking down at her lap. She began to blink rapidly and she put a trembling hand to her lips.

I gave her a verbal nudge, just to head off the tears. "Then what? After I gave you the phone number, you got in touch with Gage?"

She nodded mutely, then took a deep breath. "I had to wait till Jerry went off to work and then I called. Gage said—"

"Wait a minute. He answered the phone?"

"Uh-uh. She did. His wife, but I made sure she'd hung up the extension and then I talked so he only had to answer yes and no. I told him I knew he fucking stole the dope and I wanted it back like right then. I just screamed. I told him if he didn't get that shit back to me, he'd be sorry. He said he'd meet me in the parking lot at Mooter's after closing time."

"That was Saturday night?"

She nodded.

"All right. Then what?"

"That's all there was," she said. "I met him there at two-fifteen and he handed over the dope. I didn't even tell him what a shitheel he was. I just snatched the baggie, got back in my car, and came home. When I saw the headlines this morning, I thought I'd die!"

"Who else was aware of all this?"

"No one as far as I know."

"Didn't your boyfriend think it was odd you went out at two-fifteen?"

She shook her head. "I was back before he got home."

"Didn't he realize the dope had disappeared?"

"No, because I put it back before he even looked for it. He couldn't have known."

"What about Mooter's? Was there anyone else in the parking lot?"

"Not that I saw."

"No one coming or going from the bar?"

"Just the guy who runs the place."

"What about Mrs. Vesca? Could she have followed him?"

"Well, I asked him if she overheard my call and he said no. But she could have followed, I guess. I don't know what kind of car she drives, but she could have been parked on a side street."

"Aside from that, how could anyone connect you to Vesca's death? I don't understand why you decided to run."

Her voice dropped to a whisper. "My fingerprints have to be on that car. I was just in it two nights ago."

I studied the look in her eyes and I could feel my heart sink. "You have a record," I said.

"I was picked up for shoplifting once. But that's the only trouble I was ever in. Honestly."

"I think you ought to go to the cops with this. It's far better to be up front with them than to come up with lame excuses after they track you down, which I suspect they will."

"Oh, God, I'll die."

"No, you won't. You'll feel better. Now do what I say and I'll check the rest of it from my end."

"You will?"

"Of course!" I snapped. "If I hadn't found the guy for you, he might be okay. How do you think I feel?"

I followed the maid through the Vescas' house to the pool area at the rear, where one of the cabanas had been fitted out as a personal gym. There were seven weight machines bolted to the floor, which was padded with rubber matting. Mirrors lined three walls and sunlight streamed in the fourth. Katherine Vesca, in a hot-pink leotard and silver tights, was working on her abs, an unnecessary expenditure of energy from what I could see. She was thin as a snake. Her ash-blond hair was kept off her face by a band of pink chiffon and her gray eyes were cold. She blotted sweat from her neck as she glanced at my business card. "You're connected with the police?"

"Actually, I'm not, but I'm hoping you'll answer some questions anyway."

"Why should I?"

"I'm trying to get a line on your husband's killer just like they are."

"Why not leave it up to them?"

"I have some information they don't have yet. I thought I'd see what else I could add before I pass on the facts."

"The facts?"

"About his activities the last two days of his life."

She gave me a chilly smile and crossed to the leg-press machine. She moved the pin down to the hundred-and-eighty-pound mark, then seated herself and started to do reps. "Fire away," she said.

"I understand a phone call came in sometime on Saturday," I said.

"That's right. A woman called. He went out to meet her quite late that night and he didn't come back. I never saw him again."

"Do you know what the call was about?"

"Sorry. He never said."

"Weren't you curious?"

"When I married Gage, I agreed that I wouldn't be 'curious' about anything he did."

"And he wasn't curious about you?"

"We had an open relationship. At his insistence, I might add. He was free to do anything he liked."

"And you didn't object?"

"Sometimes, but those were his terms and I agreed."

"What sort of work did he do?"

"He didn't. Neither of us worked. I have a business here in town and I derive income from that, among other things."

"Do you know if he was caught up in anything? A quarrel? Some kind of personal feud?"

"If so, he never mentioned it," she said. "He was not well liked, but I couldn't say he had enemies."

"Do you have a theory about who killed him?"

She finished ten reps and rested. "I wish I did."

"When's the funeral?" I asked.

"Tomorrow morning at ten. You're welcome to come. Then maybe there'll be two of us."

She gave me the name of the funeral home and I made a note.

"One more thing," I said. "What sort of business are you in? Could that be relevant?"

"I don't see how. I have a bar. Called Mooter's. It's managed by my brother, Jim."

When I walked in, he was washing beer mugs behind the bar, running each in turn across a rotating brush, then through a hot water rinse. To his right was a mounting pyramid of drying mugs, still radiating heat. Today he wore a bulging T-shirt imprinted with a slogan that read: ONE NIGHT OF BAD SEX IS STILL BETTER THAN A GOOD DAY AT WORK. He fixed a look on my face, smiling pleasantly. "How's it going?"

I perched on a bar stool. "Not bad," I said. "You're Jim?"

"That's me. And you're the lady P.I. I don't think you told me your name."

"Kinsey Millhone. I'm assuming you heard about Vesca's death?"

"Yeah, Jesus. Poor guy. Looks like somebody really cleaned his clock. Hope it wasn't the little gal he dumped the other night."

"That's always a possibility."

"You want a spritzer?"

"Sure," I said. "You have a good memory."

"For drinks," he said. "That's my job." He got out the jug wine and poured some in a glass, adding soda from the hose. He added a twist of lime and put the drink in front of me. "On the house."

"Thanks," I said. I took a sip. "How come you never said he was your brother-in-law?"

"How'd you find out about that?" he asked mildly.

"I talked to your sister. She mentioned it."

He shrugged. "Didn't seem pertinent."

I was puzzled by his attitude. He wasn't acting like a man with anything to hide. "Did you see him Saturday?"

"Saw his car at closing time. That was Sunday morning, actually. What's that got to do with it?"

"He must have been killed about then. The paper said sometime between two and six."

"I locked up here shortly after two. My buddy stopped by and picked me up right out front. I was in a poker game by two thirty-five, at a private club."

"You have witnesses?"

"Just the fifty other people in the place. I guess I could have shot the guy before my buddy showed up, but why would I do that? I had no axe to grind with him. I wasn't crazy about him, but I wouldn't plug the guy. My sister adored him. Why break her heart?"

Good question, I thought.

I returned to my office and sat down, tilting back in my swivel chair with my feet on the desk. I kept thinking Gage's death must be connected to the Non Sung Smoke, but I couldn't figure out quite how. I made a call to the Vesca house and was put on hold while the maid went to fetch Miss Katherine. She clicked on. "Yes?"

"Hello, Mrs. Vesca. This in Kinsey Millhone."

"Oh, hello. Sorry if I sounded abrupt. What can I do for you?"

"Just a question I forgot to ask you earlier. Did Gage ever mention something called Non Sung Smoke?"

"I don't think so. What is it?"

"A high-grade marijuana from Thailand. Two thousand bucks a

lid. Apparently, he helped himself to somebody's stash on Friday night."

"Well, he did have some grass, but it couldn't be the same. He said it was junk. He was incensed that somebody hyped it to him."

"Really," I said, but it was more to myself than to her.

I headed down to the parking lot and retrieved my car. A dim understanding was beginning to form.

I knocked at the door of the duplex on Frontage Road. Mona answered, looking puzzled when she caught sight of me.

"Did you talk to the cops?" I asked.

"Not yet. I was just on my way. Why? What's up?"

"It occurred to me I might have misunderstood something you said to me. Friday night when you went out, you told me your boyfriend Jerry was at work. How come you had the nerve to stay out all night?"

"He was out of town," she said. "He got back Saturday afternoon about five."

"Couldn't he have arrived in Santa Teresa earlier that day?"

She shrugged. "I suppose so."

"What about Saturday when you met Gage in Mooter's parking lot? Was he working again?"

"Well, yes. He had a gig here in town. He got home about three," she said in the same bewildered tone.

"He's a musician, isn't he," I said.

"Wait a minute. What *is* this? What's it got to do with him?"

"A lot," he said from behind me. A choking arm slid around my neck and I was jerked half off my feet. I hung on, trying to ease the pressure on my windpipe. I could manage to breathe if I stood on tiptoe, but I couldn't do much else. Something hard was jammed into my ribs and I didn't think it was Jerry's fountain pen. Mona was astonished.

"Jerry! What the hell are you doing?" she yelped.

"Back up, bitch. Step back and let us in," he said between clenched teeth. I hung on, struggling, as he half-lifted, half-shoved me toward the threshold. He dragged me into the apartment and kicked the door shut. He pushed me down on the couch and stood there with his gun pointed right between my eyes. Hey, I was comfy. I wasn't going anyplace.

When I saw his face, of course, my suspicions were confirmed. Jerry was the fellow with the guitar case who'd sat next to me at Mooter's bar when I first went in. He wasn't a big guy—maybe five-eight, weighing in at a hundred and fifty-five—but he'd caught me by surprise. He was edgy and he had a crazy look in his eyes. I've noticed that in a pinch like this, my mind either goes completely blank or begins to compute at lightning speeds. I found myself staring at his gun, which was staring disconcertingly at me. It looked like a little Colt .32, a semiautomatic, almost a double for mine . . . locked at that moment in a briefcase in the backseat of my car. I bypassed the regrets and got straight to the point. Before being fired the first time, a semiautomatic has to be manually cocked, a maneuver that can be accomplished only with two hands. I couldn't remember hearing the sound of the slide being yanked before the nose of the gun was shoved into the small of my back. I wondered briefly if, in his haste to act, he hadn't had time to cock the gun.

"Hello, Jerry," I said. "Nice seeing you again. Why don't you tell Mona about your run-in with Gage?"

"*You* killed Gage?" she said, staring at him with disbelief.

"That's right, Mona, and I'm going to kill you, too. Just as soon as I figure out what to do with her." He kept his eyes on me, making sure I didn't move.

"But why? What did I do?" she gasped.

"Don't give me that," he said. "You balled the guy! Cattin' around in that green-sequined dress with your tits hangin' out and you pick up a scumbag like him! I told you I'd kill you if you ever did that to me."

"But I didn't. I swear it. All I did was bring him back here to try a hit of pot. Next thing I knew he'd stolen the whole lid."

"Bullshit!"

"No, it's not!"

I said, "She's telling the truth, Jerry. That's why she hired me."

Confused, he shot a look at her. "You never went to bed with him?"

"Jesus Christ, of course not. The guy was a creep! I'm not *that* low class!"

Jerry's hand began to tremble and his gaze darted back and forth between her face and mine. "Then why'd you meet him again the next night?"

"To get the grass back. What else could I do? I didn't want you to know I'd been stiffed for two thousand dollars' worth of pot."

He stared at her, transfixed, and that's when I charged. I flew at him, head down, butting straight into his midriff, my momentum taking us both down in a heap. The gun skittered off across the floor. Mona leaped on him and punched him in the gut, using her body to hold him down while I scrambled over to the Colt. I snatched it up. Silly me. The sucker had been cocked the whole time. I was lucky I hadn't had my head blown off.

I could hear him yelling, "Jesus Christ, all right! Get off. I'm done." And then he lay there, winded. I kept the gun pointed steadily at body parts he treasured while Mona called the cops.

He rolled over on his side and sat up. I moved back a step. The wild look had left his eyes and he was starting to weep, still gasping and out of breath. "Oh, Jesus. I can't believe it."

Mona turned to him with a withering look. "It's too late for an attack of conscience, Jerry."

He shook his head. "You don't know the half of it, babe. You're not the one who got stiffed for the dope. I was."

She looked at him blankly. "Meaning what?"

"I paid two grand for garbage. That dope was crap. I didn't want to tell you I got taken in so I invented some bullshit about Non Sung Smoke. There's no such thing. I made it up."

It took an instant for the irony to penetrate. She sank down beside him. "Why didn't you trust me? Why didn't you just tell me the truth?"

His expression was bleak. "Why didn't you?"

The question hung between them like a cobweb, wavering in the autumn light.

By the time the cops came, they were huddled on the floor together, clinging to each other in despair.

The sight of them was almost enough to cure me of the lies I tell.

But not quite.

EDWARD D. HOCH

Edward D. Hoch has written countless mystery stories over the last several decades, including one in every single issue of *Ellery Queen's Mystery Magazine* for at least the past dozen years. In his more than seven hundred pieces, he has created some very memorable series characters, including Simon Ark, Nick Velvet, and Captain Leopold, to name just a few. His work is always well reasoned, with a masterful deductive ability that closes in on the truth with an inevitability that mirrors reality too infrequently. He himself is guilty of a mystery novel set at the Mystery Writers of America Edgar Awards banquet, *The Shattered Raven*.

"The Victorian Hangman" is a period piece set in Southern California during the Gay Nineties, which is nonetheless as Victorian as its title. If we reveal more we'll tell too much.

The Victorian Hangman

Ben Snow had been to California only once before, when he visited
Sacramento in 1885. Now, five years later, as he stepped off the
Southern Pacific train at the town of Oceanfront, it seemed like a
different world. Southern California, especially the area south of
Los Angeles, was nothing like the cities to the north. There were
palm trees across the street from the station and even the air felt
different here.

When Ben was first offered the job of guarding the summer guests
at Oceanfront Gardens, he'd turned it down. "You need a Pinkerton
man," he told Douglas Ratherford. "You don't need me."

"I've been told you're a fast gun and you have a good brain,"
Ratherford said. "That's the combination I want. Most of the Pink-
ertons are nothing but strike-breaking goons."

"I'd have to stable my horse and take the train to Oceanfront."

"Would that be so difficult? I'd make it worth your while."

Ben studied the white-haired man across the table from him.
Douglas Ratherford seemed every inch the British Victorian gentleman. He had an English accent and carried a walking stick with an
ivory knob. "I could come for a month," Ben decided, "to try it
out."

"That's fine! With any luck, we wouldn't need you longer than
that."

"What is it that's been happening at the hotel? Thefts from the
rooms, things like that?"

Ratherford took a deep breath. "Last week a guest hanged himself
from the bandstand roof."

"A suicide can happen anywhere."

"Everyone calls it a suicide except the poor man's wife. She
pointed out that the noose was an elaborate one with the traditional

328

thirteen turns of the rope such as hangmen use. She claims her husband couldn't even tie a square knot."

"Still—"

"And then there's this note. It came in Monday's mail."

Ben read the simple message, printed in block letters:

ONE FOR THE HANGMAN. MORE TO COME.

"A crank," he suggested.

"Probably. But I'll feel better with you on the scene, Mr. Snow."

"I'm not a detective. I'm a hired gun."

Douglas Ratherford nodded. "I think that's what I need."

A horse-drawn carriage was waiting at the station to take Ben to the Oceanfront Hotel. He'd been expecting it, and the only surprise was the driver, a girl in her late teens who wore pants and a man's jacket and covered her long black hair with a jockey cap. "I'm Ben Snow," he said. "Are you from the Oceanfront Hotel?"

"That's right, climb aboard." She took the carpetbag he was carrying and heaved it easily onto the rear of the carriage. Then she climbed up and took her place behind the horse. As they started to move, she looked back at him with a faint smile. "I'm Emily Strait. Welcome to Southern California."

"Is it always this hot here?"

"It is in August. You picked a bad month."

"It was picked for me."

They were silent for the next ten minutes, until the carriage passed through a gate marked *Oceanfront Gardens*. "Mr. Ratherford has built this into a real seaside resort," she explained with a touch of pride in her voice. "The hotel has only thirty rooms but it's done in true Victorian style, just like you'd find at Brighton or Blackpool. There's even a small amusement park with a boardwalk and everything. Of course, the gardens are the main attraction. You can see them through the trees to your left."

Ben glimpsed the colorful bursts of tropic blossoms, but his attention was distracted by his first sight of the hotel itself. The Oceanfront was like no hotel he'd seen before—a colossal collection of towers and turrets, fancifully decorated in a style that reminded him of a gingerbread house he'd once seen in a Kansas City bakery.

"It's breathtaking," he said.

"Isn't it? My father designed it himself, after one he admired in England."

"Your father?"

"Douglas Ratherford is my father. I use my mother's maiden name with guests."

"I see. Is your mother here, too?"

"My parents are separated. She lives in Los Angeles. But I see her often."

"You don't have an accent, like your father."

She pulled up in front of the hotel and went to retrieve Ben's bag from the rear. "I was born in California. My father met my mother after he came here."

"Here, let me take that."

But she held onto the carpetbag. "No, I earn my keep here."

The lobby of the hotel was, if anything, even more impressive than the exterior. A marble floor and a great sweeping staircase were set off by potted palms and ferns that seemed to grow everywhere and even hung from the ceiling. A room clerk was busy at the desk checking in the latest guests, but Emily Strait ignored the desk and headed directly for the staircase.

Ben followed her to a small room at the end of the first-floor hall. "It's not very big, but I think you'll find it satisfactory," she told him. "My father will be in his office when you get unpacked."

She left him alone and he walked to the window to take in the view. The room looked down on the bandstand, where the body had been found. He wondered if that had been a factor in its choice for him.

Douglas Ratherford showed him around the hotel and grounds personally, and introduced him to a few of the other employees, certainly making no secret of Ben's presence. "If we do have a killer on the loose, I hope you'll scare him off," he told Ben. "Let him go down the beach to one of the other resort hotels."

"Are there many?"

"More every year. Southern California seems to have discovered Victorian England."

They passed through the dining room, where full-length windows looked out to the sea, and paused for a moment in the kitchen, where Ben was surprised to see a number of Chinese at work. "The Chinese are good cooks," Ratherford commented. "In here we have the gentlemen's bar and billiard room. Ladies are strictly excluded. This is Reno Hawkins." Ratherford introduced the tall moustached man behind the bar. "Reno, I want you to meet Ben Snow. I've taken him on as a guard after what happened last week."

Hawkins had a firm handshake. "Snow—that name is familiar. Ever been to Reno or Salt Lake?"

"Passed through," Ben admitted.

"I heard tell of a fellow by that name who was mighty fast with a gun. That was maybe ten, twelve years ago, but he was barely twenty then."

"There were some good card games in Reno the last time I was there," Ben remarked, casually changing the subject.

"We have some good ones here in the evening. Stop by if you get a chance."

Douglas Ratherford continued the tour, showing Ben the library lounge. "Something for the ladies, and gentlemen who don't like the bar," he explained. He led Ben out to the lawn next, and around back to the stable area. Then, "Here's the bandstand," Ratherford announced. The octagonal wooden structure had colored bunting draped from the roof, a reminder of the last concert.

"I saw it from my window," Ben said. "This is where the body was found?"

"Hanging right there." Ratherford pointed. "His name was Harley Foster—he was down from San Francisco with his wife. He was a newspaper editor up there."

"Did you speak to his wife about the note you received?"

"Not yet."

"Not yet?" Ben said.

"Well, she's still here. She didn't return to San Francisco with the body."

"Isn't that odd? Where can I find her?"

"I didn't hire you to investigate Foster's death, Snow. Only to prevent anything like it happening here again."

"I have to do one before I can do the other," Ben explained.

Ratherford gave Ben a long, thoughtful look. "I believe I saw her in the library when we passed through. I'll introduce you."

Linda Foster proved to be a charming, attractive woman, who wore the latest in fashion and her reddish hair in a high bun with curls against the forehead. After the introductions and a few sympathetic words, the hotel owner retreated and left Ben alone with the widow.

"Mr. Ratherford told me he has hired you to look into the matter of my husband's death. Does he agree that he didn't take his own life?"

"That's what I'd like to ask you. Did he have any reason for committing suicide?"

"None whatever."

"Has the funeral been held?"

"I—there's to be a memorial service next week in San Francisco."

"If you'll excuse my asking, why didn't—?"

Ben's question was cut short by the arrival of a dark-haired man with grey sideburns, wearing a pair of glasses clipped to his nose. "Oh, Reggie—I didn't expect you back so soon! Isn't there a game in the men's bar?"

"Reno says it won't start till after dinner. Who's this?" He eyed Ben speculatively.

"Ben Snow, Reginald Cascourt. Reggie's a new friend of mine from New York."

Ben judged the man to be in his late forties, though the grey sideburns and glasses made him appear older. "Pleased to meet you," he said.

"Likewise." Cascourt looked Ben up and down. "You dress like a cowpoke."

Ben laughed. "I do that work sometimes."

"Do you have a gun?"

Ben smiled. "It's in my room. I hope I won't need it here. I'm working for Mr. Ratherford, tending to the needs of the guests."

Reggie Cascourt nodded. "I'm glad he has someone, after what happened to Mr. Foster last week."

"What do *you* think happened to him?"

"Well, I don't believe he hanged himself. I think he had a little help from someone."

"Any idea who?"

"No."

"Let's not talk about it, Reggie," Linda said firmly. "It upsets me." She turned to Ben. "It was a pleasure to meet you, Mr. Snow. I hope we'll see more of each other."

Ben returned her smile and gave a little bow of assent. She was certainly a charming woman. He watched while the two of them left the room in the direction of the lobby. Only then did he remember he had one more question to ask her.

He glanced around the small library, picking up a copy of a new novel titled *Three Men in a Boat*. But he'd never been much of a reader and he tried a copy of the Los Angeles newspaper instead. Neither the world news—ANGLO-FRENCH CONVENTION MEETS ON NIGERIA—nor the latest from back east—NEW YORK EXECUTION IS FIRST USE OF ELECTRIC CHAIR— interested him particularly, but he did read a story on the new state of Wyoming, barely a month old.

Ben had hoped Linda Foster might return to the library following her conversation with Cascourt, but finally he drifted out and was seated in the lobby a half hour later when Ratherford found him. "Come quickly," he whispered. "There's been another one."

"Another—"

"This way."

Ben followed Ratherford out the door and around the back of the hotel, where the owner pulled open the door of a large storage shed outside the kitchen. "I noticed it was unlocked and looked inside. This is what I found."

It was one of the Chinese cooks, hanging from the overhead beam of the shed.

"His name is Kai Feng," Ratherford said. "He's worked for me for about a year."

Ben had cut him down, but it was too late. The body was already stiffening. And this time the note had been left with the body, pinned to a sleeve:

NUMBER TWO FOR THE HANGMAN. MORE TO COME.

"Did you tell anyone about the first note?" Ben asked.

"Only you."

"Then it's the same person. I just wonder why he delayed sending the first note until after the body was found."

"This one is obviously murder. I'm calling the police." Ratherford said.

Ben agreed. "Did Kai Feng have any enemies?"

"He had me! He was stealing food from this shed and from the kitchen. I caught him at it last week and threatened to fire him if it happened again."

Ratherford repeated the story to the local sheriff when he arrived a few hours later. Guests were questioned at random but it was obvious to Ben that the sheriff—a flashy dandy who didn't even wear a gun—was only going through the motions. While Ben stood by, he confided to Ratherford, "It was probably one of them other Chinks in the kitchen."

"Aren't you going to investigate further?" Ratherford asked.

The sheriff, whose name was Royce, merely shrugged snidely. "You got Snow here to do your investigating. Call me in when you get a confession—or another body."

Except for the hotel owner, Linda Foster seemed the most concerned by Kai Feng's murder. "It was the same person who killed my husband, wasn't it?" she asked Ben in the dining room that evening, stopping at the table where he was eating alone.

"I think so. It seems to be."

"And Sheriff Royce was just as uncooperative as he was last week. Does he say this one is suicide, too?"

"No."

"Will you find the person that killed Harley?"

"Here, sit down for a moment," Ben said. She took the chair opposite him. "There's something I wanted to ask you earlier. Why didn't you accompany your husband's body back to San Francisco?"

"There's to be a memorial service—"

"*Why*, Mrs. Foster?"

Her eyes were downcast as she replied. "I suppose there's no point in trying to keep it secret any longer. I'm not Mrs. Foster. We were never married. The real Mrs. Foster is back in San Francisco."

"I see. Who else knows about this?"

"Only Reggie Cascourt. He suspected something a few weeks ago and I told him the truth."

Ben nodded. "I have to ask you a frank question, Mrs.—" He hesitated. "May I call you Linda?"

"Certainly. My name is Linda Knight."

"Linda, are you having an illicit affair with Cascourt? Might he have killed Foster out of jealousy?"

She blushed at the question. "No. We're only good friends. His friendship may be one reason I stayed on here after Harley was killed, but it's been nothing more than that. He has never so much as kissed me."

"Thank you for telling me all this," Ben said. "It's a big help."

Later that evening he went in search of the card game Reno Hawkins had promised. But the men's bar was almost deserted. "Where is everyone?" he asked Reno.

"This killing has 'em all on edge. People are checking out of the hotel."

"No game tonight?"

"No game." He hesitated. "You saw the body, Snow. Is it true Kai Feng had a hangman's knot around his neck, like the one last week?"

Ben nodded. It was true. "Thirteen turns of the rope."

"I hear tell cowpokes sometimes ride on lynching parties. You ever lynch anyone?"

"No. I've prevented one or two in my time, though."

"Maybe you can prevent any more around here."

"I'm trying," Ben assured him.

There was a breeze off the ocean the following morning, but guests were still checking out of the hotel—their number had dwindled to a hand count. Ben was taking a walk around the grounds when he encountered Ratherford's daughter, Emily. "Hello, there!" she called to him. "How do you like working for my father?"

"I didn't have a very good first day of it."

"You mean Kai Feng? That wasn't your fault. I heard Sheriff Royce say he might have been killed hours before he was found, maybe even before you arrived."

"Thanks for telling me that."

"My father says you're a gunfighter. Is that true?"

They were walking along the high bluff overlooking the ocean. Down below, Ben could see fishermen with their nets in the morning surf. "I have that reputation, but it's hardly a fact. I'm a wanderer, really—a cowhand for hire. I'm good with a gun, and I suppose that's how the stories started."

"The wild west seems so far away here. Victorian England is closer somehow."

"Yet you dress like a boy and drive a carriage like a man. That's hardly Victorian."

"I suppose it's my mother's influence. My father is the Victorian." She spotted a man walking ahead of them. "Come, I want you to meet someone."

Andrew McMillan proved to be a handsome young man dressed in a striped suit and vest, with a gold chain hanging from his pocket watch. "Andrew arrived just yesterday," Emily explained, introducing him to Ben. "He's a salesman and stops by here every few months."

McMillan passed Ben his calling card. "I travel for Boss Stoves, suppliers to the finest hotel and restaurant kitchens. If you're ever in the market—"

"Different line of work," Ben said, cutting him short.

"It's a busy time for me. There are new hotels opening up and down the coast, and they all need stoves."

"How long will you be here this time, Andrew?" Emily asked.

"Probably just until tomorrow. Will there be a card game in the bar tonight?"

Ben answered for her. "There wasn't one last night. Too many people checking out. The bartender said he was going to try for one tonight."

McMillan nodded. "Will you be there, Mr. Snow?"

"I might."

McMillan left them but Ben remained with Emily until they neared the hotel and her father called to her. "Emily, I want you to ride into town for some supplies! Take the wagon!"

"All right," she agreed readily.

When Ratherford had given her a list and sent her off, he said to Ben, "She's very young. Sometimes I think she's too friendly with our guests."

"And your employees?"

"And our employees. But I know I don't have to worry about you."

"That's right."

"Have you noticed anyone acting suspicious?"

"Not yet," Ben replied.

There was a card game in the men's bar that evening. Life at the Oceanfront Hotel had returned to normal. Ben sat in for a few hands and found himself playing with Reno Hawkins, Andrew McMillan, and three strangers. One was Oriental and Ben assumed he was another of the kitchen employees.

Ben lost two hands before he drew a good poker hand—a pair of kings and a pair of aces. He upped his bet as Reggie Cascourt came through the swinging doors to watch the action. After several more raises, McMillan drew two fresh cards. Ben had been playing in frontier saloons long enough to notice a bottom deal when he saw one. Andrew McMillan was cheating. When he lost to McMillan's three sevens, Ben dropped out. "That's enough for me," he said, throwing in his hand. "Want my spot, Cascourt?"

"No, I'll just watch."

Ben drifted over and ordered a beer from the bartender. He fully expected Reno to catch onto the cheating and halt the game, but when it went on with no interruption Ben finished his beer and left. He could understand now why Douglas Ratherford warned his daughter about some of the guests.

The following morning after breakfast, Ben helped Ratherford in his inventory of the kitchen supplies, to determine how much the unfortunate Kai Feng might have stolen. He assumed his presence was mainly to serve as a warning for the other employees that such thievery wouldn't be tolerated in the future. The Chinese who had been in the poker game the previous night was one of the spectators. His name was Wei Baqun and he was a friend of the murdered man. Ben tried to speak with him after the inventory was complete, but he seemed to know very little English.

In the afternoon, Linda Knight—or Linda Foster, as Ben still thought of her—strolled with Reggie Cascourt along the beach to the nearby amusement park. Ben watched them from the top of the bluff and decided to follow along. He hadn't visited the boardwalk area yet and it occurred to him that people must work there—drifters and carnival workers—who might not be above murder. Perhaps he and Ratherford had made a mistake in limiting their investigation to the hotel.

He watched Linda ride the merry-go-round and Reggie demonstrate his strength with a mallet by ringing a gong three times straight. They then ventured onto a small gravity railroad called a roller coaster, which Ben had never seen before. The passengers screamed during the brief ride and to Ben it looked more like torture than pleasure.

Cascourt spotted him as they left the roller coaster. "Hello, there. Taking an afternoon off?"

"I just thought I'd look the place over," Ben said. "It's a short walk up the path to the hotel. Have either of you ever known any of the people from here to wander up there?"

Linda shook her head. "Never. I doubt if Mr. Ratherford would allow anyone off the premises to mingle with the guests."

Ben could see it would be an impossible task to question everyone who worked there. And it wasn't his job, anyway. His job was to protect the hotel guests. He decided to return to the hotel with Reggie and Linda.

They were halfway up the path when Ben spotted Douglas Ratherford at the top waiting for him. "What is it?" he called out.

"Come quickly, Mr. Snow! McMillan, the stove salesman, has been murdered!"

Andrew McMillan had died like the other two, with a hangman's noose around his neck, this time strung from a chandelier in the gentlemen's bar. Reno Hawkins had found the body when he opened the room at one o'clock. The note pinned to the dead man's sleeve was like the others:

NUMBER THREE FOR THE HANGMAN. MORE TO COME.

"When will this end?" Linda cried and Cascourt cradled her in his arms and led her away.

"What did Foster, Feng, and McMillan have in common?" Ben asked Douglas Ratherford.

"Nothing. Not a thing."

"McMillan sold stoves and Kai Feng worked in the kitchen."

"But to my knowledge neither of them knew Harley Foster. This was Foster's first visit to the Oceanfront, and he was already dead a week before McMillan arrived."

Ben puzzled over it. "Let's go to your office. I have another idea I want to try on you."

"I've already called Sheriff Royce on the phone. He's on his way," Ratherford said as they turned toward his office.

"I don't think Sheriff Royce is going to trap this hangman," Ben told him.

He followed Ratherford into his office behind the front desk and closed the door. "All right, Snow," Ratherford said. "What's your theory?"

"That only one of these three was intended as the real victim. Doesn't it strike you as odd that these last two had notes pinned to their sleeves, but in the first killing the note came later? Almost as an afterthought?"

"Well—"

"I think it *was* an afterthought. Suppose someone like Reggie Cascourt wanted Linda. He killed her husband, making it look like suicide. When people began to question the suicide idea, he sent you the note and then killed two other randomly selected victims so the whole thing would look like the work of a madman."

"But I never questioned the suicide until I received the note," the hotel man objected. "Nobody did except Linda."

"No," Ben admitted, and already another flaw in his theory had occurred to him. Since Linda had confessed to Reggie that she and Foster weren't married, he didn't need to kill Foster to free her. She was already free and Reggie was the one person who knew it.

"I think you're barking up the wrong tree," Ratherford told Ben. "Killing two innocent people to cover up a murder is a pretty crazy thing to do. How about this—Foster really did commit suicide and the note was sent to tie it in with the planned killings of Kai Feng and McMillan?"

Ben smiled. "And the motive for killing them? A fortune in jewels hidden inside the kitchen stove?"

Douglas Ratherford sighed. "All right, where are we?"

"Nowhere," Ben admitted. "Three murders and we're nowhere. Let Sheriff Royce do what he can. I'm no help to you. The killings have actually increased since you hired me. I'm leaving in the morning."

Ratherford seemed saddened by his decision but he didn't argue. "I'll have a check ready for you. I still think you're a good man, Snow. This simply isn't your sort of job."

When Royce arrived, Ben decided to stay out of the way. He went around back to the bandstand and pretended to be searching for something.

That was when he found it, strictly by chance, beneath the bandstand steps where an evening breeze off the ocean must have blown it a week earlier: the first note.

ONE FOR THE HANGMAN. MORE TO COME.

The first message had come late, in the mail, for the simple reason that the copy left with the body on the bandstand had blown away. So the killer had sent a duplicate.

The three killings had been tied together from the beginning. They were the work of a madman with a pattern all his own.

But what was the pattern?

And who would be next?

Ben found Linda Knight alone after dinner and spoke with her in the lobby. Sheriff Royce had finally departed after hours of asking the same useless questions. He'd been interested in the fact that Reno and Ratherford possessed the only keys to the gentlemen's bar where the body was found, but it developed that a service door to the kitchen was never locked. Anyone could have entered that way during the night or early morning when the murder was committed.

With Linda, Ben's questions took a different tack. "I want you to think carefully and tell me if Harley Foster ever mentioned knowing Andrew McMillan."

"No, I'm sure he didn't."

"Did you ever see him talking with Kai Feng or any of the other kitchen employees?"

"No, never."

"What about the bandstand where he was found? Did it have any special meaning to him?"

"No. We liked to stroll out there sometimes after dinner to enjoy that fine view of the ocean at sunset. Once he kissed me when we were out there, but that was all."

"Kissed you?"

"Yes. Is anything wrong with that? Everyone thought we were married, remember."

Ben's eyes wandered across the lobby to the doorway of the men's bar and billiard room. Reno Hawkins had swung open the doors and called out, "We're back in business, gentlemen—the sheriff's finished in here."

Ben saw Wei Baqun from the kitchen staff and a few of the guests head in. Presently there was the familiar clack of billiard balls. He imagined a poker game would soon be in progress, too.

"My God!" he gasped.

"What is it?" Linda asked.

"I need to send a telegram," he told her, and hurried off to the front desk. Sending telegraphed messages across the country wasn't something Ben ordinarily did, but the circumstances were far from ordinary.

The desk clerk put him through to the telegraph office by phone and Ben passed on the message he wanted to send. "Just this one question?" the clerk asked.

"That's all. Tell them I need a reply immediately."

"Yes, sir. Who should I charge this to?"

"The Oceanfront Hotel."

When he turned around, Ben saw that Reggie Cascourt was chatting with Linda. Reggie nodded to Ben and headed in the direction of the hotel veranda. As Ben returned to Linda's side, she asked, "Did you send your telegram?"

Ben nodded. "I only hope there's a quick reply. It's late on the East Coast. I telegraphed a reporter I know at *The New York Times*. It's a morning newspaper, so he should still be at his desk."

"Does this have anything to do with the murders?"

Before Ben could reply, they were joined by Reno Hawkins. He was wearing cowboy boots and a fancy shirt with leather fringe. "We're getting a game together if you're interested, Mr. Snow."

"Not tonight, thanks."

"Mr. Ratherford says you might be leaving in the morning."

"I hope to if I can finish up my business tonight."

Outside, the sun had set and it was growing dark. Though he'd sent his telegram only five minutes ago, Ben was already growing impatient for a reply.

"What was that?" Linda asked suddenly. "It sounded like a girl's scream!"

Then it came again, from outside, and they all heard it. Ben ran toward the veranda, with the others following. Emily stood there, pointing across the lawn at the bandstand. "It's Mr. Cascourt!" she sobbed. "He—he—"

Ben saw the figure jerking at the end of the rope, dangling from the bandstand roof as Harley Foster must have done a week earlier. He vaulted the veranda railing, pulling a jackknife from his back pocket as he ran. Then he was up on the bandstand railing, trying to support Cascourt's body as he cut through the rope.

Emily was still screaming and he was aware of her father running toward them with Reno and Linda. The kitchen staff and other guests had joined them by the time the strands of rope separated. Ben lowered Reggie Cascourt into their waiting arms. "I think he's still alive," he gasped, jumping down to the bandstand floor.

A note pinned to Cascourt's sleeve read:

NUMBER FOUR FOR THE HANGMAN.
NO MORE AFTER THIS.

"It's the end," Emily whispered, reading the note. "No more."

Linda was on her knees by Cascourt, trying to force life into him. "Breathe, Reggie! Try to breathe!"

"Did you see who did it?" Ratherford asked his daughter.

"No, not really—he just seemed to step off the railing with that rope around his neck. I didn't see anyone with him."

"There was no one," Ben verified. "He was alone."

"Alone! How is that possible? How do you know?"

Ben got to his feet and looked down at the man on the ground. The noose had been removed from Cascourt's neck and he was conscious enough to run a hand over the red welt it had left on his throat. "Because Reggie Cascourt is the Hangman. He killed three people and he just tried to kill himself."

As his strength returned, Cascourt's insane rage boiled over and he had to be restrained. Sheriff Royce had him transported under guard to the hospital before sitting down to listen to Ben's explanation. They were seated in the library along with Douglas Ratherford, Emily, and Linda Knight.

"What did they have in common?" Ben began. "Even to a crazed mind bent on murder, Harley Foster, Kai Feng, and Andrew McMillan had to stand out from all the other employees and guests at the Oceanfront Hotel. How? While they were here, *each one committed a crime*."

"Crime?" Ratherford repeated. "What crime? Kai Feng stole food from the storage shed, but what crimes did the others commit?"

"Kai Feng stole food from the storage shed, the very place in which he was hanged. Andrew McMillan cheated at cards—I saw him do it myself last night in the men's bar, the place where *he* was hanged."

"And Harley?" Linda asked. "What did Harley do?"

"I'm sorry, Linda. Harley Foster committed adultery. That's still a crime in most states, even though it's rarely prosecuted. He kissed you on the bandstand, and to Cascourt's twisted mind that was evidence of adultery, so Foster had to die on the bandstand. Tonight there was only one other criminal he knew left at Oceanfront, and that was Cascourt himself. He'd committed three murders, the first of them at the bandstand, so he chose to hang himself there."

Emily broke the silence with another question. "Even guessing the motive, how could you know Cascourt was the killer?"

"The Hangman had to know about those three crimes—the adultery, the food thefts, and the cheating at cards. Anyone might have seen Kai Feng looting the storage shed, but Cascourt was watching the game last night when McMillan cheated—he saw it, the same as I did. But how could the Hangman know about Foster's adultery? Linda told me only one other person knew she wasn't Foster's wife— Cascourt. Therefore, only Cascourt and Linda herself had the knowledge to be the Hangman. Could it have been Linda? No. She'd hardly have the strength to lift her victims into the noose, even after knocking them unconscious. This afternoon I saw that Cascourt was a strong man. He rang the bell several times with a mallet at the amusement park. Also, it was impossible for Linda to have observed Andrew McMillan cheating at cards—the games took place in the gentlemen's bar, where women are forbidden to enter."

"I might have seen him cheating elsewhere," she suggested.

"McMillan was hanged from a chandelier in the bar because that's where the Hangman saw the crime committed. The Hangman had to be a man."

Reno Hawkins entered the library and handed a message to Ben. "This telegram just arrived for you from New York."

Ben glanced at the message. It read: HOW'S CALIFORNIA? ANSWER TO YOUR QUESTION IS REG CASCOURT.

Ben handed the telegram to the sheriff. "Cascourt was from New York, and I read in the newspaper that New York State began using the electric chair this week to execute criminals. I took a chance and asked a reporter friend a question. This is his answer."

"Damn it, Snow, what was your question?"

" 'Who was the legal hangman for the State of New York,' " Ben said. "Cascourt was the man the electric chair there put out of a job."

EDWARD GORMAN

Winner of a Shamus Award for his 1987 story "Turn Away," Ed Gorman has paid a lot of dues in a relatively brief span of time. Besides being one of the editor/publishers of *Mystery Scene* magazine, he's written a series of murder mysteries featuring Jack Dwyer, an ex-cop, amateur actor, and part-time P.I. Dwyer, the protagonist of "The Reason Why," is a fine focus for this bitter-sweet story of old, bad times at a high school reunion. Dwyer's last novel, *The Autumn Dead*, was a Shamus Award finalist last year; this story is a finalist for the Shamus this year. Read it and find out why we had to publish it, despite his bad company.

The Reason Why

"I'm scared."

"This was your idea, Karen."

"You scared?"

"No."

"You bastard."

"Because I'm not scared I'm a bastard?"

"You not being scared means you don't believe me."

"Well."

"See. I knew it."

"What?"

"Just the way you said 'Well.' You bastard."

I sighed and looked out at the big red brick building that sprawled over a quarter mile of spring grass turned silver by a fat June moon. Twenty-five years ago a 1950 Ford fastback had sat in the adjacent parking lot. Mine for two summers of grocery store work.

We were sitting in her car, a Volvo she'd cadged from her last marriage settlement, number four if you're interested, and sharing a pint of bourbon the way we used to in high school when we'd been more than friends but never quite lovers.

The occasion tonight was our twenty-fifth class reunion. But there was another occasion, too. In our senior year a boy named Michael Brandon had jumped off a steep clay cliff called Pierce Point to his death on the winding river road below. Suicide. That, anyway, had been the official version.

A month ago Karen Lane (she had gone back to her maiden name these days, the Karen Lane-Cummings-Todd-Browne-LeMay getting a tad too long) had called to see if I wanted to go to dinner and I said yes, if I could bring Donna along, but then Donna surprised me by saying she didn't care to go along, that by now we should be at the point in our relationship where we trusted each

344

other ("God, Dwyer, I don't even look at other men, not for very long anyway, you know?"), and Karen and I had had dinner and she'd had many drinks, enough that I saw she had a problem, and then she'd told me about something that had troubled her for a long time . . .

In senior year she'd gone to a party and gotten sick on wine and stumbled out to somebody's backyard to throw up and it was there she'd overheard the three boys talking. They were earnestly discussing what had happened to Michael Brandon the previous week and they were even more earnestly discussing what would happen to them if "anybody ever really found out the truth."

"It's bothered me all these years," she'd said over dinner a month earlier. "They murdered him and they got away with it."

"Why didn't you tell the police?"

"I didn't think they'd believe me."

"Why not?"

She shrugged and put her lovely little face down, dark hair covering her features. Whenever she put her face down that way it meant that she didn't want to tell you a lie so she'd just as soon talk about something else.

"Why not, Karen?"

"Because of where we came from. The Highlands."

The Highlands is an area that used to ring the iron foundries and factories of this city. Way before pollution became a fashionable concern, you could stand on your front porch and see a peculiarly beautiful orange haze on the sky every dusk. The Highlands had bars where men lost ears, eyes, and fingers in just garden-variety fights, and streets where nobody sane ever walked after dark, not even cops unless they were in pairs. But it wasn't the physical violence you remembered so much as the emotional violence of poverty. You get tired of hearing your mother scream because there isn't enough money for food and hearing your father scream back because there's nothing he can do about it. Nothing.

Karen Lane and I had come from the Highlands, but we were smarter and, in her case, better looking than most of the people from the area, so when we went to Wilson High School—one of those nightmare conglomerates that shoves the poorest kids in a city in with the richest—we didn't do badly for ourselves. By senior year we found ourselves hanging out with the sons and daughters of bankers and doctors and city officials and lawyers and riding around in new Impala convertibles and attending an occasional party where you saw an actual maid. But wherever we went, we'd manage for at least a few minutes to get away from our dates and talk to each other. What we were doing, of course, was trying to comfort our-

selves. We shared terrible and confusing feelings—pride that we
were acceptable to those we saw as glamorous, shame that we felt
disgrace for being from the Highlands and having fathers who
worked in factories and mothers who went to Mass as often as nuns
and brothers and sisters who were doomed to punching the clock
and yelling at ragged kids in the cold factory dusk. (You never realize
what a toll such shame takes till you see your father's waxen face
there in the years-later casket.)

That was the big secret we shared, of course, Karen and I, that
we were going to get out, leave the place once and for all. And her
brown eyes never sparkled more Christmas-morning bright than at
those moments when it all was ahead of us, money, sex, endless
thrills, immortality. She had the kind of clean good looks brought
out best by a blue cardigan with a line of white button-down shirt
at the top and a brown suede car coat over her slender shoulders
and moderately tight jeans displaying her quietly artful ass. Nothing
splashy about her. She had the sort of face that snuck up on you.
You had the impression you were talking to a pretty but in no way
spectacular girl, and then all of a sudden you saw how the eyes
burned with sad humor and how wry the mouth got at certain times
and how absolutely perfect that straight little nose was and how the
freckles enhanced rather than detracted from her beauty and by
then of course you were hopelessly entangled. Hopelessly.

This wasn't just my opinion, either. I mentioned four divorce
settlements. True facts. Karen was one of those prizes that powerful
and rich men like to collect with the understanding that it's only
something you hold in trust, like a yachting cup. So, in her time,
she'd been an ornament for a professional football player (her college beau), an orthodontist ("I think he used to have sexual fantasies
about Barry Goldwater"), the owner of a large commuter airline
("I slept with half his pilots; it was kind of a company benefit"),
and a sixty-nine-year-old millionaire who was dying of heart disease
("He used to have me sit next to his bedside and just hold his hand—
the weird thing was that of all of them, I loved him, I really did—
and his eyes would be closed and then every once in a while tears
would start streaming down his cheeks as if he was remembering
something that really filled him with remorse; he was really a
sweetie, but then cancer got him before the heart disease and I
never did find out what he regretted so much, I mean if it was about
his son or his wife or what"), and now she was comfortably fixed
for the rest of her life and if the crow's feet were a little more
pronounced around eyes and mouth and if the slenderness was just
a trifle too slender (she weighed, at five-three, maybe ninety pounds
and kept a variety of diet books in her big sunny kitchen), she was

a damn good-looking woman nonetheless, the world's absurdity cat-
alogued and evaluated in a gaze that managed to be both weary and
impish, with a laugh that was knowing without being cynical.

So now she wanted to play detective.

I had some more bourbon from the pint—it burned beautifully—
and said, "If I had your money, you know what I'd do?"

"Buy yourself a new shirt?"

"You don't like my shirt?"

"I didn't know you had this thing about Hawaii."

"If I had your money, I'd just forget about all this."

"I thought cops were sworn to uphold the right and the true."

"I'm an ex-cop."

"You wear a uniform."

"That's for the American Security Agency."

She sighed. "So I shouldn't have sent the letters?"

"No."

"Well, if they're guilty, they'll show up at Pierce Point tonight."

"Not necessarily."

"Why?"

"Maybe they'll know it's a trap. And not do anything."

She nodded to the school. "You hear that?"

"What?"

"The song."

It was Bobby Vinton's "Roses Are Red."

"I remember one party when we both hated our dates and we
ended up dancing to that over and over again. Somebody's basement. You remember?"

"Sort of, I guess," I said.

"Good. Let's go in the gym and then we can dance to it again."

Donna, my lady friend, was out of town attending an advertising
convention. I hoped she wasn't going to dance with anybody else
because it would sure make me mad.

I started to open the door and she said, "I want to ask you a
question."

"What?" I sensed what it was going to be so I kept my eyes on
the parking lot.

"Turn around and look at me."

I turned around and looked at her. "Okay."

"Since the time we had dinner a month or so ago I've started
receiving brochures from Alcoholics Anonymous in the mail. If
you were having them sent to me, would you be honest enough to
tell me?"

"Yes, I would."

"Are you having them sent to me?"

"Yes, I am."

"You think I'm a lush?"

"Don't you?"

"I asked you first."

So we went into the gym and danced.

Crepe of red and white, the school colors, draped the ceiling; the stage was a cave of white light on which stood four balding fat guys with spit curls and shimmery gold lamé dinner jackets (could these be the illegitimate sons of Bill Haley?) playing guitars, drum, and saxophone; on the dance floor couples who'd lost hair, teeth, jaw lines, courage, and energy (everything, it seemed, but weight) danced to lame cover versions of "Breaking Up Is Hard To Do" and "Sheila," "Runaround Sue" and "Running Scared" (tonight's lead singer sensibly not even trying Roy Orbison's beautiful falsetto) and then, while I got Karen and myself some no-alcohol punch, they broke into a medley of dance tunes—everything from "Locomotion" to "The Peppermint Twist"—and the place went a little crazy, and I went right along with it.

"Come on," I said.

"Great."

We went out there and we burned ass. We'd both agreed not to dress up for the occasion so we were ready for this. I wore the Hawaiian shirt she found so despicable plus a blue blazer, white socks and cordovan penny-loafers. She wore a salmon-colored Merikani shirt belted at the waist and tan cotton fatigue pants and, sweet Christ, she was so adorable half the guys in the place did the kind of double-takes usually reserved for somebody outrageous or famous.

Over the blasting music, I shouted, "Everybody's watching you!"

She shouted right back, "I know! Isn't it wonderful?"

The medley went twenty minutes and could easily have been confused with an aerobics session. By the end I was sopping and wishing I was carrying ten or fifteen pounds less and sometimes feeling guilty because I was having too much fun (I just hoped Donna, probably having too much fun, too, was feeling equally guilty), and then finally it ended and mate fell into the arms of mate, hanging on to stave off sheer collapse.

Then the head Bill Haley clone said, "Okay, now we're going to do a ballad medley," so then we got everybody from Johnny Mathis to Connie Francis and we couldn't resist that, so I moved her around the floor with clumsy pleasure and she moved me right back with equally clumsy pleasure. "You know something?" I said.

"We're both shitty dancers?"

"Right."

But we kept on, of course, laughing and whirling a few times, and then coming tighter together and just holding each other silently for a time, two human beings getting older and scared about getting older, remembering some things and trying to forget others and trying to make sense of an existence that ultimately made sense to nobody, and then she said, "There's one of them."

I didn't have to ask her what "them" referred to. Until now she'd refused to identify any of the three people she'd sent the letters to.

At first I didn't recognize him. He had almost white hair and a tan so dark it looked fake. He wore a black dinner jacket with a lacy shirt and a black bow tie. He didn't seem to have put on a pound in the quarter century since I'd last seen him.

"Ted Forester?"

"Forester," she said. "He's president of the same savings and loan his father was president of."

"Who are the other two?"

"Why don't we get some punch?"

"The kiddie kind?"

"You could really make me mad with all this lecturing about alcoholism."

"If you're not really a lush then you won't mind getting the kiddie kind."

"My friend, Sigmund Fraud."

We had a couple of pink punches and caught our respective breaths and squinted in the gloom at name tags to see who we were saying hello to and realized all the terrible things you realize at high school reunions, namely that people who thought they were better than you still think that way, and that all the sad little people you feared for—the ones with blackheads and low IQs and lame left legs and walleyes and lisps and every other sort of unfair infirmity people get stuck with—generally turned out to be deserving of your fear, for there was a sadness in their eyes tonight that spoke of failures of every sort, and you wanted to go up and say something to them (I wanted to go up to nervous Karl Carberry, who used to twitch— his whole body twitched—and throw my arm around him and tell him what a neat guy he was, tell him there was no reason whatsoever for his twitching, grant him peace and self-esteem and at least a modicum of hope; if he needed a woman, get him a woman, too), but of course you didn't do that, you didn't go up, you just made edgy jokes and nodded a lot and drifted on to the next piece of human carnage.

"There's number two," Karen whispered.

This one I remembered. And despised. The six-three blond movie-star looks had grown only slightly older. His blue dinner jacket just seemed to enhance his air of malicious superiority. Larry Price. His wife Sally was still perfect, too, though you could see in the lacquered blond hair and maybe a hint of face lift that she'd had to work at it a little harder. A year out of high school, at a bar that took teenage IDs checked by a guy who must have been legally blind, I'd gotten drunk and told Larry that he was essentially an asshole for beating up a friend of mine who hadn't had a chance against him. I had the street boy's secret belief that I could take anybody whose father was a surgeon and whose house included a swimming pool. I had hatred, bitterness, and rage going, right? Well, Larry and I went out into the parking lot, ringed by a lot of drunken spectators, and before I got off a single punch, Larry hit me with a shot that stood me straight up, giving him a great opportunity to hit me again. He hit me three times before I found his face and sent him a shot hard enough to push him back for a time. Before we could go at it again, the guy who checked IDs got himself between us. He was madder than either Larry or me. He ended the fight by taking us both by the ears (he must have trained with nuns) and dragging us out to the curb and telling neither of us to come back.

"You remember the night you fought him?"

"Yeah."

"You could have taken him, Dwyer. Those three punches he got in were just lucky."

"Yeah, that was my impression, too. Lucky."

She laughed. "I was afraid he was going to kill you."

I was going to say something smart, but then a new group of people came up and we gushed through a little social dance of nostalgia and lies and self-justifications. We talked success (at high school reunions, everybody sounds like Amway representatives at a pep rally) and the old days (nobody seems to remember all the kids who got treated like shit for reasons they had no control over) and didn't so-and-so look great (usually this meant they'd managed to keep their toupees on straight) and introducing new spouses (we all had to explain what happened to our original mates; I said mine had been eaten by alligators in the Amazon, but nobody seemed to find that especially believeable) and in the midst of all this, Karen tugged my sleeve and said, "There's the third one."

Him I recognized, too. David Haskins. He didn't look any happier than he ever had. Parent trouble was always the explanation you got for his grief back in high school. His parents had been rich, truly so, his father an importer of some kind, and their arguments so violent that they were as eagerly discussed as who was or who was not pregnant. Apparently David's parents weren't getting along any better today because although the features of his face were open and friendly enough, there was still the sense of some terrible secret stooping his shoulders and keeping his smiles to furtive wretched imitations. He was a paunchy balding little man who might have been a church usher with a sour stomach.

"The Duke of Earl" started up then and there was no way we were going to let that pass so we got out on the floor; but by now, of course, we both watched the three people she'd sent letters to. Her instructions had been to meet the anonymous letter writer at nine-thirty at Pierce Point. If they were going to be there on time, they'd be leaving soon.

"You think they're going to go?"

"I doubt it, Karen."

"You still don't believe that's what I heard them say that night?"

"It was a long time ago and you were drunk."

"It's a good thing I like you because otherwise you'd be a distinct pain in the ass."

Which is when I saw all three of them go stand under one of the glowing red EXIT signs and open a fire door that led to the parking lot.

"They're going!" she said.

"Maybe they're just having a cigarette."

"You know better, Dwyer. You know better."

Her car was in the lot on the opposite side of the gym. "Well, it's worth a drive even if they don't show up. Pierce Point should be nice tonight."

She squeezed against me and said, "Thanks, Dwyer. Really."

So we went and got her Volvo and went out to Pierce Point where twenty-five years ago a shy kid named Michael Brandon had fallen or been pushed to his death.

Apparently we were about to find out which.

The river road wound along a high wall of clay cliffs on the left and a wide expanse of water on the right. The spring night was impossibly beautiful, one of those moments so rich with sweet odor and even sweeter sight you wanted to take your clothes off and run around in some kind of crazed animal circles out of sheer joy.

"You still like jazz," she said, nodding to the radio.

"I hope you didn't mind my turning the station."

"I'm kind of into Country."

"I didn't get the impression you were listening."

She looked over at me. "Actually, I wasn't. I was thinking about you sending me all those AA pamphlets."

"It was arrogant and presumptuous and I apologize."

"No, it wasn't. It was sweet and I appreciate it."

The rest of the ride, I leaned my head back and smelled flowers and grass and river water and watched moonglow through the elms and oaks and birches of this new spring. There was a Dakota Staton song, "Street of Dreams," and I wondered as always where she was and what she was doing, she'd been so fine, maybe the most underappreciated jazz singer of the entire fifties.

Then we were going up a long, twisting gravel road. We pulled up next to a big park pavilion and got out and stood in the wet grass, and she came over and slid her arm around my waist and sort of hugged me in a half-serious way. "This is all probably crazy, isn't it?"

I sort of hugged her back in a half-serious way. "Yeah, but it's a nice night for a walk so what the hell."

"You ready?"

"Yep."

"Let's go then."

So we went up the hill to the Point itself, and first we looked out at the far side of the river where white birches glowed in the gloom and where beyond you could see the horseshoe shape of the city lights. Then we looked down, straight down the drop of two hundred feet, to the road where Michael Brandon had died.

When I heard the car starting up the road to the east, I said, "Let's get in those bushes over there."

A thick line of shrubs and second-growth timber would give us a place to hide, to watch them.

By the time we were in place, ducked down behind a wide elm and a mulberry bush, a new yellow Mercedes sedan swung into sight and stopped several yards from the edge of the Point.

A car radio played loud in the night. A Top 40 song. Three men got out. Dignified Forester, matinee-idol Price, anxiety-tight Haskins.

Forester leaned back into the car and snapped the radio off. But he left the headlights on. Forester and Price each had cans of beer. Haskins bit his nails.

They looked around in the gloom. The headlights made the darkness beyond seem much darker and the grass in its illumination much greener. Price said harshly, "I told you this was just some goddamn prank. Nobody knows squat."

"He's right, he's probably right," Haskins said to Forester. Obviously he was hoping that was the case.

Forester said, "If somebody didn't know something, we would never have gotten those letters."

She moved then and I hadn't expected her to move at all. I'd been under the impression we would just sit there and listen and let them ramble and maybe in so doing reveal something useful.

But she had other ideas.

She pushed through the undergrowth and stumbled a little and got to her feet again and then walked right up to them.

"Karen!" Haskins said.

"So you did kill Michael," she said.

Price moved toward her abruptly, his hand raised. He was drunk and apparently hitting women was something he did without much trouble.

Then I stepped out from our hiding place and said, "Put your hand down, Price."

Forester said, "Dwyer."

"So," Price said, lowering his hand, "I was right, wasn't I?" He was speaking to Forester.

Forester shook his silver head. He seemed genuinely saddened. "Yes, Price, for once your cynicism is justified."

Price said, "Well, you two aren't getting a goddamned penny, do you know that?"

He lunged toward me, still a bully. But I was ready for him, wanted it. I also had the advantage of being sober. When he was two steps away, I hit him just once and very hard in his solar plexus. He backed away, eyes startled, and then he turned abruptly away.

We all stood looking at one another, pretending not to hear the sounds of violent vomiting on the other side of the splendid new Mercedes.

Forester said, "When I saw you there, Karen, I wondered if you could do it alone."

"Do what?"

"What?" Forester said. "What? Let's at least stop the games. You two want money."

"Christ," I said to Karen, who looked perplexed, "they think we're trying to shake them down."

"Shake them down?"

"Blackmail them."

"Exactly," Forester said.

Price had come back around. He was wiping his mouth with the back of his hand. In his other hand he carried a silver-plated .45, the sort of weapon professional gamblers favor.

Haskins said, "Larry, Jesus, what is that?"

"What does it look like?"

"Larry, that's how people get killed." Haskins sounded like Price's mother.

Price's eyes were on me. "Yeah, it would be terrible if Dwyer here got killed, wouldn't it?" He waved the gun at me. I didn't really think he'd shoot, but I sure was afraid he'd trip and the damn thing would go off accidentally. "You've been waiting since senior year to do that to me, haven't you, Dwyer?"

I shrugged. "I guess so, yeah."

"Well, why don't I give Forester here the gun and then you and I can try it again."

"Fine with me."

He handed Forester the .45. Forester took it all right, but what he did was toss it somewhere into the gloom surrounding the car. "Larry, if you don't straighten up here, I'll fight you myself. Do you understand me?" Forester had a certain dignity and when he spoke, his voice carried an easy authority. "There will be no more fighting, do you both understand that?"

"I agree with Ted," Karen said.

Forester, like a teacher tired of naughty children, decided to get on with the real business. "You wrote those letters, Dwyer?"

"No."

"No?"

"No. Karen wrote them."

A curious glance was exchanged by Forester and Karen. "I guess I should have known that," Forester said.

"Jesus, Ted," Karen said, "I'm not trying to blackmail you, no matter what you think."

"Then just what exactly are you trying to do?"

She shook her lovely little head. I sensed she regretted ever writing the letters, stirring it all up again. "I just want the truth to come out about what really happened to Michael Brandon that night."

"The truth," Price said. "Isn't that goddamn touching?"

"Shut up, Larry," Haskins said.

Forester said, "You know what happened to Michael Brandon?"

"I've got a good idea," Karen said. "I overheard you three talking at a party one night."

"What did we say?"

"What?"

"What did you overhear us say?"

Karen said, "You said that you hoped nobody looked into what really happened to Michael that night."

A smile touched Forester's lips. "So on that basis you concluded that we murdered him?"

"There wasn't much else to conclude."

Price said, weaving still, leaning on the fender for support, "I don't goddamn believe this."

Forester nodded to me. "Dwyer, I'd like to have a talk with Price and Haskins here, if you don't mind. Just a few minutes." He pointed to the darkness beyond the car. "We'll walk over there. You know we won't try to get away because you'll have our car. All right?"

I looked at Karen.

She shrugged.

They left, back into the gloom, voices receding and fading into the sounds of crickets and a barn owl and a distant roaring train.

"You think they're up to something?"

"I don't' know," I said.

We stood with our shoes getting soaked and looked at the green green grass in the headlights.

"What do you think they're doing?" Karen asked.

"Deciding what they want to tell us."

"You're used to this kind of thing, aren't you?"

"I guess."

"It's sort of sad, isn't it?"

"Yeah. It is."

"Except for you getting the chance to punch out Larry Price after all these years."

"Christ, you really think I'm that petty?"

"I know you are. I know you are."

Then we both turned to look back to where they were. There'd been a cry and Forester shouted, "You hit him again, Larry, and I'll break your goddamn jaw." They were arguing about something and it had turned vicious.

I leaned back against the car. She leaned back against me. "You think we'll ever go to bed?"

"I'd sure like to, Karen, but I can't."

"Donna?"

"Yeah. I'm really trying to learn how to be faithful."

"That been a problem?"

"It cost me a marriage."

"Maybe I'll learn how someday, too."

Then they were back. Somebody, presumably Forester, had torn Price's nice lacy shirt into shreds. Haskins looked miserable.

Forester said, "I'm going to tell you what happened that night."

I nodded.

"I've got some beer in the back seat. Would either of you like one?"

Karen said, "Yes, we would."

So he went and got a six pack of Michelob and we all had a beer and just before he started talking he and Karen shared another one of those peculiar glances and then he said, "The four of us—myself, Price, Haskins, and Michael Brandon—had done something we were very ashamed of."

"Afraid of," Haskins said.

"Afraid that, if it came out, our lives would be ruined. Forever," Forester said.

Price said, "Just say it, Forester." He glared at me. "We raped a girl, the four of us."

"Brandon spent two months afterward seeing the girl, bringing her flowers, apologizing to her over and over again, telling her how sorry we were, that we'd been drunk and it wasn't like us to do that and—" Forester sighed, put his eyes to the ground. "In fact we had been drunk; in fact it wasn't like us to do such a thing—"

Haskins said, "It really wasn't. It really wasn't."

For a time there was just the barn owl and the crickets again, no talk, and then gently I said, "What happened to Brandon that night?"

"We were out as we usually were, drinking beer, talking about it, afraid the girl would finally turn us into the police, still trying to figure out why we'd ever done such a thing—"

The hatred was gone from Price's eyes. For the first time the matinee idol looked as melancholy as his friends. "No matter what you think of me, Dwyer, I don't rape women. But that night—" He shrugged, looked away.

"Brandon," I said. "You were going to tell me about Brandon."

"We came up here, had a case of beer or something, and talked about it some more, and that night," Forester said, "that night Brandon just snapped. He couldn't handle how ashamed he was or how afraid he was of being turned in. Right in the middle of talking—"

Haskins took over. "Right in the middle, he just got up and ran out to the Point." He indicated the cliff behind us. "And before we could stop him, he jumped."

"Jesus," Price said, "I can't forget his screaming on the way down. I can't ever forget it."

I looked at Karen. "So what she heard you three talking about outside the party that night was not that you'd killed Brandon but that you were afraid a serious investigation into his suicide might turn up the rape?"

Forester said, "Exactly." He stared at Karen. "We didn't kill Michael, Karen. We loved him. He was our friend."

But by then, completely without warning, she had started to cry and then she began literally sobbing, her entire body shaking with some grief I could neither understand nor assuage.

I nodded to Forester to get back in his car and leave. They stood and watched us a moment and then they got into the Mercedes and went away, taking the burden of years and guilt with them.

This time I drove. I went far out the river road, miles out, where you pick up the piney hills and the deer standing by the side of the road.

From the glove compartment she took a pint of J&B, and I knew better than to try and stop her.

I said, "You were the girl they raped, weren't you?"

"Yes."

"Why didn't you tell the police?"

She smiled at me. "The police weren't exactly going to believe a girl from the Highlands about the sons of rich men."

I sighed. She was right.

"Then Michael started coming around to see me. I can't say I ever forgave him, but I started to feel sorry for him. His fear—" She shook her head, looked out the window. She said, almost to herself, "But I had to write those letters, get them there tonight, know for sure if they killed him." She paused. "You believe them?"

"That they didn't kill him?"

"Right."

"Yes, I believe them."

"So do I."

Then she went back to staring out the window, her small face childlike there in silhouette against the moonsilver river. "Can I ask you a question, Dwyer?"

"Sure."

"You think we're ever going to get out of the Highlands?"

"No," I said, and drove on faster in her fine new expensive car. "No, I don't."

CLARK HOWARD

Clark Howard is one of those rare writers who is equally adept at fiction and nonfiction. His book about the San Francisco Zodiac killings was a hot book, and his novels have been selling better each time out. Among his works are *The Hunters* (1976), *The Killings* (1973), and *Dirt Rich* (1986). He's been writing since the late 1950s, and his short fiction has always been tremendously satisfying reading.

"The Dakar Run" is perhaps the finest recent example of his ample narrative skills. Using the crucible of a grueling transcontinental road race as the background for a nefarious gambling scheme and at the same time a delicate bonding of an estranged father and daughter, it pulls out all the stops in delivering non-stop entertainment. Injured, middle-aged race car driver Jack Sheffield and his daughter/partner-in-extremis make a terrific pair of reluctant heroes.

The Dakar Run

Jack Sheffield limped out of the little Theatre Americain with John Garfield's defiant words still fresh in his mind. "What are you gonna do, kill me?" Garfield, as Charley Davis, the boxer, had asked Lloyd Gough, the crooked promoter, at the end of *Body and Soul*. Then, challengingly, smugly, with the Garfield arrogance, "Everybody dies!" And he had walked away, with Lilli Palmer on his arm.

Pausing outside to look at the *Body and Soul* poster next to the box office, Sheffield sighed wistfully. They were gone now, Garfield and Lilli Palmer, black-and-white films, the good numbers like Hazel Brooks singing "Am I Blue?" Even boxing—*real* boxing—was down the tubes. In the old days, hungry kids challenged seasoned pros. Now millionaires fought gold-medal winners.

Shaking his head at the pity of things changed, Sheffield turned up his collar against the chilly Paris night and limped up La Villette to the Place de Cluny. There was a cafe there called the Nubian, owned by a very tall Sudanese who mixed his own mustard, so hot it could etch cement. Every Tuesday night, the old-movie feature at the Theatre Americain changed and Jack Sheffield went to see it, whatever it was, and afterward he always walked to the Nubian for sausage and mustard and a double gin. Later, warm from the gin and the food, he would stroll, rain or fair, summer or winter, along the Rue de Rivoli next to the Tuileries, down to the Crazy Horse Saloon to wait for the chorus to do its last high kick so that Jane, the long-legged Englishwoman with whom he lived, could change and go home. Tuesdays never varied for Sheffield.

How many Tuesdays, he wondered as he entered the Nubian, had he been doing this exact same thing? As he pulled out a chair at the rickety little table for two at which he always sat, he tried to recall how long he had been with Jane. Was it three years or four? Catching the eye of the Sudanese, Sheffield raised his hand to signal that he was here, which was all he had to do; he never varied his order. The Sudanese nodded and walked with a camel-like gait toward the kitchen, and Sheffield was about to resume mentally backtracking his life when a young girl came in and walked directly to his table.

"Hi," she said.

He looked at her, tilting his head an inch, squinting slightly without his glasses. When he didn't respond at once, the girl gave him a wry, not totally amused look.

"I'm Chelsea," she said pointedly. "Chelsea Sheffield. Your daughter." She pulled out the opposite chair. "Don't bother to get up."

Sheffield stared at her incredulously, lips parted but no words being generated by his surprised brain.

"Mother," she explained, "said all I had to do to find you in Paris was locate a theater that showed old American movies, wait until the bill changed, and stand outside after the first show. She said if you didn't walk out, you were either dead or had been banished from France."

"Your mother was always right," he said, adding drily, "about everything."

"She also said you might be limping, after smashing up your ankle at Le Mans two years ago. Is the limp permanent?"

"More or less." He quickly changed the subject. "Your mother's well, I presume."

"Very. Like a Main Line Philadelphia doctor's wife should be. Her picture was on the society page five times last year."

"And your sister?"

"Perfect," Chelsea replied, "just as she's always been. Married to a proper young stockbroker, mother of two proper little girls, residing in a proper two-story Colonial, driving a proper Chrysler station wagon. Julie has *always* been proper. I was the foul-mouthed little girl who was too much like my race-car-driver daddy, remember?"

Sheffield didn't know whether to smile or frown. "What are you doing in Paris?" he asked.

"I came over with my boyfriend. We're going to enter the Paris-to-Dakar race."

Now it was Sheffield who made a wry face. "Are you serious?"

"You better believe it," Chelsea assured him.

"Who's your boyfriend—Parnelli Jones?"

"Funny, Father. His name is Austin Trowbridge. He's the son of Max Trowbridge."

Sheffield's eyebrows rose. Max Trowbridge had been one of the

best race-car designers in the world before his untimely death in a
plane crash. "Did your boyfriend learn anything from his father?"
he asked Chelsea.

"He learned plenty. For two years he's been building a car for
the Paris-Dakar Rally. It's finished now. You'd have to see it to
believe it: part Land Rover, part Rolls-Royce, part Corvette. We've
been test-driving it on the beach at Hilton Head. It'll do one hundred
and ten on hard-packed sand, ninety on soft. The engine will cut
sixty-six hundred R.P.M.s."

"Where'd you learn about R.P.M.s?" he asked, surprised.

Chelsea shrugged. "I started hanging out at dirt-bike tracks when
I was fourteen. Gave mother fits. When I moved up to stock cars,
she sent me away to boarding school. It didn't work. One summer
at Daytona, I met Austin. We were both kind of lonely. His father
had just been killed and mine—" she glanced away "—well, let's
just say that Mother's new husband didn't quite know how to cope
with Jack Sheffield's youngest."

And I wasn't around, Sheffield thought. He'd been off at Formula
One tracks in Belgium and Italy and England, drinking champagne
from racing helmets and Ferragamos with four-inch heels, looking
for faster cars, getting older with younger women, sometimes crash-
ing. Burning, bleeding, breaking—

"Don't get me wrong," Chelsea said, "I'm not being critical.
Everybody's got to live his life the way he thinks best. I'm going
my own way with Austin, so I can't fault you for going your own
way without me."

But you do, Sheffield thought. He studied his daughter. She had
to be nineteen now, maybe twenty—he couldn't even remember
when her birthday was. She was plainer than she was pretty—her
sister Julie had their mother's good looks, poor Chelsea favored
him. Lifeless brown hair, imperfect complexion, a nose that didn't
quite fit—yet there was something about her that he suspected could
seize and hold a man, if he was the right man. Under the leather
jacket she had unzipped was clearly the body of a woman, just as
her direct grey eyes were obviously no longer the eyes of a child.
There was no way, Sheffield knew, he could ever make up for the
years he hadn't been there, but maybe he could do something to
lessen the bad taste he'd left. Like talking her out of entering the
Paris-Dakar Rally.

"You know, even with the best car in the world the Paris-Dakar
run is the worst racing experience imaginable. Eight thousand miles
across the Sahara Desert over the roughest terrain on the face of
the earth, driving under the most brutal, dangerous, dreadful con-

ditions. It shouldn't be called a rally, it's more like an endurance test. It's three weeks of hell."

"*You've* done it," she pointed out. "Twice."

"We already know I make mistakes. I didn't win either time, you know."

A touch of fierceness settled in her eyes. "I didn't look you up to get advice on whether to enter—Austin and I have already decided that. I came to ask if you'd go over the route map with us, maybe give us some pointers. But if you're too busy—"

"I'm not too busy," he said. Her words cut him easily.

Chelsea wrote down an address in Montmartre. "It's a rented garage. We've got two rooms above it. The car arrived in Marseilles by freighter this morning. Austin's driving it up tomorrow." She stood and zipped up her jacket. "When can we expect you?"

"Day after tomorrow okay?"

"Swell. See you then." She nodded briefly. "Good night, Father."

"Good night."

As she was walking out, Sheffield realized that he hadn't once spoken her name.

On Thursday, Sheffield took Jane with him to Montmartre, thinking at least he would have somebody on his side if Chelsea and Austin Trowbridge started making him feel guilty. It didn't work. Jane and Chelsea, who were only ten years apart in age, took to each other at once.

"Darling, you look just like him," Jane analyzed. "Same eyes, same chin. But I'm sure your disposition is much better. Jack has absolutely no sense of humor sometimes. If he wasn't so marvelous in bed, I'd leave him."

"He'll probably save you the trouble someday," Chelsea replied. "Father leaves everyone eventually."

"Why don't you two just talk about me like I'm not here?" Sheffield asked irritably.

Austin Trowbridge rescued him. "Like to take a look at the car, Mr. Sheffield?"

"Call me Jack. Yes, I would. I was a great admirer of your father, Austin. He was the best."

"Thanks. I hope I'll be half as good someday."

As soon as Sheffield saw the car, he knew Austin was already half as good, and more. It was an engineering work of art. The body was seamless, shaped not for velocity but for balance, with interchangeable balloon and radial wheels on the same axles, which had double suspension systems to lock in place for either. The steering was flexible from left-hand drive to right, the power train flexible from front to rear, side to side, corner to corner, even to individual wheels. The windshield displaced in one-eighth-inch increments to deflect glare in the daytime, while infrared sealed beams could outline night figures fifty yards distant. A primary petrol tank held one hundred liters of fuel and a backup tank carried two hundred additional liters. Everywhere Sheffield looked—carburetor, generator, distributor, voltage regulator, belt system, radiator, fuel lines—he saw imagination, innovation, improvement. The car was built for reliability and stability, power and pace. Sheffield couldn't have been more impressed.

"It's a beauty, Austin. Your dad would be proud."

"Thanks. I named it after him. I call it the 'Max One.' "

Nice kid, Sheffield thought. He'd probably been very close to his father before the tragedy. Not like Chelsea and himself.

After looking at the Max One, Sheffield took them all to lunch at a cafe on the Boulevard de la Chapelle. While they ate, he talked about the rally.

"There's no competition like it in the world," he said. "It's open to cars, trucks, motorcycles, anything on wheels. There's never any telling who'll be in—or on—the vehicle next to you: it might be a professional driver, a movie star, a millionaire, an Arab king. The run starts in Paris on New Year's Day, goes across France and Spain to Barcelona, crosses the Mediterranean by boat to Africa, then down the length of Algiers, around in a circle of sorts in Niger, across Mali, across Mauritania, up into the Spanish Sahara, then down along the Atlantic coast into Senegal to Dakar. The drivers spend fifteen to eighteen hours a day in their vehicles, then crawl into a sleeping bag for a short, badly needed rest at the end of each day's stage. From three to four hundred vehicles start the run each year. About one in ten will finish."

"We'll finish," Chelsea assured him. "We might even win."

Sheffield shook his head. "You won't win. No matter how good the car is, you don't have the experience to win."

"We don't have to win," Austin conceded. "We just have to finish well—respectably. There are some investors who financed my father from time to time. They've agreed to set me up in my own automotive-design center if I prove myself by building a vehicle that will survive Paris-Dakar. I realize, of course, that the car isn't everything—that's why I wanted to talk to you about the two rallies you ran, to get the benefit of your experience."

"You haven't been racing since you hurt your ankle," Chelsea said. "What have you been doing, Father?"

Sheffield shrugged. "Consulting, training other drivers, conducting track courses—"

"We're willing to pay you for your time to help us," she said.

Sheffield felt himself blush slightly. God, she knew how to cut.

"That won't be necessary," he said. "I'll help you all I can." He wanted to add, "After all, you *are* my daughter," but he didn't.

As he and Jane walked home, she said, "That was nice, Jack, saying you'd help them for nothing."

"Nice, maybe, but not very practical. I could have used the money. I haven't made a franc in fourteen months."

Jane shrugged. "What does that matter? I earn enough for both of us."

It mattered to Sheffield . . .

Sheffield began going to Montmartre every day. In addition to talking to Austin about the route and terrain of the rally, he also helped him make certain modifications on Max One.

"You've got to put locks on the doors, kid. There may be times when both of you have to be away from the car at once and there are places along the route where people will steal you blind."

Holes were drilled and locks placed.

"Paint a line on the steering wheel exactly where your front wheels are aligned straight. That way, when you hit a pothole and bounce, or when you speed off a dune, you can adjust the wheels and land straight. It'll keep you from flipping over. Use luminous paint so you can see the line after dark."

Luminous paint was secured and the line put on.

A lot of Sheffield's advice was practical rather than technical. "Get rid of those blankets. It gets down to twenty degrees in the Sahara at night. Buy lightweight sleeping bags. And stock up on unsalted nuts, granola bars, high-potency vitamins, caffeine tablets. You'll need a breathing aid, too, for when you land in somebody's dust wake. Those little gauze masks painters use worked fine for me."

Most times when Sheffield went to Montmartre, Chelsea wasn't around. Austin always explained that she was running errands or doing this or that, but Sheffield could tell that he was embarrassed by the excuses. His daughter, Sheffield realized, obviously didn't want to see him any more than necessary. He tried not to let it bother him. Becoming more friendly each visit with Austin helped. The young man didn't repeat Chelsea's offer to pay him for his time, seeming to understand that it was insulting, and for that Sheffield was grateful. No one, not even Jane, knew how serious Sheffield's financial predicament was.

No one except Marcel.

* * *

One afternoon when Sheffield got back from Montmartre, Marcel was waiting for him at a table in the cafe Sheffield had to pass through to get to his rooms. "Jack, my friend," he hailed, as if the encounter were mere chance, "come join me." Snapping his fingers at the waiter, he ordered, "Another glass here."

Sheffield sat down. At a nearby table were two thugs who accompanied the diminutive Marcel everywhere he went. One was white, with a neck like a bucket and a walk like a wrestler's. The other was cafe au lait, very slim, with obscene lips and a reputation for being deadly with a straight razor. After glancing at them, Sheffield drummed his fingers silently on the tablecloth and waited for the question Marcel invariably asked first.

"So, my friend, tell me, how are things with you?"

To which Sheffield, during the past fourteen months anyway, always answered, "The same, Marcel, the same."

Marcel assumed a sad expression. Which was not difficult since he had a serious face, anyway, and had not smiled, some said, since puberty. His round little countenance would have reminded Sheffield of Peter Lorre except that Marcel's eyes were narrow slits that, despite their owner's cordiality, clearly projected danger.

"I was going over my books last week, Jack," the Frenchman said as he poured Sheffield a Pernod, "and I must admit I was a little surprised to see how terrible your luck has run all year. I mean, horse races, dog races, prizefights, soccer matches—you seem to have forgotten what it is to pick a winner. Usually, of course, I don't let anyone run up a balance so large, but I've always had a soft spot for you, Jack."

"You know about the car in Montmartre, don't you?" Sheffield asked pointedly.

"Of course," Marcel replied at once, not at all surprised by the question. "I've known about it since it arrived in Marseilles." Putting a hand on Sheffield's arm, he asked confidentially, "What do you think of it, Jack?"

Sheffield moved his arm by raising the Pernod to his lips. "It's a fine car. One of the best I've ever seen."

"I'm glad you're being honest with me," Marcel said. "I've already had a man get into the garage at night to look at it for me. He was of the same opinion. He says it can win the rally."

Sheffield shook his head. "They're a couple of kids, Marcel. They may finish—they won't win."

Marcel looked at him curiously. "What is a young man like this Austin Trowbridge able to pay you, anyway?"

"I'm not being paid."

Marcel drew back his head incredulously. "A man in your financial situation? You work for nothing?"

"I used to know the kid's father," Sheffield said. Then he added, "I used to know his girlfriend's father, too."

Marcel studied the American for a moment. "Jack, let me be as candid with you as you are being with me. There are perhaps two dozen serious vehicles for which competition licenses have been secured for this year's rally. The car my associates and I are backing is a factory-built Peugeot driven by Georges Ferrand. A French driver in a French car. Call it national pride if you wish, call it practical economics—the fact is that we will have a great deal of money at risk on a Ferrand win. Of the two dozen or so vehicles that will seriously challenge Ferrand, we are convinced he will out-distance all but one of them. That one is the Trowbridge car. It is, as you said, a fine car. We have no statistics on it because it did not run in the optional trials at Cergy-Pontoise. And we know nothing about young Trowbridge himself as a driver: whether he's capable, has the stamina, whether he's *hungry*. The entire entry, car and driver, presents an unknown equation which troubles us."

"I've already told you, Marcel: the car can't win."

The Frenchman fixed him in an unblinking stare. "I want a guarantee of that, Jack." He produced a small leather notebook. "Your losses currently total forty-nine thousand francs. That's about eight thousand dollars. I'll draw a line through the entire amount for a guarantee that the Max One will not outrun Ferrand's Peugeot."

"You're not concerned whether it finishes?"

"Not in the least," Marcel waved away the consideration. "First place wins, everything else loses."

Sheffield pursed his lips in brief thought, then said, "All right, Marcel. It's a bargain."

Later, in their rooms, Jane said, "I saw you in the cafe with Marcel. You haven't started gambling again, have you?"

"Of course not." It wasn't a lie. He had never stopped.

"What did he want, then?"

"He and his friends are concerned about Austin's car. They know I'm helping the kid. They want a guarantee that the Max One won't ace out the car they're backing."

Jane shook her head in disgust. "What did you tell him?"

"That he had nothing to worry about. Austin's not trying to win, he only wants to finish."

"But you didn't agree to help Marcel in any way?"

"Of course not." Sheffield looked away. He hated lying to Jane, yet he did so regularly about his gambling. This time, though, he swore to himself, he was going to quit—when the slate was wiped clean with Marcel, he had made up his mind not to bet on anything again, not racing, not boxing, not soccer, not even whether the Eiffel Tower was still standing. And he was going to find work, too— some kind of normal job, maybe in an automobile factory, so he could bring in some money, settle down, plan for some kind of future. Jane, after all, was almost thirty; she wouldn't be able to kick her heels above her head in the Crazy Horse chorus line forever.

And his bargain with Marcel wouldn't matter to Austin and Chelsea, he emphasized to his conscience. All Austin had to do to get his design center was finish the race, not win it.

That night while Jane was at the club, Sheffield went to a bookstall on the Left Bank that specialized in racing publications. He purchased an edition of the special Paris-Dakar Rally newspaper that listed each vehicle and how it had performed in the optional trials at Cergy-Pontoise. Back home, he studied the figures on Ferrand's Peugeot and on several other cars which appeared to have the proper ratios of weight-to-speed necessary for a serious run. There was a Mitsubishi that looked very good, a factory-sponsored Mercedes, a Range Rover, a Majorette, a little Russian-built Lada, and a Belgian entry that looked like a VW but was called an Ostend.

For two hours he worked and reworked the stats on a pad of paper, dividing weights by distance, by average speeds, by days, by the hours of daylight which would be available, by the average wind velocity across the Sahara, by the number of stops necessary to adjust tire pressure, by a dozen other factors that a prudent driver needed to consider. When he finished, and compared his final figures with the figures he had estimated for Austin Trowbridge's car, Sheffield reached an unavoidable conclusion: the Max One might—just *might*—actually win the rally.

Sheffield put on his overcoat and went for a walk along the Champs-Elysees and on into the deserted Tuileries. The trees in the park were wintry and forlorn, the grass grey from its nightly frost, and the late-November air thin and cold. Sheffield limped along, his hands deep in his pockets, chin down, brow pinched. Marcel had used the word "guarantee"—and that's what Sheffield had agreed to: a guarantee that the Max One wouldn't win. But the car, Sheffield now knew, was even better than he'd thought: it *could* win. In order to secure his guarantee to Marcel, Sheffield was left with but one alternative. He had to tamper with the car.

Sheffield sat on a bench in the dark and brooded about the weaknesses of character that had brought him to his present point in life. He wondered how much courage it would take to remain on the bench all night and catch pneumonia and freeze to death. The longer he thought about it, the more inviting it seemed. He sat there until he became very cold. But eventually he rose and returned to the rooms above the cafe.

The following week, after conceiving and dismissing a number of plans, Sheffield asked Austin, "What are you going to do about oil?"

"The rally supply truck sells it at the end of every stage, doesn't it? I thought I'd buy it there every night."

"That's okay in the stages where everything goes right," Sheffield pointed out. "But the rally supply truck is only there for a couple of hours and then starts an overnight drive to the next stage. If you get lost or break down or even blow a tire, you could miss the truck and have to run on used oil the entire next day. You need to carry a dozen quarts of your own oil for emergencies."

"I hate to add the weight," Austin said reluctantly.

"I know of a garage that will seal it in plastic bags so you can eliminate the cans," Sheffield said. "That'll save you a couple of pounds."

"You really think it's necessary?"

"I'd do it," Sheffield assured him. Austin finally agreed. "Tell me the grade you want and I'll get it for you," Sheffield said.

Austin wrote down the viscosity numbers of an oil density that was perfect for the Max One's engine. On his way home, Sheffield stopped by the garage of which he had spoken. Before he ordered the bags of oil, he drew a line through some of Austin's numbers and replaced them with figures of his own—lower figures which designated less constancy in the oil's lubricating quality.

Several days later, the garage delivered to the rooms above the cafe a carton containing the bagged oil. Jane was home and accepted the delivery. The garageman gave her a message for Sheffield.

"Our mechanic said to tell Monsieur that if this oil is for a rally vehicle, it should be several grades lighter. This viscosity will reduce engine efficiency as the air temperature drops."

When the garageman left, Jane saw taped to the top bag the slip of paper with the viscosity numbers altered. When Sheffield returned from Montmartre, she asked him about it.

"Yes, I changed them," he said, his tone deliberately casual. "The oil Austin specified was too light."

"Does he know you changed his figures?"

"Sure."

"Are you lying to me, Jack?" She had been exercising and was in black leotards, hands on hips, concern wrinkling her brow.

"Why would I lie about a thing like motor oil?" Sheffield asked.

"I don't know. But I've had an uneasy feeling since I saw you with Marcel. If you're in some kind of trouble, Jack—"

"I'm not in any kind of trouble," he said, forcing a smile.

"You're not trying to get back at Chelsea for the way she's acting toward you, I hope."

"Of course not."

"Jack," she said, "I called Austin and said I thought the garage made a mistake. I read him your numbers and he said they were wrong."

"You *what?*" Sheffield stared at her. The color drained from his face. Jane sighed wearily and sat down.

"I knew it. I could feel it."

Sheffield felt a surge of relief. "You didn't call Austin."

She shook her head. "No." Her expression saddened. "Why are you doing it, Jack?"

Sheffield poured himself a drink and sat down and told her the truth. He told her about the lies of the past fourteen months, the money he'd bet and lost, the circle of desperation that had slowly been closing in on him. "I saw a way out," he pleaded.

"By hurting someone who trusts you?"

"No one will be hurt," he insisted. "Austin doesn't have to win, all he has to do—"

"Is finish," she completed the statement for him. "That's not the point, Jack. It's wrong and you know it."

"Look," he tried to explain, "when Austin uses this heavier oil, all it will do is make the Max One's engine cut down a few R.P.M.s. He probably won't even notice it. The car will slow down maybe a mile an hour."

"It's wrong, Jack. Please don't do it."

"I've *got* to do it," Sheffield asserted. "I've got to get clear of Marcel."

"We can start paying Marcel. I have some savings."

"No." Sheffield stiffened. "I'm tired of being kept by you, Jane."

"*Kept* by me?"

"Yes, kept! You as much as said so yourself when you told my daughter I was marvelous in bed."

"Oh, Jack—surely you don't think Chelsea took me seriously!"

"*I* took you seriously."

Jane stared at him. "If you think you're going to shift onto me some of the responsibility for what you're doing, you're mistaken."

"I don't want you to take any of the responsibility," he made clear, "but I don't expect you to interfere, either. Just mind your own business."

Jane's eyes hardened. "I'll do that."

* * *

In the middle of December, the Crazy Horse closed for two weeks
and Jane announced that she was going back to England for the
holidays. "Dad's getting on," she said, "and I haven't seen my
sister's children since they were toddlers. I'd invite you along but
I'm afraid it would be awkward, our not being married and all."

"I understand," Sheffield said. "I'll spend Christmas with Chelsea
and Austin."

"I rather thought you would." She hesitated. "Are you still determined to go through with your plan?"

"Yes, I am."

Jane shrugged and said no more.

After she was gone, Chelsea seemed to feel guilty about Sheffield
being alone for Christmas. "You're welcome to come here," she
said. "I'm not the greatest cook, but—"

"Actually, I'm going to England," he lied. "Jane telephoned last
night and said she missed me. I'm taking the boat train on Christmas
Eve."

What he actually took on Christmas Eve was a long, lonely walk
around the gaily decorated Place de la Concorde, past the chic little
shops staying open late along Rue Royale. All around him holiday
music played, greetings were exchanged, and the usually dour faces
of the Parisiennes softened a bit. When his ankle began to ache,
Sheffield bought a quart of gin, a loaf of bread, and a small basket
of cold meats and cheese, and trudged back to his rooms. The cafe
downstairs was closed, so he had to walk around to the alley and
go up the back way. A thin, cold drizzle started and he was glad it
had waited until he was almost inside.

Putting the food away, he lighted the little space heater, opened
the gin, and sat trying to imagine what the future held for him. The
telephone rang that night and several times on Christmas Day, but
he did not answer it. He was too involved wondering about the rest
of his life. And he was afraid it might be a wrong number.

Sheffield finally answered the telephone the following week when
he came in one evening and found it ringing. It was Jane.

"I thought I ought to tell you, I'm staying over for a few days
longer. There's a new cabaret opening in Piccadilly and they're
auditioning dancers the day after New Year's. I'm going to try out.
Actually, I've been thinking about working closer to home for a
while. Dad's—"

"Yes, I know. Well, then. I wish you luck."

"No hard feelings?"

"Of course not. You?"

"Not any more."

"Let me know how you make out."

"Sure."

After he hung up, Sheffield got the gin out again. He drank until he passed out. It was nearly twelve hours later when he heard an incessant pounding and imagined there was a little man inside his head trying to break out through his left eye with a mallet. When he forced himself to sit upright and engage his senses, he discovered that the pounding was on his door.

He opened the door and Chelsea burst in. "Austin's broken his arm!" she announced, distraught.

On their way to Montmartre, she gave him the details. "We decided to go out for dinner last night, to celebrate finishing the last of the work on the car. We went to a little cafe on rue Lacaur—"

"That's a rough section."

"Tell me about it. On the way home, we were walking past these two guys and one of them made a comment about me. Austin said something back, and before I knew it both of them jumped him. They beat him up badly and one of them used his knee to break Austin's arm like a stick of wood. It was awful!"

In the rooms over the garage, Austin was in bed with an ice compress on his face and his right arm in a cast. "Two years of work down the tubes," he said morosely.

"It could have been worse," Sheffield told him. "People have been shot and stabbed on that street."

"I thought for a minute one of them was going to slice Austin with a razor," Chelsea said.

"A razor?" Sheffield frowned. "What kind of razor?"

"One of those barber's razors. The kind that unfolds like a pocket knife."

"A straight razor," Sheffield said quietly. An image of Marcel's two bodyguards came into focus. The thin one carried a straight razor and the other one looked strong enough to break arms.

Sheffield managed to keep his anger under control while he tried to reconcile Austin and Chelsea to the fact that it wasn't the end of the rally for them. He gave Austin the names of four drivers he knew who weren't signed up for Paris-Dakar this year and might consider an offer to make the run. Two were here in Paris, one was in Zurich, and the other at his home in Parma. "Call them and see what you can do," he said. "I'll go back to my place and see if I can think of any others."

As soon as he left the garage, he went to a telephone kiosk around the corner and called Marcel's office.

"You son of a bitch," he said when the Frenchman came on the line. "We had an arrangement that *I* was to keep Austin Trowbridge from winning."

"That is not precisely correct," Marcel said. "You agreed to take care of the *car*. I decided, because of the amount of money at risk, that it would be best to protect your guarantee with an additional guarantee."

"That wasn't necessary, you son of a bitch!"

"That's twice you've called me that," Marcel said, his tone icing. "I've overlooked it up to now because I know you're angry. Please refrain from doing it again, however. For your information—" his voice broke slightly "—my mother was a saint."

"I don't think you had a mother," Sheffield said coldly. "I think you crawled up out of a sewer!" Slamming down the receiver, he left the kiosk and stalked across the street to a bar. He had a quick drink to calm himself down, then another, which he drank more slowly as he tried to decide what to do. There was no way he could turn in Marcel's thugs without admitting his own complicity to Austin and Chelsea. And it was Marcel he wanted to get even with. But Marcel was always protected. How the hell did you take revenge on someone with the protection he had?

As Sheffield worried it over, the bartender brought him change from the banknote with which he'd paid for his drinks. Sheffield stared at the francs on the bar and suddenly thought: *Of course.* You didn't hurt a man like Marcel physically, you hurt him financially.

Leaving the second drink unfinished, something Sheffield hadn't done in years, he left the bar and hurried back to the rooms over the garage. Austin and Chelsea were at the telephone.

"The two drivers here turned us down," Austin said. "I'm about to call the one in Zurich."

"Forget it," Sheffield said flatly. "I'm driving the Max One for you . . ."

It wasn't yet dawn in the Place d'Armes where the race was to start, but a thousand portable spotlights created an artificial daylight that illuminated the four lines of vehicles in eerie silver light. A hundred thousand spectators jammed the early-morning boulevard on each side, waving flags, signs, and balloons, cheering select cars and select drivers, the women throwing and sometimes personally delivering kisses, the men reaching past the lines of gendarmes to slap fenders and shout, "*Bon courage!*"

Young girls, the kind who pursue rock stars, walked the lines seeking autographs and more while their younger brothers and sisters followed them throwing confetti. Everyone had to shout to be heard in the general din.

The Max One was in 182nd starting position, which put it in the forty-sixth row, the second car from the inside. Chelsea, in a racing suit, stood with Austin's good arm around her, both looking with great concern at Jack as he wound extra last-minute tape over the boot around his weak ankle.

"Are you absolutely sure about this, Jack?" the young designer asked. "It's not worth further damage to your ankle."

"I'm positive," Sheffield said. "Anyway, we'll be using Chelsea's feet whenever we can." Looking up, he grinned. "You just be in Dakar to receive the trophy."

"That trophy will be yours, Jack."

"The prize money will be mine," Sheffield corrected. "The trophy will be yours."

There was a sudden roar from the crowd and a voice announced through static in the loudspeaker that the first row of four vehicles had been waved to a start. The rally had begun.

"Kiss him goodbye and get in," Sheffield said, shaking hands with Austin, then leaving the couple alone for the moments they had left.

Presently father and daughter were side by side, buckled and harnessed in, adrenaline rushing, their bodies vibrating from the revving engine, their eyes fixed on the white-coated officials who moved down the line and with a brusque nod and a wave started each row of four vehicles five seconds apart.

Sheffield grinned over at Chelsea. "I wonder what your mother would say if she could see us now?"

"I know exactly what she'd say: 'Birds of a feather.' "

"Well, maybe we are," Sheffield said.

"Let's don't get sentimental, Father," Chelsea replied. "Driving together from Paris to Dakar doesn't make a relationship."

Looking at her determined young face, Sheffield nodded. "Whatever you say, kid."

A moment later, they were waved away from the starting line.

From Paris to Barcelona would have been 850 kilometers if the road had been straight. But it wasn't. It wound through Loiret, Cher, Creuse, Correze, Cantal, and more—as if the route had been designed by an aimless schoolboy on a bicycle. Nearly all the way, the roadsides were lined with cheering, waving, kiss-throwing well-wishers shouting, "*Bonne chance!*" From time to time, flowers were thrown into the cars as they bunched up in a village and were forced to slow down. Farther south, cups of *vin ordinaire*, slices of cheese, and hunks of bread were shared. The farther away from Paris one got, the more relaxed and cheerful were the French people.

Sheffield and Chelsea didn't talk much during the trip south. She was already missing Austin and Sheffield was concentrating on finding ways to relieve pressure on his weak ankle by holding his foot in various positions. These preoccupations and the increasingly beautiful French countryside kept them both silently contemplative. The Paris-to-Barcelona stage of the rally was a liaison—a controlled section of the route in which all positions remained as they had started—so it wasn't necessary to speed or try to pass. A few vehicles invariably broke down the first day, but for the most part it was little more than a tourist outing. The real race would not begin until they reached Africa.

It was after dark when they crossed the Spanish border and well into the late Spanish dinner hour when they reached Barcelona. As the French had done, the Spaniards lined the streets to cheer on the smiling, still fresh drivers in their shiny, unbattered vehicles. Because of the crowds, and the absence of adequate crowd control, the great caterpillar of vehicles inched its way down to the dock, where the Spanish ferry that would take them to Algiers waited. It was midnight when Sheffield and Chelsea finally drove onto the quay, had their papers examined, and boarded the boat. The first day, eighteen and a half hours long, was over.

Crossing the Mediterranean, Sheffield and Chelsea got some rest and nourishment and met some of the other drivers. Sheffield was well known by most of them already. (He had asked Chelsea ahead of time how she wanted to be introduced. "I don't have to say I'm your father if you'd rather I didn't," he told her. She had shrugged. "It makes no difference to me. Everyone knows we don't choose our parents." "Or our children," Sheffield added.) He introduced her simply as Chelsea and told everyone she was the vehicle designer's girlfriend.

Ferrand, the French driver, Vera Kursk, a shapely but formidable-looking Russian woman, and Alf Zeebrug, a Belgian, all expressed great interest in the Max One's structural configuration. They were, Sheffield remembered from his computations, the three favorites to win the rally: Ferrand in his Peugeot, Vera Kursk in a Lada, Zeebrug in the Volkswagen lookalike called an Ostend.

As they studied the Max One, Ferrand winked at Sheffield and said, "So, you've brought in—what do you Americans call it, a ringer?"

Vera nodded her head knowingly. "I see why you passed up the trial races, Jack. Foxy."

"Let us look under the hood, Jack," pressed Zeebrug, knowing Sheffield wouldn't.

In the end, Ferrand spoke for them all when he said, "Welcome back, Jack. It's good to race with you again." Vera gave him a more-than-friendly kiss on the lips.

Later Chelsea said, "They all seem like nice people."

"They are," Sheffield said. "They're here for the race, nothing else: no politics, no nationalism, no petty jealousies. Just the race." Ferrand, Sheffield was convinced, knew nothing about Marcel's machinations in favor of the Peugeot. Had he known, Ferrand—an honorable man and an honest competitor—would have withdrawn and probably sought out Marcel for physical punishment.

Another comment Chelsea made just before they docked was, "They all seem to like and respect you, Father."

"There are some quarters in which I'm not a pariah," he replied. "Believe it or not."

In Africa, the first stage was Algiers to Ghardaia. Sheffield stuck a handprinted list to the dashboard between them. It read:

> Ferrand-Peugeot
> Kursk-Lada
> Zeebrug-Ostend
> Sakai-Mitsubishi
> Gordon-Range Rover
> Smythe-Majorette

"These are the drivers and cars to beat," he told Chelsea. "I had a Mercedes on the list, too, but the driver was drinking too much on the ferry and bought a bottle of scotch to take with him when we docked. I don't think we'll have to worry about him."

Chelsea looked at him curiously. "I thought we were only in this to finish, so that Austin can get his design center."

Sheffield fixed her in a flat stare. "I'm a racer, kid. I enter races to *win*. This one is no exception. If you don't want to go along with that, you can get off here."

Chelsea shook her head determinedly. "Not on your life."

Sheffield had to look away so she wouldn't see his pleased smile.

During the first stage, it seemed to Chelsea that every car, truck, and motorcycle in the rally was passing them. "Why aren't we going faster?" she demanded.

"It's not necessary right now," Sheffield told her. "All these people passing us are the showboats—rich little boys and girls with expensive little toys. They run too fast too quickly. Most of them will burn up their engines before we get out of Algeria. Look over there—"

Chelsea looked where he indicated and saw Ferrand, Vera Kursk, and the other experienced drivers cruising along at moderate speed just as Sheffield was doing. "I guess I've got a lot to learn," she said.

At Ghardaia, their sleeping bags spread like spokes around a desert campfire, the drivers discussed the day. "Let's see," Zeebrug calculated, "three hundred forty-four vehicles started and so far one hundred eighteen have dropped out."

"Good numbers," Ferrand said.

Vera Kursk smiled. "This could turn into a race instead of a herd."

Chelsea noticed that the Russian woman and Sheffield shared a little evening brandy from the same cup and that earlier, when the sleeping bags were spread, Vera had positioned hers fairly close to Sheffield's. Commie slut, she thought. When no one was paying any attention, Chelsea moved her own sleeping bag between them.

It took a week to get out of Algeria—a week in which Sheffield and the other experienced drivers continued to drive at reasonable, safe speeds that were easy on their engines, tires, and the bodies of both car and driver. All along the route, vehicles were dropping out—throwing pistons, getting stuck in sand, blowing too many tires, sliding off soft shoulders into gullies, dropping transmissions, or the exhausted drivers simply giving up. The Mercedes quit the second day—its driver, as Sheffield had predicted, drinking too much liquor for the heat he had to endure and the stamina required to drive. A surprise dropout was the Mitsubishi. Driven by the Japanese speed-racer Sakai, it had hit a sand-concealed rock and broken its front axle. "One down, five to go," Sheffield said, drawing a line through Sakai's name on the dashboard list.

By the time they crossed into Niger, an additional sixty-three vehicles had dropped out. "That leaves one hundred sixty-three in," said Smythe, the Englishman driving the Majorette, when they camped that night. He was feeling good about the dropouts. At noon the next day, he joined them when the Majorette burned up its gearbox.

"Two down, four to go," Sheffield told Chelsea, and drew another line.

After camping one night in Chirfa, Chelsea noticed the next morning that Sheffield and Ferrand and the others shook hands all around and wished each other good luck. "What was that all about?" she asked.

"Everyone will be camping alone from now on," he said. "The socializing is over." Sheffield pointed toward a band of haze on the horizon. "We go into the Tenere Desert today. Now we start racing."

The terrain they encountered that day was hell on a back burner. The Max One was in ashlike sand up to its axles, plowing along like a man walking against a gale wind. The stink of the desert decay was unexpected and appalling to Chelsea. She gagged repeatedly. Huge white rats the size of rabbits leaped at the car windows. This stage of the rally that crossed the Tenere was a nightmare in glaring daylight no newcomer was ever prepared for.

Camped alone that night in some rocks above the desert floor, Chelsea saw Sheffield massaging his foot. "How's the ankle?" she asked.

"Just a little stiff. It'll be okay."

"Let's switch places tomorrow," she suggested. "I'll drive and you relieve." Up to then, Sheffield had done eighty percent of the driving. "Tomorrow," Sheffield told her, "we go over the Azbine Plain. It's like driving across a huge corrugated roof."

"Let me drive," she said quietly. "I can manage it."

He let her drive—and she took them across the rough terrain like a pilgrim determined to get to Mecca. Along the way, they saw Zeebrug lying at the side of the road, a rally first-aid team inflating a splint on his leg. The Ostend was nearby, upside down in a ditch, one wheel gone.

"Three and three," Sheffield said. He handed Chelsea the marker and she crossed off Zeebrug's name.

Into the second week of the race, both Jack and Chelsea began to feel the strain of the collective pressures: the usually unheated, quickly eaten food that wreaked havoc with their digestion, the constant jarring and jolting of the car that pummeled their bodies, the freezing nights sleeping on the ground, the scorching, glaring sun by day, the sand and dirt in their mouths, ears, eyes, noses, the constant headaches and relentless fatigue that the short rests could not remedy. Depression set in, underscored by the begging of poverty-stricken Africans everywhere they stopped.

"*Cadeau*," the black children pleaded as Sheffield adjusted his tire pressure. "*Cadeau*," they whined as Chelsea filled the radiator from a village stream.

"We have no gifts," Sheffield told them in English, in French, and by a firm shaking of his head. "Try to ignore them," he advised Chelsea, and she did try, but her eyes remained moist. As did his.

Just over the border in Mali, their physical and mental distress was displaced in priority and urgency by problems the Max One began to develop. A fuel line cracked and split, and they lost considerable petrol before Chelsea noticed the trail it was leaving behind them and they stopped to repair it. The lost fuel had to be replaced at a township pump at exorbitant cost. Later the same day, for no apparent reason, a center section of the windshield bubbled and cracked. Sheffield patched it with some of the tape he had brought for his ankle. The very next day, the odometer cable snapped and they were unable to monitor their distance to the end of the stage.

"Austin's damned car," Chelsea seethed, "is falling apart."

"It's holding up better than most." Sheffield bobbed his chin at two cars, two trucks, and a motorcycle that had dropped out at the side of the road. By then, seventy-one more vehicles had quit the rally, leaving ninety-two still in.

Near Timbuktu, Sheffield and Chelsea happened on a small water pond that no one else seemed to notice. Behind a high rise, it had a few trees, some scrub, and even a patch of Gobi grass. "We've died and gone to heaven," Chelsea said when she saw the water. She began undressing. "I hope you're not modest."

"Not if you aren't."

They took their first bath in two weeks, and when they were clean they rubbed salve on their hips and shoulders where the Max One's seatbelts and harnesses had rubbed the skin raw.

"Mother never went with you when you raced, did she?" Chelsea asked reflectively.

"No."

"Who took care of you when you got hurt?"

"Whoever was around," Sheffield said. He looked off at the distance.

Chelsea patted his head maternally. "If you get hurt in this race, *I'll* take care of you," she assured him. Then she turned away to dress, as if her words embarrassed her where her nakedness had not.

After Mali, they crossed into Mauritania. The topography of the route seemed to change every day. One stage would be a mazelike, twisting and turning trail along a dry riverbed, in turn sandy and dusty, then suddenly muddy where an unexpected patch of water appeared. Then they would encounter a long, miserable stage of deep ruts and vicious potholes, then a log-and-rock-strewn track that shook their teeth and vibrated agonizingly in Sheffield's weak ankle.

With each kilometer, his pain grew more intense. During the day he swallowed codeine tablets. At night Chelsea put wet compresses on his ankle and massaged his foot. Those days they came to a stage that was open, flat straightaway, Chelsea did the driving and Sheffield enjoyed temporary respite from the pain.

Nearly every day they caught glimpses of Ferrand, Vera Kursk, and the Australian Gordon in his Range Rover. There were no smiles, waves, or shouted greetings now—just grim nods that said, So you're still in it, are you? Well, so am I.

Into the third grueling week, the pain, fatigue, and depression evolved into recriminations. "How in hell did I let myself get into this mess anyway?" Sheffield asked as he untaped his swollen ankle one night. "I don't owe Austin Trowbridge *or* you anything."

"How did *you* get into it!" Chelsea shot back. "How did *I* get into it! I'm making the same damned mistake my mother made— getting mixed up with a man who thinks speed is some kind of religion."

"I could be back in Paris going to old movies," Sheffield lamented, "eating sausages with homemade mustard, drinking gin."

"And I could be in Philadelphia going to club meetings and playing tennis with your *other* daughter."

They caught each other's eyes in the light of the campfire and both smiled sheepishly. Chelsea came over and kneeled next to her father. "I'll do that," she said, and tended to his ankle.

Later, when he got into his sleeping bag and she was preparing to stand the first two-hour watch, flare gun at the ready, she looked very frankly at him. "You know," she said, her voice slightly hoarse from the dryness, "if we weren't blood relatives, I might find myself attracted to you."

Sheffield stayed awake most of the two hours he should have been sleeping. This was one race he would be very glad to have over— for more reasons than his swollen ankle.

From Mauritania, the route cut north across the border of the Spanish Sahara for a hundred or so kilometers of hot sand, between the wells of Tichia in the east and Bir Ganduz in the west. During that stage, with seventy-one vehicles of the original 344 still in the race, there was much jockeying for position, much cutting in, out, and around, much risky driving on soft shoulders, and much blind speeding as the dust wake of the vehicle in front reduced visibility to the length of your hood. It was a dangerous stage, driven with goggles and mouth masks, clenched jaws, white knuckles, tight sphincters, and the pedal to the metal, no quarter asked, none given.

In a one-on-one, side-by-side dash to be the first into a single lane between two enormous dunes, Chelsea at the wheel of the Max One and Gordon in his Range Rover were dead even on a thousand-yard straightaway, both pushing their vehicles to the limit, when Gordon glanced over at the Max One and smiled in his helmet at the sight of the girl, not the man, doing the driving. He had the audacity to take one hand off the wheel and wave goodbye as he inched ahead.

"You bastard," Chelsea muttered and juiced the Max One's engine by letting up on the accelerator two inches, then stomping down on it, jolting the automatic transmission into its highest gear and shooting the car forward as if catapulted. With inches to spare, she sliced in front of Gordon at the point where the dunes came together, surprising him so that he swerved, went up an embankment, and immediately slid back down, burying the Range Rover's rear end in five feet of what the nomad Arabs, translated, called "slip sand": grains that, although dry, held like wet quicksand. The Australian would, Sheffield knew, be stuck for hours, and was effectively out of the race as far as finishing up front was concerned.

"Nice work, kid," he said. Now they had only Ferrand and Vera Kursk with whom to contend.

That night they camped along with the other remaining drivers around the oasis well at Bir Ganduz. When the rally starts for the day were announced, they learned that seventeen more vehicles had fallen by the wayside on the Spanish Sahara stage, leaving fifty-four competitors: thirty-eight cars, ten trucks, and six motorcycles. Ferrand was in the lead position, one of the cyclists second, Vera Kursk third, one of the trucks fourth, another cyclist fifth, and the Max One sixth.

"Are you disappointed we aren't doing better?" Chelsea asked as they changed oil and air filters.

Sheffield shook his head. "We can pass both cyclists and the truck any time we want to. And probably will, tomorrow. It'll come down to Ferrand, Vera, and us."

"Do you think we can beat them?"

Sheffield smiled devilishly. "If we don't, we'll scare hell out of them." For a moment then he became very quiet. Presently he handed Chelsea a plastic jar. "Hustle over to the control truck and get us some distilled water."

"The battery wells aren't low—I just checked them."

"I want some extra, anyway, just in case. Go on."

As soon as she was out of sight, Sheffield reached into the car and got the flare gun. Turning to a stand of trees in deep shadows twenty feet from the car, he said. "Whoever's in there has got ten seconds to step out where I can see you or I'll light you up like the Arch of Triumph."

From out of the darkness stepped Marcel's two thugs. The one who carried a razor had a sneer on his gaunt brown face. The one with the bucket neck simply looked angry as usual. "We bring greetings from Marcel," said the thin one. "He said to tell you he is willing to be reasonable. Forget what has gone before. You and he will start fresh. He will cancel your debt and give you one hundred thousand francs if you do not overtake Ferrand."

"No deal," Sheffield replied flatly.

"I am authorized to go to a hundred and fifty thousand francs. That is twenty-five thousand dollars—"

"I can add. No deal."

The other man pointed a threatening finger. "To doublecross Marcel is not very smart—"

Sheffield cocked the flare gun. "You're the one who broke my friend's arm, aren't you? How'd you like to have a multicolored face?"

"No need for that," the thin one said quickly, holding up both hands. "We delivered Marcel's message, we have your answer. We'll go now."

"If I see you again," Sheffield warned them, "I'll tell the other drivers about you. They won't like what they hear. You'll end up either in a sandy grave or a Senegalese prison. I don't know which would be worse."

"Perhaps the young lady has an opinion," the thin man said, bobbing his chin toward the Max One, off to the side of Sheffield. It was the oldest ruse in the world, but Sheffield fell for it. He looked over to his left, and when he did the thin man leaped forward with enough speed and agility to knock the flare gun to the ground before Sheffield could resist. Then the man with the bucket neck was there, shoving him roughly until his back was against the car and driving a boot-toe hard against his painful ankle. Sheffield groaned and started to fall, but the other man held him up long enough to deliver a second brutal kick.

"That's all!" his partner said urgently. "Come on!"

They were gone, leaving Sheffield sitting on the sand clutching his ankle, tears of pain cutting lines on his dry cheeks, when Chelsea got back. She ran over to him. "My God, what happened?"

"I must have stepped in a hole. It's bad—"

The ankle swelled to thrice its normal size. For several hours, Chelsea made trips to and from the public well to draw cold water for compresses. They didn't help. By morning, Sheffield couldn't put any weight at all on the foot.

"That does it, I guess," he said resignedly. "Ferrand and Vera will have to fight it out. But at least Austin will get his design center; you can drive well enough for us to finish."

"I can drive well enough for us to win," Chelsea said. She was packing up their camp. "I proved that yesterday."

"Yesterday was on a flat desert straightaway. From here down the coast to Dakar are narrow, winding roads full of tricky curves, blind spots, loose gravel."

"I can handle it."

"You don't understand," Jack said, with the patience of a parent, "this is the final lap. This is for all the marbles—this is what the last twenty days of hell have been all about. These people still in the run are serious competitors—"

"I'm serious, too," Chelsea asserted. "I'm a racer, I'm in this run to win. If you can't accept that, if you don't want to drive with me, drop off here."

Sheffield stared incredulously at her. "You're crazy, kid. Ferrand, Vera, and the others will run you off a cliff into the Atlantic Ocean if they have to."

"They can try." She stowed their belongings on the rear deck and closed the hatchback. "You staying here?"

"Not on your life," Sheffield growled. He hopped over to the car. The passenger side.

The last lap into Dakar was a war on wheels. All caution was left behind on the Spanish Sahara. This was the heavyweight championship, the World Series, and the Kentucky Derby. No one who got this far would give an inch of track. Anything gained had to be taken.

As soon as the stage started, the Max One dropped back to eight, losing two positions as a pair of motorcycles outdistanced them. Chelsea cursed but Sheffield told her not to worry about it. "This is a good stretch for cycles. We'll probably be passed by a few more. They start falling back when we reach Akreidil; the track softens there and they can't maneuver well. Keep your speed at a steady ninety."

Chelsea glanced over. "I don't want advice on how to finish, just how to win."

"That's what you're going to get," Sheffield assured her. "You do the driving, I'll do the navigating. Deal?"

Chelsea nodded curtly. "Deal."

Sheffield tore the piece of paper from the dash and looked at the names of Ferrand and Vera Kursk. Crumbling it, he tossed it out the window.

"Litterbug," she said.

"Shut up and drive, Chelsea."

"Yes, Daddy."

They exchanged quick smiles, then grimly turned their attention back to the track.

By midmorning the Max One was back to eleventh, but Ferrand and Vera had also fallen behind, everyone being outrun by the six daredevil cyclists still in the rally. This was their moment of glory and they knew it. They would lead the last lap of the run for three magnificent hours, then—as Sheffield had predicted—start falling behind at Akreidil. From that point on, the four-wheeled vehicles overtook and passed them one by one. Ferrand moved back into first place, Vera pressed into second, and the Max One held fourth behind a modified Toyota truck. They were all sometimes mere feet apart on the dangerous track along the Mauritanian coast.

"Blind spot," Sheffield would say as they negotiated weird hairpin turns. "Hug in," he instructed when he wanted Chelsea to keep tight to the inside of the track. "Let up," he said to slow down, "Punch it" to speed up, "Drop one" to go into a lower gear as he saw Ferrand's car suddenly nose up a grade ahead.

Two of the nine trucks behind them started crowding the track south of Mederdra, taking turns ramming into the Max One's rear bumper at ninety k.p.h. "Get ready to brake," Sheffield said. Watching in a sideview mirror, he waited for exactly the right second, then yelled, "Brake!" Chelsea hit the brake and felt a jolt as one of the trucks ricocheted off the Max One's rear fender and shot across the rocky beach into the surf.

"The other one's passed us!" Chelsea shouted.

"I wanted it to," Sheffield said. "Watch."

The truck that had displaced them in fourth place quickly drew up and challenged the truck in third. For sixty kilometers they jockeyed and swerved and slammed sides trying to assert superiority. One kilometer in front of them, Ferrand and Vera held the two lead positions; behind them, Sheffield and Chelsea kept everyone else in back of the Max One to let the trucks fight it out. Finally, on the Senegal border, the crowding truck finally forced number three off the track and moved up to take its place.

"Okay!" Sheffield yelled at Chelsea. "His body's tired but his brain is happy because he just won. The two aren't working together right now. Punch it!"

Chelsea gunned the Max One and in seconds laid it right next to the victorious truck. The driver looked over, surprised. Sheffield smiled at him. Then Sheffield put his hand over Chelsea's and jerked the steering wheel sharply. The Max One leaped to the right, the truck swerved to avoid being hit, the Max One crossed the entire track, and the truck spun around and went backward into a ditch.

"Now let's go after Vera," Sheffield said.

"With pleasure," Chelsea replied.

It became a three-car race. For more than four hundred kilometers, speeding inland along Senegal's gently undulating sandy-clay plains, the Peugeot, the Lada, and the Max One vied for position. Along straightaways, it became clear that Austin Trowbridge's car was superior in speed to both the French and Russian vehicles. Chelsea caught up with and passed them both. "Yeeee*oh!*" she yelled as she sped into the lead.

"Don't open the champagne yet," Sheffield said.

When the straightaway ended and they once again encountered a stretch of the great continental dunes, the experienced drivers again outmaneuvered and outdistanced the Max One.

"What am I doing wrong?" Chelsea pleaded.

"Hanging out with race-car drivers."

"That's not what I mean!" she stormed, her sense of humor lost in the face of her frustration.

"We'll be on a sandstone flat when we cross the Saloum River," Sheffield calmed her. "You'll have a chance to take the lead again there."

When they reached the flat, Chelsea quickly caught up with Vera Kursk and passed her, and was pressing Ferrand for first place when the accident happened. A pack of hyenas, perhaps a dozen, suddenly ran in front of the Peugeot. Seasoned professional that he was, Ferrand did not swerve an inch as he felt the impact of his grille on the animals he hit and the rumble of his tires on those he ran over. Then one of the hyenas was spun up into the wheel well and, in a mangle of flesh and blood, jammed the axle. Ferrand's front wheels locked and his vehicle flipped end over end, landing a hundred feet out on the flats, bursting into flames.

"Stop the car!" Sheffield ordered, and Chelsea skidded to a halt on the shoulder. They unharnessed and leaped out, Sheffield grabbing the portable fire extinguisher, Chelsea helping him to balance upright on his swollen ankle. As they ran, hobbling, toward the burning car, they became aware that the Lada had also stopped and Vera Kursk was getting out.

At the fiery Peugeot, Sheffield handed Chelsea the extinguisher. "Start spraying the driver's door!" Chelsea pointed the red cylinder and shot a burst of Halon up and down the door. It immediately smothered the flames on that side and Sheffield was able to reach through the window, unstrap Ferrand, and drag him out of the car. Sheffield and Chelsea each took a hand and, Sheffield limping agonizingly, dragged the unconscious man far enough away so that when the Peugeot exploded none of them were hurt.

From overhead came the sound of a rotor. Looking up, Sheffield and Chelsea saw a rally control helicopter surveying a place to land. Paramedics wearing Red Cross armbands were in an open hatch waiting for touchdown.

"They'll take care of him," Sheffield said. He stood up, holding onto Chelsea for support, and they looked across the flat at the Max One and the Lada parked side by side. Vera Kursk was beside the Lada, peering down the track, where several kilometers back came the surviving vehicles. Smiling, she threw Sheffield and Chelsea a wave and quickly got into her car. Chelsea started running, dragging Sheffield with her. "The bitch!" she said.

"I'd do the same thing in her place," Sheffield groaned.

By the time they were harnessed back into the Max One, the Lada was half a kilometer ahead and the rest of the pack was moving up behind them very quickly. "We're almost to Dakar," Sheffield told his daughter. "If you want to win, you'll have to catch her."

Chelsea got back on the track and shot the car forward like a bullet. Into the African farming communities she sped, watching for animals, people, other vehicles, always keeping the Lada in sight. "Am I gaining on her, do you think?" she asked.

"Not yet."

Through the farmland, into the nearer outskirts, past larger villages, a soap factory, a shoe factory. "Am I gaining?" she shouted.

"Not yet."

Past a power station, a cotton mill, small handicraft shops at the side of the road, a huge open-air market, increasing lines of spectators in marvelously colored native garb. "Am I gaining?"

"Not yet."

"God*damn!*"

Then into the city of Dakar itself and on to the far end of Gann Boulevard, a wide, tree-lined thoroughfare roped off a mere one hour earlier, when the control aircraft advised the city that the first of the rally vehicles was approaching. The boulevard led straight to the finish line in the Place de l'Independence. The Lada was still half a kilometer ahead. "Punch it!" Sheffield yelled. He beat his fist on the dashboard. "Punch it! Punch it!"

Chelsea punched it.

The Max One drew up dead even on the right side of the Lada. The two women exchanged quick, appraising glances, saw only unyielding determination in the other, and, as if choreographed, both leaned into their steering wheels and tried to punch their accelerators through the floorboards. "Come *on!*" Chelsea muttered through her clenched teeth.

The Max One pulled forward an inch. Then two. Then three. Vera Kursk glanced over again, desperation in her eyes. Sheffield yelled, "All right!"

The cars sped down to the finish line next to the war memorial in the great plaza. Thousands cheered them on from a vast crowd that was but a blur of color to the drivers. Stretched across the end of the boulevard, a great banner with FINIS lettered on it fluttered in the breeze. The Max One was less than a car-length ahead, the Lada's windshield even with the American vehicle's rear bumper. Then Vera punched the Lada.

"She's pulling up!" Sheffield cried.

Chelsea saw Vera's face moving closer in the sideview mirror. In seconds, the Russian woman was next to her again. Biting down hard enough on her bottom lip to draw blood, Chelsea punched the Max One again.

The Max One crossed the finish line one and a half seconds ahead of the Lada.

At the banquet that night in the Saint Louis Hotel, Chelsea and Vera Kursk hugged each other and Austin Trowbridge read everyone a cable he had received congratulating him on the Max One and advising him that a bank account had been opened for one million dollars to start the Trowbridge Automotive Design Center. "I'd like you to come back to the States and be my partner," the young man told Sheffield. "Between the two of us, we can come up with cars nobody's ever imagined."

"I'll think about it, kid," Sheffield promised.

At midnight, Sheffield rode with Chelsea and Austin in a taxi out to Grand Dakar Airport, where they watched the Max One being rolled into the cargo hold of a Boeing 747 bound for Casablanca and New York. The young couple had seats in the passenger section of the same plane.

"Austin and I are going to be married when we get home," Chelsea told Sheffield. Austin had gone ahead, giving them time to say good-bye. "And we're going to start having babies. The first boy we have, I'm naming Jack. After a guy I recently met."

"Do yourself a favor," Sheffield said. "Raise him to be a doctor."

She shook her head. "Not on your life." She kissed him on the cheek. "Bye, Daddy."

"See you, kid."

*   *   *

Sheffield watched the plane rumble down the runway and climb into the starry African sky. Then he sighed and limped slowly off the observation deck and back into the terminal. When he reached the glass exit doors, he was met by the familiar face he'd been expecting.

"Hello, Marcel."

The Frenchman's two thugs were standing nearby.

"The Max One was pressing Ferrand when he crashed," Marcel accused. "You were racing to win."

"I always race to win," Sheffield replied evenly.

"Do you think you can get away with doublecrossing me?" The Frenchman's eyes were narrowed and dangerous.

Sheffield merely shrugged. "What are you going to do, Marcel, kill me?" He cocked his head in the best John Garfield tradition. "Everybody dies," he said arrogantly. And pushing through the doors, he walked painfully out into the Senegalese night.

Forgotten Writers
Jay/J. M. Flynn
by Bill Pronzini

The subtitle of this book is "The Year's Best Suspense and Mystery." That suggests a book filled with fiction. But just as we think news of the field is a germane topic for discussion, so, too, are articles concerned with the history of the field within our purview when we talk about the year's best.

In the following article, Bill Pronzini writes about an author who is likely to be unknown to many readers. Jay Flynn's lack of fame doesn't mean, however, that his story isn't an important one. On the contrary, it makes him a perfect example of the writers who formed the backbone of American hardboiled detective fiction for decades. His story isn't unique, but Pronzini's skilled, poignant telling of it packs a wallop only rarely found in this kind of reporting.

Jay Flynn was a character. The tragicomic variety, with accent on the tragic.

In many ways he was a throwback, a stereotype. Hard-drinking, rough-living, blarney-spouting Boston Irishman. Ex-GI, newspaperman (ten years as a crime reporter on the *Portland Express*, Portland, Maine; stints on the *San Jose Mercury* and other California papers), bartender, editor, mystery writer, sex novelist, bootlegger, security guard, caretaker, and (so he claimed) prisoner in a hellhole Mexican jail on a trumped-up charge and "writer-in-residence" at a Nevada whorehouse. A screw-up of the first rank, with sometimes hilarious results. Lousy luck with women and games of chance, much of it of his own making. Restless, peripatetic; "everybody's got to be someplace," he said once, "but it don't always have to be the same damn place." Lazy, ambitious, apathetic, energetic, generous, selfish, cynical, sentimental, don't-give-a-damn, care-too-much—all the schizophrenic contradictions that make up most of us, but that in him seemed magnified to an even greater degree. As has been said about Hemingway, he was just a little larger—and just a little smaller—than life.

There is a schizophrenic quality to his fiction as well. He was like the proverbial little girl: When he was good he was very good, but when he was bad he was very, very bad. His characters and his plots, like Flynn himself, were full of BS and on the screwball side. Big, tough, occasionally inept Irish heroes with names like McHugh, Tighe Slattery, Joe Mannix (no relation or resemblance to the Mike Conners TV character), Burdis Gannon, Matt Tara, Burl Stannard, John Christian Fifer. Beautiful, willing, treacherous women. Ultra-nasty villians. Action fast and furious—and scatterbrained and often implausible. Storylines, some solidly constructed and some riddled with holes, involving elaborate capers, hijackings, modern-day boot-legging, the hot-car racket, military-base intrigue, the Mafia, vigilante cops and serial killers, Nazi war spoils, spy stuff, even a treasure hidden inside an Irish pub's thirty-foot, hand-carved mahogany bar. Typical paperback fare of the sixties and seventies, in one sense; atypical, in another, because of Flynn's slightly skewed perceptions and not inconsiderable (when he worked at it) storytelling skills.

His first published work and only published short story, "The Badger Game," as by Jay Flynn, appeared in the November 1956 issue of the hardboiled, J.D.-oriented mystery magazine, *Guilty*; his first novel, *The Deadly Combo*, as by J. M. Flynn, was an Ace Double two years later. The short story isn't such-a-much; the novel is a pretty fair maiden effort. There is a similar dichotomy among his six other Ace Doubles published between 1959 and 1961, all as by J. M. Flynn. Four are varying degrees of good: *The Hot Chariot, Ring Around a Rogue, Drink with the Dead, The Girl from Las Vegas*. The other two, *One for the Death House* and *Deep Six*, are rather awful.

His best novels of the period are a pair of capers, *Terror Tournament* and *The Action Man*, and the five titles that comprise his series featuring an off-the-wall San Francisco bar owner and secret agent named McHugh. *Terror Tournament* (Bouregy, 1959, his only hardcover) is an effective tale of the carefully planned heist of the gate receipts of a golf tournament modeled after the one at Pebble Beach. Even better—his magnum opus, in fact—is *The Action Man* (Avon, 1961, as by Jay Flynn). The caper here is a bank heist, and its mastermind, antihero Denton Farr, is Flynn's most complex and believable protagonist. A high level of suspense and a savagely ironic ending are two of the novel's other pluses.

If Denton Farr is Flynn's most complex and believable character, McHugh is his most memorable. In *McHugh, A Body for McHugh,*

It's Murder McHugh, Viva McHugh!, and *The Five Faces of Murder* (Avon, 1959–62, all as by Jay Flynn), this two-fisted Irish-American James Bond blithely brawls and blusters his way through dizzy plot-swirls concerning a missing electronics expert, Mafia hit men, a couple of Navy flyers mysteriously AWOL in Mexico, a Caribbean island dictator and his army of thugs, and a fortune in hidden Nazi loot. Along the way he drinks prodigious amounts of booze, trades quips with his fellow agent, Bud Chapman, and his boss, General Burton Harts, and has more problems than sack time with bevies of good and bad women. None of his adventures make much sense, really, but there is a good deal of energy in each, plus plenty of sly humor, breakneck pacing, and some lean, evocative writing. As in the barbed narrative hook that opens *It's Murder McHugh*:

McHugh pushed the Polish girl away and went on watching the door of the cantina. *He wished Bramhall would show up. It would be even better if Long was with him.*

That would make his job easier, because he could kill both of them at the same time.

(Flynn once told me that the McHugh series was the result of a drunken lunch with his agent and an editor at Avon. The agent, he said, began extolling the virtues of "a great new series" Flynn had concocted, and did such a good selling job that afterward the three of them lurched back to the Avon offices, where the editor immediately put through a request for a three-book contract. The only problem was, Flynn had not concocted *anything* at this point; had never heard the name McHugh until his silver-tongued agent mentioned it, nor had any idea of who or what McHugh was going to be. This anecdote may be true and it may be apocryphal. With Flynn, you just never knew what was fact and what was bullshit.)

I read most of his Ace and Avon novels either when they were first published or at some point in the sixties. One of my favorites was *Drink with the Dead*, which has a modern-day bootlegging theme, and in early 1969 I recommended it to friend and fellow writer Jeff Wallmann. Jeff liked it so much he suggested we write a story with a similar theme, which we proceeded to do. The result, "Day of the Moon," was published in *Alfred Hitchcock's Mystery Magazine* in 1970 under our William Jeffrey pseudonym. Much later, we expanded the story into a novel that was published under the same title and same pseudonym.

One evening after we'd written the story, over too many drinks in Wallmann's house near San Francisco, we got to talking about Flynn and his work; to wondering why he hadn't published a new novel in seven years, and whether or not he was still living on the Monterey Peninsula, where much of his fiction was set and where a brief bio in one of the Ace Doubles said he made his home. As a lark, we began that night to track him down. It took us a while, following a cold and circuitous trail, but we finally found him—not on the Monterey Peninsula but in a VA facility in Portland, Maine. On the phone he claimed to be recuperating from a buckshot wound—in the ass, no less—administered by an irate husband. He also claimed to be writing a new McHugh novel to pay his medical expenses, which proved definitely to be hooey because no such book was ever published.

That was Flynn.

I exchanged a couple of letters with him shortly afterward, but at that point none of us seemed inclined to keep up a regular correspondence. It would be almost two years before Wallmann and I got to know Flynn well. And how that came about requires a couple of paragraphs of relevant autobiography.

In mid-1969 Jeff and I succumbed to an offer to write sex books for an outfit called Library Press—partly for the money, which was top market dollar in those days ($1200 per title), and partly because it enabled us to finance our legitimate work. Soon we were collaborating on a book every two months for LLP. We churned them out in four or five days of intensive effort, so we could spend the rest of our time writing fiction we cared about.

Late that year LLP moved its base of operations from California to the Mediterranean island of Majorca, where the high-rolling publisher (an Ivy-League American) had rented a palatial villa. For tax and other reasons he preferred his writers to also live on Majorca— or at least somewhere in Europe—and so he offered to pay the way of anyone who was willing to make the move. Wallmann and I were willing. We took a freighter for Amsterdam in February of 1970, and arrived on Majorca in a broken-down VW station wagon five weeks later.

Neither of us remembers corresponding with Flynn while we were on Majorca; and we have only dim recollections of receiving some kind of communication from him at Christmas of 1970, when we returned to California for a brief holiday visit. But we're both sure that after we moved from Majorca to a small Bavarian town near Munich in the spring of 1971, we were not only in touch with him again but exchanging frequent letters.

Toward the end of that year Flynn wrote saying he was broke and looking for work—a letter that arrived at about the same time LLP's publisher decided to move his headquarters to Paris and to increase the number of books he was publishing. LLP was in need of writers; Flynn was in need of work, and claimed to have been writing sex books off and on since his legitimate paperback markets dried up in 1962 (which was probably true). So we got them together, Flynn submitted some sample material, and LLP put him on the payroll.

It was six months or so before the publisher offered to pay his way to Europe. By that time Jeff had made up his mind to move again, this time to France. He and Flynn arrived in Paris not long apart, and met there for the first time in the fall of 1972.

I was doing well enough with legitimate fiction by then to quit the sex-book racket, and I opted to get married and to stay in West Germany. But I continued to correspond with Flynn, and the better I got to know him through his letters (he wrote great letters), the more he intrigued me. I used him as the model for the boozy ex-pulp writer, Russell Dancer, who first appeared in the "Nameless Detective" novel, *Undercurrent*, in 1973 and who made encore appearances in *Hoodwink* and *Bones*. There are a number of differences between Dancer and Flynn, but none of them is fundamental; the lines Dancer speaks in the three "Nameless" novels either were or might have been spoken by Flynn.

He stayed in Paris for a while, at LLP's expense, and then moved to Majorca, at least in part because Wallmann and I had extolled the island's virtues to him on numerous occasions. He somehow managed to rent the same small villa Jeff and I had occupied in Palma Nova, and stayed there for about a year, getting himself into and out of a series of minor misadventures with LLP (he was fired at least once, briefly, for delivering "unacceptable" material), a group of other LLP writers living on the island, and the owners of several bars and discos. Then his wanderlust got the best of him and he hied himself off to Monte Carlo, near where Jeff and his girlfriend had moved from Paris.

In Monte Carlo, Flynn fell passionately in love with a 25-year-old suicidal West Germany beautician named Hildegarde. But their romance didn't last long; she threw him over for a randy Bulgarian and went back to Germany. This so upset Flynn that he, too, fled Monte Carlo. He went first to Ireland, on the mistaken assumption that any writer could live there cheaply and tax-free. When he found out that in order to obtain the tax-free status he would have to exchange his American citizenship for an Irish one, he figured it was time to return to the States. Specifically, to New York to look for writing work, since the bottom was already beginning to drop out of the sex-book market.

He took a room in Rosoff's, an old and now-defunct hotel-and-restaurant on West 43rd just off Times Square, and managed to scrounge up a contract to write several books in the then-popular Lassiter paperback Western series. The job didn't last long; he screwed up somehow on one of his manuscripts and was fired. But it so happened that Wallmann arrived in New York just about then, on a business trip; and Jeff, who was doing a book for Belmont-Tower, one of the lower echelon paperback houses, learned that B-T was in need of an assistant editor and house writer. He recommended Flynn, and Flynn got the dual job.

This was 1975. By which time I had been back in the U.S. myself for well over a year, living in San Francisco and also making periodic business trips to New York. So it was in Rosoff's in early '75 that Flynn and I finally came face to face.

He was shorter than I had envisioned him, less bulky, not at all imposing. No outstanding features, except maybe for a bristly salt-and-pepper mustache. I was vaguely disappointed. Flynn in person was nowhere near as impressive as he was in the abstract.

Over the next couple of years we got together every time I went to Manhattan. On one occasion he took me up to see his ex-agent (they were still friendly even though they could no longer work together), because the agent kept a bottle of 30-year-old Scotch for after-hours visitors and why pay for cheap booze, Flynn said, when you could get vintage stuff free? Mostly, though, we sat in the bar at Rosoff's and drank cheap liquor and talked shop. One of the things we talked about—and wrote each other about from time to time—was collaborating on a novel, but somehow we never got together on a mutually appealing idea. I wish we had; the finished product may not have been much good, but it would have been interesting.

Once when I went to see him, he announced that he was on the wagon for good. I asked him why. "Damn croaker said I'd be dead inside a year if I didn't," he said.

Two days later he was drinking again.

But he was still alive and kicking when the year was up.

That was Flynn.

During his association with Belmont-Tower, he published several novels as by Jay Flynn under their B-T and Leisure imprints—all of them bad. Sexed-up Westerns about a World War I-era operative for the Gallows Detective Agency, Jim Bannerman; sexed-up adventure tales featuring a drifter named Venable; sexed-up, violent cop melodramas starring San Francisco police sergeant Joe Rigg. Worst of the lot were the Joe Riggs': *Trouble Is My Business* (1976, no apologies to Chandler), about a psycho who chopped off his victims' heads with a Bowie knife, which Flynn had the puckish audacity to dedicate to Wallmann and me; and *Blood on Frisco Bay* (1976), a scandalous anti-police diatribe about the murder of a San Francisco socialite. He inscribed my copy of the latter: "For Bill Pronzini—a jolly tosspot [sic] and a hell of a fine friend. After this

thing, let on you know me and the S.F.P.D. will have your ass—
sit tight." I took his advice and sat tight.

Flynn did publish one reasonably good novel during this period,
though it was written a year and a half to two years earlier while
he was in Ireland. *Warlock* (Pocket Books, 1976, as by J. M.
Flynn) features psychic detective John Christian Fifer and his 15-year-old
daughter, Fiona, a full-fledged, spell-casting witch. Fey stuff, mixing
crime and fantasy—not wholly successful but with some of the same
positive energy that made his Ace and Avon novels so enjoyable.
It was supposed to be the first of a series, and in fact he wrote and
delivered a second book; but that second manuscript was close to
200,000 words in length and *very* eccentric, and when Flynn refused
to cut or revise a word, his editor rejected it outright and canceled
the series. My copy of *Warlock* carries this inscription: "For Bill
Pronzini—who knows where it's at—from the founder of the Day
Late & Dollar Short Writers' Assn."

It took Flynn just about two years to wear out his welcome at
Belmont-Tower, which for him was quite a long time. One of the
reasons for the wear-out was the increasing eccentricity of the contract novels he delivered; another reason was his failure to deliver
at all on other contracts; a third reason was that he had begun to
foul up on his editorial duties because he was drinking on the job.
His bosses knew he had booze stashed in the office; he would get
increasingly oiled as each day wore on, without ever leaving the
premises. He would also lurch into the john periodically to freshen
his breath from a bottle of Listerine he kept in his desk. It took
them weeks to figure out that he had his booze in the Listerine bottle
and the Listerine stashed somewhere else.

That was Flynn.

After B-T fired him, and he couldn't find any other contract or
editorial work, he quit New York and the writing business for good.
The first place he went was to Richmond, Virginia, for reasons that
never were quite clear to me. Inside of a year he was broke and
living on Richmond's skid row, where he fell in with a bunch of
white-lightning bootleggers; for a time he ran an illegal "nip shop"
for them in the rear of a neighborhood barbershop. Then, also for
obscure reasons, he quit the bootleggers and took a legit job as a
uniformed security guard—a job that required him to carry a
handgun.

One night during a heavy rainstorm, drunk on white-lightning or
the like, he noticed that the ceiling of his furnished room was bulging
strangely. Maybe he thought he had the DTs and demons were
coming after him; maybe he was just too drunk to know what he
was doing. In any event he grabbed up his revolver and pumped

five shots into the ominous bulge. Whereupon the entire ceiling collapsed and the ensuing deluge of trapped rainwater knocked him flat, broke his leg, and almost drowned him.

That was Flynn.

I had lost touch with him again by this time, but he and Wallmann (who had also returned to the States and was quartered in Eugene, Oregon—still is, in fact) continued to exchange an occasional letter. So I found out that after his leg healed Flynn left Richmond, broke and jobless again, and went to Connecticut, where he talked his ex-agent into letting him live on the agent's estate as a nominal care-taker. He stayed out of trouble there, for the most part, but he still and inevitably managed to wear out another welcome. In February of 1985 he decided to move back to Richmond. But he'd been feeling poorly, he wrote Wallmann just before he left, and so he intended to put himself into a VA hospital enroute for a checkup.

He never got back to Richmond because he never got out of the hospital. Within a week of his admission, he was dead.

Ironically, it wasn't the booze that killed him; the damn croakers never did get that right. It was cancer. A tumor the size of a beer bottle. Doesn't seem possible, but he was still a relatively young man, still in his fifties. Wallmann and I each thought he was that age the first time we met him, thirteen and ten years earlier.

Yeah, Jay Flynn was a character.

The tragicomic variety, with accent on the tragic.

Recommended Reading

Novels

Braun, Lillian Jackson, *The Cat Who Sniffed Glue*, Putnam.
Collins, Max Allan, *The Neon Mirage*, St. Martin's Press.
Constantine, K. C., *Joey's Case*, Mysterious Press.
Cook, Thomas, *Sacrificial Ground*, Putnam.
Diehl, William, *Tai Horse*, Villard.
Emerson, Earl, *Black Hearts and Slow Dancing*, Morrow.
Estleman, Loren D., *Downriver*, Houghton Mifflin.
Ellroy, James, *The Big Nowhere*, Mysterious Press.
Grafton, Sue, *"E" Is for Evidence*, Henry Holt.
Harris, Thomas, *The Silence of the Lambs*, St. Martin's Press.
Healy, Jeremiah, *Swan Dive*, Harper & Row.
Kaminsky, Stuart M., *A Cold Red Sunrise*, Scribners.
Lutz, John, *Kiss*, Henry Holt.
MacLeod, Charlotte, *The Silver Ghost*, Mysterious Press.
Paretsky, Sara, *Blood Shot*, Delacorte.
Pickard, Nancy, *Dead Crazy*, Scribners.
Preiss, Byron, ed., *Raymond Chandler's Philip Marlowe*, Knopf.
Pronzini, Bill, *Shackles*, St. Martin's Press.
White, Teri, *Fault Lines*, Mysterious Press.

Short Fiction

Aird, Catherine, "Home Is the Hunter," *John Creasy's Crime Collection 1988,* edited by Herbert Harris, Victor Gollancz.
Allyn, Doug, "Deja Vu," *Alfred Hitchcock's Mystery Magazine*, June.
Bankier, William, "Losers," *Ellery Queen's Mystery Magazine*, May.

Barnard, Robert, "A Good Deed," *EQMM*, August.

Braly, David, "Desert Kill," *AHMM*, July.

Brandner, Gary, "Mark of the Loser," *Post Mortem: New Tales of Ghostly Horror*, edited by Paul F. Olson and David B. Silver, St. Martin's Press.

Braun, Lillian Jackson, "Phut Phat Concentrates," *EQMM*, April.

———, "Stanley and Spook," *EQMM*, October.

Bryant, Edward, "The Cutter," *Silver Scream*, edited by David J. Schow, Dark Harvest.

Cady, Jack, "By Reason of Darkness," *Prime Evil*, edited by Douglas E. Winter, New American Library.

Cody, Liza, "K.K.," *Murder & Company*, edited by Harriet Ayres, Pandora Press.

Collins, Michael, "Black in the Snow," *An Eye for Justice*, edited by Robert J. Randisi, Mysterious Press.

———, "Criminal Punishment," *A Matter of Crime*, edited by Richard Layman and Matthew Bruccoli, Harcourt, Brace & Jovanovich.

de Lint, Charles, "The Soft Whisper of Midnight Snow," *Pulphouse: The Hardcover Magazine*, fall issue #1.

Egan, Greg, "Scatter My Ashes," *Interzone 23*.

Ferrars, Elizabeth, "Justice in My Own Hands," *Winter's Crimes 20*, edited by Hilary Hale, Macmillan.

Ford, John M., "Preflash," *Silver Scream*.

Fremlin, Celia, "Dangerous Sport," *Murder & Company*.

Garton, Ray, "Sinema," *Silver Scream*.

Gault, William Campbell, "The Kerman Kill," *Murder in L.A.*, edited by Jon L. Breen and Martin H. Greenberg, Morrow.

Gores, Joe, "Detectivitis, Anyone?" *EQMM*, January.

Gosling, Paula, "I Wonder if She's Changed," *Murder & Company*.

Healy, Jeremiah, "Till Tuesday," *AHMM*, April.

Howard, Clark, "Silhouettes," *EQMM*, October.

Kantner, Rob, "Duck Work," *AHMM*, February.

Lamburn, Nell, "Jack's Place," *EQMM*, March.

Lansdale, Joe R., "Night They Missed the Horror Show," *Silver Scream*.

Lewin, Michael Z., "Family Business," *Winter's Crimes 20*.

Martin, Carl, "Fatherly Love," *EQMM*, July.

McInerny, Ralph, "The Dutiful Son," *AHMM*, May.

Nolan, William F., "The Cure," *The Horror Show*, 1988 issue.

O'Daniel, Janet, "A Heart for Murder," *AHMM*, mid-December.

O'Neill, Judith, "Bridey's Caller," *AHMM*, May.

Perry, Ann, "Digby's First Case," *AHMM*, August.

Powell, Talmadge, "The Jabberwock Valentine," *14 Vicious Val-*

entines, edited by Rosalind M. Greenberg, Martin H. Greenberg and Charles G. Waugh, Avon Books.

Pronzini, Bill, "Something Wrong," *Small Felonies*, St. Martin's Press.

Reasoner, James, "In The Blood," *An Eye for Justice*.

Sanders, Lawrence, "A Case of the Shorts," *Timothy's Game*, Putnam.

————, "One from Column A," *Timothy's Game*.

————, "Run, Sally, Run!" *Timothy's Game*.

Savage, Ernest, "The Suicide Theory," *EQMM*, April.

Shepard, Lucius, "Life of Buddha," *Omni*, May.

Simmons, Dan, "Two Minutes Forty-Five Seconds," *Omni*, April.

Strieber, Whitley, "The Pool," *Prime Evil*.

Symons, Julian, "A Theme for Hyacinths," *Creasey's Crimes 20*.

Taylor, L. A., "The Moebius Trick," *AHMM*, June.

Twohy, Robert, "Highway Girl," *EQMM*, July.

————, "Maggie," *EQMM*, February.

Washburn, L. J., "Hollywood Guns," *An Eye for Justice*.

Wasylyk, Stephen, "The Alley," *AHMM*, November.

Wettering, Janwillem van de, "Friends," *EQMM*, November.

Yorke, Margaret, "Such A Gentleman," *Creasey's Crimes 20*.

A Short History of *Mystery Scene* Magazine

In 1984, Edward Gorman and Robert J. Randisi decided that the mystery field needed its own news magazine, a living record of the writers, editors and readers who make up the field in our era.

Thus MYSTERY SCENE was born.

After several format changes, after several modifications of the magazine's scope, *Mystery Scene* is today the world's leading news magazine about mystery fiction. It is now sold throughout the world.

Interested readers may request a free sample copy simply by writing to: *Mystery Scene*, 3840 Clark Road S.E., Cedar Rapids, Iowa 52403 (319) 363-7850. Subscriptions are $35 for 7 issues.